THE BEGINNING

Janelle
Best Wishes
Patrick D Smith J.
11-5-13

Novels by Patrick D. Smith

The River Is Home
The Beginning
Forever Island
Angel City
Allapattah
A Land Remembered

THE BEGINNING

A Novel by
Patrick D. Smith

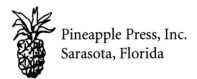

Pineapple Press, Inc.
Sarasota, Florida

Inquiries should be addressed to:
Pineapple Press, Inc.
P.O. Box 3889
Sarasota, Florida 34230
www.pineapplepress.com

Library of Congress Cataloging-in-Publication Data
Smith, Patrick D., 1927-
The beginning : a novel / by Patrick D. Smith.
    p. cm.
ISBN 978-1-56164-152-9 (hb : alk. paper)
ISBN 978-1-56164-450-6 (pb : alk. paper)
ISBN 978-1-56164-569-5 (e-book)
    I. Title.

PS3569.M53785B44 1998
813'.54--dc21 97-32635

First Edition
Hb 10 9 8 7 6 5 4 3 2 1
Pb 10 9 8 7 6 5 4 3 2

Design by Jennifer Kamberg
Printed in the United States of America

INTRODUCTION

The Beginning was written on the 1960s at the height of the Civil Rights movement, and its publication in 1967 brought varied reactions. As a whole, the novel was favorably received, but not without its share of controversy. There were those who agreed that the novel was an accurate reflection of the times, and there were those who objected to the way certain levels of society—both white and black—were portrayed. It would have been impossible back then to write a novel about race relations in the South without taking shots from someone.

Back in the 1960s, white Southerners—and especially Mississippians—were often stereotyped as violent racists, most painted with the same brush. There were those who resorted to violence, but the vast majority did not. Only those who advocated and committed violent acts were given notice in the national media; thus, the many efforts to solve racial problems without violence remained virtually unknown.

For those who did commit violent acts, what motivated them to do so? Was it fear or hate? What lay deep in their backgrounds that caused them to react as they did, making segregation a form of religion? This novel attempted to peel off the veneer and look inside.

Most of the civil rights workers who invaded the South in the 1960s came with a sincere desire to help, but there were also those who came masquerading as civil rights workers and seeking only adventure. Some of their actions opened wounds that will take generations to heal, if ever.

Much has changed in the South and the nation since those turbulent times just a few decades ago, but much change is yet to come—especially in the hearts of the people, both white and black. Perhaps enough time has now passed so that readers can view *The Beginning* as what it was intended to be: a look into a changing South where even issues of relations between races were not simply black and white but as complex as the motivations within the human heart.

—Patrick D. Smith
Merritt Island, Florida
1998

THE BEGINNING

One

"Thornton, you got to do somethin about them niggers."

Ike Thornton pushed away the ledger and looked up into the ruddy face of Sim Hankins. "What you want me to do, Sim?" he asked. "You want me to go out and shoot several down in the streets?"

"It ain't my job to say what to do, but you better do somethin," Hankins replied harshly. "You're the sheriff; I ain't. It's all over town that them niggers is havin a meetin tonight at the church, an they're goin to come into town and take over the vote."

Ike got up from the desk, walked over to the counter. "Who told you that the Negroes were going to take over the vote? Currey said the other day that only a few have been in to register."

"Don't matter how many it's been," Hankins snapped. "You let one of them in an then first thing you know the whole goddam courthouse will be swarmin with niggers. They's goin to be trouble at that meetin tonight."

"They've got as much right to hold a meeting as anybody," Ike said with annoyance. "You want me to put them in jail because they're having a meeting?"

Hankins' eyes bulged as his face flushed. "I done told you I ain't tellin you what to do, but if you don't do somethin there'll be somethin done anyway. You goin to stand up for the white folks or the niggers?"

"Hankins, if you're threatening me," Ike said angrily, "or if you start trouble in this county, so help me God I'll see you in the state pen! I didn't make this voting law and I didn't put it through Congress. I'm a sheriff, not a lawmaker. And I don't intend to let this county be ripped to pieces because a few Negroes have registered to vote."

As Hankins started to leave he said, "Thornton, you come from a good white family, an the white folks elected you sheriff. Now you better think of somethin to do about them niggers." He turned quickly and left.

Stonewall County lay in the rolling pine hills of south Mississippi. The county seat, Midvale, was the home of fourteen hundred white people and nine hundred Negroes. The main highway from Jackson to the Gulf Coast passed through the center of the town.

There were no grandiose antebellum mansions falling to ruins in Stonewall County, for none had ever been there. And there was no decaying aristocracy. Since the time the pine hills had been wrenched from the Choctaw Indians, the people who lived on this land survived by scratching a poor living from the hostile soil. The men who had left Stonewall County to fight in the Civil War entered the Confederate forces as privates, and had limped home with the same rank when it ended. There was no statue of a famous-son Confederate general on the courthouse lawn.

The Negroes of Stonewall County were not all ex-slaves of native landowners, for there had been few farmers who could afford slaves. The Negroes had drifted into the pine hills from north Mississippi and the Delta, from Alabama, Louisiana and Georgia. Some had squatted on the land and started small farms; some had come to work in the sawmills and in the town. But when too many swarmed on the land a Klan was formed; the nights were filled with fiery crosses and the screams of terrified Negroes. This was just another skirmish to the men of the rolling hills, not violence against Negroes because they were Negroes, but a survival movement aimed at retaining the land, which at the time was not even worth fighting for. It would have been the same if this invasion had been by Hopi Indians or Eskimos. Possesion of the land meant survival, such as it was.

In the early days, life in Stonewall County for both whites and Negroes centered around the daily problem of feeding hungry stomachs. Both races were equally miserable. And from this life of perpetual toil there emerged two classes of society among both whites and Negroes—the haves and the have-nots, those with a bin full of corn and those without, those with two mules and those with none, those with a frame house and those with a tarpaper shack, those who ate pork and those who ate opossum, those who gradually emerged from the wilderness of ignorance and poverty and those who did not.

Some Negroes owned farms and others worked on the farms of white people. Those who moved into town worked at the mill and did manual labor; the women worked in the houses of the whites. The whites and the Negroes lived in peace with each other, a peace maintained by an invisible yet concrete wall over which the Negro could not, dared not pass. Although neither really tried to understand the other, the white and the Negro gradually established a bond between themselves, a bond of unique friendship which was unbreakable until the wall was breached by some dark shadow who ran amuck and violated the unwritten code that ruled the two worlds—a code that centered mainly around the white man's woman. There would be a court trial and a hanging, then peace would again settle over Stonewall County.

Until recently the past two generations of white people were not conscious or concerned with Negroes as such or with race relations or civil rights. They had taken the Negro and his way of life for granted, just as the Negro had done with the white man. But now a set of new laws had been passed by Congress, laws giving the Negro the legal right to do everything the white man had always done. Months had passed and the white man and the Negro had not discussed this new thing. Both ignored it, acted as if it did not exist. But a feeling of apprehension, a slight restless movement of winds, was beginning to move over Stonewall County

Ike Thornton looked out the window and down the main street of Midvale. From the courthouse he could see the entire business section of the town, which consisted of three blocks of stores running from the courthouse to the highway. On both the south and north edges of Midvale there were sawmills, and a string of filling stations lined the highway. South of the highway, along Town Creek, were the Negro quarters.

Ike Thornton was a product of Midvale, a product of its society, its mores. He had been born there, raised there, spent his life there except for four years at the state university and two years in the army. He had been born Isaac Delmar Thornton, son of Benjamin Horatio Thornton, Midvale's leading lawyer of the Depression era. His father had been a kind yet stern man, one who could have gone far in county and state politics except for his trait of being a bit too uptight and a bit too concerned with helping others rather than looking out for his own welfare.

Everyone in Midvale was poor in those days, yet no one was in danger of starvation. For entertainment the boys roamed the woods, hunting, camping, exploring, swimming in the creeks and rivers, smoking rabbit tobacco when told not to, attending prayer meeting on Wednesday night, Sunday School and church on Sunday, revival meeting in the spring and Bible School in the summer. The Baptist church was the center of community life, and the preacher of that time filled the people with visions of hellfire, damnation and brimstone. Religion was the dominating influence in Midvale life.

Ike's mother had died when he was eight, and he had been brought up by their Negro cook, Doshie, who had continued to live with them after his mother's death. His father had built a small cottage for Doshie behind their house, and she had always been present, feeding him, loving him, doing the washing and ironing, house cleaning, serving as mother, teacher and companion. Many times when he was bad she had whipped him, saying, "Ike, whut fo you acks lak a nigger boy? You a white chile, so you ack lak one." Then she always gave him a slice of cake to make up for the whipping.

Doshie died during Ike's junior year in college. He had come home for the funeral, sat there in the Negro church, crying, had helped carry the casket to the grave. Later, after his graduation, he placed a granite stone on her grave, with the inscription: *Doshie, Loved by All, Missed Forever and Forever, God Grant Her Peace.*

Ike had played with Negro boys all his early life, swam with them, fished with them, played basketball with them, fought with them. White and Negro boys of Midvale were companions during

4

the daytime, never saw each other after darkness. Somehow they were afraid of each other at night. There had been tales of how Negroes turned into devils in the dead of night, did strange tribal dances, pierced each other with knives, lusted after white man's blood. And Negro boys had passed-down visions of bonfires and burning crosses. No white boy would dare venture into the Negro quarters after dark, just as no Negro boy would cross the railroad tracks at night.

Ike's father had once been elected county attorney, and his first case as a prosecutor had been the trial of a Negro for rape. The man was accused of raping a farm girl in beat four; lynch fever ran high over the county. The case would have been won had his father not even opened his mouth, but it was his first case, and he wanted to make a good showing.

Ike had slipped into the gallery of the courtroom to watch the conclusion of the trial, although his father had given him stern orders to stay away. He peered through the iron grill-work and listened as his father told the jury that the buck nigger had grabbed the little white girl, ripped off her clothes, thrown her naked to the ground, put that black thing in her as she screamed for mercy; and the little white girl had lain there with the buck nigger on top of her like a savage animal, and she screamed and pleaded until she finally fainted. When a woman in the courtroom fainted and fell into the aisle, the judge ordered the room cleared of women before the trial could be continued. By the time his father had finished, the faces of the jurors were flushed red, their mouths snarled; even the Negro had turned as pale as a quarter-moon. A group of spectators had then grabbed the frightened Negro, rushed him out and hanged him from the courthouse balcony. That night when his father came home he didn't eat his supper. Later, Ike heard him on the back porch, vomiting into the yard; then a few days later he resigned as county attorney. For years afterward Ike had recurring nightmares, seeing hundreds of buck niggers lurking in the shadows, leaping out and raping thousands of white girls, but more than anything else, seeing the frightened Negro hanging on the courthouse balcony.

During Ike's senior year in college his father had died of a sudden heart attack, and Ike had dropped his goal of studying law. He had taken the bachelor's degree and volunteered for two years of military service. After that, he came back to Midvale, married Peggy Jo Dale, his childhood sweetheart, and accepted a job teaching history and coaching football at Midvale High School. He had been a good but not great football player in college, and even at thirty-five he still had the trim build of an athlete. Ike was six feet tall, weighed a hundred and seventy-five pounds. His eyes were deep brown, and always seemed to have the expression of a hurt little boy. His hair was black, had not started to recede, and was always curled around his ears when he needed a haircut. He looked nearer twenty-five than his actual age.

Ike had never given up an early political ambition, although he remembered vividly what had happened to his father at the very start of his career as an elected official. Two years before, Ike had decided to run for sheriff and had won in his first effort for public office; and after only two years in office, there was talk of his being the next state senator from Stonewall County.

Ike had followed the civil rights movement closely. He knew that its effects would sooner or later come to Stonewall County, that it would come either peacefully or violently, that it could be voluntary or forced. He had read in the newspapers and seen on television what had happened in other parts of Mississippi and in other Southern states, what had happened at the state university when the federal government had sent in marshals and army troops to enroll a Negro. He wanted to keep violence and federal force out of Stonewall County. He thought that he could since he had friends among the Negroes and friends among the whites. It was a problem that could be reasoned out peacefully among all the citizens of the county. There would be no need for force or violence to settle a thing which had really already been settled without the counsel, consent or advice of anyone in Stonewall County. Whether they liked it or not, it was only a matter of time.

Hankins parked the old Ford in front of his small dingy grocery store and walked inside. His wife, Bessie, was sitting behind the counter. She was a lean, stringy woman of fifty, with coarse hair and a complexion yellow as tallow. She got up when he entered.

"Bessie, you mind the store for a while more," he said, not really looking at her. "I'm goin out to Big Springs to see Jud Miller." He went into a back storeroom and returned with a gallon jug of moonshine whiskey.

"You ought to stay away from such as Jud Miller," she said, blinking her eyes like an owl. "Jud Miller don't mean nothin but trouble."

"You mind your goddam business," he snapped as he walked out the door. He got into the car and headed away on the gravel road that led to the Big Springs community.

Sim Hankins was sixty years old, slim and rawboned at six-foot-three, red-complexioned with little splotches of brown, like freckles yet not freckles, on his skin. He had bushy red eyebrows, red hair streaked with gray, huge hands gnarled by arthritis. He looked like a gangling human scarecrow in need of a good meal.

He had been born in a cottonhouse on a plantation in Georgia. His father was a migrant farm worker. In a small Georgia town his father had taken up with a town whore who stayed with him as wife without marriage, had brought Sim into the world legally a bastard. As a child he lived on so many farms and in so many tenant shacks Sim could not remember or name any one particular town or county in which he had lived. But he could remember going into the fields when he was barely able to walk, with a hoe in his hand, working in the hot blistering sun until his head ached, his eyes swelled, then at noon going into the woods, digging roots to chew for his lunch; and sometimes the bitter roots made him sick; he would vomit, wash his face in the creek, go back into the long hot endless parched blistering hellish fields, then at night eat his piece of hard corn pone, eat his chunk of salty sow belly, lie on the floor with his bastard brothers, listening to his father mount the slut, then listening to his father snore until dawn when it was time for him to eat another piece of corn pone and sow belly, go back into the fields—endless days of work, endless nights, then move on to another farm, be turned away because a nigger family also wanted the job and would work cheaper. The niggers would always have more kids, always twice as many nigger children. The white man would hire the niggers because it would mean more hands in the fields, more work for less money. The Hankins clan would be turned away, and his stomach would ache. They would ramble along in the creaky wagon, move into another county, find a job the niggers with their snot-nosed kids didn't want; then back to the fields, at night listen to his father mount the slut; then at Christmas the town ladies from the Missionary Circle would drive out into the country, past the shack where the white trash lived; and he would watch them, watch them go past the shack where the white trash lived, go to the nigger house, give the niggers croaker sacks of grits, ham hocks, rock candy, meal and flour, bags of apples and oranges; then they would drive back past where the white trash lived, not stopping, turning their heads away, not looking. Soon the nigger kids would walk by, grinning and sucking on oranges, spitting the seed through their teeth, sucking and grinning; and he would run under the shack and cry, beat his fists into the rank earth until his father would come out and whip him with a strop because he hadn't slopped the white man's hogs; and when the white people had clothes they no longer needed, they would give them to the niggers, and he would watch; they would give him nothing, then the niggers would wear the clothes to church on Sunday, because the niggers always had a church—there was no church anywhere anyplace for white trash; and he would sit on the porch of the shack, watching, watching the niggers come by in their coats either too large or too small, their loud ties, white shirts with frayed collars and mismatched buttons, on their way to the nigger church; they would grin and laugh, and he would run under the house and cry, beat his fists in the rank earth; and sometimes he would go into town on a Saturday night, stand on the street; the niggers would stand on the same street, and a white man would come along and give the niggers a nickle to buy a popsicle; they would come out of the store sucking on the popsicle, grinning and sucking, and he would watch; there would be no popsicle for the white trash; then he would strike one of the niggers in the face, and they would gang around him, kick him in the stomach, beat him when he doubled up in pain, throw the white trash in an alley; and later he would go along the railroad track, because he knew the niggers sat on the railroad track on Saturday night, sat on the railroad track and stared into darkness; and he would walk until he found one alone, then take a stick and hit him on the head, kick him in the stomach, then run all the way home; and when his mother died they buried her in a cardboard packing box the white man gave them; then one night he came home from town and found his father drunk, in bed with a nigger woman, kissing her, kissing a nigger, and he had run from the shack, run and run and run, never looking back, drifting down through Georgia and Alabama, to countless farms, countless jobs, dreaming at night of unending legions of niggers sucking on oranges, spitting the seed through their teeth, walking and grinning with their coats either too large or too small, loud ties, white shirts with frayed collars and mis-matched buttons, grinning and sucking, his father kissing the nigger, ladies from the Missionary Circle passing by, not stopping for the white trash; then wandering into Stonewall County, living on peck-erwoods and jaybirds and opossum, saving a nickel here and a dime there, finally buying a small farm for fifty cents an acre during the Depression; then hiring a nigger family to work for him, and at Christmas walking past the nigger shack, sucking an orange and spit-ting the seed through his teeth.

Hankins stopped the car when he reached a bluff overlooking the small farm he had once owned, parked by the side of the road and sat under a tree. He looked out over the valley, seeing the unpainted frame house still standing, the bare yard, the hog pen to one side, the privy in the rear. He remembered back to the day he had purchased the land, his hands trembling so badly he could hardly make his mark on the deed. He had thought at the time that here was the tool with which he could remove the brand that had been placed on him at birth, here was his avenue of escape. He would be a landowner, a farmer, a man in his own right. But it did not work out that way. He was still branded, still isolated, still shunned by the Negroes and ignored by the white man. He was neither white nor black but trapped between the two, an unwanted untouchable unchangeable human nonentity.

But he had not given up. He worked hard, plowing the land, planting the seed, reaping what the poor soil would offer, saving, doing without, seeing that each of his children graduated from high school so they could leave Stonewall County, get jobs in Memphis or St. Louis or Chicago where they were not known, each sending back a five- or ten-dollar bill when they could, an atonement for their never coming back, never allowing their new-found friends to see and to know. And then he was struck down with arthritis in his hands, stopping him from plowing the fields, milking the cow, shucking the corn. He sold the farm, bought a small store in Midvale and moved to town. In Midvale he partly achieved his goal. He was allowed to join the Baptist Church, to vote, to attend town meetings, speak up if he wished, at least be heard. But he was still held at arm's length socially, still kept waiting just outside the white man's magic circle.

Hankins got back in the car and drove down the road, across Wildcat Creek; then he turned onto a dirt lane that led to a shack perched on the side of a hill. The front yard was bare clay partially covered by pine straw. Two hounds ran from under the unpainted weathered shack and bayed halfheartedly. Sitting off to one side of the house was a rotted cotton wagon, a rusted hay rake; on the other, a 1940 Ford with the wheels missing. The front porch was cluttered with old plow points, well buckets, car batteries, bicycle wheels and assorted junk. A tin washtub hung on one wall, a mirror on the other. Croaker-sack curtains flapped in the breeze. The hot June sun was making him sweat, so he pulled a red bandana from his back pocket and wiped his brow. When a tall bearded man came around the corner of the house, Hankins reached to the back seat of the car and brought out the jug of whiskey.

"Howdy, Jud," he said, wiping his brow again. "Thought I'd come out and visit for a spell." They didn't shake hands, just looked at each other.

The two men squatted on their haunches, facing each other. Jud took the jug and drank deeply, then wiped his mouth with the back of his hand. He handed the jug to Hankins, who also drank deeply.

"You want to go huntin?" Jud asked. "We seed deer tracks over by the crick this morning."

"Naw," Hankins replied lazily. "Let's just sit a spell."

"I'll call in the boys." Jud put his thumbs in his mouth and let out a shrill whistle.

Jud Miller was fifty-five, tall, slim, black-bearded, with coarse hair that swirled down and covered the back of his neck. He wore a wide-brimmed black felt hat, with sweat stains around the band. His eyes were narrow and deep-set, his mouth thin, almost bloodless. He had on a black denim shirt and faded blue overalls.

Jud Miller lived in the woods with his three sons, Bester, Berl and Coney. Bester, thirty, the oldest, was an exact replica of his father; Berl and Coney were identical to the other two except that each was two inches shorter on a graduated scale, each one a year younger than the next. All wore beards, overalls and wide-brimmed black felt hats.

The woman had died giving birth to the youngest, Coney. They had buried her in a box made of pine slabs, beneath a hickory tree on a hill, without prayer, without tears, the grave unmarked.

Jud had walked into Stonewall County in 1935, leading a mule, the woman riding and moaning, pregnant, ready to give birth to Bester under a pine tree, unaided. He had come down out of the mountains of Tennessee, leaving a trail of slaughtered hogs, chicken feathers, pulled-up turnips, anything he could steal. He had left the mountains from necessity, having killed a man in a fight over a coon hound.

His father had come on a schooner from Liverpool to Boston, where he worked on the docks, drank and fought in the taverns at night, killed a whore with a whiskey bottle and moved south just ahead of the law. In Charlotte he had married his woman, the daughter of a blacksmith, stolen a wagon and mule, then headed for the Tennessee mountains. He built a shack beside a creek, planted just enough corn to make whiskey, and lived off game and what he could steal from neighbors. He sired seven sons, all wild, unloved, taught to respect nothing and take everything, doomed from the beginning, stunted in morals and mentality to the level of animals.

Jud had not bought his land, just squatted, took possession; after one visit by the sheriff had ended in near-disaster, no one tried to move him. He was left alone to go his own ways. At first he tried farming the Stonewall County land, but after three years he had given up and then lived off the woods, killing game, taking what he wanted from neighbors who dared not protest. At one time he had been called "Pig" because so many of his neighbor's hogs had disappeared, all in the direction of his land and shack. When he made his occasional trip into Midvale, walking, the three bearded boys in line behind him, he was given a wide berth by both white and Negro. No sheriff had ever tried to collect taxes from him, few people visited him, and many in Stonewall County didn't even know he existed. The five men had been squatting in a circle all afternoon, saying nothing, drinking whiskey and spitting into the dust. Hankins finally looked at Jud and said, "Jud, we got to do somethin about the niggers."

"Whut they done now?" Jud asked.

"The government done passed some new laws," Hankins said, looking disgusted, "an they aim to give the whole dern county to the niggers."

"They's six of 'em buried up in the pine woods," Bester said. "We caught the last one'bout five years ago, stealin a hawg. Ain't no nigger goin to steal a hawg from us and live to tell about it."

"Best you don't talk like that except around here," Hankins said. "Seems like Sheriff Thornton done turned to a nigger lover. I went to see him this mornin, told him the niggers were havin a meetin tonight, an he said they have a right to have a meetin, said he'd see me in the state pen if I started trouble."

"Whut you want us to do?" Jud asked. "You want us to shoot up a few niggers?"

"Not yet," Hankins said, taking another drink from the jug. "We'll wait a mite an see what the sheriff's goin to do. Looks like it's goin to be left up to me and you and Con Ashley an a few others to keep the niggers in their place. Back in the old days them niggers wouldn't be havin no meetin. Not for long they wouldn't."

"That's the God's truth," Jud said.

"Shore is," Berl said.

Sim got up and stretched, then he wiped sweat from his eyes with the red bandana. "I got to go now," he said, starting toward the car. "You fellows keep the rest of the whiskey."

The four Millers followed Hankins to the car. "You come back anytime, Sim," Jud said, "an let us know whut you want us to do about them niggers."

Hankins got in the car and headed back to Midvale.

Two

Ike Thornton had worked on the tax books that morning, still thinking about his short conversation with Sim Hankins. He did not really believe Hankins would cause trouble that night, but he knew Hankins was capable of it. He felt uneasy, nervous.

Ike did not like the job of being sheriff. He had run for the office merely as a stepping stone in politics. He had never visualized himself as a person carrying a gun, engaging in gunfights, being caught in the middle of violence, or actually ever having to shoot anyone. He did not wear a uniform as did his deputies, nor carry a gun except when on calls or on special patrol duty.

Ike had three deputies, Sam Cummings, Billy Hargrove, and Lon Macey. Lon was a Negro. Ike had caused a mild rumble of protest when he first appointed Lon. In the past it was unheard-of for any Stonewall County sheriff to have a Negro deputy. Ike had assigned Lon to patrol the Negro quarters of Midvale and Dry Ridge, a section of farming land five miles south of town which was an all-Negro community. It had worked out well. After the initial newness of seeing a Negro wearing a badge had worn off, the business and civic leaders of Midvale had overwhelmingly approved of Ike's action.

The bulk of the work of the Stonewall County sheriff's office involved collecting taxes and keeping various records. Mrs. Fleming, a widow, had worked for four sheriffs preceding Ike, and he had retained her as his clerk. Ike and Mrs. Fleming ran the business end of the office, and the deputies handled the routine chores of arresting drunks, brawlers, thieves and traffic violators, and serving warrants. Stonewall County still had its occasional murder, but none had occurred since Ike had been in office.

All of the deputies were natives of Stonewall County. Sam Cummings and Billy Hargrove had come from farm families in different beats of the county. Ike had appointed them in return for the support of their families and relatives. Both were graduates of Midvale High School, and both were in their late twenties. Lon was thirty. He also came from a farm family, and his parents still lived in the Dry Ridge community. He had graduated from the Negro high school, worked in New Orleans for a year on the docks, then returned to Midvale to work at the sawmill. Lon was a good credit risk and had never been in trouble. He had always been liked and respected by the white community. He was flattered and pleased when Ike appointed him a deputy, and he took his job seriously.

Ike left the office and drove the patrol car down Main Street, across the highway and railroad tracks, and into the Negro quarters. He drove slowly, looking at the dwellings. He had been in this section of Midvale thousands of times yet he had never really looked at it.

The row of houses along the paved street were neat, painted, with screen porches and picket fences. Off this street there were six dirt streets that led for five blocks to Town Creek. Along these pock-marked dusty streets were the rental shacks, unpainted, weathered, each one built exactly alike, row upon row, mesh wire fences surrounding each backyard to keep in the chickens that pecked at the bare soil; outdoor privy just behind each shack (no sewer line had been run down these side streets), the air smelling vile, like a stockyard. Half-naked children played in the dust, rolling old car tires up and down the streets.

Along the creek, in a small clearing bounded by magnolia, pine and sweet gum, stood the Midvale African Baptist Church, a whitewashed frame building with stained glass windows in front and a steeple over the entrance. Under the trees on the right side of the clearing there were several rows of picnic tables where the families spread their dinner on Sunday afternoons following services. This building was also their community center and meeting hall.

The pastor of Midvale African Baptist Church was Reverend Emanuel Holbrook, sixty-five, fat, gray, polite to the point of being humble, uneducated in formal schooling but self-made by the light of dozens of oil-lamps during thousands of nights in untold numbers of tenant shacks; thought of as a saint by most of the Negro community, respected by the white community, called a "white man's nigger" by a few of his own race.

Reverend Holbrook was a descendent of slaves, originally from north Mississippi. He had come to Stonewall County in 1930, after "the Lord called him" to help his people and spread the gospel. He arrived in Midvale with six sweet potatoes and a tattered Bible. For five years he almost starved, eating with different Negro families when invited, sleeping more often on the ground than in a bed, holding services beneath a magnolia tree, baptizing his converts in the waters of Town Creek. In 1935 the white people of Midvale had taken up a collection, built him his church, and each year since had donated one Sunday's collection from the Midvale Baptist Church to the Midvale African Baptist Church.

Ike turned the patrol car around in front of the church and drove slowly back along the dirt street. He suddenly realized that these people were strangers; he knew their faces, their names, but he did not actually *know* them. They had talked thousands of times about the weather, about families, about crops, about hunting and fishing, but they had never *really* talked to each other about anything significant to their lives. And the invisible wall had not been built by anyone in Ike's generation, or in the generation before him. No one now living in Midvale had ever told a Negro that he could not eat in the white cafe, that he could not vote, that he must sit in the balcony section only at the local movie theater. There were no town laws saying this. It was just understood between the races, unquestioned, a part of a way of life. The Negroes did not *seem* to resent this, the whites did not *seem* to think of it as some special privilege reserved for themselves. Whites and Negroes worked together, hunted together, ate together on camps, laughed together and grieved their dead together. Negroes sat in a reserved section of the ballpark, watching whites play ball; and no Negro football game was ever played in Midvale without a section of white spectators. But they did not eat together in the cafe, sit together in the theater, go to school together. They were as close as brothers in some things and as distant as continents in others. Yet no one had ever asked *why*.

The answer to the unasked question lay partly here in the filthy streets, the unkempt yards, the dilapidated and neglected houses with television antennas but no paint, the dirty children with unwashed clothes, the men and women living together who had not yet recognized the advantages of holy matrimony, the stench which could be partially eliminated with soap and water. If the white community was to be held mainly responsible for these conditions, it was also evident that the people who lived in the shacks had not attempted self-improvement. Neither could rightly accuse the other of being totally responsible. Both must share the guilt, and both must work together to eliminate this human cesspool which furnished most of the bricks in the invisible wall with its invisible sign saying STAY IN YOUR PLACE, NIGGER.

Ike returned to the paved street and turned left, driving slowly past Albert Leslie High School, a modern brick air-conditioned building with an attached gymnasium. The school was named after Albert Leslie, who had been the pioneer Negro educator in Stonewall County. The county school board had floated a bond issue in 1958 to construct the new Negro school as a gigantic forward step in eliminating the myriad shortcomings of Negro education in Stonewall County — and also to reduce any attempt to integrate the white school. Albert Leslie High was far superior physically to Midvale High, which had been built during WPA Depression days and had since received only an occasional face lifting. The imposing Negro school was in sharp contrast to the unpainted shacks only four blocks away.

Ike turned the patrol car and started back along the paved street lined with neatly painted houses, yards with flower beds and white picket fences. It was in this section of the Negro quarters where the property owners lived, the teachers, school administrators, Negroes who owned their own businesses, those who held supervisory jobs in the mills, several elderly retired farmers who had sold their land and moved to town. There was more than one level of society even here in the Negro section.

When Ike came to the home of Reverend Holbrook he parked the car and walked into the yard. The old Negro, sitting in a rocker on the porch, got up when he recognized Ike. He said cordially, "Well, my goodness, how do, Mistuh Ike. Come on in an sot a spell." His front teeth were all gold capped, and when he smiled the bright sunlight made his face glint.

"Thanks," Ike said, taking a rocker from against the wall, feeling awkward knowing what he must ask the preacher. They both sat down and Ike said nervously, "How's everything with you, Reverend?"

"Fine, Mistuh Ike, jus fine," Reverend Holbrook replied, adjusting himself back into the rocker. "Looks lak it's goin to be a fine summer. I was out in de country dis moanin an de fields looks good. Jus might be a mighty fine summer."

Ike said hesitantly, "Reverend Holbrook, I hear you folks are having a meeting at the church tonight."

"Dat's right, Mistuh Ike," he replied, the smile fading. "We havin a town meetin."

"Are you going to talk about civil rights?" Ike asked.

"Dat's part of de meetin," the reverend answered cautiously. "We never talked 'bout it befo, an lots of folks say we ought to have a town meetin and talk some 'bout it."

"Well, I think that's the thing to do," Ike said reassuringly. "I'll send Lon to the meeting. If you have trouble afterwards, let me know right away."

"Mistuh Ike, we don't 'spec no trouble," he said, relieved that the sheriff approved of the meeting. "We jus goin to discuss some of de things we all been readin 'bout."

"Just the same, I want to know immediately if anything develops from this," Ike insisted.

"I'll sho let you know, Mistuh Ike," Reverend Holbrook said, the smile returning. I 'preciate yo bein consarned."

Ike got up and walked back to the patrol car, Reverend Holbrook following. The preacher scratched his ear for a moment and then said, "Mistuh Ike, we not goin to do anythin to rile up de white folks. We got too many white friends to do somethin foolish."

"I know that," Ike said, a trace of worry in his voice. "I know, but there might be some folks who don't."

Reverend Holbrook looked puzzled as he stood by the side of the street, watching the patrol car move back toward the railroad tracks.

Ike sat at the table, picking at the sandwich. Peggy Joe was at the range, making a pot of coffee. The two children, Ike Jr. and Cindy, were having lunch with neighbor friends.

Peggy Jo put a cup of coffee in front of Ike and sat down. She was three years younger than Ike. She wore her black hair long, swirling down onto her shoulders; her thin lips and wide-set blue eyes gave her an almost sultry look. Ike had always claimed that she had the sexiest look in Stonewall County.

"What's the matter, Ike?" she asked, stirring sugar into her coffee. "You look tired. Been real busy this morning?"

He ignored her question, then he said suddenly, "Peg, do you know that I've never talked to a Negro?"

She stopped stirring, looked at him curiously and said, "What on earth kind of a statement is that? You've talked to Negroes thousands of times, all of your life."

"No, I've never *really* talked to one," he repeated seriously. "I'm going to talk to Lon this afternoon."

"Ike, did something happen this morning about this civil rights business?" she asked, worry coming into her eyes.

"No," he replied quickly, afraid that his behavior had alarmed her. "Not anything much. Sim Hankins came in and made sort of a vague threat, but I don't think it meant anything. The Negroes are having a meeting at their church tonight, to discuss civil rights." He stopped for a moment, in deep thought, then said to her, "Peg, we've got to do something for the Negroes now. It doesn't matter about our philosophies, our personal convictions, what we've thought about this whole thing in the past. We've got to do something now or we're inviting trouble."

"What do you mean?" she asked, disturbed by the tone of his voice and the sudden outburst. "Do you think the Negroes are going to act up tonight?"

"No, it's not that," he replied, sinking into deep thought again. He sat there blankly for a moment, then looked at her and said, "Peg, the government is backing the Negroes all the way, and the laws are all in their favor. If we don't do something on our own, right here in Midvale, something to start them on the way up, somebody is going to step in and do it for us, force it, and that's when all hell could break loose. Every redneck in Stonewall County would probably start packing a gun. We'll have some objections and criticism no matter what we do, but we've got to do something. This thing must be worked out right here among ourselves, not by outsiders."

"What is it you think should be done?" she asked, perplexed. "What can we do?"

"I don't know," he replied uncertainly. "I just don't know. Maybe we could start by cleaning up that stinking Negro quarters. I was down there this morning, and that place almost made me puke. Whatever we do, though, they'll have to help, be as much a part of it as we are. It must be a partnership deal with a lot of patience on everybody's part."

"You know I'm behind you, whatever you decide," she said reassuringly. "I hope we don't have trouble in Midvale like they've had in some places."

"I better leave now," he said, getting up quickly, preoccupied again. "I'll talk to Lon this afternoon."

She followed him to the door, kissed him lightly on the cheek and said softly, "Don't worry too much, Ike. It will work out some way."

"Maybe," he said absently. "Maybe. I just hope we're not too late."

Ike was at the counter, making out a car tag application, when Lon came in. He handed the book to Mrs. Fleming and motioned for Lon to follow him into the private office. They went in and Ike closed the door.

"Sit down, Lon," Ike said casually, taking a chair himself. "Have any trouble on your run?"

"No, sir, Mistuh Ike," Lon replied. "Everybody's in the fields out on Dry Ridge." Lon was a deep black Negro, with short-cropped kinky hair and a wide nose. He was stocky, five-ten and a hundred eighty pounds, quick on his feet with alert eyes that reflected a devotion to Ike.

Ike looked at Lon seriously and said, "I want to ask you something and I want you to give me a truthful answer. I mean a *really* truthful answer, Lon."

"Yes, sir, mistuh Ike," Lon said, puzzled, worried that he might have committed an error on his job. "You know I always tell you the truth."

Ike hesitated a moment, then he said, "Lon, can you sit here and talk to me not as a black man to a white man, or as a deputy to his boss, but just as two friends having a discussion?"

Lon fidgeted with his hands, shifted his weight, glanced downward and replied solemnly, "I believe so, Mistuh Ike. We've never had trouble talkin before."

"I know," Ike said earnestly, "but this time I really want us to be honest with each other."

"I'll do my best," Lon said, becoming more puzzled.

Ike hesitated again, then said quickly, in rapid sentences, "Lon, what are your people saying about this civil-rights movement? What are they thinking? What do they intend to do? What do they want us to do?"

Lon backed up mentally from the onslaught, trying to digest what had been thrown at him. He said, "You've asked me a heap of questions, Mistuh Ike." He sat silent for another moment, scratching his head. He said slowly, "They're not sayin too much yet, but they're doin some thinking. You can feel it, feel it in the air, like a rain coming, or a thunderstorm. But they know nothin is going to change in one day, no matter what the new laws say. They's some white folks who pure hate a colored man. I know that, and you know that. And they's some colored folks who has as much hate in their hearts as the whites. It all started a long time ago, and it's not going to change in one day. It'll take some time."

"Do you know what your people want us to do as a beginning?" Ike asked, going a bit slower with him. "What is it *you* want, Lon? I've got to know."

"Mistuh Ike, you'd be surprised," Lon said, still speaking slowly, forming his answers carefully. "My people don't want too much all at one time. They want to vote, sure, but they don't want some of the old folks to vote before they're taught to at least read a ballot. They want it on the same basis as a white man. They want the white man and the colored man to qualify the same. And they don't care nothin about coming up here in town and eating at a white cafe. If a colored man is on a trip he'd like to go into a cafe and eat without getting his butt kicked, but it don't mean anything here in Midvale. Maybe in a city it does, but not here. Most of the cafe cooks here are colored, so why would a black man go into a white cafe and pay two bucks to eat his own wife's cookin?" He hesitated for a moment, then said, "An Mistuh Ike, I swear I haven't heard a single colored man say he wants to send his children to the white school, not now anyway. Maybe later, but not now. We got a good school, an we're proud of it. Colored folks got pride just like white folks. Not all colored folks, or white folks either, are like those people we throw in jail ever Saturday night for hell raisin. We got pride too, Mistuh Ike, and we're not all bad folks."

Ike and Lon were both feeling better, more relaxed, glad that it was finally coming out, pleased that they could be frankly honest with each other. Lon looked back into Ike's eyes and said eagerly, "You really want to do something to help the colored folks, Mistuh Ike, to start things on the way they ought to be?"

"Yes, Lon, I do," Ike replied.

"Try to get somebody to do something about the quarters," Lon said. "Those folks livin in those shacks aren't interested in fixin them up themselves, not while they're just payin rent an livin on dirty streets with no sewer. Nobody can have pride if they live in a pig sty. Somebody's got to help them before they want to help themselves. Give them some hope, then sit down an talk with them, just like we've been talkin. Try to understand what they'd like out of life. That's all you need to do, Mistuh Ike. Just give them a push, and then listen."

"I believe you're right," Ike said, toying further with Lon's suggestion. "The quarters is what I thought of first myself. We've got to do something, and that may be it. I'll talk to the mayor this afternoon." Ike suddenly shifted the subject. "There's another matter I wanted to discuss. Do you know about the meeting tonight at the church?"

"Yes, sir, I know."

"I want you to go to that meeting," Ike said, concerned. "If you see either Sim Hankins or Con Ashley around there, watch them closely. And if anybody tries to disturb that meeting I want you to call me immediately."

"I will, Mistuh Ike," Lon said apprehensively, "but I sho' hope Mistuh Ashley don't come around. I don't want to mess with that man 'less I have to. He's plain mean. He's tole me a dozen times that he's constable in this beat an for me to stay out of his way. Last Saturday he came up to me down in the quarters an said that if there were any niggers to be arrested he'd do it, an if I didn't like it he'd cram this badge down my throat."

"He may be constable," Ike said angrily, "but I'm still sheriff, and that's about ten steps up the ladder from him. If he bothers you I want to know about it."

"I'm not gone run from him, Mistuh Ike," Lon said, "but I'm sure not gone run into him 'less it's necessary. I've seen too many colored folks he's worked over with a club."

Ike left the courthouse and walked down Main Street toward City Hall. He had telephoned Sidney Grenlee at his insurance agency and asked to meet him in the mayor's office. The position of mayor in Midvale was only a part-time job since the amount of city business did not warrant the cost of having a full-time mayor.

Sidney Grenlee and Ike were the same age and had been friends and classmates all through grammar school and high school. They had hunted together, fished together, camped together and pulled pranks together. They had also attended the state univeristy together. Upon graduation, Grenlee had accepted a job with a savings and loan association in Memphis, where he lived for five years. He had returned to Midvale to take over the family insurance agency after the death of his father. He had a twinkling eye, always something good to say to everyone, had won the mayor's office without opposition and was now in his third two-year term. His hair was beginning to turn prematurely gray, and a slight bulge was showing around his waist.

Grenlee was waiting, a fat cigar clenched between his teeth, when Ike entered the office. He propped his feet on the desk, leaned back in the swivel chair, blew a mushroom cloud of smoke and said humorously, "Well, how's Midvale's gift to the Wild West? Had any shoot-outs today?"

"I'm afraid not," Ike grinned. "All the banditos are afraid to come into town since they know I'm on the job." Ike pulled up a chair and sat down.

Grenlee took his feet from the desk, leaned forward and said, "What can I do for you, Ike? I know you don't want to buy insurance or you'd have come to my other office."

Ike looked at Grenlee seriously. "We've got a problem, Sid, and we may as well face it now, right away."

Grenlee became attentive. "Sounds bad. Just what is it?"

"The civil rights movement," Ike said emphatically. "This thing is not going to be confined forever to other places. It could come to Midvale at any time, and God knows we've got some tough characters in these Stonewall County hills. This place could be torn wide open."

"Well, what are you suggesting?" Grenlee asked, blowing smoke across the desk.

Ike looked uncertain for a moment, then he said, "We've got to do something to help the Negroes, something to buy enough time to work this thing out among ourselves. The Negroes here are not going to sit still forever, and you know that. They're having a meeting tonight to discuss this thing. I talked to Reverend Holbrook this morning, and he said they don't intend to do anything that will rile anybody or start trouble. But you know, Sid, we can't continue to just wait. We've got to move ahead with something."

"I know, Ike, I know," Grenlee said with slight anguish. "To tell you the truth, I've been worried myself. And I've been a coward. I haven't spoken out because I didn't want to be branded a nigger-lover. I don't have to stay in the mayor's office, but I do have to sell insurance here in Stonewall County for a living. This thing could rip hell out of both of us, Ike."

"I'm aware of that," Ike replied. "But I believe that most of the people in the county, no matter how they feel personally, or what they've done or said in the past, realize this thing is legally ended, that to shout 'never' is stupid and can lead only to disaster. It's pure folly. There's not many people here who would actually kill a Negro over anything, and we generally know who the ones are who would. I believe this thing can be worked out peacefully if we go on and act now."

"I'm with you, Ike," Grenlee said firmly, "no matter what the consequences might be. I guess if necessary I can always go back to Memphis. It's just a damned shame we didn't start something a long time ago. What do you suggest for a beginning?"

"I talked to Lon, my Negro deputy," Ike said, "and he says we ought to do something about the rental section of the quarters. Does old man Bingham still own all those houses?"

"Yes, he does," Grenlee said, putting out the cigar. "He owns the entire south quarters except for those lots he sold off on Front Street and the land around the church."

"You think we could talk him into adding bathrooms and repairing the houses?"

"Jeremiah Bingham?" Greenlee said, squinting at Ike. "Hell fire, no! That old skinflint wouldn't give Jesus a lift with the cross unless he was paid to. We'll have to buy the houses and do it ourselves."

"Buy them?" Ike questioned, puzzled. "Sid, we can't buy those houses. Even if he would sell, I don't have any money to put into them."

Greenlee scratched his ear, then he said, "I think I can persuade him to sell to the city. I'll tell you what we can do. We'll buy those houses for a hundred dollars each. The city can purchase surplus bathroom fixtures from the state for about fifty dollars a set. We'll call it a slum clearance project in order for it to qualify. We can get lumber and other building materials from the mill at cost. Jim Bailey's construction crew isn't doing anything now, so he would probably furnish the labor at cost. If we can get the materials and the labor at cost, we can add bathrooms, repair the woodwork, put on new roofs and paint the houses for maybe nine hundred dollars per house. We'll sell each Negro his house for a thousand dollars and get the bank to finance them with payments the same as the rent has been. In about four or five years, everybody will own their own house, free and clear. How does that sound?"

"Almost too good to be true, if we can do it. But what about the sewer lines and the streets?"

"I'm sure we can get the sewer pipe free from the county," Grenlee replied. "Instead of contracting, we'll do the job with a rented ditch digger and our own street crew. Then we can take a motor patrol, smooth out the streets, put down gravel and then cover it with asphalt. By doing it ourselves it won't cost too much, and we can do it with city funds."

"How long do you think the sewer lines and the street work will take?" Ike asked.

Grenlee toyed with a pencil for a moment, then said, "About six weeks, doing it with our own crew. The houses will take longer. Can you be here at nine in the morning?"

"Yes."

"I'll call Bingham and have him meet with us in the morning."

Ike stood up and said, "Sid, this all sounds like a real beginning, but I just don't believe that Bingham will sell those houses for a hundred dollars each."

Grenlee popped the pencil against the desk. "We'll see. Be here at nine in the morning."

Three

The sun was casting its last dim red streaks through the June sky when Lon Marcey parked the patrol car off to one side of the Midvale African Baptist Church. The church was already filled, and a small group of men were standing outside, talking in low tones. Light from a single light bulb, set flush against the front of the frame building, paled the clearing and seeped gently into the surrounding trees. Town Creek made a bubbling, tinkling noise as it rounded a sharp bend in the edge of the woods.

Lon came around the side of the building and past the cluster of men. "Evenin'," he said. "Evenin'," they responded in unison. He went inside and took a seat in a back pew.

A center aisle ran through the rows of wooden pews to a raised platform in the rear of the church. On the platform there were four cane-bottomed chairs and a pulpit, the front of which was draped in black velvet with a white cross in the center. An eight-foot framed lithograph of Christ on the cross hung on the wall directly behind the platform. To the far left there was an upright piano of early American vintage. Three naked light bulbs hung on cords attached to the exposed rafters.

Reverend Holbrook came down the aisle and stepped up to the pulpit. He stood there, silent, immobile, almost dreamlike, his head tilted slightly upward, his arms crossed on his chest. Without moving his head he cast his eyes downward, looking out at the faces before him: old faces, young faces, weathered faces, shining faces; cotton dresses, calico dresses, black dresses, red dresses, rainbow dresses; hats with feathers, hats with wide brims, hats with black mesh partially covering the faces of the wearers; freshly-washed overalls, khaki pants, black wool suits; denim shirts, starched white shirts, some with ties, some without.

The reverend looked up at the ceiling and said in a deep rumbling voice, "Praise de Lawd!"

"Praise the Lawd," chanted the voices before him.

"Blessed Jesus!"

"Blessed Jesus," returned the chant.

"Jeeeeeesus my Jesus!"

"Jeeeeeesus my Jesus," echoed the voices.

"Does you love God?" he asked in a higher pitch.

"Yes!"

"Does you *really* love God?" he asked in a higher pitch.

"Yes!"

"How can you be saved?"

"Obey the Lawd!"

"Praise God, yes, brothers an sisters," Reverend Holbrook chanted mesmerically, "Praise God, obey de Lawd an you shall be saved, saved from de damned, de eternal hell fires, praise God an obey de Lawd an you'll be washed in de Blood of de Lamb!"

He took a handkerchief from his back pocket, mopped his brow and then said, "Turn to page sixty, hymn number nine."

The choir leader stood beside the pulpit and motioned for everyone to stand. When the piano player struck a chord the hymn was begun. The high-pitched, beautifully-blended Negro voices drifted through the windows and out into the still, peaceful night.

"Shall we gather at the rivvvv-er, the beautiful the beautiful rivvvv-er. . ."

Con Ashley came out of the house and got into the 1952 Dodge parked in the driveway. Red flasher lights were mounted on the front bumper just beneath each headlight. A large chrome star was attached to the center of the bumper. On the front seat lay a sawed-off double-barrel twelve-gauge shotgun, a wooden billy stick, a lead-filled blackjack and two pairs of handcuffs.

He started the car and drove north along the highway. When he reached the traffic light at the foot of Main Street he turned left, crossed the railroad tracks and drove into the Negro quarters. He turned off Front Street and drove slowly, without lights, down the dirt road that led to the church. Just before he reached the clearing he stopped, backed the car behind a clump of bushes and maneuvered so that he could see the church without being seen. He could hear the singing coming from inside the building. He picked up the billy stick and popped it continuously in the palm of his hand as he watched and waited impatiently for the meeting to end.

*   *   *

Reverend Holbrook stepped from behind the pulpit and walked to the edge of the platform. He adjusted his tie, scratched the back of his head and crossed his arms over his chest. He said slowly, "Brothers an sisters, we's gathered here tonight, in de House of de Lawd, to discuss some matters of pertnance an importance to de community."

A deathly stillness fell over the congregation, an overwhelming quietness, smothering even the sound of breathing. The reverend pursed his lips, displaying the gold teeth, closed his eyes and stood motionless, immobile, muscles frozen, rigidly erect like a statue carved from black granite, praying silently. He swayed slightly, then opened his eyes and said, "Brothers an sisters, de Lawd moves in ways unbeknown to common folk. What we do, we does in de name of de Lawd. God made us all, an God say blessed be de meek, fo' dey shall inherit de earth. Dey's another world comes after dis one, an in dat other world dey's great mansions, an peace, an rest, an no toil or trouble, an everbody be's equal, an dey ain't gwine be no sufferin, no misery, no worry 'bout makin a livin, no frettin, brothers an sisters, no cotton to chop an we all gwine be angels of de Lawd, an everbody gwine be happy, an we all gwine sing, and we gwine be together, an we all gwine be brothers, you an me, an de white folk too, we gwine be brothers 'cause de Lawd say He make a place fo' all people, colored folk an white folk, an He say live in peace, brothers an sisters, live in peace, 'cause if you don't, dey ain't gwine be no mansion. Whut we do here on dis earth, brothers an sisters, whut we do here tonight in de House of de Lawd, we do in de name of de Lawd, for de glory of de Lawd. Live in peace, brothers an sisters, live in peace."

"Amen," came a chant.

"Praise God," said another.

"Yes Jesus," echoed a voice.

"Blessed be the name of the Lawd," they said in unison.

Reverend Holbrook then continued, "Brothers an sisters, de fedral govment has passed some laws sayin de colored folk an de white folk be's equal. Dey say we got a right to vote, to send de chillun to de white school if we want to, a right to do as we please, lak all other folk. We all gwine have a better life. But brothers an sisters, dey ain't no law whut can put love in a man's heart, make a man yo brother. Only de Lawd can make us all brothers. All de white folk ain't bad. De white folk built dis church, brothers an sisters, an de white folk helped us back in times when dey couldn't hardly help demselves. All us been hurt by bad white folk, brothers an sisters, but dey's bad colored folk jus like dey's bad white folk, an most white folk got love in dey hearts. Brothers an sisters, if you got hate in yo heart, git down an pray, git down an pray, brothers an sisters, to de Lawd, 'cause if we does anything in hate, wid a heart full of hate, we gwine vilate de law of de Lawd, an de Lawd gwine look down on us, an He gwine know, an He gwine say, *fogive yo white brother, colored man!* jus lak yo white brother got to fogive you *yo* sin, and de Lawd gwine say, *colored man yo ain't widout sin, colored man don yo cast no stone!* An brothers an sisters, de Lawd He know we all are sinners and we done sinned 'gainst each other, an de Lawd gwine say, *fogive fogive fogive fogive fogive!* Git de hate outen yo heart, brothers an sisters, oh Lawd God Jesus Christ blessed Jesus! Brothers an sisters, git down an pray! Git down an pray! Fall on yo knees, brothers an sisters! Ask de Lawd git de hate outen yo heart an make us all brothers, brothers in de name of de Lawd!"

The reverend fell to his knees on the platform, bent forward and placed his head near the floor. The congregation began swaying back and forth, sideways, a moving mass, transformed, moving, swaying, chanting, kneeling, first one by one, then in groups, sliding from the pews, kneeling, crying "Praise the Lawd! Forgive! Forgive!" finally rendered silent and motionless by exhaustion. Reverend Holbrook finally got up, his expression peaceful, and said in a calm voice, "Brothers an sisters, rise up out of sin, out of hate, brothers an sisters, an stand tall in de sight of de Lawd." His congregation returned to their seats, some helping others, faces bright as if just washed, tranquilized but attentive.

Reverend Holbrook paced along the front of the platform for a moment, then he said, "Brothers an sisters, I knows I ain't no smart man, no wise man, not book smart lak de young folk wid education, but I loves de Lawd, an knows de Lawd, an tries to do whut de Lawd say do, an I knows in my heart de Lawd gwine look down on us, an be wid us, an guide us durin dese troublin times, an He say love yo neighbor, colored folk, then you gwine reap de blessins of de Lawd. I say to you, brothers an sisters, let's do it de Lawd's way, wid love, an talk to our white brother, an see whut he say, an work in peace wid our white brother, an keep love in our hearts. Sheriff Thonton a good white man. He hired Lon Marcey, made him a law man, a colored law man, an I knows he got no hate in his heart. Fo we do anything, let's have a deacon meetin, an have Sheriff Thonton come meet wid us, an ax him whut's de best thing to do. Whut is de will of de church?"

"Aye," rang a chorus of voices.

"De Lawd has spoken, brothers an sisters," Reverend Holbrook said, smiling. "Tomorrow I'll see Sheriff Thonton, see when he can meet, den call in de deacons."

A gnarled, stooped woman with a crown of gray hair got up and said, "Reverend, is we all gwine git to vote?"

"I don't know, sister, I jus don't know," he replied. "De new law say yes, buy dey's some white folk dey don't 'low to vote. We'll ask de sheriff. An now, brothers an sisters, de meeting is ended. Blessed be de name of de Lawd. Kneel an pray fo all of us durin de troublin times ahead."

Lon stood outside the church, watching the procession of cars and trucks as they left the clearing, churning up a cloud of dust. When one car made the turn from the clearing to the street Lon saw a headlight beam momentarily flash against the outline of a chrome star. He turned and went back into the church.

Lon walked up to Reverend Holbrook, who was stacking hymn-books on a table, and said, "Reverend, you go on an leave. I'll stay around till Montique finishes up and closes the church."

"Bless you, Brother Lon, bless you," he said. "I is tired. I's gettin old, Brother Lon. Dis old man ain't much fo' de world. You young folk gwine soon have to put us old folk out to pasture."

Lon said teasingly, "Aw, Reverend, you'll probably be here when I'm dead an in the grave."

"I don think so, Brother Lon. Sometime I think I hear de Lawd callin me, sayin come on, old colored man, come on an rest. Good night, Brother Lon, an bless you." When he reached the door he turned and said, "Montique, you be sho an turn off dem lights when you leave."

Montique was a small Negro, five feet tall, skinny, fifty and bald, wide-eyed and thick-lipped, with a short right leg that turned back at the knee and wouldn't bend. He had to use a crutch to walk. He had no other name, and no one knew where he came from or just when he had arrived in Midvale. It was sometime during the thirties. He had fallen off a boxcar as a freight train passed through town and had never bothered to leave. He had built a shack out of pine slabs and roofing tin on the bank of Town Creek and lived there alone. For a living he shined shoes in Bradley's Barber Shop, janitored for three stores, and was custodian of the church. Everyone in Midvale liked him. His one vice was excessive drinking.

Lon finished stacking the hymnbooks, turned and said, "Montique, why don't you marry some good woman, move out of that shack, an start gettin some grub in your belly? You look like a good wind would blow you 'cross a corn field."

"Lawd have mercy, Mistuh Lon," Montique said, laughing, "who you think would have a old skimp lak me? One time I was out in de woods drunk, an I went to sleep in a buzzard nest. When dat ole mammy buzzard come along, an found dis here nigger dere, she crammed a dead possum in my mouf 'cause she thought I were another buzzard, an she kep me in dat nest fo a week, feedin me all kinda dead junk, an I finally got to feelin lak a buzzard. I s'pose I'd still be dere 'cepin one day I fell outen de nest, an dat ole she-buzzard seed I couldn't fly, an after dat she wouldn't have no truck wid me. Even a buzzard don't want dis ole nigger, Mistuh Lon."

"Good Lord, Montique," Lon exclaimed, "it's a wonder you don't get struck by lightnin, tellin such a whopper here in the church."

32

"Dat ain't no lie, Mistuh Lon," Montique said seriously. "Sometime I'll take you up in de woods an show you de nest. I's through now. Let's git." Montique turned off the lights after Lon stepped outside.

"You go on, Montique," Lon said. "I'll be along after a while. An watch out that ole mammy buzzard don't get you."

Lon stepped around the corner of the building and watched Montique hobble across the clearing. Just after Montique reached the street a set of headlights flashed on in the bushes, and a car pulled out, blocking the road.

Con Ashley stepped out. "You drunk, nigger?" he asked harshly."

"Naw suh, Mistuh Ashley," Montique said, blinking his eyes. "I ain't done no drinkin tonight. I's been in church."

"Goddammit, don't lie to me," Ashley said, cracking Montique across the right knee with the billy stick.

Montique fell to the ground and doubled up in pain. "Lawd God-a-mighty, Mistuh Ashley," he cried, "don't hit me lak dat. I ain't done nothin. I swear 'fo God I ain't!"

"Stand up, Montique," Ashley demanded, "before I bust hell out of you!" Montique pulled himself up with the crutch and leaned against the car. Ashley said, "Now you tell me, an you better not lie, what you niggers been doin in that church tonight."

The giant Negro had been sitting beside a bush, watching, his eyes gleaming. He came across the ditch as quietly as a fox. The stick made a loud *pop*! as it cracked across the back of Ashley's head. The constable crumpled to the ground beside the car.

"Git, Montique!" the dark form said.

"Dat white man kill you, Hamibel, he find out you crack him wid dat stick!"

"I said *git!*" he repeated.

Montique hobbled up the street as the dark form disappeared into the brush. Lon got into the patrol car and drove across the clearing. Ashley was still on the ground when he passed and headed toward Front Street.

Four

Ashley finished breakfast and walked out to his car. He opened the door and stood there, hesitant, wondering if he should go to Montique's shack again, look for the Negro alone, or first see the sheriff. He got in and sat down, undecided, still feeling a dull throb in his head, trying to think.

Ashley was a hulk of a man, forty-eight years old, red-faced, bald except for a trace of hair around each temple, splotches of purple on his neck, huge wrinkled hands, six feet three inches tall, two hundred eighty pounds with a stomach that bulged out and draped over the wide black leather belt he wore tightly around his lower waist, almost down to his hips. Permanent puffs were beneath each eye, and his blue eyes were surrounded by areas of faded brown that resembled the color of dried tobacco leaves.

Con Ashley had been born in Midvale, in a shack on Town Creek just north of the Negro quarters, of parents who had tried farming, failed, moved to town and subsequently failed in everything they tried, including mill work and any sort of steady manual labor. His father had ended up being the town medicine man, digging herbs and roots in the woods, selling them to the Negroes and to the few whites who believed in their mystical powers. His mother competed with the Negro women, taking in washing, a huge black iron pot in the back yard; standing there hour after hour, clomping the dirty clothes up and down with a broom stick in the boiling water, hanging the steaming garments on a barbed-wire fence that separated their yard from their neighbor's cow pasture.

Four Ashley children had been born in this shack, one a girl who at age fourteen had become pregnant by a Negro and had mysteriously vanished from Midvale. Of the boys, all but Con left Stonewall County as soon as they were old enough to hop a freight train, and had not been heard of since.

Con dropped out of school after the third grade and had tried a series of occupations including chicken-stealing, pilfering rural mailboxes, shoplifting, and selling home-brew to the Negroes. He kept the family in milk by slipping out each day before dawn and milking the cows in the pasture behind their shack. He sold the surplus milk to the Negroes, who never questioned the origin of cutrate milk coming from someone who didn't own a cow. By age fifteen he was a connoisseur of moonshine whiskey and a tobacco smoker of the addicted-bummer variety.

After the death of his parents he had sold the small plot of land and used the money as a down payment on a second-hand log truck, then obtained a contract from the mill and gone into the logging business. This ended six months later when the bank repossessed the truck for nonpayment of notes. He then took a job at the mill as a lumber stacker. He had few friends in Midvale, either white or black. The townspeople tolerated him in much the same manner they tolerated the garbage dump.

In 1951 he had run for sheriff of Stonewall County on a "bash the nigger" platform, and had received forty-six votes from an electorate of over three thousand. Four years later he again ran for sheriff, this time capturing thirty-one votes. In the next election he ran for beat one constable and received six votes. Undaunted, he entered the next race for constable, and three days before the election his opponent was killed in a car wreck, leaving him the sole candidate. The county election commission had shrugged its shoulders and declared him the winner. He immediately imagined himself the law-enforcement czar of beat one and started making good his 1951 campaign promise of "bash the nigger."

The town citizens were deeply disturbed over the rough tactics of the constable but did not know how they could legally remove him from office before the next election, or force him to be more humane. Once he had jailed and pistol-whipped three Negroes who were tenants of a farmer in the southern end of the beat. The farmer had come into town with a shotgun, shoved the barrel into Ashley's fat stomach and threatened to blow his guts into the next county if he ever "tetched my niggers again." He became more particular whose Negroes he whipped.

Ike was behind the counter when Ashley stormed his huge bulk into the office, blowing in like a tornado. "Goddammit," he bellowed, "have you seen that Montique nigger this mornin?"

"No," Ike said, looking up from his work. "I don't usually go around looking for 'niggers' when I first get to work. I would imagine he's down at Bradley's where he always is this time of morning."

"No, he ain't!" Ashley snapped, pushing his stomach against the counter. "I done been down there this mornin, an they ain't seen the little bastard. I looked all over the quarters for him, too, an he ain't there. He's hiding sommers."

Ike closed the ledger and came over to where Ashley stood. He said, "What do you want with Montique? I haven't seen him drunk in over three weeks."

"I'm goin to kill the little bastard, that's what!" Ashley said roughly. "I was questionin him down in the quarters last night an the son-of-a-bitch cracked me over the skull with a stick."

"Montique hit you with a stick?" Ike questioned and laughed. "*Montique?* Come on now, Ashley, Montique wouldn't hit a snake with a stick."

"Well, he shore as hell whomped *me!*" Ashley said, angered by Ike's attitude. "Damned near busted my head! I was just talkin to him, askin him 'bout somethin, an when I turned to leave he cracked me with a stick. I'm gone charge him with assultin an officer an lock his black ass up till it turns orange."

"You got a witness that Montique assaulted you?" Ike asked.

"Don't need no witness. It'll be his word 'gainst mine."

"I wouldn't be too sure how that would come out."

"Are you insenuratin I ain't tellin the truth?" Ashley asked, his face flushing.

"If you're asking me if I believe that Montique attacked you, the answer is no. But if that crippled little Negro did get the best of you, if I were you I wouldn't go around telling it. You might get laughed out of town."

"Well, you just wait'll I get my hands on him!" Ashley roared. "He sure as hell ain't goin to laugh."

Lon had been sitting in a chair, leaning against the wall, listening. He got up and came over to the counter. "Mistuh Ike," he said slowly, "I was there. I saw the whole thing. Montique didn't hit him."

"Why, you goddam lying black son-of-a-bitch, I'll . . ."

Ike rushed from behind the counter and stepped between Ashley and Lon. "Now you wait a minute, Ashley!" Ike said, his voice filled with anger. "You touch one of my deputies and you'll be behind bars so fast you won't even remember the trip to the jail! Now what *did* happen, Lon?"

Lon stepped back further away from Ashley and said, "After the meetin at the church last night I saw a headlight beam strike Mistuh Ashley's car, parked across the street behind some bushes. When Montique finished an closed up I stayed behind a corner of the church an watched. Ashley drove out an stopped him. He hit Montique 'cross his bad knee with that club he carries an knocked him to the ground. Then he made him get up an lean 'gainst the car. Somebody came out of the bushes behind Mistuh Ashley an hit him over the head. When Mistuh Ashley fell to the ground, Montique left."

"Thornton, you gone stand here and listen to a goddam nigger lie?" Ashley asked.

Ike stared at Ashley. "Yes, I'm going to stand here and listen, but not to any lie. And if you beat up that little Negro I'm going to have him swear out papers against you for assault and battery."

The purple splotches on Ashley's neck seemed to deepen, and the tips of his ears became violent red. "Well, Mister Sheriff," he said, putting his hands on his hips, "I'll tell you what you are. You're just a goddam nigger-lover, an the white folks in this county'll take care of you. You an your nigger deputy! You ain't got the guts to git out an help us keep the niggers in their place. Sit here behind a desk, with that fancy coat of yourn, an let me handle all the rough stuff. You ain't got the guts!"

Ike stepped to within a foot of Ashley's face and said harshly, "Let me tell you something, too, fat man! I was born here in Midvale, spent half my life in the woods around Midvale, and by the time I was twelve I could hit a squirrel with a rifle at fifty yards. I don't go around packing a gun and beating hell out of people just because I enjoy it, but if I ever do have to strap one on, especially against you, you better damned sure remember I'll know how to use it! Now you get the hell out of this office! And if you ever put so much as one finger on Lon, you'll wish you'd never seen that constable badge!"

"This ain't over yet, Sheriff," Ashley said. Then he turned and left.

Ike said to Lon, "You better see if you can find Montique and get him to go on back to work. Tell him if Ashley comes around trying to start something for him to come on up here to the office."

Ike and Sidney Grenlee sat in the mayor's office, waiting for Jeremiah Bingham. The old man, who was pushing eighty, was one of the wealthiest men in Stonewall County. He had been the local railroad agent for thirty years but had always traded on the side in timber, land, and loaning money to the Negroes at fifty per cent interest. He had gained possession of several small farms by foreclosing a two-hundred-dollar mortgage loan on which he had already collected six hundred dollars in interest. When Bingham's wife had died twenty years before, it was common gossip that he had starved her to death. He had never been known to spend more than two dollars at one time on food in any store in Midvale. Each Sunday he put fifty cents in the collection plate at church. Once he donated a dime to the Red Cross.

"Sid, that old man's going to think we're crazy," Ike said doubtfully. "He'll never turn loose the money to fix those houses, and I don't believe he'll sell. You'll probably just make him mad."

"Don't care how mad he gets," Grenlee replied. "Can't lose a vote by it. I checked the books and he isn't even registered. Hasn't voted in over thirty years. I guess he was too tight to pay the poll tax."

Bingham pushed open the door and walked in without knocking first. He was short, potbellied, gray and sullen, with false teeth that didn't fit because they came from a discount mail order house.

Grenlee got up and placed another chair in front of his desk, saying cordially, "Have a seat, Mr. Bingham. Good to see you so chipper."

Bingham sat down and lisped, "What do you want? I haven't got all day. Don't need insurance and don't have any business with a politician."

"Well, Mr. Bingham," Grenlee said, "Sheriff Thornton here and myself have got up a little slum clearance project for the Negro quarters. We want you to add bathrooms to all those houses you own down there and fix them up a little."

"Must be out of your mind!" he snapped. "Wouldn't spend a dime on them. They're good enough for nigger houses."

Grenlee leaned back in the swivel chair and relaxed. He said calmly, "Well, I thought you wouldn't want to put out any money, so we're prepared to buy them from you for one hundred dollars per house."

Bingham thrust out his false teeth, then sucked them back in and said, "Wouldn't consider it! I draw twenty dollars a month rent from each house."

Grenlee straightened up quickly and leaned forward, a gleam in his eyes. "Twenty dollars a month! Well, it's like this, Mr. Bingham." He took a pencil and a piece of paper, started writing and said, "I looked on the books. According to the records, you own sixty houses down there, if you want to call them houses. They're shacks. Built them thirty years ago at a cost of one hundred dollars per whatever they are. We'll call them houses. Twenty dollars a month. That amounts to twelve hundred dollars a month, fourteen thousand four hundred per year. For thirty years that's four hundred and thirty-two thousand dollars you've drawn from a six-thousand-dollar investment, and haven't spent a cent on upkeep or repairs. Not bad, Mr. Bingham, not bad at all."

Bingham said indignantly, popping his teeth, "That's none of your damned business! My finances are my own affair!" He moved forward in the chair, sat ramrod straight and said briskly, "I won't sell!"

Grenlee leaned back again, creaking the swivel chair, and said nonchalantly, "Don't be too hasty, Mr. Bingham. It says on the tax book that those houses were valued for tax assessment at fifty dollars per house and have been that way for thirty years. You've been paying taxes on a three-thousand-dollar valuation. Now we're going to change the valuation to five hundred dollars per house— you know, bring things up to date. That will be a thirty-thousand-dollar tax valuation. We're also going to pave all those streets. Put down six inches of gravel base, four inches of asphalt with a slag topping, with concrete curbs and gutters. On street assessments the city pays one-third and the property owners on both sides of the street pay one-third. Now, you own property on both sides for five blocks down six streets. That's going to make your street assessment come to around a hundred and eighty-five thousand dollars. And we haven't come yet to what the new sewer lines will cost."

Ike sat immobile, fascinated, intrigued.

The old man sputtered, his teeth popping wildly, a lisping sucking wheezing rattling animal-like gurgle coming from his mouth and nose. He stammered, "Why . . . why . . . that's pure blackmail!" He shoved the vibrating teeth back in place, made a grinding noise with the lower and upper plates and said, "I won't have it! I won't have it! I'll sell to someone else for a fair price!"

Grenlee said innocently, in a hurt tone of voice, "Why, Mr. Bingham, I've *offered* you a fair price. I've offered you your full investment back after thirty years of depreciation." He lit a cigar, blew smoke across the desk and continued, "Of course, you've hauled in almost a half-million dollars from the Negroes. And who else would offer you such a good deal knowing about that thirty-thousand-dollar property valuation and nearly two hundred thousand dollars in street assessments?"

Bingham's face turned ash gray, then pinkish red, then gray

again, changing colors like a chameleon. "Well, goddammit, what's all this sudden interest in the niggers?" he asked. "They've never complained about those houses, and not a one of them has ever fixed a house up themselves. Plenty of people make improvements on rental houses."

"That's not the point, Mr. Bingham," Grenlee said. "This is a city project. You know, we have to have a project every now and then, and we just thought that you were tired of having to collect all that rent every month. Must be a real pain in the neck keeping track of all that."

Grenlee leaned back and put his feet on the desk. "Don't you think it's about time you got out of the real estate business, Mr. Bingham? You're getting old. You ought to relax and have some fun. Hell, get a good woman, take some pills, live it up, spend some of that dough." He blew a stream of cigar smoke just over the top of Bingham's head. "You want the six thousand, Mr. Bingham?" he asked suddenly.

"Dammit! Dammit!" Bingham sputtered.

Grenlee straightened up quickly in anticipation and said hurriedly. "Just sign this contract, Mr. Bingham, and we'll have you a check as soon as the board meets. Look on the bright side, think of all the taxes you'll be saving."

Bingham took a pen from his pocket and signed the papers. He stood up, thrust his teeth out at Grenlee, then sucked them back in, grinding them into place. "Good day, Mr. Grenlee," he snapped, and left abruptly.

"Jesus Christ, Sid," Ike said, laughing. "You missed your calling. You're a born con man. If I weren't in on this deal I think I'd have to arrest you."

Grenlee leaned back and propped his feet on the desk. "It just took a little reasoning. I'll call a board meeting for Friday morning and we'll be on our way. I want you to be at that meeting to help explain what this is all about."

Five

Ike left the courthouse early that afternoon, stopped by the florist to purchase a bouquet of yellow chrysanthemums, then drove south past Town Creek to the Negro cemetery, which was on a knoll of land, isolated, two miles off the gravel road, accessible only by a dirt lane that was, according to the season, either dust or slush, bounded on one side by woods, on the other by cotton fields. There was no fence to set off the plot, to keep out straying cattle or distinguish this earth from the fields or the nearby woods. It was circled by a tall growth of sagebrush.

Ike walked through a sea of grave markers, wooden crosses, half-rotten, crumbling, crudely fashioned stones, leaning, fallen, store-bought granite with angels on top, pieces of broken concrete, some unmarked, sunken, forming a jumbled reasonless pattern. Covering the graves were bottles: blue, green, red, purple, brown, yellow, clear, some turned amethyst by long exposure to the elements; snuff bottles, pop bottles, liniment bottles, milk of magnesia bottles, Black Draught bottles, cough syrup bottles, whiskey bottles, whole, broken, crushed, scattered; pieces of dishes, plates, platters, bowls, pots and pans, things once used and treasured in life by those who now lay at rest in this plot of Stonewall County land, surrounded by sage and cotton fields and woods, not known to exist save by those who had an interest here, or a hunter who chanced to pass this way, or the dogs that occasionally dug into the graves, or the local funeral director who charged three hundred dollars to lower a cheap pine casket into this ground reserved for those who came by way of dust or slush, in a hearse used only for nigger funerals.

Ike knelt by the grave, read the inscription, DOSHIE, LOVED BY ALL, MISSED FOREVER AND FOREVER, GOD GRANT HER PEACE. Mother, companion, member of a generation, a way of life, a complex yet simple intimate unexplainable civilization found only in the South, soon to vanish, be destroyed by time, age, death, the passing of a legend, a love, a bond, a relationship both beautiful and ugly, precious and valueless, criticized, bitterly assailed, scorned, maligned, ruthlessly distorted, understood only by those who had been a part of it, lived it, known its happiness and sadness, virtues and faults, known the warmth, love, friendship, the mystical link that was now broken, gone, vanished, severed forever and forever, never to return, to be replaced by something which was yet in the embryo stage, unborn, unknown, uncertain, frightening, restless, strange, sired not by love, friendship and understanding but conceived in violence, fear and hatred.

Ike closed his eyes, and he could see her standing there, her short fat body, the red-checkered apron, head tied in a cloth, the fat hands, twinkling eyes, shoes slit down the sides to relieve the pressure on her corns, round black face, fiercely loyal, commanding, domineering, humble, sometimes arrogant, anger that could flash in a moment and be gone the next, culinary genius, teller of tales, a member of the family yet not a member of the family, but more a member than not, believing in God, trusting, dependent yet independent, gone now, gone forever. *Ike, whut fo you acks lak a nigger boy? You a white chile, so you ack lak one.*

Ike placed the flowers on the grave, walked over to a tree, sat on the ground and leaned against the trunk. His mind was whirling, thinking, wondering. *Nigger-lover.* Con Ashley had called him that, as if the term meant something vulgar, evil. What did it mean? If it meant that a white person can love a black person, then he was a *nigger-lover*, and there were *nigger-lovers* all over the South. He had loved Doshie, and other Negroes, many Negroes, and this had been a simple accepted part of his life. Now it seemed that they must be enemies, form two distinctive armies, clash, never again be friends, companions, must destroy each other. He remembered when he was a child, and the family went on vacation trips, with Doshie along; they would stop at a restaurant, and his father would go in first, ask if Doshie could come inside; most times she could not, but sometimes she could; but if she couldn't, they would bring out her food, and she would eat in the car; when they stayed in a tourist court or a tourist home, Doshie would sleep on a cot, in the room with them, and thousands of tourist courts and tourists homes across the South had been integrated in this manner a generation ago, without notice, without fanfare; but when force was mentioned, this ceased to be; on Saturday afternoons they had gone to town to attend the Western movie, Doshie holding his hand, walking down Main street, hand in hand and it was natural, and she had taken him into the movie, sat with him in the white section, but suddenly this ceased to be, and now would never be; there would be no more traveling with a Doshie, no more eating with a Doshie, no more sleeping with a Doshie, no more sitting in the theater with a Doshie, no more loving a Doshie; it was gone, vanished almost immediately because when a government said that it *must be* it immediately *was not* and would now never be what once was. *Nigger-lover.* Was it because of the Sim Hankinses and Con Ashleys of the South? Those who had been called white trash by their own race, shunned, ignored, risen up now through violence and threats of violence with that fiery brand of *nigger-lover*, that vague unexplainable term, now dictating to the former masters what they could and could not do, at last after generations of waiting become masters; or was it old fears rekindled? Fears that had long been submerged just beneath the conscious, now come to the surface, fears born of agony after a Civil War in which these people were defeated, crushed, smitten into nothingness, trampled upon, degraded, not helped, not forgiven, punished, punished, no Marshall Plan, no federal aid, no rebuilding of destruction, no attempt to regain friendship, understanding, only revenge, degradation, carpet-baggers, Negroes who couldn't read or write put into the legislature, in the Governor's Mansion, wild uncivilized Negroes protected as they pillaged, raped, slaughtered, not doing this to former slave owners only but to everyone, not to fellow human beings but to eternal enemies, rebels, former fighters for an unholy cause; now a people only a few generations removed from a nightmare, a people who had fought back for survival, in hoods and bedsheets, for survival, and had won, and forgotten, the fears submerged, lost for two generations, now brought back to the surface, white trash created by a hos-

tile unforgiving government after the Civil War, now being con-
demmed and dammed by his father because of his violent actions
which the father himself had created, put in his loins and made necessary three generations ago, once forgotten, now returned, and now
it must start again, the same cycle, same pattern, and it would eventually end, be done with forever, but it would never be the same
because the key to the dilemma had been lost, destroyed, gone,
stamped out in a single decade because of a simple meaningless
unexplainable term *nigger-lover* wielded by a minority that had never
led, never built, never attempted, never created but had been des-
tined to destroy because at one time it had been born of destruction.

Ike wondered about himself, about his own true honest personal feelings. He had never tried to classify himself as conservative,
moderate, liberal, all of which were abstract terms which overlapped
each other and were rendered meaningless. He knew that he did not
hate the Negro, that he wanted to help him, wanted to do what he
could to better the life of all Negroes. He knew that he could accept
some of the radical changes. But he also knew that deep within himself he did not want his children totally integrated with Negroes, that
this did not stem from hatred but from fear, a deep-seated genera-
tion-after-generation-instilled fear of interracial sex, going back to
the Reconstruction era and lingering on for one hundred years; this
was the one overwhelming dominating fear of intimate contact with
Negroes: sex. And he knew that this would be with him during his
lifetime, perhaps for generations to come. He could adjust to any
concept of change but this. He would accept school integration
because of the futility of resisting, but he would do it in fear.

Ike got up, walked to the patrol car, and started back along the
dusty lane. He left the lonely plot of land with a troubled mind.

Six

Ike left the sheriff's office and walked down the hall to the office of the circuit clerk. Buford Currey had been circuit clerk of Stonewall County for sixteen years, and he ran the office in such an efficient manner that he had been unopposed in the past two elections. Among the duties of his office were keeping the records of the circuit court, issuing marriage licenses, and the registration of voters.

Curry was sitting in a chair by a window, idly gazing out at the grounds around the courthouse, when Ike entered. He was a man of forty-five, already gray, of medium build, the type of person who never attracted attention when he walked down the street. He looked up when he heard Ike's footsteps on the wide-plank floor.

"Well, have a seat, Ike," he said. "I was dreaming that I was out at Horsetail Lake, with a big fat worm on a hook, watching the cork, and it had just started bobbing when you came in."

Ike sat down, stretched his legs and said, "I'm sorry to have spoiled your day. Now you'll never know if you caught that fish or not."

"Never mind," Currey quipped. "I'll have a go at him some other time. I take five minutes every day and go fishing out this window. I never have to dig worms, haul a boat around, or clean fish. But I have all the fun of catching them. What can I do for you?"

Ike frowned. "Buford, it's about the Negroes registering to vote. What are your plans? What are you going to do?"

Currey turned from the window, pulled his chair closer to Ike and said, "There's no plans for me to make. When they come in to register we use the new form the state legislature authorized. If they can read and write, we register them. It's as simple as that."

"Have many come in lately?" Ike asked.

"Nope. About a dozen. And I didn't register two of them because they were illiterate."

Ike then said, "What about the new federal law that says you have to register them even if they can't read or write?"

Currey scratched his ear, a perplexed expression crossing his face. He said, "Ike, that's where they've really got us in a bind. If I register anyone, white or black, who's illiterate, I'm breaking a state law. But the federal government says we have to register people who are illiterate. So I'm breaking somebody's law no matter what I do."

"What do you intend to do?"

"Follow the state law," Currey replied. "The governor sent a letter to all the circuit clerks, instructing us not to register illiterates, white or black. He says the state is going to challenge the federal law in the courts. If the Negroes raise a ruckus, and demand that we follow the federal law, we'll have a federal registrar sent into Midvale to register them, and I won't have anything to do with it. Maybe that won't happen, and maybe it will. We'll see soon enough."

Ike remained silent for a moment, and then he said, "Did you hear about the meeting the Negroes had in the church the other night?"

"Yes, I heard. I suppose everybody in Stonewall County has heard about it by now."

"Reverend Holbrook came to see me this morning and said they don't know what is the right thing for them to do at this time. They don't want to stir up trouble if it can be prevented. They're having a deacon's meeting tonight and want me to come talk to them about this. Do you have any suggestions?"

Currey leaned his chair against the wall. "Ike, I don't know of but one thing that could stir up trouble, and that's for the Negroes to come up here in a mass. It takes me about five minutes to register a person with the new state form, so if they'll come a few at a time I don't think it'll even be noticed. And hardly anybody cares now anyway. I've talked about this with everybody who has come into my office lately, and I've made three trips out into the county, talking with country folks. Aside from a few hotheads, everybody seems to understand that the Negro now has the right to vote. It's the law. Even the governor has come out into the open to let the Negro vote, and the legislature has backed him. It's over."

Ike got up, walked to the window for a moment, then returned and said, "Buford, it's simple on the surface, but it takes only one hothead to start a fire, and I don't want that fire started. If you have the least bit of trouble I want to know about it."

"Don't worry, Ike," Currey said. "You'll be the first to know."

Hankins left his store early that morning and drove into beat two to the farm of Simon Weatherby, where he had once worked before buying his own land. The old farmer had fought a break-even battle with the Stonewall County land for thirty years and had then converted from cotton to dairy farming, had prospered to the point of owning a new brick home, two trucks, an automobile, and an aluminum barn complete with electric milking machines.

When Hankins pulled into the driveway he saw Weatherby out by the barn, working on a hay bailer. Weatherby stopped when he saw Hankins coming across the lawn, then he walked to meet him.

"Howdy, Sim," the old man said, extending a callous-lined hand. He had on a pair of blue overalls and a wide-brimmed straw hat. "Ain't seen you in a coon's age. How's the grocery business?"

Hankins shook hands, then scratched his thigh absently. "'Tain't too bad, Mr. Weatherby. It's a livin, 'bout all. Ruther be on the farm, though, if I could work. Can't do much with my hands anymore."

"What brings you out here, Sim?" Weatherby asked. "Something I can do for you?"

Hankins scratched again, this time with both hands, then he said hesitantly, "Just visitin around." He shuffled his feet, kicking up a small cloud of dust, pulled on his left ear, then said quickly, "Mr. Weatherby, you heard 'bout the niggers lately?" His mouth made a whooshing sound after he said it.

"Niggers?" Weatherby said, puzzled. "Naw. What is it I'm supposed to have heard about?"

Hankins got excited and moved closer to Weatherby, as if to impart a secret. He said earnestly, "They had a meetin, an they gone have more meetins, an then they gone take over the vote, an ain't no tellin whut'll come next, maybe the whole dern county'll be taken over by niggers! We got to pertect our wommenfolk, Mr. Weatherby! We got to do somethin 'bout the niggers!" Hankins' eyes were gleaming, his face flushed.

Weatherby reached up and shifted the straw hat to the back of his head. He gave Hankins a penetrating look, hooked his thumbs on his overall straps and said, "What's votin got to do with protectin our womenfolk?"

Hankins shuffled his feet again, almost doing a softshoe dance there in the dust, and said in a booming voice, "If'n the niggers take over the vote, an we git a nigger sheriff an a nigger constable an a nigger judge, then the niggers can run wild, do anything they want to, an us white folks can't do nothin 'bout it!"

Weatherby gave Hankins another piercing look, then shifted his hat forward and said, "What you got in mind, Sim? You want to burn a few crosses, whup some niggers, maybe shoot a few just to show the others we mean business?"

"That's right, Mr. Weatherby, that's right!" Hankins said excitedly, hopping around in a small circle, his arms dangling, his hands jerking. "We'll throw a scare in the niggers! We'll scare hell out of 'em!"

"Let me tell you something, Sim," Weatherby said firmly, "an you listen good!" The old farmer spoke deliberately, slowly. "'Bout all I been hearing for the last few years is niggers, nigger, niggers. You see that antenna over there? I got a TV set, an ever night on the national news I see niggers, niggers, niggers, floppin in the streets, shoutin an singing like a bunch of damned circus freaks, an I'm sick an tired of it. I got a farm to run, a mortgage to pay off, an I ain't in the nigger business no more. Few years back I was ready to take a gun an start shootin, but I'm sick of it. I got two nigger families livin on my farm, an if they come to the house an tell me they want to vote, I'm goin to take them to town in my car an register them, an if anybody comes out here makin trouble over it, includin you, Sim, I'm gone get out my shotgun an fill their ass full of buckshot! I'm sick of hearin 'bout niggers! An you'd be a whole lot better off if you'd start tendin to your own business an let the goddam niggers alone!"

Hankins froze, his face drained white, every muscle tingling. He opened his mouth, sputtered, hissed, tried to speak but only made a clucking sound, a trickle of saliva running out of one corner of his mouth, down his chin.

"But ... but ... but ..."

"I got work to do, Sim," Weatherby said. "You're welcome on my farm anytime, but don't come back out here talkin 'bout niggers." He turned and walked back to the barn.

Hankins stood there for a moment, immobile, stunned, breathing heavily like a dog that has run a fox all night. He was dumbfounded, speechless, a blank, smashed to the ground by a barrage of unexpected alien hostile incomprehensible words, coming from a man he had once watched whip a Negro with a gin belt for stealing a chicken. Slowly the blood began to pump again, boiling blood, the corpuscles replaced by small cockleburrs of anger, grating his insides, pricking his veins. *Goddam nigger-lover!* He turned and got in his car, raced the motor, slammed in the shift and sent a shower of gravel across Weatherby's yard. He drove north toward Jud Miller's shack.

Ike turned down the dark lane and into the pale yellow of the clearing in front of the church. Several cars and trucks were parked there. When he walked inside, Reverend Holbrook and the deacons were waiting. The reverend rose and came over to him, not shaking hands, but slapping him gently on the shoulder. The others turned and looked. Ike walked to the back of the church where Holbrook had place two cane-bottomed chairs in front of a pew.

Twelve deacons of the Midvale African Baptist Church were sitting in the pew. Some were dressed in khaki, some in denim, some in overalls and some in black wool suits. A few looked as if they had come straight from work to attend the meeting, had not washed the salty sweat-streaks from their faces. Each man, while serving his term as a deacon, assumed the name of one of Christ's disciples and was called by that name during church meetings and services. Each was also designated as a messenger, to carry word from the Midvale church to the other Negro churches scattered across the county.

The room was solemn, quiet, tomblike, the air stuffy with apprehension. Even the light seeping down from the hanging naked bulbs seemed uncertain. Ike could feel the tension radiating from the deacons when he sat in front of them in the cane-bottomed chair.

Reverend Holbrook stood before them, straightened his shoulders, reared back slightly, cupped his hands beneath his pot belly, applied pressure with his hands and emitted a tremendous belch. The sound of it ricocheted around the room like a thunderclap. The solemn deacons came unglued, fell into fits of laughter, slapping their legs and swaying. Ike suspected that the belch was not accidental.

The reverend raised his hands and said solemnly, "Brothers! Brothers! Let's have peace in de church." The laughter receded in waves until only a dying snicker was heard. "Brothers, you all know Sheriff Thonton, a fellow servant of de Lawd. Mistuh Ike, you start de meetin." Reverend Holbrook took a seat in the chair beside Ike.

Ike started to speak, thought about the belch, and began giggling. Then the deacons giggled. If anyone had happened to pass they would have thought the church was filled with a gathering of idiots. What had begun as two tense, suspicious forces facing each other on a sea of apprehension had suddenly turned into a giggling contest.

Reverend Holbrook cleared his throat and said loudly, "Aaaaahum! Aaaaahum!"

Ike regained his composure, sat straight in the chair and said, "As you all know, Reverend Holbrook asked me to talk to you about the new voting laws. First, I'll explain how they work, then you can ask questions."

The deacons became attentive. Ike continued, "There are two new voting bills, one a state bill and one a federal bill. Under the state bill you have to be able to read and write to qualify. Under the federal bill you don't. Buford Currey, the circuit clerk, is following the provisions of the state bill, because it's state law, and he has to administer his office under state laws. If you can read and write, you can go to the circuit clerk's office and register. That's all there is to it." Ike hesitated a moment, then he said, "If your people force the issue about having to read and write, the federal government will send in a registrar and register you without any qualifications. But the state government intends to contest the federal bill in the courts."

One deacon stood up, clasped his hands together and said nervously, "Mistuh Thonton, is dey white folk in Stonewall County who can't read an write but is registred?"

"Yes," Ike said, squirming. "There are some on the books, but under the new state bill nobody, white or black, can register if they're illiterate. From now on the qualifications will be the same for everyone."

Another deacon, an old stooped gray-haired man, stood up and said, "Mistuh Thonton, I's illiterate, soes if'n I regster under de fedral bill, an I can't read, how's I gwine know who I's votin fer on de ballot? Do dey be's a man in de votin booth wid me to 'splain it?"

"No," Ike replied. "That's the whole point of the new state qualifications. This thing should have been changed a long time ago. If a person can't read or write, white or black, he or she can't possibly cast an intelligent vote in an election. If you can't read the name of an office, you don't know who or what you're voting for. If there's a tax referendum on the ballot, and you can't read it, you might vote yourself a new tax increase even if you don't want it." Ike stood up, walked behind the chair, placed his hands on the top rung and said, "I want to be honest with you. In the past the voter qualifications have kept most Negroes from registering, and it hasn't been used the same with white people. But that's all past now. This new bill is equal to all."

The same old man stood up again and said, "Mistuh Thonton, I's de only deacon whut's illiterate, so whut 'bout me? Cepin I register wid de fedrals, how's I gwine ever vote?"

"Learn to read and write," Ike replied. "Just the simple basics. Just enough to qualify. Become familiar with the names of all elective county offices, and learn how to recognize them in print. Learn enough to know the difference between a 'yes' and a 'no' vote on a ballot. As far as writing is concerned, learn how to write your own name. You can't just mark an X on the ballot. Just learn the basics.

You've got plenty of time to do this before the next election. There aren't too many of your people who can't qualify now, but for those who can't read and write, the older folks, set up some classes at your school and teach them. If anybody really wants to vote, they should be willing to give a little time to learning."

Another deacon, known as Brother Luke, stood up. Ike knew this man. He was Albert Hopkins, superintendent of the Negro school. He said, "You're right, Mr. Thornton. Our teachers at the school will volunteer their time, and we can set up day and night classes, teach all the illiterates who want to vote to read and write. There's not anyone who can't learn just the basics. We won't develop any scholars, but we can teach them enough."

Reverend Holbrook stood up and said, "Brothers, de Lawd has shown de way. We all got to live wid each other here in Stonewall County, an we don't need no fedral man down here. Brother John, you jus gwine have to do you some larnin. Mistuh Ike, whut is de best plan fer us to use?"

"Well," Ike said, gratified by their agreement, "I talked to Mr. Currey about this, and he said it takes about five minutes for a person to register, that it would be much better if a lot of people don't come at once. There's not another election for two years, so your people have plenty of time. Just come a few at a time and everything will work out fine."

"Whut is de will of de deacons?" the reverend asked.

"Aye," they responded.

"De Lawd has spoken," Reverend Holbrook said, smiling. "Dis Sunday we'll send messengers to ever church in de county, tellin de people 'bout dis meetin, an 'bout de plan. Brother Luke, you be's in charge of settin up a school fo' all de old folks. Brother Mark, you be's in charge of instructin de messengers. An bless you, Mistuh Ike, fo' meetin wid us. We 'preciate it. Dat's all, brothers."

The deacons got up and filed down the aisle toward the door. Ike waited for a moment, then he said to Holbrook, "I want to ask you something, Reverend Holbrook, and please give me an honest answer."

"Why sho, Mistuh Ike," he replied. "Whut you want to know?"

"The other night, after your meeting here, Montique had some trouble with Constable Ashley. I've talked to Ashley about it, and he's not going to bother Montique. I sent Lon Marcey to find Montique and tell him to come back to work, that he might lose some of his jobs if he doesn't come on back, but Lon couldn't find him. I know Montique's scared and hiding out somewhere. Do you know where he is?"

The old Negro shifted his eyes, then he looked back at Ike and said, "Mistuh Ike, I ain't supposed to say, but Montique he's hid out in dat house of Hanibel Felds, de last house down on de second street. But Mistuh Ike, don you go over dere tonight. Don you go 'round Hanibel Felds at night."

"All right, Reverend, I won't," Ike said, puzzled. "And thanks. I just want to help Montique."

"I knows you do, Mistuh Ike," Reverend Holbrook said, his eyes reflecting deep concern. "But you stay 'way from down dere at night."

Reverend Holbrook turned off the lights and they walked outside.

"Good night, Reverend," Ike said, getting into the patrol car.

"Good night, Mistuh Ike, an bless you," Holbrook responded.

Across the street, behind a clump of bushes, Sim Hankins lay on the ground, watching. He breathed heavily when he saw the sheriff and the Negro preacher come from the building together.

Seven

All of the deputies had already left on their patrol routes when Ike arrived at the office the next morning. He had intended to send Lon after Montique but now decided to go himself. He left the office and drove toward the Negro quarters.

Ike had not recognized the name of Hanibel Felds, but he knew many Negroes by sight and not name. He followed the directions Reverend Holbrook had given him and parked the patrol car in front of an unpainted clapboard shack. He walked across the bare yard, stopped at the steps and knocked on the porch floor.

The Negro was in the kitchen, slicing salt pork with a butcher knife, when he heard the knock. He walked through the unlit hall, opened the screen door and stepped onto the porch. When he saw the patrol car, with the sheriff's star painted on the door, he tightened his grip on the knife.

Ike took a backward step when he looked up at the giant Negro. He was seven feet tall and weighed over three hundred pounds. He had a small head that didn't fit the huge frame. His eyes were narrow slits, and his thick lips were curled back in a permanent snarl. He wore faded blue overalls, three sizes too small, no shirt, and brogan shoes slit down the sides. Ike had never seen this man before, this Negro who stood there staring at him, holding the butcher knife.

"Whut you want, white man?"

"I'm Sheriff Thornton," Ike said, shocked by the Negro's appearance. "I'm looking for Montique."

The Negro took a step forward, the butcher knife clasped like a dagger. Ike took another backward step.

"Whut you want, white man?" he repeated.

"I said I'm looking for Montique," Ike said, feeling extremely uneasy. "I want to talk to him. I'm a friend of his."

Ike backed up further and bumped into the gate. A sawed-off double-barrel shotgun was lying on the front seat of the car. He felt behind him, not wanting to make a quick move, trying to find the gate latch. The Negro took another step forward, looming over him like a black holocaust, and repeated, "Whut you want, white man?"

Montique hobbled through the door and onto the porch. He shouted, "Hanibel! Hanibel! Dat my friend! Dat my friend!"

The giant Negro took another step forward, the knife drawn

back to his shoulder. Ike pressed back against the gate, desperately trying to find the latch.

Montique hobbled down the steps, across the yard to the giant Negro, and bashed him behind the head with the crutch. Felds turned and looked at Montique blankly.

"Hanibel! Dat my friend!" Montique screamed. "You go back in de house whilst I see whut he want!"

The Negro retreated to the steps, the knife still raised, his eyes boring into the sheriff.

Montique turned to Ike. "I's sorry, Mistuh Ike. Hanibel he go kinda crazy he see dat sheriff car. He a good nigger, Mistuh Ike. He don mean no harm."

Ike tried to steady his trembling hands. He turned and unlatched the gate as a safety measure. He wiped sweat from his forehead and said, "He may not mean any harm, Montique, but I was sure glad to see you come out of the house. He scared the hell out of me."

"You gwine 'rest me, Mistuh Ike?" Montique asked calmly.

"No, I'm not going to arrest you. I've had Lon looking for you for a couple of days. You better get on back to work or you'll lose your job."

"Mistuh Ike, I can't," Montique said, his face now marked with anxiety. "Dat constable he'll kill me if'n I go back uptown."

Ike put his hand on the little Negro's shoulder and said, "No, he won't. He won't touch you. I've already talked to him about this."

"Is you sho, Mistuh Ike?" Montique asked, looking directly into Ike's eyes.

"Yes," Ike said firmly. "Do you want to ride to town with me now, or come later?"

"I come later," he said, the worry beginning to fade. "I'd best cool Hanibel down some first. He a good nigger, Mistuh Ike. Hit dat sheriff car whut done it."

Ike started out of the yard. "Well, you better tell your friend to watch out how he handles that knife. He could get himself killed that way."

"I tell him, Mistuh Ike," Montique said quickly. "He a good nigger."

Ike got into the patrol car and drove back up the dusty lane. Montique hobbled across the yard and into the shack.

Felds stood in the doorway, watching, watching the small crippled Negro hobble up the street, watching, seeing not an old crippled man but a boy, skipping along, with a book satchel, skipping along, the woman in the kitchen, singing, packing a lunch pail, always singing a hymn, *Glory be to God*, feeling the cold steel, a man but not a man, watching, feeling the pain, watching, watching until the small Negro was gone, the boy gone, gone from sight, gone and then forever gone, forever and forever, *Glory be to God*. . . .

He walked back into the kitchen and sat at the table, the slab of salt pork before him, the knife in his hand, the chunk of salty white meat with lean streaks of brown; then he stabbed it, stabbed it again, then stopped and propped his elbows on the table, cupping his head in his hands, the small head in the giant hands; then crying not a man's cry but a child's cry, a giant Negro crying, tears dropping down and making little splotches in the salt, crying and remembering: on a creek bank in Alabama, fishing, then walking up a trail, coming on her suddenly, unexpected, and she froze, started screaming, the white girl standing there screaming, and he was afraid, and she ran from the woods screaming, and he stood there, afraid, and that afternoon they came for him, in a car with a star on the side, came for the thirteen-year-old nigger, took him to jail, brought in a set of pincers, pincers used to make a steer of a bull, to crush the tubes without cutting, to fatten a steer for slaughter, and the white men held him, pulled down his pants, and he could see the white man with the pincers, standing over him with the pincers, and they held him on the floor, and he could feel the cold steel, feel but not see, then a sudden pain, a searing pain, and he vomited, and didn't know, didn't realize, thinking they had only hurt him, not knowing, not realizing; then a year later, in a cotton field, with a nigger girl, he knew, realized, and he ran through the wood screaming, wild, running and screaming, running through the woods until he went over a bluff, lay there senseless, a human steer, knowing; then wandering from town to town to town, working in the fields, hauling garbage, odd jobs, growing larger and larger; and the slut in Florida, in a cafe, a nigger cafe, coming to him, teasing him, and he hit her and hit her, almost killing her, and they came for him in a car with a star on the side, took him to jail, beat him with a rubber hose, white man with a rubber hose, pain, then took him out of town and said *git, nigger! stay away, nigger!;* wandering, a hundred jails, a hundred hoses, sometimes becoming confused, lost, not knowing, then knowing, striking out blindly, then jail, working on the county farm, chopping cotton, cleaning ditches along the highway, the white man with the gun watching, watching, then wandering, a man but not a man, capable of eating and sleeping and endless toil, not capable of love, denied, fattened, growing larger, *git, nigger!;* then wandering into Stonewall County, living alone, always alone, working at the mill only at night, a dark shadow, lurking, slipping to work along the creek bank, not being seen, dodging the white man, never daring to approach Main Street or any other part of the town; twenty-five years of being a man but not a man, wandering alone, lurking, hating, hating, remembering, not being seen, denied, sometimes confused, knowing and then not knowing, the white girl screaming, watching the crippled Negro hobble up the dusty street, seeing not an old crippled man but a boy with a book satchel, the woman in the kitchen, *Glory be to God,* then gone, forever and forever gone. . . .

The giant Negro picked up the butcher knife and slammed the blade through the top of the table.

Eight

When Ike left the courthouse and walked down Main Street toward City Hall he was still emotionally shaken from his encounter with the strange giant Negro. He wondered what he would have done had the shotgun been in his hands instead of in the car, what would have happened except for the appearance of Montique. It puzzled him that he had not seen this Negro before, this huge hulking black man who was so different physically that he could not possibly escape notice. He thought of the warning Reverend Holbrook had given him to stay away from that shack at night, and of Montique's words, "He a good nigger, Mistuh Ike. Hit dat sheriff car whut done it."

Ike paused when he reached Bradley's Barber Shop, looked through the window and saw that Montique was back at his shoeshine stand. He had not seen Con Ashley since their verbal encounter in the courthouse. He did not trust Ashley, and had a dubious feeling about his own role in persuading Montique to come out of hiding so soon. But had the Negro not come back he would have been replaced in at least his janitorial jobs.

For a few moments Ike stood on the curb, thinking about the physical proximity of the white and Negro sections of Midvale, separated merely by a railroad track, a narrow strip of earth, juxtapositioned yet as far apart as two civilizations, two worlds, could possibly be. White and Negro shared this small insignificant plot of earth, this tiny part of even Stonewall County, bound together by the land, crowded together for a century yet not knowing each other at all, strangers, fellow sojourners who could as well have been on different continents, both afraid to ask *Who are you?* because of an underlying fear of each other passed down through generations. Only a few seconds were required to cross those railroad tracks, yet a century had not been enough time to penetrate the invisible boundary.

Ike crossed the street and walked toward the one-story stucco building that was governmental headquarters of Midvale. He was the last to arrive for the meeting. The others were gathered around a pot of coffee Grenlee had ordered from the Ritz Cafe. He crossed the room and poured a cup of the steaming liquid.

The Midvale board of aldermen was composed of four men: Roy Kelso, editor of the *Stonewall Weekly Gazette;* Jefferson Bennett, owner of Bennett Mercantile and Farm Supply; John Branch, a service station owner; and Edward Kelley, owner of the Stonewall County Lumber Company, the largest employer in the county; and Sidney Grenlee, the mayor, chairman of the board who cast a vote only to break a tie. Major Sylvester Beecham served as city attorney.

The *Gazette* had been in the Kelso family since it was established in 1879. Roy Kelso, who had been editor for twenty years, was an intelligent man in his fifties, but had never been a crusading editor, having been more interested in the weekly ad from City Grocery announcing a weekend special on lard and black-eyed peas than in creating or fighting for a cause. His editorials usually reflected the sentiment of the times. For several years after the 1954 Supreme Court decision on public school desegregation he had denounced the federal government, damned the Supreme Court, compared the defiant state legislature to the disciples of Christ, and branded all liberals as Communists. As the futility and disaster of blind resistance became clearer, and the state leadership expressed a more moderate view, he had called for respect for law and order and obedience to the law no matter how distasteful it might be. His only brush with fame and glory, or the excitement of journalistic intrigue, had been during a political campaign when he endorsed a candidate for supervisor and the man's opponent had stormed into the news office and dumped a washtub full of fresh cow manure on his desk.

Jefferson Bennett had come into the family firm after his graduation from a university in Louisiana, and now ran the business. The Bennett family was one of the pioneer families in the county. Jefferson, in his late thirties, had two married sisters, and both of his brothers-in-law worked in the huge firm which sold everything from farm tractors to cow feed to hog chitterlings. Jefferson had at one time or another served as president of every civic organization in

Midvale, and he endorsed and fought for anything that would bring progress to the town and county. He was outspoken and quick to reach a decision, had no tolerance for anyone who straddled the fence on any issue. He had been one of the most influential people in persuading the school board to build the new Negro school.

John Branch, also in his late thirties, was the sort of politician who donated twenty dollars to every candidate in a particular race and later told the winner he had backed him to the hilt and fought his opponents to a shirt-tail finish. After his graduation from high school he had gone to work at the mill, where his father was a lumber stacker, and saved enough to buy the service station. The bulk of his business in gasoline, oil and tires came from the beat one county supervisor, who received a five per cent kickback each month on every dime of county money spent at Branch's place. It was said that Branch was the only man in Stonewall County who could pump thirty gallons of gasoline into a county truck with a twenty-gallon tank. In the alderman's race, he received the votes of those who respected anyone who could cheat the county and get away with it, and the votes of lower-income people because he could chew plug tobacco, spit and cuss with the best of them.

Edward Kelley, at sixty-five still trim and muscular, had come to Stonewall County in 1930 from North Carolina. When he saw the giant virgin pine trees, as thick as hairs in a brush, he knew he had found his utopia. With a hundred dollars he borrowed on his Ford model-T truck, he purchased a used shotgun sawmill and set up a three-man operation which included himself and two Negroes. For years he cut trees, hauled them to the mill site, ran the saw, helped stack the rough timber, shipping it out of Midvale in boxcars to buyers in other states. His operation gradually grew to include a finishing mill and building supplies, a business employing over six hundred people. He now owned thirty thousand acres of Stonewall County timberland. He still occasionally went out into the mill yard and helped stack lumber "just for the hell of it." He lived in the largest house in Stonewall County, owned the longest car in Stonewall County although in his everyday travels he drove only a pickup truck and knew almost everyone in the county by name. His political influence reached into every beat, and all candidates eagerly sought his support, which he gave only to the candidate he thought best qualified. He could often be found out in the county, at a country store, sitting on a barrel playing gin rummy with a group of straw-hatted farmers.

Major Sylvester Beecham had lived in Midvale for ten years, after having retired from the army at age forty-three with twenty-five years of service. He had earned a law degree from Georgetown University while stationed in Washington following World War II. He was born on an army post in Oklahoma, son of a career army officer, raised on army posts from Georgia to California, and appointed to West Point in 1930. He had twice been stationed in the South and wanted to live there after retirement. He preferred small-town living and had selected Midvale because of its location between the state capital and the Gulf Coast, where he owned a beach cabin and spent many of his weekends. Major Beecham was a good lawyer, one who knew every facet of the law, but one who believed in stretching a point of law to fit human needs. When he believed himself right he would speak out on any issue regardless of public sentiment. Before he became city attorney he had filed a suit to force the city to build a sewage lagoon and discontinue pumping raw sewage into Town Creek just above the Negro quarters, a fifty-year practice which he found repulsive as well as unsanitary. He had won, and in the process gained the humble gratitude of the Negro citizens. The major enjoyed the respect of Midvale's white and Negro population and was regarded as a valuable import in spite of his outspoken and sometimes controversial ways.

Grenlee stood behind a chair at the head of the conference table as the others took their places. The major was at the far end of the table, Bennett and Branch on the left, Kelso and Kelley on the right. Ike sat in a chair against the wall, a spectator.

Greenlee said, "I asked Sheriff Thornton to sit in on this meeting because what I'm going to bring up was his idea in the first place, and if there are any questions he can answer them."

In the formality of getting down to business, the men pulled their chairs closer to the table, making scraping noises on the concrete floor. The major sat ramrod straight, the others relaxed.

Grenlee continued. "What we propose is a little slum clearance project."

"Slum clearance?" Branch broke in, propping his elbows on the table. "We ain't got no slums in Midvale."

"I believe we have," Grenlee said. "What we propose is for the city to buy all the Bingham property in the Negro quarters and make some changes down there."

"God-a-mighty!" Branch broke in again. "What does the city want with the nigger quarters?"

"Why don't you shut up, Branch," Kelley snapped, "and let's hear the proposition."

"Well, this is the deal," Grenlee said, eying Branch distastefully. "Old man Biggham owns sixty houses down there. We'll buy them for one hundred dollars per house. Using surplus bathroom fixtures, cost material and cost labor, we can add bathrooms, repair the houses and paint them for nine hundred dollars per unit, then sell them back to the renters for a thousand dollars each, and it won't cost the city a cent. I've already talked to the bank and they'll finance the houses with the payments the same as the rent they're now paying, twenty dollars a month. With interest added on, in less than five years all the Negroes will have their houses paid for and we'll have that eyesore down there cleaned up."

"There's no sewer lines on the Bingham property," Bennett said. "What good will bathrooms do with no lines. You can't put sixty septic tanks in such a small area."

"That's another part of the proposition," Grenlee said. "I've already asked, and the county will give us the sewer pipe. We'll use our own street crew, rent a ditch digger, put in the lines, and then we'll blacktop the streets."

"Sounds like a good idea to me," Kelley said, "but I've never heard of a project like this one. Major Beecham, is this thing legal?"

"I don't see why not," the major replied. "I don't see any problems. Eventually it will be bank money financing the property purchase and the house repairs."

"What do you estimate the sewer and street project will cost?" Kelso asked.

"Well," Grenlee said, scratching his head, "we won't be out anything on the sewer project except rent on the ditch digger, because our crew would have to be doing something anyway. We'll use our own crew and motor patrol on the street project, so that will mean only the cost of gravel and asphalt. Best we can figure, the entire thing will run between four and five thousand dollars."

"That's not bad," Bennett said. "I spent that much paving the lot where our tractors are displayed. Have we got the money in any fund?"

"Yes," Grenlee said, lighting a cigar. "But this is where you come in, Roy. We've got the money in our road and bridge fund, but if we do this job, we'll have to delay paving a street in your ward for about six months."

"I don't think that will matter too much," Kelso said. "That's a good gravel street, and I haven't heard any complaints. It can wait six months for paving."

"Now all of you wait just a minute," Branch said, pushing his chair back from the table. "I ain't for this one bit! I got three streets in my ward that needs paving, and if we go paving them nigger streets first, ahead of the white streets, somebody's going to raise hell."

"Who's going to raise all the hell?" Kelley asked, giving Branch a contemptuous look. "There's one house on one of those streets you're talking about, two houses on another, and the third street runs around a cow pasture you happen to own and have been trying to sell lots on for twice what they're worth."

"I ain't for it!" Branch said belligerently. He took a plug of tobacco from his pocket and bit off a chunk. "What's all this interest in the niggers anyway?" he asked, chewing fiercely. "Them niggers don't pay no taxes, so what the hell we want to spend tax money down there for?"

"You ever heard of anybody paying taxes on a rented house?" Bennett asked. "They *will* be paying taxes as soon as they own the houses."

"Well, they won't ever pay taxes like the white folks do," Branch said, shifting the cud to the other side of his mouth.

Grenlee rapped on the table with his knuckles. "Let's hold up a minute. Branch has brought up something Ike can answer. Ike, you take over and tell everybody what you told me."

Ike had been sitting unnoticed, listening to the banter of talk, the others having forgotten he was in the room. He got up and stood at a corner of the table next to Grenlee. For a moment he hesitated, looking at the faces of those around the table, and then he said slowly, "I'm just the one who suggested this project. Sid is the person who worked out the details. The reason for this, which John has questioned, is that we've got to do something for the Negroes, something to start them on the way up, or we might inherit some of the trouble other places have been getting. We've got to make a start, and we can't wait any longer. We haven't had trouble here yet. I've already talked to the Negro leaders, and they don't intend to start any, but things aren't going to stay the way they are forever unless we make some changes for the better. We can do it ourselves, or somebody will do it for us. It's up to us which way it will be."

"You're exactly right," Major Beecham said, standing up and moving behind his chair. "And we should do this not only to keep peace, but because we owe it to ourselves and to them. The Negroes who live in those shacks are human beings. They eat, they sleep and they bleed, just like anybody else. They work their butts off all day, go home at night and can't take a decent bath or even take a crap without going outside to a latrine. How would any of you like that, especially you, Branch?"

"I've taken plenty of craps in an outdoor privy in my lifetime," Branch said, lobbing the cud into a spitoon. I still ain't for it! What the hell we want to spend tax money for just so some nigger can come uptown, cash his welfare check and then sit at home all day crappin in a fancy commode? If they suddenly got to take so many craps they can go down to the creek!"

Major Beecham turned a livid red and moved back to the chair, drumming his fingers on the table. "Branch, you know what you are," he said, his fingers making a steady rhythm, "you're just a —"

"Wait a minute!" Grenlee broke in, banging on the table. "Let's not get personal with this thing! Roy, you haven't said much, and you'll have to report the project in the *Gazette*. What's your opinion?"Kelso leaned forward, his eyes on the major. "I agree with you, Major Beecham. I don't feel proud of myself for having buried my head in the sand over the past few years, looking the other way when I didn't want to see something so obvious. I'm not for all these new civil rights laws, but there's a lot of things we could have done that wouldn't have been civil rights, that would have been just plain human rights. We're late now, but we've got to start sometime."

"I agree too," Bennett said, "but there's just one little catch to the whole thing. We'll never get all that property from old man Bingham for six thousand dollars."

"Oh yes we will," Grenlee said, a triumphant gleam in his eyes. "I have a signed contract at the price of six thousand."

"How the hell did you do it?" Bennett asked. "You must have pulled a gun on the old man."

"That's not important," Grenlee said. "All that's important is that we've got the contract."

"Seems to me," Kelley said, "that on a project such as this, the board ought to cast a unanimous vote so we can say we're all behind it in case somebody does put up a gripe."

"Well, I'm still not for it!" Branch said, his expression defiant, "and they ain't nothing nobody can say that will make me change my mind!"

Kelley leaned across the table, stared straight into Branch's eyes and said, "Give me a try. Let me see if I can say something that will make you for it. I say that if you don't vote yes, I'm going to the supervisor in this beat and tell him if he ever spends one more single dime at that place of yours I'm going to beat him in the next election if I have to spend fifty thousand dollars on his opponent to do it! Now you think about that for exactly ten seconds." Kelley started watching the second hand on his watch.

Branch squirmed in his chair, fidgeted with his hands and said, "Ain't no use to get mad, Mr. Kelley. I'm outvoted anyway, so I'll go along. I'll vote yes if it means all that much." He suddenly straightened up and said loudly, "But I ain't going to like it! And I'll tell all of you that you're wrong! You gonna regret this 'fore it's over. You just wait and see. They ain't nothin in the world you can do for a nigger that he won't turn around and whomp you in the back for it. You just wait and see!"

Grenlee rapped on the table again. "Well, is it settled? Does anyone vote no? No objections? Everybody agrees?" No one raised a dissenting voice, although Branch looked completely dejected. "Then we'll do it!" Grenlee said, a smile flashing across his face. "We'll start as soon as the Negroes are informed about the project. Major, can you draw up the deed transferring the property from Bingham to the city and then start on the individual deeds?"

"Yes, I can draw the Bingham deed this afternoon and have his check cut. I'll start on the others Monday. But I don't think we should convey the individual deeds until all of the work is completed. Any rent money paid during the project can be held in escrow and applied to the purchase price when the work is completed."

"Fine," Grenlee said. "That'll be just fine. Well, gentlemen, that's all. The meeting is adjourned." Grenlee stopped Ike on his way out and said, "Do you think Reverend Holbrook will let us have a few minutes in his church Sunday to explain this thing? If he will, we can talk to almost everyone in the quarters at one time."

"I'm sure he will," Ike replied. "I'll see him this afternoon."

Ike crossed the tracks and drove down Front Street to the home of the Negro preacher. He parked the patrol car, crossed the yard and knocked on the front door. It was several minutes before the knock was answered; he felt awkward and conspicuous standing there alone.

Reverend Holbrook opened the door and said, "Well, suh, Mistuh Ike, dis a pleasant suprise. Come in de house."

When Ike entered the dark room he felt that he had been transported backward several decades in time. There was a red velvet Victorian love seat with two matching chairs, a bentwood chair and rocker, two marble-top tables, one with a banquet lamp and one with a "pickle jar" lamp, a blockfront secretary, a pillar and scroll clock on a whatnot shelf—all worn but sturdy, things discarded years ago by white Stonewall County families, given to the Negro preacher, thought to be junk by the previous owners, replaced with "modern" things—junk now valuable and irreplaceable, given to the Negro preacher who could not afford to purchase anything himself, new or old. The walls were covered with framed lithographs, scenes picturing the Crucifixion, the Last Supper, Moses on the mount, Jesus in the temple, Peter casting a net, and one of a black Mary holding a black Baby Jesus.

"Sot down, Mistuh Ike," the reverend said. "It's a pleasure to have you in my home. Make yoself comfortable." Ike sat on the love seat, immediately enjoying the sinking comfort of the faded worn cushion. He said, "Reverend, I want to ask a favor of you, if I might."

"Why sho," the old Negro smiled, flattered and pleased that the sheriff had come to his home to ask a favor. "I be pleased to do anything I can fo you, an you knows that."

Ike could feel the pleasure radiating from the Negro preacher. He said, "Reverend, Mayor Grenlee and I would like to have a few minutes before your services Sunday morning to explain something of interest to your congregation. We thought it would be the best opportunity to speak to most of your people in one gathering. Do you think this is possible?"

"Lawd have mercy, Mistuh Ike," he said, his eyes gleaming, "you know you be's welcome in our church at any time. You an de mayor come right on. You can have de flo' whenever you wishes. Whut's it about? Is it somethin mo 'bout de votin law?"

Ike smiled and said, "No, it's not about voting, but I'd rather not say what it is. It's something good. Let's wait until Sunday and make it a surprise."

"Why sho, Mistuh Ike. I shouldn't a' asked, but you knows how curious a old man is. You be's most welcome Sunday."

Ike leaned forward, crossing his arms in his lap. He asked, "Reverend, who is this big colored man, Hanibel Felds? He almost attacked me when I went to his house looking for Montique."

Reverend Holbrook shook his head, a swaying sideways motion, then he rocked back and forth. "Lawd, Mistuh Ike," he said, his eyes closed, "I was 'fraid of dat. Hanibel a strange man. Sometime he be's as gentle as a kitten, an sometime he be's lak somethin I never seen befo. He a good man, Mistuh Ike, when he be's all right, but he has spells, lak he been hexed, filled wid de debil, an when he git day way, it best no white man go 'round him. He don't bother de colored folk, but he sho do hate a white man. He been hurt powerful bad by somethin, Mistuh Ike, powerful bad, and when he have a spell it seem he even hate de Lawd."

"What could have happened to fill a man with so much hate?" Ike asked, realizing immediately he should not have asked the question, thinking of Sim Hankins and Con Ashley, knowing the old Nergo could ask him the same question.

Reverend Holbrook paled, his black skin turning momentarily brown, the color of a chinquapin. He closed his eyes, rocked back and forth again, then looked at Ike and said, "Mistuh Ike, I can't 'splain it. Lawd God I wish I could. Some white folk hate a colored man jus cause he be's a colored man, hate him so much dey beat him down lak a dog, beat de life outen him, an then he ack lak a dog, snarlin an snappin at everbody. Dey beat a colored man down lak dey done beat Hanibel, an he got nothin but hate in his heart. Then he be's as bad as de white man whut hurt him, be's jus as bad. I's been down there a dozen times, down on my knees, prayin wid Hanibel to get de hate outen his heart, come to de church, take de Lawd in his heart, foget all de hate an pain, but it too late, Mistuh Ike, too late. He been hurt too much, he jus cuss me an de Lawd. An he not de only one. I be's afraid of whut I see, be's so afraid I gets down on my knees ever night an prays, prays to de Lawd fo dem to get de hate outen dey hearts, de young folk too, Mustuh Ike, get de hate outen dey hearts, live in peace, give the white folk a chance, 'cause dey changin, do it de Lawd's way, live in peace, give de white folk a chance, fogive, git de hate outen dey hearts."

The old Negro's eyes were open wide, staring, but he was not seeing Ike Thornton, not seeing this room, this place, this time, not present in this house on this afternoon in Midvale with a white man in his parlor; now transposed, spinning through decades of being a Negro, seeing the hurt, the pain, the dilapidated tenant shacks, the persecution for being born Negro, WHITE ONLY, seeing frustration and resignation, yet seeing the good, the bright specks in the darkness, like fireflies, faint rays of hope, seeing the white man build his church because the white man *wanted to*, seeing the white man help a Negro family because the white man *wanted to*, seeing the white man in the quarters at Christmas with carloads of food and toys because the white man *wanted to*, faint rays of hope, a beginning, feeling the white man's fear, fear not developed or nourished but inherited, passed down without reason, *wanting to* understand yet afraid, feeling the wind shift and change, a slight rustle yet a beginning, a strange subtle perceptive tingling breeze moving gently across this land, a beginning, praying for patience, praying for time, a little more time, just a little more time, knowing an explosion could create a vacumn and send this gentle breeze spinning off in a thousand directions, destroying all in its path, like a tornado.

As Ike watched the old Negro mesmerize himself into mental oblivion he felt a sudden, overwhelming, unexplainable humiliation sweep through his own body. He felt ashamed, deeply ashamed, but did not understand why. He also felt that he had passed through a barrier he had never before breached, entered a room in which he had never been. Without knowing, without being aware, he was absorbing the emotional waves radiating from the old Negro, subliminally entering a world not his own, perceiving what it meant to be born Negro, live Negro, depend on the white man for physical existence because the white man owned the bank, owned the mill, owned the land, dependent as a hog for whatever comes, living under a Midvale government in which he had no voice, following rules which he could not help make, moving with the white man through time, attached to him like a flea on a hound, without choice, suddenly being set free, but without the knowledge or ability to manage freedom because the white man had not taught him, had not prepared him for the inevitable.

Reverend Holbrook suddenly returned to awareness and became alert. "Lawd, 'scuse me, Mistuh Ike," he said, a startled expression on his face, as if seeing the white man in his home for the first time. "'Scuse my manners. I done sot here an ignored my guest. . . . Hanibel." He scratched his head, thinking back to what the original conversation had concerned. "Mistuh Ike, don you worry too much 'bout Hanibel. He don have dem spells very often."

Ike got up and said, "I guess it's not that important. We appreciate the time you're giving us Sunday. We'll be there shortly before your services begin."

When Ike reached the door he turned and extended his hand, for the first time extended his hand to Reverend Emanuel Holbrook, a Midvale Negro preacher. The two hands were then clasped together, not in capitulation to the other's wishes or desires, not in the solving or dissolving of complex problems, but in a sense of understanding.

Nine

Ashley drove up Front Street, the drunken Negro on the back seat, silent, his eyes blurred and blinking, his mouth twitching, breathing heavily, filling the car with the sour rancid odor of moonshine whiskey, manufactured in the Pearl River swamps, brewed in oil drums, fermented with rabbit guts, sold to the Negroes for three dollars per gallon, consumed on Saturdays as an established ritual.

Ashley crossed the railroad tracks and stopped at the traffic light on the main highway. The area surrounding the railroad station house was crowded with pickup trucks, cattle trucks, log trucks, cars of all models, some with coon tails tied to the radio antennas, some freshly washed, some covered with dust and mud, groups of people, white and black, standing, leaning against trucks, sitting on fenders, milling, squatting, talking, some silent, watching the traffic flow along the highway.

The drunken Negro weaved, made a gurgling sound, then leaned forward and vomited on the floor of the car. Ashley turned and looked, a grimace on his face. He muttered, "Goddammit!"

The traffic signal turned green, and the constable's car joined a procession moving slowly up Main Street, cars and trucks, going nowhere, killing time on a Saturday afternoon, going up the business street, around the courthouse, back down the business street, across the highway, turning back up the business street, around the courthouse, back down the business street, pedestrians following the same pattern, up the sidewalk, then back down. Farmers, cattlemen, loggers, white and black, leaned against storefronts, laughing, eating bananas, sweating, buying groceries, talking, milling, loafing, looking, kids chasing each other, sucking on popsicles.

Ashley turned left at the courthouse, drove north one block and parked in front of the Stonewall County jail, an imposing structure that resembled a miniature medieval Scottish castle, two-storied, constructed of stone blocks, on one end a circular tower looming twenty feet above the roof level, complete with indented ramparts, with ramparts running around the entire main roof level. The second-story windows were covered with iron bars and heavy steel mesh wire.

The first floor was used as living quarters for the jailer and his wife, and the second floor contained the cells. A circular stone stairway ran between the two levels, and on each end of the stairway were massive iron doors. The grounds were surrounded by a ten-foot iron picket fence. All of the flower beds around the building and the fence were planted solidly with collard greens, which the jailor's wife cooked and fed to the prisoners.

No one could remember who had designed the sixty-year-old jail, but it was the only building in town that distinguished Midvale from hundreds of similar small towns across the state.

Ashley opened the back door of the car and ordered the drunken Negro to get out, which he managed to do after three unsuccessful attempts.

"Clean up that puke with your shirt," Ashley demanded.

The Negro leaned against the car, his eyes blinking.

"Goddammit, I said clean it!"

The Negro fumbled with the buttons, tearing two loose, removed the shirt, then climbed into the car and slowly mopped up the vomit. He fell out the door, pushed himself up and leaned against the car, the shirt in his hands.

"Put it on!" Ashley said, popping the billy stick in the palm of his hand.

The Negro put on the fouled shirt and stood there blinking, his nose twitching like a rabbit's.

"Now tuck it in!" Ashley commanded.

When the Negro unbuttoned his pants he fell backward against the car, the pants dropping to the ground. He stood there swaying, making no attempt to cover himself.

"Goddammit, git on in the jail!" Ashley boomed.

The Negro walked slowly, reeling, stumbling, hobbled by the pants around his ankles. He managed to cross the yard and climb the steps, then he fell headlong into the front hall.

The jailer, a retired farmer named Ance Clayton whom Ike had appointed to the job, came into the hall. "Gettin a early start, ain't you, Con?" he asked, looking at the prostate black body. He dreaded each Saturday, because the jail would be filled with drunks, and the next morning he would have to mop the vomit from the cells.

"Yeah, they already got one goin down at the Froggy Bottoms Cafe," Ashley replied. "By sundown they'll be drunk niggers whoopin an hollerin all over the place. Will you get this son-of-a-bitch on upstairs? I got business to attend to."

"I guess so," Clayton said without enthusiasm. He leaned down and turned the Negro on his back, pulled the pants up and fastened them. He held his nose, then said, "Phew! What'd he do, puke all over hisself?"

"Naw," Ashley said disgustedly. "He lobbed it on the floor of my car, an I made him clean it up with his shirt. They ain't nothin smells exactly like moonshine puke. I got to go. You take care of the nigger."

When Ashley left, Clayton pulled the Negro to a sitting position, took off the shirt and carried it to the washroom.

Ashley parked the car in front of Hankins' grocery and walked inside. The store was housed in a small wooden frame building, the back of which was made into living quarters for Hankins and his wife. It was located on the highway, near the mill, and Hankins got most of his business from the Negroes who stopped there to pick up items after work rather than going to one of the larger stores on Main street. At noon each day he did a brisk business in sardines, soda crackers, onions, hoop cheese, bologna, white bread, Moon Pies and 'belly washers,' the sixteen-ounce soft drinks.

Hankins was sitting in a cane-bottomed chair, leaning against the counter, swatting flies, when Ashley entered, causing the sagging wood floor to creak.

"Howdy, Con," Hankins said, throwing the swatter on the counter. "What can I do for you?"

Ashley took a chair from behind the counter, sat next to Hankins and said, "You can help me teach a nigger a lesson."

Hankins became interested immediately. He pushed himself away from the counter, shuffled the chair closer to Ashley and asked, "What you got in mind, Con?"

"That little Montique nigger done made a fool out of me," Ashley said. "I'd like to take him out to Jud Miller's for a few days.

You reckon Jud will be at home tonight?"

Hankins' eyes were gleaming with anticipation. He said, "Yeah. He'll be at home. What did the nigger do?"

"One of his friends lopped me behind the head with a stick the other night," Ashley replied, "an Sheriff Thornton threatened to arrest me if I fooled with the little son-of-a-bitch. I'm gittin damned tired of Thornton messin with me. I'll fix that nigger if you'll help me."

Hankins leaned forward and said quickly, "I'll help! I'll help! What you want me to do?"

Ashley leaned back against the counter. "Well, I don't want nobody to see me with the nigger, so soon as it gits dark, you go down to his shack and tell him you got some work for him here at the store. I'll park my car by the station house an walk back here. Then we'll take him out to Jud's in your car."

Hankins was becoming more excited. He enthused, "I'll tell him I need some help unpacking boxes, that it won't take long, an I'll offer him a dollar an a hunk of cheese. I'll go after him soon as it gets dark."

"He'll git somethin besides cheese out at Jud's," Ashley grinned. He got up and walked to the door. "I got to go run in a few more drunks. I'll come back soon as it gits dark. I got some chain an a couple of locks I want to leave here."

Hankins got up and followed Ashley out to the car. Ashley opened the car trunk, handed Hankins a box and said, "You put this in your car. An on your way to git the nigger stop by the Ritz Cafe an pick up their garbage."

"O.K.," Hankins said, his voice still tingling with excitement. "I'll have everthing ready."

Ashley got in the car and drove back toward the Negro quarters.

Hankins parked the car at the end of the street, turned on a flashlight, then walked along the narrow trail that led to Montique's shack on the bank of Town Creek. The blaring jukebox music and shrill laughter coming from the Froggy Bottoms Cafe, three blocks to the west, blended into a wild melody that drifted through the silence. The moon was creeping out of a cloud, and the tips of magnolia leaves along the path were catching little blobs of dancing silver that sparkled like fireflies.

The trail took a sharp left turn and Hankins came upon the shack suddenly, a dim light inside silhouetting the screen door and two rocking chairs sitting on the sagging front porch. The sides of the shack faded into the darkness, making it seem that nothing existed but the screen door and small porch.

The boards creaked under Hankins' weight. He did not have to knock before the small Negro emerged into the cone of yellow light.

"Who dat?" The voice was apprehensive, the Negro hesitant to come nearer.

"It's Sim Hankins," Hankins said, peering inside. "I got a job for you."

Montique hobbled over, opened the door and said, "Come on in, Mistuh Hankins. I were jus makin a pot of soup. Mistuh Green at de grocery give me a big soup bone when I finished cleanin up an I got it goin on de stove."

"Ain't got time," Hankins quipped. He was nervous, impatient, not wanting to linger any longer than necessary. "I got some boxes to unpack," he said. "I'll give you a dollar an a pound of cheese to help, an I'll bring you back."

"How long it take?" Montique asked. "Dey's someone comin here soon to help me et dis soup."

"Won't take but a few minutes," Hankins said, wanting the Negro to hurry. "I'd do it by myself but I got a bad back. I'll have you back here in a half hour."

"I guess I help you den," Montique said. "Let me turn off de stove fust. I owes de butane man fo dollars now, an I sho don't want to run out 'fo I gets some mo money."

The small Negro hobbled toward the back of the shack, the crutch making a dull *thomp* on the plank floor. Then he came out and followed the white man along the dark path.

Hanibel Felds had just turned down the trail when he saw the bobbing beam of light coming toward him. He slipped silently behind a bush and squatted, watching the light float through the darkness, come even with him and pass, hearing the muffled sound of a crutch striking dirt, hearing the thud of a shoe heel hit the ground before the sole, the way a white man walks. He crept alongside the trail like a cat, on his hands and knees, stopping just before the yellow glow of a street light penetrated weakly into the woods. The giant Negro froze, not a muscle moving, not even a slight sound of breathing breaking the silence, and watched, watched the small crippled Negro get into the car with the white man, watched them drive up the street and disappear into the night.

When Hankins crossed the railroad tracks he cut to the right and drove beside the station house, between the building and the tracks, and came back to the highway around the end of the station, avoiding the traffic light on the highway at the bottom of Main Street, not wanting anyone to see the Negro in the car with him. When he reached the store he parked the car in the darkness behind the building. He got out and led Montique through the door to the living quarters.

"You wait here," Hankins said. "I'll be back in a minute." He walked up a narrow unlit hall toward the front of the store.

Montique was in a small room that served as both kitchen and dining area. It contained a round table covered with a red and white checkered oilcloth, four straight-back chairs, an ancient refrigerator with the motor unit on top, a stove and sink, and an open cupboard stacked with once-white dishes that had turned brown with age. The smell of fried sausage lingered in the air.

The small Negro stood there in the quiet room, waiting, wishing the white man would hurry so he could get back to the shack, finish cooking the soup bone, then share it and the cheese with Hanibel Felds. Later, they would sit in the rockers on the porch, listening to the faint music and laughter drifting through the woods from the cafe. He heard Hankins come back down the hall, enter the room. Then he saw and he knew he had been tricked. He felt a sickening paralysis grip him as Con Ashley came into the room and stood before him.

"Well, well, Montique," Ashley said, placing his hands on his hips. "You hongry? I hear you want some cheese. Give him some cheese, Slim. He's hongry."

Hankins opened the refrigerator, broke off a small chunk of cheese from a slab and handed it to Ashley. Ashley spat on it, then handed to Montique and demanded, "Eat it!"

Montique put the cheese into his mouth and chewed. He tried to swallow but couldn't, the yellow glob lodging in his throat, choking him. He coughed violently, managed to swallow, then looked up and said, "Whut you gwine do, Mistuh Ashley? Shuff Thonton he say you ain't mad wif me, say dat you ain't gwine mess wif me."

"Thornton ain't here now though, is he," Ashley said menacingly. "I'm gonna mess with you some, all right. You gone learn a little lesson 'bout hittin a white man with a stick." Ashley moved closer.

"I ain't hit you, Mistuh Ashley," Montique pleaded. "I swear 'fo God I ain't hit you! Whut you gwine do? You gwine kill me? I swear 'fo God I ain't hit you!" He was becoming hysterical with fear, trembling, cringing backward against the wall, his eyes wide and wild.

"Then who did?" Ashley asked, moving a step closer, waiting expectantly.

"I don know, Mistuh Ashley," Montique answered, "but I swear 'fo God it warn't me!"

"You lyin bastard" Ashley snapped. Then he said teasingly, "Tell you what, Montique, we gonna take a little ride out in the country. You gonna get on the back floor of the car, an if you so much as open your mouth one time, you ain't never comin back. You understand?"

"Sho, Mistuh Ashley, I onderstan," Montique said. "I gwine keep my mouf shet, jus lak you say. Don't you kill me, Mistuh Ashley! I swear 'fo God I ain't hit you!"

Ashley turned and looked at Hankins, who had broken off another chunk of cheese and was eating it. "You ready, Sim?" he asked.

"Yeah," Hankins replied. "Tole my wife to mind the store, that I was goin coon huntin."

"You got the slop?"

"It's in the trunk."

"Well, let's go," Ashley said. "It's time to get the show on the road."

Montique hobbled out the door in front of the two men and climbed onto the back floor of the car.

The four Millers were sitting on the edge of the porch, in the darkness, when they saw the car headlights brighten the tops of the pine trees, come closer, then invade the clearing. They sat still as the car came to a stop, its headlights still on but its engine now silent. They recognized Hankins and Ashley as they crossed through the beams of light and walked to the house.

"That you, Jud?" Ashley asked, peering at the forms sitting in the darkness.

"Yeah," Jud answered flatly. "You an Sim have a seat. Go git a lamp an light it, Bester."

One of the dark forms got up, went into the house and returned with a kerosene lantern. He raised the globe, struck a match to the wick and a round circle of orange light sprang across the porch and onto the bare ground.

Now they looked at each other, the four bearded black-hatted men sitting on the plank floor, the two visitors mounting the steps. The car headlights still bathed the nearby pine trees.

"Jud, we got a nigger in the car," Ashley said, taking a seat on the top step.

"Whut you gone do, whup him or shoot him?" Jud asked calmly.

"Well, we ain't goin to shoot him," Ashley replied. "You got any hogs in your pen?"

"Got a shote an two boars," Jud said. "Ain't much to 'em. Them boars is skinny as rails an don't do nothin but fight all the time. Been meanin to make sausage out of 'em."

"You mind if we put the nigger in there for a few days?" Ashley asked. "We not gone put you out any. We brought a tub full of slop so you won't be out any vittles feeding him."

"Naw, I don't mind none," Jud said, not showing any surprise by the request. "Them hawgs will be glad to share the slop with the nigger. They ain't had nothin to eat but deer guts fer two days. Whut'd the nigger do, steal somethin?"

Ashley shifted his weight and said, "He hit me with a stick. Leastwise, somebody did, an he won't say who."

Jud got up and stretched. "If the nigger hit you, or had somethin to do with it, how come you didn't just whup him 'stead of bringin him out here?" he asked.

"Don't do much good to whup a nigger anymore," Ashley replied. "It's a whole lot better to scare hell out of him."

Jud scratched his head and said, "Let's get him on out there if that's whut you want to do. Me, I'd whup him. Bester, you an the boys go down to the car an fetch him. An turn off them damned headlights."

Ashley walked to the car with them and took the box from the car. When they came back into the circle of light at the porch, Montique was terrified, trembling, dwarfed by the group of huge men surrounding him.

"Ain't much to him," Jud said, looking at Montique as he would a horse or a cow. "He better be kerful them boars don't et him."

The strange procession moved around the corner of the house and across the back clearing, the circle of light moving with them, the Negro hobbling in front, his eyes shining, his body trembling. The boars ripped the silence with grunts and squeals as they fought over an acorn that had fallen into the pen.

Jud opened the gate and they took Montique inside. Ashley wrapped one end of the chain around a fence post, tied it, then snapped on one of the locks. He wrapped the other end around Montique's left ankle and locked it; then he took Montique's crutch, left the pen, shut the gate and threw the crutch to the ground. They all moved to the fence and watched the Negro, the small black man sitting on the ground, his eyes fixed on the boars, his frail body shaking as if seized with a fit.

"Don leave me in dis pen, Mistuh Ashley," he pleaded, "don leave me wid dem hawgs! I swear 'fo God I ain't hit you!" The voice was uneven, wavering, almost shrill.

"Sloppin time be's at six," Jud said, "an you better slop fast or you won't git nothin. Them hawgs is powerful hongry."

The group turned and went back across the clearing, back to the front porch, leaving the hog pen in darkness.

They climbed the steps and squatted on the porch in a circle, the lantern in the center. "Go get a jug of corn, Bester," Jud said, "an bring that hind quarter of smoked deer." Bester got up and went into the house.

"The sheriff's taken up with the niggers," Hankins said suddenly, absently, bouncing up and down on his heels. Bester came back out and handed the jug to Jud and threw the chunk of deer meat and a knife on the floor. Jud took a deep drink, and then the jug started around the circle. Ashley cut a slab of meat and started chewing.

"Whut you gone do 'bout the sheriff?" Jud asked, cutting a slice of meat.

"Let's shoot up his house," Coney said, speaking the first words he had uttered all night.

"Naw, not tonight," Jud said. "The moon ain't right."

"We could burn a cross on his yard," Hankins said, wiping corn whiskey from his chin.

"Naw, not tonight," Jud said. "Druther sot here an drink."

"Whut you want to do, Jud?" Ashley asked.

"Damned, Con," Jud said, his voice agitated, "are you deef? I done said I want to sot here an drink!

Not even Ashley wanted to argue with Jud. The subject of cross-burning was dropped. The jug was making its third round when Jud threw up his hands and said sharply, "Listen!"

It was coming from across the clearing behind the house "Aaawhooooo. Aaawhooooo. Aaawhooooo."

"What the hell is that?" Ashley asked. "Sounds like a hound has a wildcat treed."

"Hit's thet durn nigger," Jud said. "He's bayin. He don't shet up, he'll stir up the dogs for sure. Bester, you go put a stop to thet."

Bester got up and disappeared into the darkness. The sound came again, "Aaawhooooo. Aaawhooooo. Aaawho—"

"That's better," Jud said, taking a deep drink. He cut another chunk of deer meat as Bester came around the corner of the house and rejoined the group.

Hankins took another drink, cut a piece of meat and said, "The sheriff's taken up with the niggers."

"Whut yo gone do?" Jud asked.

It was three in the morning when Hankins parked the car behind the store, staggered into the kitchen and fell across a chair, cursing the darkness. He got up and felt his way along the hall to the bedroom. When he snapped on the overhead light his wife looked up at him from the bed. "You kill him?" she asked calmly.

"Kill who?" Hankins said, glaring at her.

"The nigger."

"Goddammit, I ain't seen no nigger!" Hankins exploded. "I been coon huntin. I told you that."

"The Lord gone judge you someday, Sim."

"Dammit, shut up," he mumbled. He threw his clothes on the floor, snapped off the light and tumbled into bed, snoring instantly, spraying the woman with the foul odor of half-digested corn whiskey.

Ten

Grenlee came from the house, a fat cigar in his mouth, and got into the car with Ike. They drove around the courthouse, down Main Street, and across the railroad tracks.

"This will be something new to me," Grenlee said. "I've never been inside a colored church, and to tell the truth, I'm kinda nervous."

"I can't imagine you being nervous about anything," Ike teased. "And besides that, you're their mayor. Next time you run they'll be voters, and you'll be wanting their votes. Just talk to them like you would your other constituents."

"Say, I never thought about that," Grenlee said, flicking cigar ashes out the car window. "I might make a hundred votes down here this morning." His expression then changed, becoming serious. "Ike, do you really think we could have trouble in Midvale?" he asked.

"Nobody believes they could ever be hit by a train," Ike replied, "but some do. It can happen to the other fellow, but not to me. Best thing we can do is get off the tracks, if that's possible. And that's what we're trying to do."

"Maybe so," Grenlee said, "but some of the stuff I see on television scares the hell out of me. So much violence and hate. I sure hope we don't get a dose of it here."

"I don't believe we will," Ike said. "Midvale is not that important to anyone."

Ike turned off Front Street and drove slowly down the dusty lane toward the church.

"You know, Ike," Grenlee said, looking at the dilapidated shacks, "times have really changed. A few years ago, no white man would have encouraged a Negro to fix up his house and make it look nice. Nobody cared. And if a Negro did fix up his place on his own and painted it, he would have been branded an 'uppity nigger.' I'm glad we're able to get this project going without any trouble from anyone."

Ike parked the car at the edge of the clearing and they walked across the parched grass toward the church. Reverend Holbrook stood in the door, greeting each member of his congregation. He smiled when he looked down and saw the two white men coming up the steps, then extended his hand to Ike.

Ike took the hand and said, "Good morning, Reverend Holbrook."

"Good moanin, Mistuh Ike," the reverend replied pleasantly. "An good moanin to you, Mistuh Grenlee." The two shook hands hesitantly.

"Good morning, Reverend," Grenlee then said, feeling awkward.

"We sho mouty proud to have you both wid us dis moanin," Reverend Holbrook said cordially. "We gwine have dinner on de grounds after services, an you sho be's welcome to stay an et."

"Thanks, Reverend," Ike said, "but we can't this time. The mayor has another engagement. Maybe next time."

"Dat's too bad," the reverend replied, disappointed, "but you be's welcome any Sunday. Come on in de church an take all de time yo needs befo de services."

The two men followed the Negro preacher down the aisle of the church, with every eye in the congregation turned to them, following each step, wondering in unison why the two white men, the sheriff and the mayor, were in their church. Ike and Grenlee stepped up on the platform and took seats in the cane-bottomed chairs while Reverend Holbrook went behind the pulpit. Not even a hint of sound came from the pews.

Reverend Holbrook stood silent for a moment, then he said, "Brothers an sisters, we's privileged dis moanin to have wid us de mayor an de shuff, Mistuh Grenlee and Mistuh Thonton. De mayor has asked could he speak to de congregation befo de services. Mistuh Mayor, we welcome you to our church."

Reverend Holbrook took a seat beside Ike as Grenlee got up

and walked to the pulpit, his steps on the wooden floor sounding like claps of doom. As he stood there before the Negro congregation, every eye became magnetized to his face, every expression asking, *Why is he here?*

Grenlee was wondering if he should say "fellow citizens" or "ladies and gentlemen" or what? He cleared his throat twice, then said, "Reverend Holbrook, I want to thank you for allowing me to break in on your services this morning to speak on something of importance to your congregation."

Grenlee stopped, cleared his throat again, then continued, "Now this may not affect all of you, but I'm sure you'll all be interested. The city has bought all the Bingham rental property here in the quarters and we're going to start a new project down here tomorrow morning."

A unified sucking of air made a whooshing sound as those who lived in the rental houses took a deep breath, thinking, *The white man is going to put us out and destroy our homes.* A shuffling rumble came from the pews.

Grenlee noticed the abrupt change of expression in his audience and decided he had better get straight to the point. He again cleared his throat and continued. "As I said, the city has bought all the Bingham rental property. Tomorrow a ditch digger will begin work laying sewer lines down all the streets, and we're going to pave the streets. Each house will have a bathroom added to it, repairs made, including new roofs, and then painted, and then we'll sell the property to the renters for one thousand dollars per house. The bank has agreed to finance each house with the payments the same as you're paying now for rent. In less than five years, each person will have his house completely paid for."

The stunned Negroes sat silent, faces blank, staring at the white man behind the pulpit, wondering if he had really said what it sounded like he had said, unable to immediatly comprehend.

Reverend Holbrook jumped up and said, in a full booming voice, "You see! You see, brothers an sisters! I done tole you! Do things de Lawd's way an de Lawd will smile down! Praise God, praise de Lawd!"

An "Amen!" drifted from the congregation, then another, then a chorus of "Praise the Lawd!" rang through the church. The Negroes stirred and came back to life, releasing the breath they had been holding in dread.

Grenlee suddenly felt a surge of pleasure course through his veins, a tingling exhilaration. He smiled. "Are there any questions about the project?"

One man stood and asked, "How much do we have to pay for the bathrooms?"

"Not anything," Grenlee answered. "That's included in the price of the house. You don't pay anything extra."

"Another: "How much will de taxes be?"

"Leaving the houses assessed as they are now, the tax will be between five and ten dollars a year," Grenlee replied. "Later on, when you qualify for homestead exemption, you won't owe any property tax.

Another: "Whut do we do if we has to move away? Do we has to give the house back to the city?"

"No. It will be your house. You can sell it or do whatever you wish with it."

Another: "Whut about the sewer pipe an streets? Who gone pay for that?"

"The city will assume the entire cost of the sewer lines and paving the streets. There won't be an assessment." Grenlee was enjoying answering the questions, for each answer brought a better response from the audience.

Another: "When we gwine own dem houses?"

"As soon as the project is completed you'll be given a deed to the house," Grenlee said. "Any rent money paid during the project will be held in escrow and applied to the mortgage payments."

Same man: "Whut's dat?"

"What's what?" Grenlee asked, puzzled.

"Dat es-crow."

A ripple of laughter swept through the pews.

Grenlee smiled, trying to choke back the laughter that was knotted inside him. He said, "Putting the payment in escrow means we put it in a fund at the bank and hold it there for you until the project is complete. Then it will be applied to your payments."

"Sho nuff."

Another: "Mistuh Mayor, I ain't got no question, but I wants to say bless yo. I's seventy-five yar old, an I ain't never sot in no bathtub an biled myself in hot water. I been askin de Lawd befo I go, let me sot one time in a bathtub an bile myself in hot water. Bless yo, Mistuh Mayor, bless you. I's gwine bile myself ever day 'fo I die."

Grenlee decided he had better quit while he was still ahead. He said, "Well, if there are no more questions, I'll turn the meeting back to Reverend Holbrook. And I want to thank you again for letting us come. It's been a pleasure."

Reverend Holbrook stood up and said, "Sistuh Pearly an Sistuh Dothy, you go out an fix our friends some plates to take home. An bless you, Mistuh Grenlee and Mistuh Thonton. You be's welcome in our church anytime." The Negro preacher extended his hand to the two white men, and this time Grenlee clasped the black hand without hesitation.

Ike and Grenlee walked back along the aisle, the same aisle they had walked a short time before in trepidation, now seeing a host of smiling faces that previously had borne anxiety, apprehension and doubt. They followed two plump Negro women out the door.

Sister Pearly, who reminded Ike of Doshie, said, "White folks, you come wif us. We gwine fix you some food."

Ike said, "Don't bother, please. Don't go to any trouble for us."

Sister Pearly then said, in a commanding voice, the lost voice of a Doshie come back, "'Taint no bother! Now you come wif us! We gwine fix you some food!"

Ike and Grenlee followed the two wobbling women across the clearing to the table under the trees at the edge of the woods. Both women wore black dresses, red high-heeled shoes, and strings of red glass beads around their necks. Sister Pearley was topped by a red hat with a foot-wide brim. Sister Dorothy's white hat perched on top of her head and was decorated with artificial flowers. The tables were covered with red-and-white-checkered cotton tablecloths, and a white cloth covered the food. The two women took paper plates and started bustling around, throwing back the cloths, uncovering dishes.

"Now Sistuh Bet make de best chicken an dumplin," Sister Pearly bubbled, "an Sistuh Carry de best fried chicken, an be sho an git some of Sistuh Lucy's fresh poke backbone an collard greens, an Sistuh Jane's pot roast, an don't foget Sistuh Larry's pecan pie, an Sistuh Martha's choclate cake, an put on some roast'n ears, an some sugared sweet 'taters, an some spare ribs."

The two men watched in awe as the women piled mountains of food on the plates, making them sag in the middle; then they took two more plates and filled them. Sister Dorothy found cardboard boxes in a nearby pickup truck, put two plates in each box, and covered them with paper napkins.

Sister Pearley was bursting with enthusiasm as she handed a box to each man. Ike and Grenlee thanked them profusely.

"You sho be's welcome, white folks," Sister Pearly said, a wide grin splitting her face. "When you get home, you an yo family eat ever bite!"

As they walked back to the car Grenlee said, "Man, smell that aroma! I'd swap the best chef in France any day in the week for a good Negro cook. You just can't beat it."

"Tell me about it," Ike said knowingly. "I was raised on it."

They drove back up the dusty lane and turned onto Front Street. Grenlee said, "You know, Ike, I really enjoyed that meeting. I've been dreading going down there this morning, really doubtful about how we would be received. I felt like I was going into a foreign country and couldn't speak the language. Why didn't you think up this idea before? We should have started this project a lot sooner."

"Yes," Ike said, "we should have started a long time ago."

Eleven

Peggy Jo and the children had just returned from church services when Ike arrived home with the unexpected but welcome gift from the ladies of the Midvale African Baptist Church. The usual Sunday lunch of soup and a sandwich was supplanted by a feast that took Ike back to the days of his childhood when the Sunday noon dinner was a thing looked forward to during the entire week. Doshie never missed a church service, so she would be up at dawn, banging pots and pans in the kitchen, filling the house with odors of delights to come, getting the meal prepared in time to leave for services, then rushing home afterwards to spread the table with her culinary masterpiece. Then she would stand off to one side, smiling, waiting for the compliments she knew would come, the little verbal gifts that were the treasures of her life.

The Baptist Church had planned an afternoon of games for the children as the opening activity of the annual summer Daily Vacation Bible School, a thing Ike had always looked forward to eagerly when he was a boy, not for the Bible lessons he and his cohorts endured, but for the games and cookies and candy and iced lemonade that were used as enticements to lure the Midvale boys to the church. After they dropped the children at the church playground, Ike and Peggy Jo drove out into the country, on a paved road that ran from Midvale to a farming community in the lower Pearl River section of the county. Although he had never been a farmer, Ike loved the land and enjoyed riding on a Sunday afternoon, looking at the fields, the farm houses, the crops that were pushing back the earth and springing into the sunlight. June was a time of reckoning for the farmers of Stonewall County, a time when all planting was finished, a time when nature could create with her gentle rain or destroy with her blistering sun, a time of transition from moderate spring to sweltering summer.

The road twisted and turned, like a snake in agony, following property lines, cutting through banks of red clay, over hills and into little valleys bounded on both sides by woods, areas of swaying broomsage, pastures, fields, gulleys where erosion had created miniature canyons. Ike could remember when the only paved road in the county was the main highway that ran through Midvale. Now there were few roads that were not paved. He could also remember the changes in the land, the times he had driven this same road, spewing gravel, seeing fields being plowed with mules, animals that had almost completely vanished, replaced by tractors; seeing dilapidated farm houses with clay chimneys, cords of firewood stacked in the yard, a lone chinaberry tree for decoration; now replaced by neat houses, wood and brick, with power lines, telephone lines, butane tanks, yards with flower beds, modern houses belonging to these people, white and Negro, who had suffered with strength and fought the land, determined to win against seemingly unsurmountable odds, and had eventually won, won over poverty and squalor, won by converting worthless scrub acres to cattle pastures, filling former cotton fields with row upon row of chicken houses, won by feeding the worn tired soil with chemicals and planting different crops only in cycles, giving the soil a new life, won by dotting dry hilltops and gulleys with pine trees that would yield cash crops, won by sheer determination not to surrender to a life of miserable endless toil without compensation, a life of sow belly and corn pone. He could also see evidence of those who had not won, those who were yet losing, shacks covered with tarpaper, the wood yet stacked in the yard, the lone chinaberry tree, chickens pecking at bare ground, a leaning rotting barn that housed a mule—a minority yet present, both white and Negro, perhaps permanently defeated, resigned, overwhelmed and drowned in a surging sea of progress, unable to cope or keep pace, left behind.

Ike had tremendous respect for these men of the soil who fought a day-by-day and year-by-year battle with nature, asking no quarter and void of complaint. He knew their weaknesses, faults, shortcomings and virtues; their false premises, fears, desires and prejudices. He had bonded with them spiritually and could speak their language, and during his campaign for sheriff, he received the majority of their votes.

Ike turned north and drove along another country road that circled back to the west side of Midvale, following the banks of Strong River. Peggy Jo, who had been silent, also absorbed in the landscapes they had seen so many times previously, realized where he was heading, knew that he was taking her to Old Mound, their secluded place of dreams and reality. She did not speak, for she sensed that he was in deep thought, perhaps troubled thought.

He parked the car off the side of the road and they walked along a trail leading upward, beneath tall pines, over ground matted with decades of accumulated pine needles that gave way beneath their feet, like a plush carpet. She walked ahead of him, and he watched the sensuous movement of her body, the flow of dark hair around her shoulders, watching her as he had done when they walked this trail the day before he had left her for college, the day before he left her for the army, and countless other times. He stepped forward and took her hand gently, and they walked together beneath giant trees whose tops were entwined, forming the roof of a cathedral here in the piney woods, a place he had always loved.

They came to a bluff that towered over the banks of Strong River. Ike and Sidney Grenlee had camped on this bluff each summer when they were boys, digging with shovels and picks, looking for a sealed cave which was said to hold the skeleton and treasures of a once-great Indian chief, looking for something they never found but always believed in—something that probably never existed. Ike had brought Peggy Jo here for the first time when she was fourteen, and they had returned often, sometimes riding bicycles, sometimes hiking, climbing down the steep bluff and wading in the cool waters of the river. A giant boulder, which still occupied its precarious perch on the edge of the bluff, was scarred with crudely-cut words, now blackened by time and the elements: IKE + PEGGY JO. He had always wished he could someday own this bluff and fence it away from the world, keeping it as his private sanctuary.

They sat on the edge of the bluff, listening to the wind sing through the pines, watching and listening to the flow of the river as it bubbled over rocks far below. It was a mesmerising sound, and it suddenly transported Ike backward in time to the carefree days of his youth, to a time when he had no knowledge or conception of a Sim Hankins or a Con Ashley or a Reverend Holbrook or a Hanibel Felds, not even an inkling that something was not right in the small world in which he lived. It would have been inconceivable to him to believe that someday he would be caught in the middle of violent winds of change.

When the spell was finally broken, and they got up to leave, Ike did not know that he would never again return to this hallowed ground with even a trace of the innocence of his youth.

Twelve

Ike and Grenlee stood by the patrol car, watching the machine cut a black trench in the dusty soil. They were in a crowd of more than a hundred Negro spectators who were also watching every move the machine made, visually examining each speck of soil as it was scooped up and cast aside. The day before had been the same, with the operator of the ditch digger commanding an audience that watched with awe. From an adjoining street came the staccato rhythm of hammers and the hum of electric saws as the carpenters went about the task of face-lifting and expanding the sagging shacks. The two white men watched with amusement as a lumber truck drove past them, churning a cloud of dust, pursued by a dozen Negro children who were whooping and hollering as if to frighten the truck along. During the first two days of the project the entire quarters had taken on the gala atmosphere of a carnival.

Ike dropped Grenlee at his insurance office and drove to the courthouse. He went past his office and walked down the hall to the circuit clerk's office. Currey was standing by the window, and Ike supposed that he was engaged in his daily five-minute imaginary fishing trip.

"How're they biting this morning?" Ike asked.

Currey looked at Ike in simulated annoyance and said, "Dang it, Ike, you do that every time! I almost had him in the boat."

Ike grinned and said, "I did you a favor, Buford. If you'd caught that fish you wouldn't have anything to look forward to. Now you can go after him again tomorrow."

Currey smiled and said, "What can I do for you?"

"Just wondering about the voter registration," Ike replied. "How's it been going since I had that meeting at the church?"

"Just a few at a time, and not a one has been in this week who couldn't qualify. They're coming in at scattered intervals, and I haven't had more than three in the office at one time."

"That's good," Ike said, pleased, "just the way they said they would do it. Better luck next time with the fishing."

"Yeah," Currey said wryly. "And you come again, Ike."

When Ike entered his office the giant Negro, Hanibel Felds, was standing at the counter. Ike stepped behind the counter and said, "Something I can do for you?"

Felds looked at Ike with a blank expression, without the slightest hint of recognition, as if he were seeing Ike for the first time. "You de shuff?" he asked.

"Yes," Ike replied, surprised that the Negro did not know who he was. "I'm Sheriff Thornton. Don't you remember me?"

Felds ignored the question and said slowly, "Montique gone. He been gone three day. Montique say de shuff his friend. He left Saddy night an ain't been back since. Left wid a white man. I seen him."

A sudden sickness boiled inside Ike's stomach. He asked apprehensively, "Who was the white man?"

The Negro stood straight, still expressionless. "Dat white man who own de sto down by de mill."

Sim Hankins? Not Con Ashley? Ike rubbed his forehead, puzzled, wondering if the Negro were telling the truth. He said doubtfully, "Are you sure that's who it was?"

"I seen him."'

Then it came to Ike, a realization that Ashley would be too cunning to risk being seen with Montique, that he would enlist the aid of Hankins in whatever it was he intended to do. But he also wondered if he were concluding too hastily. Montique had been known to stay drunk for several days without coming to work or sending word to his employers. He looked up into the slit eyes that were fixed on him and asked, "Have you been by his cabin to see if he's there?"

"He gone," Felds said firmly. "Left wid de white man. I seen him."

Ike came from behind the counter and walked into the outer office. Sam and Billy were sitting at a desk, working on warrants that had been brought in by the justice of the peace.

"Where's Lon?" Ike asked in a harsh tone.

"He went down into the quarters just a few minutes ago," Billy said. "Has something come up?"

"Yes," Ike said, "something has come up." Both men sensed that something important to Ike had happened. Ike said, "Billy, you go find Lon, and both of you come back to the office and wait here. Sam, you follow me in your car down to Sim Hankins' store."

"What's happened, Ike?" Sam asked curiously.

"Montique's missing," Ike said, "and we might have a murder on our hands. You better rush it, Billy, and come straight back here."

Ike went back to the counter where Felds still stood motionless and said, "You come with me, Felds, and identify the man you saw leave with Montique."

"I seen him," Felds said again. "Montique been gone three day."

The giant Negro followed Ike outside and to the patrol car. Ike opened the door and got in, expecting Felds to come around and get in beside him. He looked up and the Negro was standing by the car, staring at the star on the door, a wildness in his eyes.

"Let's go!" Ike commanded. "Come on around and get in!"

Felds stared at the door, then he took a step backward.

Ike got out of the car, faced the Negro and said, "I'm Montique's friend. I want you to help me. Don't you want us to find Montique?"

Felds looked at Ike and then back to the star. He said, "Montique say you his friend." He walked around the rear of the car, opened the door and got in reluctantly, having to hunch forward to keep his head from bumping against the inside roof.

Ike took a side street away from Main Street and came to the highway two blocks south of the traffic signal. The Negro sat rigid, looking straight ahead, his hands trembling against the dashboard, his eyes blinking. Ike gave the car a burst of speed, then turned off the highway and parked beside the wooden building. As they got out Sam pulled in and parked beside them. Ike took the shotgun from the front seat.

When they entered the store Hankins got up from a chair and leaned against the counter. He said, "Howdy, Sheriff. What can I do for you?

"Is this the man?" Ike asked Felds.

Felds stared at Hankins, still expressionless, then he said, "Dat him. Dat's de man. I seen him."

Hankins looked at the Negro, then back at Ike and Sam. His face was beginning to turn crimson. "What the hell is this?" he asked, his voice mixed with curiosity and anger.

"Where's Montique?" Ike asked, looking straight into Hankins' eyes.

Hankins' crimson flush disappeared immediately, replaced by a marble-white face. "Montique? What you mean? I don't know nothin about Montique." He pressed back against the counter as Ike stepped toward him, the shotgun in his right hand, pointing downward.

"Montique's been gone since Saturday night," Ike said harshly. "Felds here says he saw him get in the car with you. Where is he, Hankins?"

Hankins looked at Felds, his face flushing from white to crimson. He said angrily, "Why, you goddam black son-of-a-bitch, I'll—"

Ike stepped in quickly and shoved the shotgun barrel into Hankins' stomach as he moved toward Felds. Hankins stopped, then retreated backward to the counter.

"Where's Montique, Hankins?" Ike demanded. "Did Con Ashley put you up to it?"

Hankins face was now white again, and beads of sweat appeared on his forehead. "That nigger's lyin, Thornton," he said, his voice dropping down an octave. "I ain't seen Montique in two or three weeks."

"I seen him," Felds said, staring at Hankins. "I seen Montique get in the car with him."

Hankins' hands were trembling. He started to move forward, then hesitated when he looked at the shotgun. "All right," he said. "I did pick him up. I had a job for him to do here at the store. He was here about a half hour an left when I paid him." Hankins' mind was so jumbled under pressure that he had not thought to say this when Ike first entered and asked about Montique. He was now completely addled, thinking only of what would happen to him if he told on Con Ashley or Jud Miller.

"Why did you lie to begin with?" Ike asked.

"I didn't lie," Hankins said, mopping his brow with a handkerchief. "I just didn't remember. I git niggers all the time to do odd jobs, an I don't go around makin a big thing of it."

Ike was becoming even more agitated, tired of this game he knew Hankins was playing. He stepped closer and said, "Hankins, if you don't tell me what has happened to Montique, I'm going to take you up to the jail and charge you with kidnapping. And if something bad has happened to Montique, you're going to be an accessory, even an accessory to murder. Now would you like to say where he is?"

Hankins was thinking, the word murder banging around in his brain, thinking that if he told them, they might go away, and he could beat them out to Miller's place and let the Negro go. But what if the Negro was dead, and they got there first? And even if Montique was not dead, and the sheriff found him first, then what? He knew that either Con Ashley or Jud Miller would have him in the pen next, maybe dead, to be eaten by hogs. He was more afraid of Con and Jud than the sheriff. He said firmly, "I don't know nothin about it!"

Ike turned crimson, his hands trembling, shaking the shotgun. "Hankins, you lie!" he snapped. "I ought to bash your head in with this gun butt! Let's go!"

None of them had noticed the woman silhouetted behind the thin cotton curtain separating the hallway from the store. She stepped out unnoticed and said, "The nigger's out at Jud Miller's place."

All of them stood silent for a moment, frozen, looking at the frail woman as they would a suddenly appearing ghost.

"Jud Miller's?" Ike muttered. "That bunch of bearded hermits out at Big Springs? Why there?"

"They took him," the woman said directly to Ike. "Sim and Con Ashley took him."

"You bitch!" Hankins suddenly boomed, his lips quivering and puckering as if sucking a lemon. "You filthy bitch! I told you I was goin coon huntin!" His lips were popping and jerking so fast he couldn't continue talking. He then just stood there, staring at the woman, clucking like a hen.

"I know you'll whup me, Sim," she said, now looking at him. "But it warn't right with the Lord." She turned and disappeared behind the curtain.

"Cuff him, Sam," Ike said. "Take him to the jail and hurry on back to the office."

Sam snapped a pair of handcuffs on the sputtering red-faced man, then the small procession left the dim interior of the store and got into the patrol cars. Felds walked away alone up the railroad tracks.

Lon and Billy were waiting when Ike entered the office. He walked straight to his desk, opened a drawer, took out an army .44 and strapped it to his hips. He came back around the counter and said, "Sam will be here in a minute. He's taking Hankins to the jail.

Montique is out at Jud Miller's place. We better take pistols and shotguns.

"Jud Miller's?" Billy said, surprised. "What's he doin out there with that bunch of wild monkeys?"

"I don't know," Ike replied. "Hankins and Con Ashley took him out there. Billy, you come in the car with me. Sam and Lon can follow. Put cuffs and leg irons in the car. And be damned sure those guns are loaded."

Mrs. Fleming was standing behind the counter, listening with concern. "Ike," she said, "all of you be careful. You be real careful."

Ike was not aware she was even in the office. "Yes, we will," he said, not conscious of what he was saying, thinking ahead to how they would approach the place. "Let's wait outside for Sam."

When they reached Ike's car, Sam was driving up. Billy got into the car with Ike and they headed toward the road leading to Big Springs, the other car following.

Ashley had been driving north toward town when he spotted the two patrol cars at Hankins' store. He pulled off the highway and watched as they led Hankins outside and took him away. He sat there for several minutes, thinking of what he must do, knowing that this must have something to do with Montique. He thought first of racing out to Jud's and taking Montique away, but then there was the chance that Hankins had not told them where the Negro was. But if he had not told them something they would not have led him out handcuffed. And he did not want to run the risk of being caught by Ike at Jud's place. He would have to find out what Hankins had told them. He drove into town, past Main Street, then turned onto a back street that led to the west side of the jail, away from the courthouse.

Ashley could see the courthouse from where he was parked, and he watched Ike and his deputies as they drove away. When the patrol cars were out of sight he drove to the jail and parked. Clayton was standing in the doorway when he came up the steps.

"Howdy, Con," Clayton said. "They brung ole Sim Hankins up here a while ago. What you suppose they got him fer?"

"I don't know," Ashley said impatiently. "Maybe he owes somebody some money an won't pay. Let me have the keys. I got to see somebody up there a minute."

"Shore," the old man said, handing Ashley the ring of keys. "But I ain't never seen 'em bring nobody in handcuffed 'cause of a debt. Ole Sim musta stepped in it good 'bout somethin."

"Yeah," Ashley said, unlocking the downstairs door. "I'll bring the keys back in a minute."

He climbed the circular stone stairway, unlocked the upper door and walked down the corridor that divided the two rows of cells.

Hankins was in a cell alone, at the end of the corridor. He was sitting on a bunk, nervously popping his knuckles, when he saw Ashley approach. He got up quickly and came to the bars. "You got to git me out of here, Con!" he said. "I was just doin you a favor by helpin! You got to get me out of here!"

"Keep your fool voice down," Ashley said. "Now what the hell did you tell Thornton?"

"I didn't tell him nothin, I swear I didn't," Hankins said desperately.

"If you didn't tell him nothin, what the hell are you doin in that cell?"

"My old woman tole him," Hankins said, lowering his head, casting his eyes downward.

"Told him what?"

"That me an you took Montique out to Jud's."

"Son-of-a-bitch!" Ashley muttered.

"I didn't know she even knew, Con, honest I didn't," Hankins said apologetically. "She must have overheard us talkin."

"You ought to ram a cross-tie up her when you get out of here!"

"She's really got religion lately," Hankins said, "just as if she's about to pass on, and knows it. She didn't mean no harm. I'll whup her, though, soon as I get back to the store."

Ashley glanced up the corridor, making sure no one was listening. Then he pressed against the bars and said in lower tones, "If that's all she told him, Thornton don't really know nothin, except where Montique is. Ain't no law against us takin him out there. We can say he told you he had a job out there, an just asked us for a ride. Jud ain't gone say nothin, so unless the nigger talks, they ain't got no legal right to do anything. You remember, now, he had a job, an we just took him out there as a favor."

"You think the nigger will talk?" Hankins asked anxiously.

"I don't know," Ashley replied, scratching his head. "But would you, with them Millers around?"

"He won't say nothin," Hankins said, relieved.

"You remember, we just did him a favor an drove him out there," Ashley said firmly.

"I'll remember, Con. We just drove him out there. I shore would hate to be Thornton right about now, facing them Millers."

"How'd Thornton get on to you anyhow?" Ashley asked.

"A goddam big nigger named Felds told him!" Hankins' voice boomed through the corridor and startled Ashley.

"What you tryin to do, you damned idiot," Ashley exclaimed, "tell everbody on Main street?"

"I didn't mean it, Con, I swear," Hankins said quickly. "But I'm gonna fix that big nigger, just you wait an see!"

"I got to get on out of here before Clayton suspects somethin," Ashley said, glancing around. "Now you remember what to say."

"I will, Con," Hankins said, pressing against the bars. "I swear I will."

The two patrol cars pulled off the narrow lane and into the woods just before they reached the clearing in front of the shack. The men gathered around the lead car. Each carried a shotgun and a pistol. Ike said softly, "I don't know what we'll find here, if anything, but be alert. This Miller clan hasn't joined the twentieth century yet. All of you stay in the edge of the woods and keep out of sight. I'll walk up to the house alone. It would be best not to startle them with a show of force before we know what to expect. Montique may not even be here now. He might be buried in the woods somewhere."

Billy said, "What you want us to do if these fools start shootin?"

"What I'm going to do is get the hell out of there and hide behind a tree," Ike said, grinning. "I'd suggest you do likewise. Then throw every bit of lead you've got into that shack."

"You be careful, Mistuh Ike," Lon said. "If anybody starts shootin, you get on the ground so's we can shoot over you an blast that place full of holes."

"Don't worry, Lon," Ike replied, "I won't do anything foolish. We're just trying to find Montique — not become heroes, alive or dead."

Ike cradled the shotgun in his arms, stepped from the woods and walked forward slowly, moving across the clearing toward the shack. Not a sound came from anywhere, not even the slight rustle of a breeze in the pines. He glanced right and left without turning his head, stepping lightly as if approaching a covey of quail. The distance to the shack seemed to increase with each step. He could feel gun barrels pointed at him from every direction, expecting at any moment to hear the crack of rifles and the boom of shotguns. Then the shack loomed larger and larger, like a monstrous mouth open and awaiting him, breathing hot air that caused sweat to roll down his forehead and into his eyes.

He paused for a moment at the porch steps, trying to see through the screen door and into the dark interior of the shack. Still not a sound could be heard except his own labored breathing. He knocked on the porch floor, waited, then knocked again, skinning his knuckles on the rough planks but not feeling it. Still he waited, hearing nothing, the shack specterlike, somber and silent.

He went up the steps, one foot placed cautiously ahead of the other, gun cocked and pointing straight ahead; then he crossed the porch and shouted through the screen door, "Miller! Jud Miller! This is the sheriff! I want to talk to you!"

Nothing. Silence so intense it banged in his head louder than thunder. He retreated backward, glancing behind quickly, backward down the steps and into the yard; then he turned and motioned for the others to join him. They came out of the woods and across the clearing, the sound of their footsteps breaking the silence, breaking the tension, releasing a reservoir of strain that flooded through his pores.

"Well," Ike said, drawing the back of his hand across his forehead, "we're still here. Looks like I've been stalking a turkey after it flew away."

"When you knocked on the porch floor I damned near let go both barrels," Sam said. "This place gives me the creeps. It reminds me of something I had nightmares about when I was a kid."

Ike then said, "Lon, you stay here and watch the front. The rest of us will look around in back. Billy, you spread out to the left. I'll take the center, and Sam, you move to the right. And don't get too relaxed. We're not out of here yet."

"Who's relaxed?" Billy said. "I still feel like I've got ants in my pants."

The three men walked around the side of the house, and Sam and Billy moved off in opposite directions. Ike waited until they had reached each side of the clearing, then he started straight across the center, toward the woods. All three moved slowly, deliberately, glancing sideways at each other. They halted momentarily when they heard the hogs squeal, then moved forward again.

Ike came to the hog pen, turned and looked back toward the shack, trying to decide if they should search the woods or go back to the patrol cars and wait for the Millers to return. Sam and Billy stood motionless, waiting for Ike to signal them what to do.

"Dat you, Mistuh Ike?" a voice said weakly, breaking the silence.

Ike's heart stopped for what seemed an eternity but was only a split second. He whirled around instinctively, almost dropping the shotgun. He looked into the pen, staring at the rail-thin hogs, then he realized that one of the dirt-caked forms lying on the ground was not a hog but a man, a small Negro chained to a post, looking up at him with eyes as big as washtubs.

"Dat you, Mistuh Ike?" the voice came again.

"Montique!" Ike exclaimed in disbelief. "Good God-a-mighty!"

Ike just stood and continued looking for a moment, looking at

Montique lying there, filthy, lying prostate in a hog pen. He felt a rage boil up within him, a furious surge of anger, an overwhelming desire to shoot someone, hit with his fists, pound the guts out of someone, rip something with his trembling hands.

"Sam! Billy!" he finally shouted. "Over here!"

The two deputies crossed the open space quickly and stood by Ike, staring into the pen, at first not realizing, as Ike had not realized, that they were looking at a man, not a hog. All three of them leaned against the fence rails and stared silently, trying to comprehend, Montique now sitting up and staring back, blinking, his face muscles twitching, his lips quivering.

"Mistuh Ike, you looks jes lak Jesus," Montique said, a broad smile splitting his face.

"The fust one of you who moves is goin to meet Jesus face to face!" Jud said loudly. "Put them guns down real easy an turn around."

Ike and his deputies froze, the shotguns clutched limply by their sides. They backed away from the fence.

"You fellows ain't deef, air you?" Jud said, his voice flat. "I ain't goin to tell you again to put them guns down."

None of them had heard even the slightest sound when the Millers came up behind them. They put the shotguns on the ground, turned and faced the four bearded men, looking into the barrels of four rifles.

"You know whut we do to a hog thief?" Jud asked. "If'n you don't, you gone find out."

"The Negro," Ike said, his voice faltering. "We came for the Negro. We're not hog-stealing. I'm the sheriff. We came for Montique."

"Whut nigger?" Jud asked.

"In the pen," Ike muttered. "In the hog pen."

"You must be loco," Jud said, staring at Ike. "They ain't no nigger in the hawg pen."

Ike was watching, watching without letting them know, seeing Lon creep silently across the clearing, as silently as the Millers had come out of the woods.

"The first one moves gets two barrels of buckshot!" Lon said, his voice hard. "Whoever wants it, just move! I'll blow a hole through you like a stovepipe. Ease them guns down on the ground. Do it now! My finger is just itchin to pull this trigger."

The four bearded men dropped the rifles to the ground. Coney looked around and said, "Pa, hit's a nigger! Hit's a nigger done got the drop on us! I ain't never been drawed on before by a nigger!"

Ike, Sam and Billy picked up their guns, pointing them at the Millers. Lon stayed behind them.

"You got the keys to those locks?" Ike asked, turning to Jud.

"Whut you bring that nigger with you fer?" Jud asked, ignoring Ike's question. "We ain't never had a nigger out here with a gun."

"Dammit, Jud," Ike said, the anger surging back, "have you got the keys or not? In about five seconds I'm going to wrap this gun barrel around your head!"

"Ain't no need to get riled up," Jud said calmly. "We don't know nothin 'bout no nigger. Somebody musta left him here by mistake. We don't keep niggers in our hawg pen. Ain't enough fer the hawgs to et, much less feed a nigger. I ain't got no keys."

"Get an ax!" Ike shouted. "Get an ax and chop that damned fence post down!"

"Ah shucks, Sheriff," Jud said, "'taint no use cuttin up a good fence post. I chop up that post the hawgs will get out fer sure, an them boars is hell to catch in the woods."

Ike had lost all patience. He wanted to make Jud get down on his hands and knees and chew the post in half with his teeth. He said, "Billy, march this idiot down to the shack and make him get an ax and bring it back here. Ram that barrel up his rear if you have to. And Lon, go get handcuffs from the car and put them on these three."

"Whut you gone do that fer?" Coney asked. "We ain't done nothin. Ask the nigger."

"Don't worry," Ike said, "I'll ask the nigger. I'll ask him plenty."

Ike opened the hog pen gate as Billy marched the lumbering bearded man toward the shack. He walked over to Montique, knelt beside him and said, "Who put the chain on you, Montique?"

"I done it myself, Mistuh Ike," Montique said, glancing at the Miller brothers.

"Did it yourself?" Ike questioned. "Come on now, Montique. Who did it, Sim Hankins or Con Ashley or Jud Miller?"

"I done it myself," Montique repeated. "I were drunk, an done it myself.

"Never mind," Ike said, exasperated. "We'll talk about it when we get back to town."

Jud entered the pen, an ax in his hand, Billy one step behind with the shotgun pressed against his back.

"Chop," Ike said.

"Aw shucks, Sheriff," Jud said, looking at the post.

"Dammit, chop!" Ike shouted.

When Jud smashed the blade into the post a shower of chips peppered the pen. The two boars and the shote jumped and squealed, kicking like mules, then tore out through the open gate and disappeared into the woods, still kicking and squealing.

Jud turned to Ike and said, "You see, I tole you! I done tole you you'd let them hawgs git out! Them dern critters will be in the next county 'fore we can ketch 'em."

"Chop!" Ike said. "You won't need any hogs for a while."

Jud cut the post and Ike pulled the chain off. He went outside the pen and brought Montique's crutch to him. Montique got up and they all walked back out of the pen.

"We'll have to wait and use a hacksaw to get that chain off your leg," Ike said. "Lon, give this bearded hyena a set of bracelets and let's get going."

Lon walked over to Jud and snapped the handcuffs on his wrists.

"Sheriff, you gone let a nigger do that?" Jud asked. "Whut'd you bring a nigger fer? I ain't never had no dealins with a nigger 'cepin when I catch one stealin a hawg."

"You had one chained in your pen," Ike said. "What kind of dealings do you call that?"

"Don't know nuthin 'bout it," Jud said calmly. "Don't know how that nigger got in the hawg pen. That's the fust time I ever seed a nigger who'd want to chain hisself in a hawg pen. Must be loco."

"We'll see," Ike said. "Sam, you and Lon put these buzzards in the car with you and take them straight to the jail. We'll bring in Montique."

"You gone blow the siren?" Coney asked. "I ain't never been in one of them police cars with the siren blowin. You gone let him blow the siren, Sheriff?"

"Let's go," Ike said. "Let's get on away from here before I blow my own brains out."

"Whut would you do that fer?" Jud asked seriously. "If'n you gone shoot somebody, shoot the nigger."

"Good God!" Ike muttered. "Let's get out of here!"

Mrs. Fleming's jaw came unhinged when she looked up and saw Ike leading Montique into the office, the filthy hobbling Negro with a chain around his ankle, looking as if he had been dragged through a swamp bottom. She watched wide-eyed as they went into Ike's private office.

"Sam," Ike said, "go down to the hardware store and get a hacksaw. On the way back stop at the Ritz and pick up a sack of sandwiches and a quart of milk. I imagine Montique could use something to eat."

"Sho could, Mistuh Ike," Montique said, his eyes gleaming at the mention of food. "I didn't git much out dere 'cause dem hawgs kept rootin me out of de trough. I sho could use some vittles."

Ike closed the door and sat on the edge of his desk. He looked straight into Montique's eyes and said, "Montique, we can put this whole bunch, including Con Ashley, away for a long time if you'll just tell me the truth. Tell me exactly what happened."

"Mistuh Ike, I don know," Montique said, trying to sound convincing. "I were drunk. Dem white men didn't do nothin."

"I know you're afraid of them," Ike said, "but they can't hurt you if they're all in the state prison."

"I were drunk, Mistuh Ike," Montique repeated, not looking into Ike's eyes. "I done it all myself."

When he heard Billy and Lon come in Ike got up and went into an adjoining room with them. He said to Billy, "Go find Ashley and bring him here just as soon as possible. If he puts up an arguments, arrest him and bring him in cuffs if you have to."

"OK, Ike," Billy said. "I'd rather be out arresting Ashley than be around that Miller bunch. First thing they asked when they got in the cell was when they could eat. Old man Clayton almost swallowed his false teeth when we brought them in. I don't think he'll go upstairs even with the cell locked."

"When you get here with Ashley take him into your office and let me know right away," Ike said.

Ike walked back into the room with Montique and closed the door. He said to him, "Montique, Hanibel Felds didn't say you were drunk when he saw you get into the car with Hankins. Why don't you tell me what happened?"

"Hanibel de one who led you to me?" Montique asked, surprised.

"Yes. He came to me this morning and said he saw you get in the car with Hankins Saturday night. Why did you go with him, Montique?"

"I did a little job at his sto," Montique replied. "He paid me."

"Then how did you get out to Jud Miller's?" Ike asked, not expecting a truthful answer."

"I don't know, Mistuh Ike," Montique said again. "I were drunk."

Ike got up and walked back and forth across the room, then he stopped and said, "Montique, do you expect me to believe that you somehow got out to the Miller place, got in that hog pen and chained yourself to a post? I know that Hankins and Ashley took you out there. Who put the chain on you?"

"I done it myself," Montique repeated. "I were drunk."

"Don't you want to help me?" Ike pleaded.

"Don't you want to see those men in jail?"

"They ain't done nothin, Mistuh Ike," Montique said calmly. "I were drunk. I done it myself."

A sickening feeling swept through Ike. He knew he was defeated. Montique was afraid, deathly afraid, and he could understand why. All of the others would lie too, and he knew they would stick together and not change their story. "Montique," Ike said, staring directly into the Negro's eyes, "would you get up in a court of law and say that those men did not do anything to you, that you chained yourself to that post because you were drunk?"

"Yassah, Mistuh Ike, I sho would," Montique said quickly, wanting the questioning to end. "Dem white folks ain't done nothin to me. I done it myself."

Ike went to the window and looked into the courtyard, gazing at nothing in particular, seeing the Negro chained in the hog pen, seeing the men who did it, seeing the men laugh as they fed the Negro slop, seeing Sim Hankins and Con Ashley and the Miller clan going free, laughing at him, laughing at the Negro, free because the Negro was afraid. He turned when Sam entered, then he watched the small Negro take the bag of sandwiches, rip off the napkins and wolf the sandwiches down like a starving dog; then gurgling milk and letting it run down his chin through the dirt, forming a small rivulet of milk-mud on the floor.

"Montique," Ike said, walking back to the desk, "we've got to put a stop to the sort of thing that happened to you. It has to end. But without your help, there's nothing I can do, and there's nothing a court can do. Please tell me all about it."

Montique swallowed a mouthful of sandwich, looked up at Ike and said, "I's sorry, Mistuh Ike. I were drunk. I done it myself." He crammed another half of sandwich into his mouth and started chewing.

The saw blade cut through the last bit of metal and the chain fell to the floor. Sam picked it up and put it against the wall. "You want to keep this as evidence, don't you, Ike?" he asked.

"No, not as evidence," Ike said absently. "As a souvenir."

Lon opened the door and told Ike that Ashley was in the next room.

"Stay in here, Lon." Ike said. "When Montique finishes eating, take him home. Stop on the way and buy some soap. He'll need lots of soap." Ike then turned to Montique and said, "I'm going to put the whole bunch, Hankins and Ashley and the Millers, under a peace bond. That means that if they bother you again, they'll all go to jail immediately. Now get yourself cleaned up and go back to work, and don't be afraid. They can't touch you again. Do you understand?"

"Yassah, Mistuh Ike, I understan," Montique said untruthfully, knowing nothing about the meaning of a peace bond.

"Sam," Ike said, taking his arm and pulling him over to the window, "I want you to do something. Go over to the jail and look around upstairs, just like it is part of your job. Then stop at the Millers' cell and tell them that Ashley is over here laying this whole thing on them, saying that it was all their idea and they did it all. Tell them Ashley is putting all the blame on them."

Sam looked at Ike quizzically and said, "What for, Ike?"

Never mind what for!" Ike said firmly. "Just do it! And get on over there right now."

Ike walked out and went in to Billy and Ashley. Ashley jumped up from a chair and said, "What the hell you mean sendin a deputy out after me? I'm the constable in this beat!"

"I'm the constable in this beat!" Ike mimicked sarcastically. "Why'd you do it, Ashley?"

"Do what?" Ashley asked, keeping the anger in his voice."

"What you did to Montique," Ike responded, watching Ashley's reaction.

"I don't know what you're talkin about," Ashley said calmly, "and I don't know nothin about Montique. He did a job at Sim Hankins' store, then he said he had a job out at Jud Miller's place. We just done him a favor an took him out there. I ain't seen him since."

Ike stared into the red-brown eyes and said, "So that's your story. You just did him a favor."

"That's all!" Ashley snapped. "If that nigger said anything else he's lyin!"

"Oh, he hasn't said anything else," Ike said, moving closer. "But I'm going to say something. I'm putting you and Hankins and those Millers under a peace bond, and if any one of you, just any one of you, so much as look at that Negro again, you're all going straight to jail. Now you tell the rest of them, and make it good and clear, that if anyone touches Montique, everybody goes to jail. And right now, you're going to jail with the rest of them."

"Goin to jail!" Ashley bellowed. "What for? You ain't got no right!"

"I'm holding you for investigation," Ike said. "You'll get out, but for now you're going."

Ashley's face paled. He walked over to Ike and said, "You mean you're really goin to put me in jail?"

"That's right," Ike said briskly. "Billy, I want to see you in private for a moment."

Billy followed Ike outside and closed the door. Ike said, "Take him over and put him in the cell with the Millers. Don't leave, though. Stay around for a few minutes and then take him to a doctor."

"He don't need a doctor, Ike," Billy said, puzzled. "He's as healthy as a stud horse."

"He will," Ike said, a wry smile on his face. "Take him on over there now."

Billy gave Ike another puzzled look, then he opened the door and said, "Come on, Ashley. Let's go over to the pokey house."

Billy and Ashley walked across the courthouse lawn and down the street to the jail. Clayton met them at the door. "Gimme the keys," Billy said. "You got another boarder."

"What's goin on?" Clayton asked. "What's all this sudden traffic? An how come you got Con here? What'd he do?"

"Ain't nothin to worry about," Billy said. "Don't sweat it." He unlocked the bottom door and climbed the stairs, Ashley following. They walked down the corridor and stopped at the cell where four bearded men were squatting in a circle on the floor. They got up when they saw Ashley.

"Got another customer," Billy said. He unlocked the cell door and Ashley stepped inside.

"Howdy, Jud," Ashley said. "We'll be out of here 'fore you know it. They can't hold us long."

"Let me be fust," Bester said.

"Hit ain't right," Berl said. "Jest 'cause you're the oldest you allus want fust go at everthing. Hit's my tarn to be fust."

"Now, boys, don't fuss 'bout it," Jud said. "They'll be enough fer everbody. We'll take tarns."

"Take turns doin what?" Ashley asked. "What're you all talkin about?"

"We'll odd man out," Jud said, ignoring Ashley. He took four pennies from his pocket and gave one to each of them; then they flipped them into the air. The coins made ringing sounds when they hit the concrete floor.

"You're out, Berl," Jud said.

"What the hell are you doin?" Ashley asked.

They flipped the coins again. "You're out, Bester," Jud said.

Billy stood outside the cell, watching, becoming as puzzled as Ashley.

"Heads an tails," Jud said. "You win, Coney. You got fust go."

"Gee, thanks, Pa," Coney said, grinning. "I won't be a hawg. I'll leave some fer everbody."

Without speaking further, Coney rammed his fist into Ashley's stomach. Ashley doubled up and made a sound like a cat with a fish bone caught in its throat. Coney then brought his knee up in a swift movement and smashed it into Ashley's face. This straightened Ashley back up, and he moved into a corner and snorted.

"Goddamit," he babbled, "what the hell's gone wrong with all of you? You sons-of-bitches lost your minds?"

Coney walked over and stomped his heavy brogan shoe onto Ashley's foot. Ashley grabbed the foot and hopped around the cell, Coney following. Ashley started screaming, "Let me out of here!

Goddamit, let me out of here!"

"It's my tarn now, Coney," Bester said. He walked over and smashed his fist into the side of Ashley's face, causing his jaws to fly open. A blow to the kidney doubled Ashley up, then a knee to the face straightened him back to a standing position. He backed into a corner and started braying like a mule. Another fist caught him in the stomach and he started an alternate series of squeals, brays and grunts.

"Jee-e-sus!" Billy muttered, watching with disbelief. "They're beatin the do-do out of him. He's goin to need a doctor for sure. Maybe I better not leave him in there too long."

Thirteen

The chief topic of conversation on Main Street the next day was that some sort of ruckus had taken place at the jail, but no one knew exactly what it was. Con Ashley had been seen coming from Dr. Saley's clinic, limping badly, his face plastered with bandaids. Ike had let Hankins and the Millers spend the night in jail. When he released them the next morning, he watched as they walked away free, the bearded clan headed for the piney woods, Hankins on his way to the store to whip the woman, to beat her senseless with his fists. Ike's only consolation was that he felt reasonably sure none of them would bother Montique again.

Ike had been down in the Negro quarters that morning, viewing the progress with satisfaction. Sister Pearly was in the crowd of onlookers, and when Ike told her how much they had enjoyed the food from the church, she insisted that she would make him a chicken pie and bring it to his office. He asked her not to go to so much trouble for him, but he hoped she would.

Ike had been back in the office but a few minutes when he received a call from Grenlee, asking him to come to the City Hall.

When the entered the office Roy Kelso was also there.

"Come on in, Ike," Grenlee said. "Pull up a chair. Heard you had quite a day yesterday. What was it all about?"

"Yes, it was quite a day," Ike said, taking a seat. He did not want to go into too much detail about the episode because he was still disgusted at having to set the men free. He continued, "Con Ashley had a run-in with Montique last week, and Saturday night he and Sim Hankins took Montique out to that place of Jud Miller's near Big Springs. They chained him in a hog pen. We found him out there yesterday morning, but Montique claims he did it himself while drunk. He's too afraid of them to tell the truth."

"Chained in a hog pen!" Grenlee exclaimed. "I wouldn't have thought something like that could happen in this day and age. What about Ashley? They say he looks like he fell into a cage full of wildcats."

"The Millers got mad and worked him over pretty good," Ike said. "I've got the whole bunch under a peace bond, so I hope it's ended."

"To be honest," Grenlee said, "I'm glad Ashley got stomped. There ought to be some way we can get him out of office." Grenlee lit one of his cigars, leaned back and said, "Ike, we've got a problem."

"Problem?" Ike questioned, shifting his thoughts away from Montique. "What's that?"

"Roy says he's been getting a lot of complaints at the newspaper office about the project in the quarters. And I've had some myself."

"Complaints?" Ike asked apprehensively. "What kind of complaints?"

"Not about one part of it in particular," Grenlee said. "Just about the project as a whole, the fact that we're doing it."

"What's there to complain about?" Ike asked. "We've had street and sewer projects before. I don't get the point."

"One man came into my office this morning," Kelso said, "and wanted to know why the city is paying out tax money to fix up a bunch of nigger houses. I tried to explain that the city isn't paying out anything on the houses, but he kept ranting that we could fix his house free too."

Grenlee said, "Several have called me wanting to know why we're working on the Negro streets before we pave their street. Branch might be putting them up to it just to stir up trouble."

"What are you going to do," Ike asked. "A few complaints won't affect the project, will they?"

"No," Grenlee said. "We're not going to stop the project, but Roy suggested we call a public meeting in the school auditorium and let everybody have their say. I think it's a good idea. This project could be the turning point in our relations with the Negro community. It's time for us to have a general discussion and bring this whole civil rights business out into the open, not just talk about it in little groups on street corners, or keep silent. We've got to face it straight on."

"I agree," Ike said, "but why are some people tying this project only to the civil rights movement? The purpose of the project is to take us in another direction."

"Hell, Ike," Grenlee said, propping his elbows on the desk, "it's got to the point nowdays that any dealings you have with a Negro, somebody will connect it to this civil rights business. You know that! Sometimes I've been hesitant about talking to a Negro on Main Street, afraid somebody will say I'm plotting some big civil rights deal. And I'll bet that ninety per cent of the people in town have felt the same way at one time or another, afraid to have simple communication with Negroes they've known all their lives because somebody might be looking over their shoulder and start a stupid rumor. Well, who is this somebody? Just who am I supposed to be afraid of? I think that if we stick a pin in this overblown balloon and let the hot air out, it will shrink down to the size of a peanut."

"Maybe you're right," Ike said. "It's impossible to really know what's on a person's mind and how he feels unless he speaks out.

Maybe if everyone knows where everyone else stands it will help solve a lot of problems."

"What about Friday night?" Kelso asked. "I can run an article in tomorrow's paper announcing a public meeting and it will cover the county before Friday."

"That's fine," Grenlee said. "You can say that the meeting is being called to discuss the new city project. You don't need to use the word *Negro* in the article. Everybody knows. And they'll be there. We'll have all the board members on the stage. Ike, you might have a couple of deputies there just in case somebody does get hotheaded. I don't think they'll be needed, but it wouldn't hurt for them to be there."

"Will do," Ike said, getting up to leave. "No problem. This meeting will sure be something new for Midvale."

"That it will," Grenlee agreed. "And it will be interesting. Most interesting."

Cars and trucks were parked for two blocks on both sides of the street as Ike and Peggy Jo walked along the sidewalk leading to the high school auditorium. Grenlee had been correct in his prognosis that the word *Negro* would not be needed in the news article about the meeting. When the citizens of Midvale and Stonewall County read the article, knowing that the project mentioned was in the Negro quarters, they assumed immediately that the meeting would develop into an open discussion of the "Negro problem." Their reasons for assembling on this Friday night were varied. Some would come out of curiosity, wanting to hear what others might say; some would come because they wanted to express an opinion; and some would come because they had nothing better to do. Many would not come because of indifference, concerned only with the immediate problem of earning a living and not caring if toilets were put in the Negro houses or not, or if the Negroes rode on asphalt or dirt streets, or even if the Negro actually existed. To many citizens of Stonewall County, the Negro was there and not there. He was there on the streets, in the stores, in the mill yard and on the railroad tracks, but he was not there with them on a tractor in a sweltering field, not there milking seventy-five cows or cleaning up the droppings of twenty thousand chickens in a chicken house, and not there when the barn roof rotted and had to be replaced. They could see no real connection between themselves and the Negro population other than the fact that both white men and black men have to work in order to have groceries in the kitchen, pay the electricity bill, buy shoes, and own an automobile or a pickup truck.

The Midvale High School auditorium had a seating capacity of six hundred. Fifteen minutes before the meeting was to begin, all of the seats were occupied and chairs were brought in from classrooms and placed in the aisles. The auditorium was not air conditioned, which meant that on a warm June night there would be a profusion of sweating. Constant fanning—with hats, caps, newspapers and anything else available—made whooshing sounds that competed with the drone of conversations.

Being in this auditorium brought back a flood of memories to Ike and Peggy Jo. In earlier days, before the advent of television, this auditorium could be filled merely by dressing a group of clumsy children as fairies and elves and letting them prance around the stage. It had been not only the center of Midvale's social life, but almost the entire social life. Now it was used only for graduation exercises, and never before had it been used as a meeting site to discuss something pertaining to Negroes.

A podium had been placed in the center of the stage, and to the left there was a table and five chairs. The four aldermen and Major Beecham were sitting at the table; Grenlee was behind the podium. Branch was busy ramming his elbow into Bennett's ribs and saying, "I told you, didn't I? I told you there'd be trouble over the nigger project!"

Grenlee coughed several times, trying to attract attention. He said loudly, "Ladies and gentlemen . . . ladies and gentlemen."

The dull grating roar of six hundred voices mumbling gossip gradually subsided, and every eye in the auditorium became fixed on the mayor.

"Ladies and gentlemen." Grenlee stopped, took a handkerchief from his back pocket and mopped sweat from his brow.

"You done said that three times now," came a voice from the front row of seats. A wave of snickering ran through the auditorium.

Grenlee continued, "Ladies and gentlemen—"

"There he goes again," broke in the voice from the front row, this time bringing on a roar rather than a snicker.

Grenlee's sweat seemed to increase. He mopped his brow again, then said, "Fellow citizens, there seems to be some confusion about the project we have begun in the Negro quarters. We've called this meeting to explain the project and to answer any questions. You can stand up at any time and ask a question.

"First, I'll explain what we're doing down there and clear up the confusion. The city is not spending tax money to repair houses free. We've purchased all the Bingham property, and the people who are renting the houses are buying them and paying the entire cost of alterations and repairs. The only tax money being spent is for the sewer and street project. We're doing the work ourselves to eliminate the cost of contracted labor."

One man stood and asked, "What is the cost of this project, Mayor?"

"Between four and five thousand dollars," Grenlee replied.

Another: "What is the purpose of this project anyway? Why has the city suddenly become concerned about old man Bingham's nigger houses that have been down there now for over thirty years?"

Grenlee leaned across the podium and said, "One of the purposes of the project is to clean up an eyesore that should have been eliminated years ago. That place is a health hazard. Another reason is that we've got to start something to help the Negro population, and this is as good a beginning as any."

Another: "What do you mean when you say we've got to help the Negroes? Nobody helped me build my house, and nobody helps keep it painted or repaired. Why can't they do it the way I've done it?"

"Am I correct in assuming that you own your house?" Grenlee asked.

"Yes. I own it."

"If you rented it, would you spend money on it?"

"Well, no. But I'd raise hell and make the landlord fix it up."

"What kind of hell do you suppose a Negro could have raised that would force a white landlord to repair or maintain a house?" Grenlee asked. "We're talking about only the rental houses in the quarters, not the ones the Negroes own themselves and keep in reasonably good condition."

Another: "Why are you paving the streets in the quarters before you finish all of the streets in some white sections?"

"Because they're in worse shape than any others in town," Grenlee answered. "They don't even have gravel, only dust and mud, according to the weather. And this won't delay any other street project but for a few months."

The questions were coming faster than Grenlee expected, and he was irritated by the tone of some questioners. He mopped his brow again, wishing he had a large glass of cool water.

Another man stood and said harshly, "I'm not for spending a cent down there till we see what the niggers are going to do. If they're going to try to integrate our school, I'm for letting those houses rot to the ground. I don't want my kids in school with niggers."

"Now wait just a minute," Grenlee said, "You're—"

"Let me answer that one," Major Beecham broke in, getting up and walking to the edge of the stage. "You say you don't want your kids in school with niggers. I don't recall anybody saying you did, or that anybody here tonight does. But if a Negro applies for admission to this school he's going to be admitted. That's a settled question. You could stand in the school yard, do something foolish and fill the town with federal marshals, or you could take your kids out of school and make ignoramuses of them. You just tied the repair of those houses in the quarters to school integration. Part of the work on those houses will be to add bathrooms for the first time, so let me ask you this question. If you're going to have a Negro child in school with your kids, and there's nothing you can do about it, which would you rather have, a 'filthy nigger' or a 'clean nigger'?"

The man who had made the statement stood silent, staring at the major.

"Well, come on," Major Beecham said, "answer my question! Which would you rather have?"

"A clean nigger," the man said meekly.

A ripple of laughter came from the audience as the major walked back to the table and sat down.

Another: "What about the voting? I hear the niggers are signing up every day. If we end up someday with a nigger mayor, you think he'd pave a white street?"

Grenlee gripped the podium again and said, "The Negroes are not trying to take over the vote! That's just an untrue rumor. They are starting their own classes to teach illiterates to read and write before they even attempt to register. They don't have to do that. If they want to they can raise hell and get a federal registrar sent here, then anyone can register, illiterate or not. The new voting laws are on the books, so you're trying to beat a dead horse. As far as having a Negro mayor is concerned, and what he would or would not do, I can't answer that. But anyone, black or white, who would want this job at this particular time must be crazy. Sometimes I think I am. If I were you, I wouldn't lose any sleep over who is going to be mayor somewhere way down the road from now."

Grenlee walked from behind the podium, came to the edge of the stage and stood there silently, looking out at the audience, people he had been born among, grown up with and known all his life, people he would die with and be buried with, tied to each other by physically inhabiting a plot of earth called Stonewall County. Then he started speaking slowly and deliberately, choosing each word carefully as he went along. "There's one thing we should all understand," he said, "and that is we've got to change some things. There's some things we must do that we don't particularly like, but we must do them. I'm not up here tonight advocating that you invite a Negro family into your home for dinner, or go dancing together. There's not any law that can force anyone into your private lives if you don't want them there. What I'm saying is, let's do the decent thing. I've lived in this county all my life and known all of you all my life, and there's not a person here tonight who won't admit that the Negro is on the short end of the stick. He's been there so long he needs help, our help. Those people who live down there across the tracks are human beings, and I know that none of you would want to live like most of them are living. They're citizens of Midvale too, and the federal government has given them citizenship rights. So what are we going to do? Are we going to help them and make them good citizens, or are we going to let things stay as they are? I don't know of any Negroes in Midvale who want to beat us over the head with a civil rights club, although they've been banged plenty of times in the past. They want the same thing all of you want, a better shake out of life. That's all. With just a little understanding, we can all live together and work together without stepping on each other's toes. And if fixing up some houses and paving some streets is a beginning, then by God that's what we ought to do, and we should do it because we want to."

The silence of the auditorium was overwhelming. Not a person moved, not even to fan the heat away. Grenlee walked back behind the podium, leaned forward and said, "Most of you here know the Negroes in Midvale. You work with them, hunt with them and tell jokes together. Many of them work in your homes and are treated like members of the family. Now which one of you here tonight would go up to a Negro friend, stare him straight in the eyes and tell him you're against paving his street simply because he's a Negro? Who would do it, face to face, with a Negro friend? Or tell him you're against his living in a decent house because he's a Negro? Who would do it? We're going to find out who would. We're going to find out how many of you want to do the decent thing because we *want to*, and how many don't. We have some slips of paper to pass out, and we want you to write a simple yes or no on them and cast a straw vote on this project. A group of ladies will take the slips into a classroom and count them. Then we'll know."

Ten women got up from the front row and passed the slips of paper down the rows of seats. When the slips were returned, they put them into boxes and left the auditorium.

Grenlee was sweating profusely, clinging to the podium as if exhausted. Kelly got up from the table, walked to the edge of the stage and said, "Regardless of how this vote turns out, the board has approved the project and we're going to finish it. This ballot is just for the purpose of determining public sentiment, to see if we have your backing, which I certainly hope we have. I agree with everything Mayor Grenlee said. I employ several hundred Negroes at the mill. A few years ago, if one of them had tried to register to vote, I would have passed the word that anyone who even sets foot in the courthouse is immediately unemployed. Not anymore. That's all ended now, a part of the past best forgotten. I'll tell you how I personally feel about this project. I'm going to pull two crews out of my home construction division and put them to work down there to speed things up, and it won't cost anyone a cent. I'll foot the bill. Like the mayor said, this project isn't any world shaker, but it is a beginning."

Kelley hesitated for a moment, as if to say more, then he turned and went back to the table. Grenlee stood still at the podium, looking out at an audience that seemed to have frozen in rigid positions, stunned by unfamiliar words.

Seconds moved into minutes, minutes compounded themselves into a half hour; no gossiping, no glancing sideways at neighbors, no fanning with newspapers; the men on the stage facing the audience, the audience facing the men on the stage; Branch nervous, cracking his knuckles, wishing he were pumping gasoline and not here on this stage as a part of this meeting; Grenlee sweating and mopping his brow, waiting anxiously. The click of high-heeled shoes striking concrete moved up the center aisle and to the stage. Grenlee came forward and received a slip of paper, a small piece of white paper containing an expression of attitude.

Grenlee looked at the paper, then faced the audience and announced, "The vote is six hundred seventeen yes and five no." For a moment silence prevailed, then pandemonium broke loose. There was a mass shifting of positions, a creaking of joints made stiff by sitting rigid, a fanning of air, a flood of broken tension, and a clapping of hands. Grenlee shouted gleefully, "Thank you for coming! Thank you for being here! There's no other business! The meeting is adjourned!" He spoke in clipped words, like a track runner out of breath.

A roar of chatter filled the building as the audience moved toward the exits. Kelly was smiling, Branch looked confused, Kelso and Bennett broke into broad grins, and Major Beecham seemed to be contemplating the meaning of the night's proceedings. All came over and shook Grenlee's hand, all except Branch who left quickly, dodging the public handshake lest those five negative votes observe and interpret such an act as meaning he had changed his mind and now approved of the project. He had voted yes in the board meeting but immediately made certain that his true convictions be known to a select circle of cohorts.

Ike and Peggy Jo moved with the crowd, the human river flowing through the center door and spilling onto the school grounds. No one seemed in a hurry to leave. They broke into small groups, milling, laughing, talking, talking about crop prospects, trips, children and grandchildren, parties, food, the weather, talking about anything and everything but the subject of the meeting and the results of the vote. That was finished and behind them, done and gone, and now other things could be discussed. Everyone was relieved that an inevitable moment had arrived and passed without an emotional bloodletting.

Ike and Peggy Jo left the school grounds and walked along the street toward their home, strolling slowly beneath a clear sky sprinkled with stars, listening to the melancholy sermon of a nightingale. She took his hand and said, "It's over, isn't it, Ike? The trouble's ended."

They stopped, and for a moment he didn't answer. He took both her hands and said, "No, Peg, it's not ended. We passed a milestone tonight, but it's not over. We have a way to go, but it's not as far now as it has been."When they walked away, he was thinking of Sim Hankins and Con Ashley.

Fourteen

The perpetual Saturday morning sidewalk dispensers of gossip did not dwell long on the outcome of the public meeting. Those who didn't attend were told briefly; those who participated felt the event to be past history and deemed prolonged conversation about it to be unnecessary. The negative minority, both those who had been present and not present, were stunned and angered by the overwhelming approval. To them, those who voted yes must have temporarily lost their sanity. But predominantly, an atmosphere of relief blanketed Main Street.

An opposite situation existed in the Negro quarters. News that there was a meeting clacked off tongues up and down every alley, but no one yet knew the outcome.

Ike was in the quarters that morning as a member of the spectator audience visually supervising the ditch digger. Reverend Holbrook sidled up to him, an expectant look on his face. He said, "Moanin, Mistuh Ike."

"Good morning, Reverend," Ike replied. "How're things with you?"

"Fine, Mistuh Ike, jus fine."

The Negro preacher pretended to be absorbed with watching the ditch digger but was constantly glancing sideways at Ike, hoping that Ike had more to say to him. When he could bear the silence no longer he turned and said, in hesitant tones, "Mistuh Ike, 'bout dat meetin in dis week's Gazette, at de white folks' school last night, whut —"

Ike broke in and said, "The vote was six hundred seventeen for the project and five against."

"Sho 'nuff, Mistuh Ike?" Reverend Holbrook asked, grinning broadly.

"Yes," Ike replied matter-of-factly. "Biggest one-sided vote we ever had on a city project." He kept looking at the machine, being

123

nonchalant about the news he knew had stunned and delighted the Negro preacher.

Reverend Holbook immediately took his leave from Ike and began spreading the word about the white folks' meeting. Those who comprehended the meaning of the expression of support by the white community were in succession surprised, awed and pleased, pleased not only by the passage of the sample vote, but by the decisive margin. Those who did not understand that this represented more than just the approval of a construction project were simply glad that they were now assured of a bathroom, that the white man wouldn't snatch their anticipated bath away before they could take it.

Saturday was passing as usual in Midvale, with the constant procession of cars and trucks up and down Main Street, the sidewalk walkers, gawkers, grocery buyers, loafers, squatters by the highway, and kids chasing each other; but the busiest man in town that afternoon was Con Ashley, who was going about his routine of hauling drunks from the quarters to the jail with unusual vigor.

Ashley had maintained his own personal volcano within himself since the Millers beat him nearly senseless in the jail cell. His anger was not directed at the Miller clan but at Sheriff Thornton, his deputies, Montique, Hanibel Felds, and all Negroes in general. Hankins had explained to him why he had received the beating, that he overheard the deputy tell the Millers that Ashley was in the courthouse putting all the blame for the Montique affair on the Millers. Ashley held no grudge against the Millers, but this benevolent attitude toward his assailants did not stem so much from forgiveness because of false information and trickery as it did from the fact that Ashley was no fool and harbored not even the faintest desire to carry on a feud with the bearded clan or have them as his enemy.

Ashley had depleted the existing supply of drunks from the Froggy Bottoms Cafe by nightfall, so on his next trip he parked across the street from the cafe, watching and listening for the hysterical laughter that signaled an overdose of swamp whiskey, a Negro ready for the ride north above Main Street. The Negroes, expecting the constable each Saturday afternoon and night, had devised various methods of fooling him, including carrying their whiskey in liniment bottles and hiding the containers under loose planks in the floor when someone warned that he was about to enter.

Froggy Bottoms was known in the white community as a notorious hellhole, but the whites were not concerned with the rowdyism and occasional violence so long as the Negroes kept it in the quarters and out of sight.

The cafe was housed in a square wood-frame unpainted building set on stump blocks. A string of red and blue lights decorated the front roof line, and one yellow light was set flush above the door, which opened into a room containing a dozen tables and a jukebox. Behind this room was a small kitchen. The menu consisted of fried chicken, fried catfish, hog chitterlings, hamburgers, sardines, onions, and soda belly washers.

Ike's deputies invaded Froggy Bottoms only when there was a serious knife fight, but some of the violence had ceased when Lon was made a deputy and started a regular patrol route past the place. The Negroes had a fear of Ashley, fear of physical harm, and would run from him if they could, but they respected the black deputy, and sometimes his mere presence stopped a seemingly inevitable knife fight, which at one time had been a nightly occurrence. Because of the amount of blood spilled in and around Froggy Bottoms, it was sometimes referred to as "the bloody bucket."

Ashley was being observed as well as observing while he sat in the dark car across the street. Several Negroes who occupied two benches against the outside front wall of the cafe were watching him, and if he made a move they would knock three times on the wall. This would set off a chain reaction of plank-pulling, bottle-hiding and scurrying out the rear door. Ashley's interest was aroused when a seventeen-year-old Negro girl came from the cafe. Her tight cotton dress revealed a pair of large breasts as she turned and silhouetted herself against the soft yellow light. Ashley got out of the car and limped over to her.

"You drunk, nigger?" he asked.

"Naw, sir, I ain't done no drinkin," she replied, frightened. "I had a sardine an onion sanwich an a big orange." She started backing away.

"Dammit, hold up!" Ashley said, advancing toward her. "What's your name?"

"Rosie," she said, her eyes wide and blinking. "I got to go now."

"Let me smell your breath!" Ashley demanded.

The girl took another backward step, then stopped. Ashley bent down and placed his nose to her mouth. "Blow," he said. The girl made a deep sucking sound. Ashley's bushy eyebrows vibrated as she blew into his face, filling his lungs with the odor of sardines and raw onion. Ashley grabbed his nose, jumped back and shouted, "Goddammit to hell!" He backed off another step and snorted, then said harshly, "Let's go, nigger!"

She stepped back again and said, "I had a sardine an onion sanwich and a big orange. I got to go now."

Ashley grabbed her wrist, pulled her to the car and shoved her onto the back seat. The men on the benches watched as they drove away.

When Ashley reached Front Street he stopped and looked back at the frightened girl. "You want to go to jail or to the woods?" he said.

"What you mean?" she asked, her eyes blinking rapidly. Then she straightened up and sat rigid on the seat.

"I mean do you want to go to jail, spend the night and pay a fifteen-dollar fine, or go to the woods and be back home in a hour?"

"I ain't got no fifteen dollars," she said weakly.

Ashley was beginning to pant. He said quickly, expectantly, "You want to go to the woods?"

"Yassah, I guess so," she said in a resigned tone of voice. "I ain't got no fifteen dollars."

"Lean up here a minute," Ashley said. The girl leaned forward and Ashley reached back and squeezed one of her breasts. Her body jerked when she felt his grip tighten. Then he turned, slammed the car into gear and roared off toward the railway station.

When he reached the tracks he drove around the side of the

building, dodging the traffic light. Then he turned south on the main highway, hunching over the steering wheel as if in command of a fire truck, his mind absorbed in the silhouetted body of the Negro, the feel of the firm breast. The girl sat motionless, limp, hands clasped together in her lap, eyes blinking at the huge form of the constable. He left the highway when he reached Hankins' grocery store and parked behind the building.

"You wait here," he said. "You run off and I'll come after you."

"Yassah," she said. "I ain't got no fifteen dollars."

Hankins was alone in the store when Ashley entered. He came from behind the counter and said, "Howdy, Con."

Ashley eased up close and whispered, "You want some nigger cooter? I got some in the car."

Hankins' face went blank for a moment, his mind subconsciously racing backward in time, spinning back through the decades, seeing his father in bed with the nigger slut. He blinked and said, "No! No! I don't want none!"

Ashley looked at him quizzically. "It's real young stuff. They's enough for both of us."

"No!" Hankins repeated. "I don't want none!"

Ashley said disgustedly, "What's the matter, Sim, ain't you ever had no nigger cooter?"

Hankins went blank again, then he muttered, "No. And I don't want none."

"Well, O.K.!" Ashley snapped. "You want to go with me anyway? We'll go out to Jud's. I took a bottle of sto-bought whiskey off a nigger."

"Yeah, I'll go," Hankins said, his expression returning to normal. "I'll have to close up, though. My woman took sick right after I got out of jail. She ain't feelin so good." He turned off the lights and set the night latch; then they went around the side of the building to the car.

When the two men got in the car the girl became rigid, but as they drove away she went limp again. Hankins did not look back at her. He stared straight ahead, ignoring her, acting as if she didn't exist.

A mile down the gravel road Ashley turned off on a timber lane and parked. "You go out in the woods, Sim," he said. "I'll blow the horn when I'm done."

Both men got out, Hankins disappearing into the darkness, Ashley climbing into the back of the car. Hankins walked about fifty yards and sat on a tree stump. He started thinking again, seeing the bed, seeing his father with the black slut. He heard a half-shriek come from the car, a flat wailing sound, then all was silent except for the incessant chatter of katydids and the rustle of wind in the pines.

Hankins' mind began shifting in cycles, racing from the shack to his father to the black slut and to Ashley there on the back seat of the car. He gradually focused his attention on Hanibel Felds, the giant small-headed slit-eyed nigger who had made a liar of him in his own store, caused him to be thrown in jail, hauled out of his own store in handcuffs, shoved behind bars like white trash. Felds was becoming a sore on his brain, festering, entering the bloodstream, growing larger, flowing through his veins like poison.

Hankins was startled when he heard the sound of the car horn. He had no conception of how much time had passed, how long he had been sitting on the stump. He got up and walked back through the woods. Ashley and the girl were standing outside the car, silent, not looking at each other.

"Git in an let's go," Ashley said.

The girl opened the rear door and stared to get in.

"Not you," Ashley said to her as he moved to the front of the car.

The girl stepped back, closed the door and said, "Ain't you gone take me back to town like you said?"

"Hell no!" Ashley snapped. "You walk! And keep your mouth shut! You open your mouth about this I'll have your ass in jail ever night. You understand?"

"Yassah," she said weakly, moving out of the way.

Ashley turned on the lights and backed down the lane. The

beams centered on the girl, standing in the middle of the lane as she watched the car back away, turn, and move off into the night, leaving her alone in the woods.

"Sonuvabitch," she muttered.

Hankins did not look at Ashley. He stared straight ahead, sitting rigid.

Ashley said, "Open the car pocket, Sim, an git out the bottle. I need a shot. All I can smell is onions." Hankins got out the bottle, took the top off and handed it to Ashley. He heard a gurgling sound as the whiskey poured down Ashley's throat. He took the bottle back, turned it up and drank deeply, then returned to normal again.

"You shore Jud an them boys know I didn't say nothin to the sheriff?" Ashley asked.

"Yes," Hankins said, now looking at Ashley. "I told them after we got turned loose. I told them the deputy lied."

"You better had," Ashley said. "I ain't wantin no more of that. My gut still hurts."

They drove the remaining distance in silence. When Ashley turned up the narrow lane and entered the clearing, the headlights revealed four bearded men sitting on the porch. One of them got up and went inside, returning with a lantern.

Ashley and Hankins climbed the steps. Then in ceremonial fashion they all formed a circle and squatted.

"Howdy, Jud," Ashley then said. "I brung some sto-bought whiskey. Cost ten dollars a bottle if you buy it. Good stuff."

Jud took the bottle, drank and started to swallow. Then he spit into the yard and said, "Phew! Taste like shote piss."

"How you know, Jud?" Ashley asked. "You ever drunk any?"

Jud craned his neck forward like a goose in flight, staring straight into Ashley's eyes. Ashley knew at once he had committed an error. He said quickly, "Ah shucks, Jud, I didn't mean nothin. I were just kiddin. I know you ain't drunk no shote piss."

Jud pulled his neck back in and said, "Get a jug of corn, Bester. I ain't drinkin that crap."

After the gallon jug made one round of the circle, Jud said, "We wouldn'ta whupped you, Con, if we'd knowed that deputy lied 'bout you blabbin on us."

"That don't matter none, Jud," Ashley said, "You had a right. I'd a' whupped your butt under the same circumstances."

Jud's neck shot out again, and Ashley decided he'd better take a tack in another direction. "It's the sheriff's fault," he said quickly. "The whole thing's Thornton's fault. They ought to be some way to get that nigger-lover. A white man havin truck with niggers. It ain't natural."

"Costed me three hawgs," Jud said. "Ain't no nigger wuth three hawgs."

"It's the big nigger's fault," Hankins said. "The big nigger, he's the one who caused it all."

"You gone git the one we had in the hawg pen?" Jud asked.

"Naw," Ashley said, "we better leave him be. Don't you know what a peace bond is?"

"I know it costed me three hawgs," Jud said.

The jug made another round. Hankins said, "The sheriff's taken up with the niggers."

"Whut you gone do?" Jud asked.

"We could burn a cross on his yard," Hankins said.

"Whut you allus wantin to bern a cross fer?" Jud asked. "You want to do somethin, shoot the big nigger or bern the jail."

"Druther shoot the nigger deputy," Coney said. "Ain't never had no nigger draw down on me before."

"They had a meetin at the school last night," Hankins said. "Voted to put toilets in the nigger houses."

"'Taint sanitory," Jud said. "Man ain't suppose to do his job in the house. The woods is the place fer that."

"Ain't right for a white man to have truck with niggers," Ashley said. "It ain't natural."

"Git some deer meat, Berl," Jud said. "I'm hongry."

Berl went into the house and returned with a chunk of meat and a knife. Jud took the knife, cut a slice of meat and crammed it into his mouth. Then he drank again from the jug.

Hankins took a deep drink and said, "It's the big nigger's fault. The big nigger, he's the one."

"Whut you gone do?" Jud asked.

"We could burn a cross in front the shack where he lives," Hankins said.

"Whut fer?" Jud asked. "Jest shoot the nigger."

Ashley cut a slice of meat, chewed and said, "It ain't natural. A white man havin truck with niggers. It just ain't natural."

Fifteen

The red sports car bearing California license plates pulled off the highway and stopped. The driver looked at the sign and read: "Midvale City Limits." Then he turned to his companion and said, "Well, Sylvia, here it is."

"Yes, at last, thank goodness," she replied, sighing. "I don't believe I could have made it another mile today."

Jeffrey VanDolan pulled the car back onto the highway and drove slowly into town, past the traffic light to the mill, then back to the traffic light, up Main Street and around the courthouse, past the jail, turned at the high school and retraced his route, then across the railroad tracks and down Front Street to the Negro school, then back to the railroad station, where he parked.

"Well, what do you think?" he asked.

"I like it," she smiled. "It's a pretty little town. I'll be glad to get started and know more about the people."

It was late in the afternoon, and stores on Main Street were closing for the day. The street would soon be deserted, bringing on the lull hour in Midvale, a time of going home.

"What do you suggest we do?" VanDolan asked.

"Let's find the mayor or the police official and explain why we're here," she suggested.

"No, it's probably after office hours now. Let's find the Negro pastor first. We can see the mayor tomorrow."

Two old Negro men were standing beside the station house. VanDolan got of the car and walked over to them. He extended his hand and said, "I'm Jeffrey VanDolan. Could you tell me where your pastor lives?"

The two Negroes stared at the small white man with the red beard on his chin. They blinked at each other, then turned their eyes back to the stranger whose hand was still extended toward them. Each touched the hand briefly, then glanced around, seeing that no one was watching them.

"Yassuh, Mistuh Van," one said. "Whut you want to know?"

"No, not Van," he said. "VanDolan. Jeffrey VanDolan. Where does your pastor live?"

"You mean Reveren Holbook?" one asked.

"Is that his name?" VanDolan responded.

"Whose name?" the Negro asked.

"Your pastor's name," VanDolan said, beginning to shuffle his feet.

"You mean Reveren Holbrook?" the Negro asked again.

"Yes," VanDolan said, exasperated. "Where does Reverend Holbrook live?"

"He live on Front Street."

VanDolan hooked his right foot behind his left foot, clasped his hands and said, "Where-is-Front Street?" He enunciated each word separately, slowly.

One of the men pointed and said, "Welsuh, you goes down heah two block, turns lef, goes fo block, an Reveren Holbrook live in de fouth house on de lef."

"Thank you," VanDolan said, backing away.

"You sho welcom, Mistuh Van." The two Negroes blinked at

each other again as they watched the white man go back to the car.

VanDolan got into the car and said, "Christ!"

"What's the matter?" the girl asked, disturbed by the tone of his voice.

"Nothing," he replied briskly.

"Did they tell you where the pastor lives?"

"I think so," he said. "I'm not sure."

VanDolan followed the directions the Negro had given him. He turned onto Front Street, driving slowly, examining the dwellings, then parked in front of the house he supposed to be the home of the Negro pastor. Both of them got out of the car and walked to the house.

Reverend Holbrook was sitting in the parlor when he heard the knock. He opened the door and was startled by the strange white man and the white girl on his porch. After a moment he stepped outside.

"Are you Reverend Holbrook?" VanDolan asked.

"Yas, suh, I's Reveren Holbrook," he replied, eyeing them closely.

VanDolan extended his hand. "I'm Jeffrey VanDolan, and this is Sylvia Landcaster."

The Negro preacher took the hand briefly, a perplexed expression on his face. For a moment they all remained silent, then Reverend Holbrook said, "Is dey somethin I can do fo you?"

"Yes," VanDolan said. "May we come in for a moment?"

Reverend Holbrook became more perplexed, furrows forming across his brow. He thought perhaps they were selling something, for white people often went door to door through the quarters, selling insurance and cooking utensils. But he had never seen a salesman dressed in blue jeans, T-shirt and leather sandals without socks. They usually wore suits, and none were accompanied by a girl.

"Come in de house," he said reluctantly, stepping back so they could enter. "I were jus preparin my text fo prayer meetin. We allus has prayer meetin at de church on Wednesday night."

The two white people came in and sat on the sofa. Reverend

Holbrook took a seat in a chair across the room from them. The girl looked around the parlor, studying each article of furniture. She said, "You have lovely things. It must have taken you a lifetime to acquire such a collection."

"White folks give dem to me after dey built de church."

"Gave them to you?" she questioned, surprised. "Some of these articles are genuine antiques."

"Don know 'bout dat," the reverend said, "but dey does fine fo me. Now whut kin I do fo you?"

"You can help us find a place to stay," VanDolan said, crossing his legs. "We're here to set up a school. Miss Landcaster and I are students at the University of California, and this summer we're with the National Student Freedom League. We're setting up schools all over the South."

Reverend Holbrook felt greatly relieved, glad that they weren't salesmen because he always hated to turn anyone away. He said, "Dey's a small motel on de highway jus past de mill, where de lumber buyers stay when de here, an I's 'fraid you got de wrong pusson. I don have nothin to do wid de schools. De man who be's in charge of de schools is Mistuh Blackmon, and he has a office in de cotehouse."

"No, you don't understand," VanDolan said, uncrossing his legs and leaning forward. "We're here to set up a school in your section of Midvale, to help the Negro people. We want to live here with you this summer."

The Negro preacher became rigid, trying to grasp the meaning of the words. He said, "Us got a school. Brother Hopkins is de supentindent. He be's in charge of de school."

"No," VanDolan said, "you still don't understand. We want to start a freedom school in your church and live here among your people."

Reverend Holbrook's face flushed with anxiety. He clasped his hands tightly and said, "You means you wants to live here in de quarters?"

Miss Landcaster had been sitting quietly, letting VanDolan talk.

She leaned forward and said, "Reverend Holbrook, we want to be friends with your people. We want to live among you and learn your mores. That way, we can understand better how to develop our school."

The reverend became even more rigid, saying in broken tones, "Moes? Moes? Whut you mean? We ain't got no moes."

"Your customs, your habits, the way you live," she said, trying to put kindness in her voice. "We're here to help your people, to help in any way we can."

VanDolan said, "We're on your side, Reverend. We're civil rights workers. Don't you understand, we're on your side."

Reverend Holbrook's hands trembled noticeably, and his face became contorted. For a moment he closed his eyes. Then he looked at them and said with a quivering voice, "Naw suh! Naw suh! We gwine do it de Lawd's way! We ain't gwine march in de streets an hate de white folks! Naw suh! De Lawd say live in peace, brothers an sisters, live in peace an git the hate outen yo heart! Do it de Lawd's way an de Lawd smile down on you!"

The two white people sat silent, surprised by the outburst, caught unaware by an attack on their motives. They had not expected this sort of reception from a Negro.

Miss Landcaster got up, crossed the room and sat in a chair next to the preacher. She said softly, "Reverend Holbrook, you still don't understand. We're not here to start demonstrations or cause trouble. We're here to teach. We won't do anything you don't want us to do. We're college students, and we've given up our summer vacation to come here and help your people. We're here only to help, not harm."

Reverend Holbrook became calmer. He looked at her and said, "Whut exactly do you want to do?"

She said, "We want to set up a school anywhere we can, but in your church if you will let us. We'll teach classes to anyone who wants to come, young or old. We can teach civics, economics, history, English grammar—anything your people want us to teach. It will be like a summer school, or a summer camp for the young people, and it won't conflict with courses at your school this fall."

"Why you want to stay in de quarters?" he asked, his voice troubled again. "No white folk ever stayed down here befo. Dat could mean trouble, Miss, bad trouble, an we don want no trouble. Naw suh, we don want no trouble!"

Miss Landcaster leaned forward and touched the back of his wrist. "We won't cause trouble," she said. "We won't bother anyone."

"Well," Reverend Holbrook said hesitantly, "I don know 'bout de church. Dat be's up to de boad of deacons. But is you sho you jus wants to run a school?"

"Yes, that's all," she replied convincingly. "I give you my word."

"I guess it be's all right if you talks to de boad," he said cautiously. "You can come after prayer meetin, 'bout eight. De church is at de end of de next street down."

"Thank you, Reverend," she said, pleased. "Thank you very much. Do you think you might help us find a place to stay?"

"I don think so, Miss," he said, frowning again. "Dat don be's no good idea. You ought to talk to de sheriff fust. Sheriff Thonton a good man. He be's a friend of mine."

"The sheriff is your friend?" VanDolan questioned, doubt in his voice.

"Yas, suh. Mistuh Ike be's a good friend."

"We'll see him tomorrow," Miss Landcaster said, glancing at VanDolan. "Now, can you tell us the name of the nearest restaurant in your section?"

"Resrant here?" he said, puzzled. He scratched his head and said, "You mean de Froggy Bottoms Cafe?"

"Froggy Bottoms," she repeated. "What a quaint name. Yes. We can go there and have dinner, and come to the church later."

"No, ma'am!" Reverend Holbrook said emphatically. "You don want to go dere! You go up on Main Street to de Ritz Cafe."

"Well, all right," she said. She got up and walked to the door, VanDolan following. Then she said, "Thank you, Reverend Holbrook. We'll see you later at the church."

"Yes ma'am, miss," he said, still wary of the situation.

The couple got in the car and drove back toward the railroad crossing. VanDolan said approvingly, "You sure handled that old geezer."

"What do you mean by 'handled him'?" she asked. "I didn't 'handle' him. All I did was explain the project. He's a nice man, and I liked him."

"Don't be so touchy," VanDolan said, glancing at her indifferently. "I was just admiring your diplomacy."

"You'd be better off if you used some yourself," she said sharply.

VanDolan drove across the highway and parked in front of the Ritz Cafe on Main Street. He turned to Miss Landcaster and said, "Well, let's sample the local cuisine. I suppose we'll get such gastronomic delights as hog jowl, blackeyed peas, collard greens and corn pone."

"I don't know about you," she said, ignoring his intended humor, "but I would settle for a hamburger. I'm hungry. Better still, I want fried chicken, some of that real Southern-fried chicken.

The two got out of the car and went into the small cafe.

Jeffrey VanDolan and Sylvia Landcaster were part of a program instigated by a national civil rights organization to establish "freedom schools" in Southern states. Personnel for the summer project had been recruited from colleges and universities in states outside the South. The stated purpose of the program was to teach illiterate Negroes how to read and write, thus qualifying them for voter registration, and to also offer a variety of subjects to others of all ages. The recruits had also been given instruction on how to go limp when being taken to a paddy wagon, how to shield the head from billy sticks, and how to organize and conduct demonstrations. They had been told not to stage street marches and voter registration drives unless the local situation warranted such action, and the decision of what needed to be done was left to those assigned to the areas and towns. Midvale had been selected at random from a list of small Mississippi towns. A state headquarters for the program had been established in Jackson.

Jeffrey VanDolan and Sylvia Landcaster were opposites in physical appearance, temperament, and purpose. Miss Landcaster was a tall girl, five-foot-eight, twenty years old, a junior majoring in elementary education. She had long blond hair that swirled to her shoulders, green eyes, and suntanned skin splotched with freckles on her arms and shoulders. VanDolan was five feet three, thin, pale-complexioned, brown eyes, with fiery red hair that covered the back of his neck, and a goatee. He was twenty-one and still classified as a sophomore after three years of college.

Sylvia Landcaster was from a small town in North Dakota, where her father had served for ten years as a teacher of history and fifteen years as superintendent of the local school. She grew up amid a world of books and read the classics at an early age. In high school she won academic honors and participated in such extracurricular activities as choir, 4-H Club, Girl Scouts and Beta. She had a love of the outdoors and knew every foot of field and stream around her hometown. Sylvia was ten years old when she first saw a Negro, and this first one was an old man, standing on a street corner in Bismarck, strumming a guitar with a tin cup on the sidewalk in front of him. She had stopped and stared at the man, stared until her mother jerked her arm to move her away. She felt a deep sympathy for the sad-eyed black man with the guitar, and for years she pictured all Negroes as being old and stooped and carrying tin cups.

Jeffrey VanDolan was from New York, son of an advertising executive, an only child, shuffled aside in a world of cocktail parties, weekend trips to Cape Cod, nights at the theater, and bitter quarrels. He was raised by a succession of governesses, none lasting more than six months. Because of his size he had never succeeded in any sport and grew to hate anyone who did. He antagonized his teachers and all other children, which resulted in his never becoming a part of any childhood activity. His first year of college he had gone to Dartmouth and quit during the second semester because he did not receive a fraternity bid. He then joined causes, any cause that would attract attention to himself; but he never attained the role of leader, always a follower, always in the shadow of others. He became restive and moved to California, where he entered a new university and joined the "beat generation" of rebellion. He experimented with reefers, bennies, LSD, and all varieties of alcohol, spending more time in coffee houses and on park benches than in the classroom. He read books of philosophy, volumes of history dealing with the lives of the Caesars, Alexander the Great, Genghis Khan, Napoleon, and books of ancient mythology. For more than a year he wore only T-shirts, stone-washed jeans, and leather sandals, giving all his New York clothes to the Salvation Army.

Sylvia Landcaster joined the National Student Freedom League summer project to aid people she thought needed help. Her parents had misgivings about her doing this, but consented because they knew she would use good judgment and avoid bringing trouble or injury to herself or to others. Jeffrey VanDolan volunteered for the project because he thought that perhaps here at last was a way he could reach the head of the procession and become a leader, bringing attention to himself, finally escaping from the ranks of obscurity. His parents were not worried about his participation in a civil rights project in Mississippi because they did not know he was in Mississippi. He left a forwarding address in California for his weekly check from New York.

Jeffrey VanDolan and Slyvia Landcaster had not known each other before being assigned together to the Midvale project and attending the training school in California. Neither knew the other's background, motives or desires. But Sylvia Landcaster was already beginning to suspect that Jeffrey VanDolan was something less than the dedicated servant to humanity he pretended to be.

The deacons of the Midvale African Baptist Church were waiting expectantly when VanDolan and Miss Landcaster entered the building. Reverend Holbrook got up from the front pew and stood nervously as the white couple walked down the aisle. The deacons watched silently as the two strangers rounded the last pew and stood before them.

Reverend Holbrook said uncertainly, "Brothers, dis be's Mistuh

Vanlander an Miss Lancoster. Dey wants to discuss a subject wid de boad."

"No," VanDolan said, glancing at Reverend Holbrook. "it's VanDolan. Jeffrey-Van-Dolan. And this is Miss Sylvia Landcaster."

"'Scuse me," the reverend apologized. "Which one wants de flo?"

"I'll speak." VanDolan said quickly, stepping in front of Miss Landcaster, who then walked over and sat on the edge of the platform. He said vigorously, "Gentlemen, we represent the National Student Freedom League, and we're here to set up a school in Midvale, to be of service to your people." The deacons were fascinated by the bobbing red goatee. VanDolan noticed this and placed his right hand on his chin. He continued, "We're college students, advanced in our major fields, and are qualified to teach such subjects as political science, economics, mathematics, American history, sociology and other useful courses."

Reverend Holbrook interrupted and said, "Mistuh VanDolar, dis be's Brother Luke, de school supentindent. He wants to ax some questions."

"Yes, Mr. Luke, what is it you wish to know?"

"The name is Hopkins," the man replied. "Albert Hopkins."

"But he said Luke," VanDolan said, confused.

"Brother Luke is the name I assume as a deacon," Hopkins said. "My name is Albert Hopkins."

"Yes, Mr. Hopkins?" VanDolan began again.

Hopkins cleared his throat and said, "What is the purpose of this school you wish to organize?"

"Well, as I said," VanDolan replied, "we're here to help your people. We want to educate your people. We're here to advance the cause of the Negro."

"What group do you intend to teach?" Hopkins asked.

VanDolan looked puzzled. "What do you mean?"

"Are you going to teach the fourth grade, the sixth grade, the eighth grade, the seniors, or what?" Hopkins asked. "And do you intend to offer the same courses they had last year or more advanced courses?"

"Well, you see," VanDolan said, hooking his right foot behind his left foot, "the Negro of the South has been deprived of his constitutional rights, and we're here to help your people, to—"

"Mr. Hopkins," Miss Landcaster broke in, getting up quickly and walking over to the pew, "we don't know what group to teach. That's why we are asking your help. We want you to tell us. We had thought about teaching the old people."

VanDolan backed over to the platform and sat down, crossing his legs and pulling on his goatee. The deacons stared at him for a moment more, then looked at Miss Landcaster.

"Miss Landcaster," Hopkins said softly, "I'm not trying to be rude, but what good would it do to teach such courses as you suggest to people who can't read or write? And it would not be wise for you to teach our school children, especially since you don't know what courses they've had and how advanced they are."

"You're exactly right, Mr. Hopkins," she agreed. "It would be unwise for us to break in on the academic routine of your school, and teaching sociology to someone who can't read or write would be questionable. Why not let us teach reading and writing to the older people?"

"Well, it wouldn't hurt anything," Hopkins replied without enthusiasm. "We intended to start our own classes with volunteers from the school, but this could be delayed until fall." He hesitated for a moment and then said, "Miss Landcaster, I have another question, and I would appreciate an honest answer."

"Why yes, Mr. Hopkins,"

"Is operating a school all that you have in mind?"

"Yes," she answered firmly. "That is our only purpose, to operate a school."

Hopkins looked directly into her eyes. "Reverend Holbrook may have told you that we wish to avoid any sort of trouble here. Several things are happening to our advantage, and we want to give them a chance to succeed. You don't know anything about our situation here, but we are making progress. Do you understand what I am saying?"

"Yes, I understand," she said.

"Reverend Holbrook says you both intend to live here in the quarters," he said, continuing to stare. "Do you know how much trouble this could bring?"

Miss Landcaster looked at VanDolan and then back to Hopkins. She was beginning to have doubts about this part of the project. She said meekly, "This is a part of the program, to live among your people and get to know you better. But I guess it's not necessary if it will cause problems. We could stay in another part of the town if you think our living here would jeopardize the project."

"No!" VanDolan objected harshly, getting up and coming over to the pew. "That's a necessary part of the program. We agreed to this before we were accepted to participate. We're obligated. This is one part of the program we cannot change."

"You seem pretty insistent," Hopkins said, eyeing VanDolan closely.

"Yes!" VanDolan snapped. "We agreed to it! We're obligated!"

Miss Landcaster glared at VanDolan and started to speak, then decided to keep silent and not start an argument with him in front of the deacons, perhaps losing the support they seemed to be gaining.

"You know, don't you," Hopkins said warily, "that if you do a foolish thing and bring trouble, you won't be bringing it on yourself alone, but on all of us."

VanDolan remained adamant. "Trouble how? Whose business is it where we stay? Who are you afraid of? Is it the whites? If it is the whites, that's why we're here, to be on your side, against them. I'm not afraid of them. I have my rights!"

"We're not against the white people!" Hopkins snapped emphatically, getting up and facing VanDolan. "We're trying to work things out! I thought you said you are here to run a school! If you have any idea of coming here and—"

"Gentlemen!" Miss Landcaster said, stepping between the two.

"We're here only to establish and operate a school. Mr. VanDolan and I will discuss lodgings later. I believe we've taken too much of your time already. Could you please give us a decision on using your church?"

Hopkins sat down as Reverend Holbrook arose and faced the deacons. All of them had been absorbed in the conversations, letting Hopkins do all the talking. They now turned their attention to the reverend.

Reverend Holbrook spoke slowly, "Brethren, you's all heard de proposition 'bout de school. Dey's not much more I can say, 'cepin I abides by de will of de boad. Whut we do, we does in de name of de Lawd, so let's go to de Lawd an see whut He say."

The Negro preacher dropped to the floor on his knees and bowed his head. The deacons all knelt and joined him in silent prayer. Miss Landcaster, seeing what was happening, knelt beside the reverend. VanDolan remained standing, watching them, seeing his partner bowed in prayer with the Negro deacons. He removed a small bottle from his pocket, opened it, rolled two pills into the palm of his hand, popped them into his mouth and swallowed. The reverend said "Amen," and they all got up from the floor.

Reverend Holbrook said, "Brothers, whut is de will of de boad?"

For a moment they all remained silent, glancing at the small white man and his companion, thinking, wondering what results their decision would bring to the black community.

Hopkins finally broke the silence and said, "If they want to run a school to teach the old folks to read and write, I'll vote to let them use the church on a trial basis. But that's all I'm voting for, a school."

"Whut is de will of de boad?" Reverend Holbrook asked again.

"Aye," came a chorus of voices, audible but not strong.

Miss Landcaster smiled. VanDolan just stood there, seeming not to hear the decision. Hopkins glanced at VanDolan, then centered his gaze on Miss Landcaster and said, "I strongly suggest that as soon as possible in the morning the two of you see Mayor Grenlee and explain this project thoroughly. You will also need the cooperation of

Sheriff Thornton."

"We will see them in the morning," she said agreeably. "And we thank all of you very much. You won't regret this decision."

Reverend Holbrook looked at Miss Landcaster and said softly, "Miss, do whut you do in de name of de Lawd, 'cause de Lawd be's walkin wid all of us."

"We will, Reverend Holbrook," she replied. "And thank you again. We'll say good night now."

The Negro men walked outside the church and stood beneath the yellow light, watching the tall blond girl and the small man get into the car, the red sports car with wire-spoke wheels with an engine that rumbled as their car motors did not rumble. They continued watching silently as the car pulled away and disappeared from sight.

VanDolan stopped when he reached Front Street. He said, "We ought to get that preacher in one of your classes. He can't speak English. I can't understand half what he says."

She leaned against the door, as if completely exhausted, and said weakly, "Jeffrey, you almost ruined it for us before we even got started. I'm beginning to wonder what you've got in mind. What do you really want?"

"Not a thing," he said, lighting a cigarette, "not a thing but what you want. Teaching. But I'll tell you one thing for sure. We both signed up for this deal and we'll follow the agreement to the letter, right down the line, the whole bit. We're going to stay down here in the Negro section. While you're setting up the school tomorrow I'll find us a place to live. We'll sleep in the motel tonight, but that's all. We're doing the whole bit, right down the line."

She looked at him but didn't speak. She was too tired to argue. And it had been part of the agreement, part of their mission to Midvale, to live in the Negro section.

Sixteen

Ike was in Bradley's Barber Shop, getting a shoeshine from Montique, when Billy came in and said, "Ike, Mayor Grenlee called and said he wants to see you in his office right away. Sounded like it was important."

"Thanks," Ike said, curious. "I'll go right on over there."

When Montique finished, Ike stepped down from the stand, took a half-dollar coin from his pocket and handed it to the small Negro.

"Naw, suh, Mistuh Ike," Montique said, refusing the coin. "You don owe me nothin. I be's obliged to shine yo shoes fo as long as I kin make it to de shop."

"Ah, take it, Montique," Ike insisted, pressing the coin into the Negro's hand. "You can't make a living if you don't charge people."

"Dat be's O.K. too, Mistuh Ike," he said firmly. "I ain't gwine take dat money. You don owe me nothin."

"Well, all right," Ike said, resigned. "If that's the way you want it. But I'd rather pay you."

"You come back, Mistuh Ike," Montique grinned. "I'll keep them shoes lookin lak glass."

Ike left the barber shop, crossed Main Street and entered the mayor's office in City Hall. Grenlee got up from behind his desk and said, "Ike, this is Jeffrey VanDolan and Sylvia Landcaster." Then he looked at them and said, "This is Sheriff Ike Thornton." The couple stood briefly, then returned to their chairs.

Grenlee said nervously, "Mr. VanDolan and Miss Landcaster are from California. They're here to start some sort of a school in the Negro quarters."

"School?" Ike questioned, looking from VanDolan to Miss Landcaster. "What kind of school?"

"To be brief," VanDolan said, "we're civil-rights workers from the National Student Freedom League. We're going to start a school in the Negro church."

"We're not really what you think of as civil-rights workers," Miss Landcaster said quickly. "We're teachers. Our school will be operated to teach old people to read and write."

"Let's just take a few minutes and discuss this thing," Grenlee said, looking directly at VanDolan. "Who asked you to come to Midvale? Was it someone in the quarters?"

"Nobody asked us to come," VanDolan replied, crossing his legs. "We were sent here."

"What do you mean," Ike asked, "when you say you were sent here? Who sent you?"

VanDolan sighed and said slowly, "The - National - Student - Freedom - League."

"What is that?" Grenlee asked.

"Mayor Grenlee," Miss Landcaster said, "the league is an organization that uses volunteer college students to open schools in towns across the South. We're here simply as teachers, to help the Negro people."

"That's not the kind of civil-rights workers I know about," Grenlee said. "The ones I know about march in the street, pray on the courthouse lawn, flop all over the sidewalks, and throw rocks when it suits their fancy."

Miss Landcaster's face flushed. She decided not to be as condescending as she had been with the Negro preacher and deacons. She said harshly, "We're not here to do any of those things! We're here only to operate a school! If you've had trouble in the past it's certainly not our fault!"

"That's just the point," Grenlee said, leaning across the desk. "We haven't had trouble here. We're trying to avoid it. God knows we're trying, and we've got a start. It may not seem like much to you, but it's a beginning."

"I gathered as much from Mr. Hopkins," Miss Landcaster retorted.

"You mean Albert Hopkins?" Grenlee asked, surprised.

"Yes," she replied, "the school superintendent. We met with the church board last night. Mr. Hopkins was as concerned about our motives as you are."

Ike looked at her and asked curiously, "Did the board grant permission for you to use their church?"

"Yes. Reluctantly. Only on a trial basis to see if it works."

"What's all the flap about?" VanDolan asked. "Do we have to have a license to teach non-credit classes that have nothing to do with your county schools? Do we have to have your permission?"

"No, you don't have to have our permissiom!" Grenlee snapped irritably. "But this town is our responsibility, and you're our responsibility while you are here, whether you know it or not. Don't you think that fact deserves a bit of discussion?"

"I only asked if we must have your permission," VanDolan said. "And I still don't see what all the flap is about."

"The flap is, Mr. VanDolan," Grenlee said, trying to calm his voice, "that whether we like it or not, there are still some people who would burn a church rather than see it used by someone like you, and if some fool burns a church, then we've really got a 'flap' on our hands."

"What do you mean by 'someone like me'?" VanDolan asked, leaning forward and glaring at Grenlee.

"Hell fire, man, look at yourself!" Grenlee shouted. "You don't look like any teacher I've ever seen! You're like a red flag in a bull pen Why don't you put on some decent clothes and get a haircut and a shave?"

VanDolan jumped to his feet, grabbed the edge of Grenlee's desk and yelled, "What the hell has my choice of attire got to do with this project? My personal appearance is none of your damned business!"

Grenlee leaned back and closed his eyes. Miss Landcaster sat on the edge of her chair, rigid. Ike glanced at VanDolan, not knowing what to expect next.

Grenlee said, without opening his eyes, "You're right. It's none of my business. I'm sorry I shouted. Perhaps I'm prejudiced. I guess I'm as bad as the rest of them. Your appearance has nothing to do with the project."

VanDolan returned to his chair as Grenlee opened his eyes and put his arms back on the desk.

"Mayor Grenlee," Miss Landcaster said, "I can appreciate your concern and your apprehension. The people at the church last night felt the same way. I can only tell you, as I told them, that we are not here to cause trouble. Our only purpose is to operate a school to help the Negro people. Are there really those among you who would object to our doing this?"

"No, Miss Landcaster, I don't think so," Grenlee replied. "I don't believe anyone here would object to your simply operating a school for Negroes, but it goes far beyond that. It's not just your project, and I don't really know how to explain what I mean. You see, we're undergoing a change, a painful change, painful for both white and Negro. A lot of the changes hurt, but we're doing them. Slowly, yes, but we're moving along. And the people want to feel that they're doing this themselves and not being forced to by outsiders who have never lived here. It's something we must do ourselves, white and Negro together, and somehow do it in such a manner that it doesn't turn us against each other permanently. I don't know how to explain it, but it's a constant part of our lives. I don't believe that anyone who wasn't born here and spent their lives here could ever understand."

"I understand more than you believe I do," she said. "And I'm sure Reverend Holbrook understands. He said the same thing you are saying, only in a different way. Mr. Grenlee, I am from a Christian family in North Dakota. My father is a school superintendent. I give you my word that I am not here to cause harm, only to help the Negro people. We will operate our school regardless, but we would like your support."

Grenlee leaned forward and said, " Miss Lancaster, I believe you are sincere in what you intend to do. But in my opinion, your project won't be worth two cents to the Negro people. They're starting their own classes for old people, so whatever you do here will be of no lasting value. It wouldn't even begin to balance against the harm it could cause. But I respect your motives. I'm sure you wouldn't have come all the way from California to Mississippi if you didn't think you were doing the right thing. I will say that I don't approve of your project, but I won't stand in your way or do anything to impede you. Now what is it you want me to say officially as the mayor of Midvale?"

"Nothing, really," she said, pleased that he at least would not interfere. "Perhaps our mission here is worthless. Perhaps not. But if we can instill a spark of self-motivation and pride into the Negro people and encourage them to become more useful citizens, don't you believe this will be worth something?"

"Yes, it would," Grenlee agreed. "We've got a project started now that could do just that. But no one thing alone will solve all the problems we face. It's too complex. And we don't want to create false hope. Not now, anyway. We can move forward just one step at a time. There's no magic transformation going to take place when a Negro walks into a voting booth for the first time, or sits in a classroom with white children for the first time. And it won't bring about instant equality. We don't have equality here among whites and Negroes, whites and whites, or Negroes and Negroes, never have, and never will. To say otherwise is a cruel hoax."

"I'm not so naive as not to know that," Miss Landcaster said, "and I don't have any intention of deceiving anyone. But I do believe that you would have never taken that one step forward without being forced to. You have been forced to make changes you should have made on your own a long time ago, and you probably will have to be forced to do so in the future."

"You're right and wrong," Grenlee replied quickly. "Force might have been necessary to get these civil-rights laws on the books, but force alone cannot get the Negroes here in Stonewall County a better life. When all the hoopla is ended, when the marching and singing and demonstrating stops and the civil-rights workers go home, and all the smoke is cleared away, the white man will still own the bank, still own the mill, and still run the credit department in a store.

Whatever gains the Negro makes in his personal life will come through friendship and cooperation, not force. Congress can put a hundred laws on the books and it won't really change anything. There is no law that can force anyone to be your friend and want to help you. If our racial problems are ever really solved, it will be on a man-to-man basis in friendship, and not by force. And it will have to be done here, not in Washington or in California."

"Mr. Grenlee," Miss Landcaster said, "I don't intend to sit here and debate the entire scope of the civil-rights movement with you. If I did, we might be here for the summer, so let's get back to the subject of our school."

"As I said before, I won't do anything to impede your project," Grenlee responded. "I personally hope your school is a success. I rather admire you, Miss Landcaster, and I find myself liking you already. I'll do everything possible to keep the atmosphere calm and inform everyone that you're here as teachers, not agitators, as we call some so-called civil-rights workers."

"Well, thank you," she replied pleasantly. "I find you to be rather nice, too, especially for a redneck, as I've heard Mississippians often called."

"What about police protection?" VanDolan asked. "If we do run into trouble, what can we expect from the city?"

"Police protection?" Grenlee questioned, turning his attention to VanDolan. "Our Midvale police force consists of two men, and one of them is past the age of being able to hit a snake with a stick. We use him for traffic control at the school, and we use both of them at ball games and other such events. We depend on Sheriff Thornton and his deputies for law enforcement. I don't think you will need police protection around your school. You might be called a few names you've never heard before, but all the police in the country couldn't prevent that."

"We're going to live in the Negro section," VanDolan said, "and the Negro preacher said this could cause trouble. We want protection if something happens."

"Did I hear you right?" Grenlee asked in disbelief. "Did you say you're going to live in the Negro quarters?"

"Yes," VanDolan replied, watching the mayor closely. "It's part of the project. We agreed to it."

"Why?" Grenlee asked, completely confounded. "Do you also intend to do this, Miss Landcaster?"

"Yes," she said, concerned by his reaction. "We did agree to it as part of our project."

"Part of your project," Grenlee repeated. "How is living in the Negro quarters part of operating a school?"

"We need to understand our students," Miss Landcaster said, afraid that she was losing the ground she had gained. "We want to be an actual part of the Negro community. Our purpose is to learn Negro customs and lifestyles firsthand, and to become a part of them if possible."

"I still don't understand why living down there is necessary just to teach people to read and write," Grenlee said, exasperated.

"Do we have to have your permission?" VanDolan asked, staring at Grenlee.

"No, goddammit!" Grenlee exploded. "You don't have to have my permission! You don't have to have my permission to crap in the middle of the street, but somebody might bust your ass for doing it!" Grenlee put his hands across his face and covered his eyes for a moment, then said, "I'm sorry I shouted. I didn't mean to say that. But you don't understand. You would be violating the most emotional taboo there is, a white girl living with Negroes. It just isn't done in a small Southern town. You would be inviting unnecessary trouble. Why would you do something that would deliberately make people turn against you?"

"Would it really be that bad?" Miss Landcaster asked. "Would it be so tremendously evil for us simply to stay in the Negro section?"

"Miss Landcaster," Ike broke in, speaking slowly, "it would be bad for several reasons. We have more than one class of Negroes here, just as we have more than one class of white people. There are some fine Negro people you would be perfectly safe with, and there are some Negroes who are downright mean. I know. I've seen them.

I've seen stomachs ripped open and throats slit over a ten-cent bottle of pop. You could get yourself hurt down there, especially at night. And besides that, there's nothing you could do that would create more ill will than living in the Negro quarters. It's a no-win situation."

"I don't know about you, Sylvia," VanDolan said, "but I've got things to do today besides sit here and argue." He got up and walked to the door. "Let's go. You made certain agreements when you volunteered for this project and you are obligated to carry them out. Are you coming with me or not? You can be replaced, you know."

"Don't do it, Miss Landcaster!" Grenlee urged. "You can stay in my home with my family. We've got an empty guest room. If VanDolan wants to live down there, fine, but you stay with us."

Miss Landcaster looked from Grenlee to Ike, doubt once again flooding her mind. She hesitated for a moment, then she got up and said, "I'm sorry, but they could replace me. I want this school very much. I've come a long way to do this, and I must carry it through. I do appreciate your concern, but I'm sure I will be all right."

"It's not only you I'm concerned about," Grenlee said. "I don't want anything to happen to you, but I'm also concerned for all of us."

"I understand that too," she said, "but perhaps your people won't be as disturbed as you imagine. And thank you for everything. You and Sheriff Thornton have been very kind, and I appreciate it. We'll keep you informed of our progress." She turned and followed VanDolan from the office.

Grenlee got up from his desk and walked over to the front window. He watched as the couple got into the red sports car and drove away, then came back to the desk and said, "This could be our worst nightmare come true, and all at the wrong time."

"Maybe not," Ike said, trying to calm Grenlee. "We don't know that everyone will react to this as we think they will. We're surmising. Perhaps it doesn't make that much difference anymore."

"You know better than that," Grenlee said. "As soon as word gets around that a white girl is living with the Negroes she'll be treated like a leper, and she could draw every crackpot out of the hills. As far as that kook VanDolan is concerned, I don't think anyone will give a damn. But Miss Landcaster is something else."

"I'll keep Lon down there all the time during the day," Ike said, "and double the patrol at night. Let's don't form storm clouds if they're not necessary."

"You're right," Grenlee agreed. "I'll call all the aldermen and tell them about the project, and explain that the two white people are harmless. I don't know about Branch, but I'm sure all the rest of them will try to calm the waters."

Ike left as Grenlee picked up the telephone.

Seventeen

Reverend Holbrook was sitting on the porch when the car pulled in and parked in front of his house. The sight of the two young white people brought back the apprehension. He got up as they crossed the yard and came up the steps.

"Hello, Reverend Holbrook," Miss Landcaster said cheerfully. "How are you today?"

"I be's fine," he said, the apprehension soothed by her friendly tone. "How is you an Mistuh VanDolar likin Midvale?"

VanDolan stared at the Negro but didn't respond. He shrugged his shoulders and ignored the mispronunciation of his name.

"It's very nice," Miss Landcaster said. "We had a meeting this morning with Mayor Grenlee and Sheriff Thornton and discussed our project."

"Whut dey say?" Reverend Holbrook asked.

"They weren't enthusiastic, but at the end of the meeting they wished us success. They were concerned, however, about our living in your section of town."

"You folks 'scuse my manners," Reverend Holbrook said apologetically. "Have a chair." He waited until they were both seated before returning to his rocker. "Now whut did dey say 'bout you livin down here, Miss?"

"I told them it wasn't any of their business," VanDolan said. "This is a free country, and a person can stay anywhere he damn well pleases without the permission of some hick mayor or sheriff."

"You say dat to Mistuh Grenlee an Mistuh Thonton?" Reverend Holbrook asked, alarmed. "You oughten to do dat, Mistuh VanDolar. Dey be's fine men, de best friends us colored folk got. Mistuh Thonton he been here in my house, an both of dem been in our church. Dey fine men, Mistuh VanDolar."

"Well, it's nothing to get excited about," VanDolan said, lighting a cigarette and flipping the match into the yard. "And sometime when you've got nothing better to do I want you to tell me why they're such good friends."

Miss Landcaster spoke quickly to prevent the reverend from answering VanDolan. "About the school," she said. "I think we will offer classes three times a day, at ten in the morning, two in the afternoon, and eight at night. That will give everybody a chance to attend. The classes will last about two hours per session. Do you think we could start this afternoon?"

"I don know, Miss," he said doubtfully. "We got to get de folks to come fust. I'll spread de word aroun 'fo den an see how many wants to come. Might not be too many at fust."

"What's all the banging and hammering down here?" VanDolan asked. "Sounds like somebody is tearing the place apart."

"Dat de 'struction crews," Reverend Holbrook said, smiling. "Dey puttin toilets in de houses an fixin 'em up, an dey puttin down sewer lines, an dey gwine pave all de streets."

"Toilets?" VanDolan looked hard at the Negro, blew a stream of smoke into the air and said, "You mean that some of the houses here don't have toilets?"

"Yassah, dat's right," the reverend answered, still smiling. "Dem rental houses don't, but dey soon gwine have. Mayor Grenlee an

Mistuh Thonton got de city to buy all dem houses, an dey gwine fix 'em up good an sell 'em back to de renters wid de payment same as de rent."

"That sounds like a wonderful project," Miss Landcaster said.

"Sounds like a con racket to me," VanDolan quipped. "How much they soaking everybody for? A hundred down and fifty bucks a month for the rest of their lives?"

"Nawsuh!" Reverend Holbrook said emphatically. "Dey gwine put in de toilets, fix de houses up an paint dem, an sell everbody de house dey now rents fo a thousand dollars. And dey puttin in de sewer line and fixin de streets fo nothin. De city payin it all."

"You mean they're going to do that much work on a house and then sell it and the lot for a thousand bucks?" VanDolan asked, frowning. He scratched his head and said, "They'll put a five-hundred-dollar per year tax on the house and take it back for non-payment of taxes, then sell it again."

Reverend Holbrook was becoming agitated. He clasped his hands together and said crisply, "Nawsuh, dat's not right. Mistuh Grenlee an Mistuh Thonton came to our church, an dey 'splain de whole thing, an dey say de tax run fo-five dollar a year. And all de white folks had a meetin at de school, an dey voted six hundred seventeen fo de project wid five against it. Dey ain't tryin to cheat nobody. Dem's fine men."

VanDolan hunched forward in deep thought, trying to figure some other angle to the project.

"Did they start this all by themselves?" Miss Landcaster asked.

"Yassum, Miss, dey sho did," Reverend Holbrook said. "De good Lawd He smilin down on us at last, 'cause we follow de Lawd's way."

"De good Lawd hell," VanDolan muttered. "He's never put a toilet in a house and sold it for a thousand bucks."

"Whut you say, Mistuh VanDolar?" Reverend Holbrook asked, startled.

"What? Me?" VanDolan mumbled absently. "I didn't say anything."

"It's a fine project," Miss Landcaster said quickly, glaring at VanDolan. She had heard the muttered words, but VanDolan ignored her, seemingly unaware of her anger. "Getting back to our school, Reverend Holbrook," she said, "is it all right if I go on to the church early and get things set up? I have an easel and some other supplies in the car, and I'd like to go now and arrange things."

"Yassum, Miss, dat be's fine," he replied, still startled by VanDolan's attitude. "Might not have many folks at fust, but I'll do de best I can."

Miss Landcaster got up and said, "Well, it will probably take a few days to get the school operating. I will have everything ready in case someone does show up this afternoon."

Reverend Holbrook followed them into the yard and said hesitantly, "Miss, 'bout you an Mistuh VanDolar stayin in de quarters, whut you decide 'bout dis? Where you gwine stay?"

"We haven't located a place yet," Miss Landcaster said, "but we'll be staying here somewhere."

"I'll take care of it this afternoon," VanDolan said. "Do you have any suggestions, preacher?"

"Nassuh," Reverend Holbrook said, frowning. "I jus don't know 'bout dis idea."

"Don't worry about it," VanDolan said. "I'll take care of it."

VanDolan drove away from the reverend's house and along Front Street, then turned onto the lane leading to the church. "Dem dey dat, dem dey dat," he mimicked. "I don't see why the people put up with that old fool as their pastor. Jesus! They're bound to have someone better than that."

"He may not speak good English," she said, "but he has better manners than some people I know. At least he's honest and sincere."

VanDolan ignored her remark. "When we get this stuff unloaded at the church I'll find a room somewhere. I'll come back and pick you up later."

They drove across the clearing and parked in front of the clapboard building. Then the white couple climbed the steps and entered the silent sanctuary.

*   *   *

Con Ashley stormed into the sheriff's office, panting and wild-eyed, looking like a bull trying to escape the executioner. He rammed his bulky stomach into the counter, bounced back a step, glared at Mrs. Fleming and bellowed, "Where's Thornton?"

Mrs. Fleming looked up from her work and squinted into the blinking eyes of the flustered man. She said calmly, "He's in the outer office with Sam and Billy. You want to see him?"

Ashley was already moving toward the door when she asked the question. He burst into the office and stopped short just before he went over to the desk where Ike was sitting. Billy and Sam were in chairs to the right of the desk.

Ashley looked at Ike and made inaudible sounds, then said with a gush, "Thornton, they's civil-rights workers in the nigger quarters! After I heard about it I drove down there an seen the car! It's got a California license plate! An one of 'em is a white girl! I seen the car, Thornton, parked at the church!"

"I know," Ike said, watching Ashley pant. "Mayor Grenlee and I talked to them this morning."

"You talked to 'em?" Ashley said, looking at Ike with awe. "You tell 'em to git out of town fast?"

"No, I didn't tell them to get out of town," Ike said calmly.

"You goin to arrest them?" Ashley asked, the awe changing to consternation.

"No, I'm not going to arrest them," Ike said, mixing a fading degree of calm with agitation.

"Well, if you ain't goin to arrest 'em I am!" Ashley boomed.

"On what charge?" Ike asked.

Ashley exploded, "Who the hell needs a charge! When I git through with 'em they gone be mighty anxious to move along!"

"Now wait a minute," Ike said, getting up and coming to the front of the desk. "Those people haven't broken any law. They're here to operate a school for Negroes, to teach reading and writing."

"School my ass!" Ashley snapped. "The only thing they'll be teachin is how to march in the street, flop on the sidewalk, an throw rocks! Who the hell ever heard of a civil-rights worker operatin a school? I'll have 'em out of town 'fore sundown!"

Ike sat back on the edge of the desk. "Ashley, we better get something straight right now. Don't you ever read a newspaper? You make a false arrest on a civil-rights worker, or do them bodily harm, and you'll have the whole town swarming with federal agents. Is that want you want?"

"I don't give a damn 'bout federal agents!" Ashley countered. "Them sons-of-bitches would be here anyway if they could git a chance, leadin the parade up Main Street, marchin with the niggers, right at the head of the line! Are you goin to go agin the white folks again, Thornton?"

"Listen, Ashley," Ike said, getting up and ramming a finger into the fat stomach, "Grenlee and I talked to those people at length, and we both believe they're here only to operate a school. They aren't breaking any law. We're not going to allow anyone to make trouble over this when it's not necessary, and that includes you. I'm keeping a man down there all day every day, and a double patrol at night. We won't tolerate trouble from you or anyone. You better understand that right now, or you'll end up in jail. Leave those people alone, Ashley, and I mean it!"

Ashley stepped back to the door and said, "You're a fine sheriff, Thornton! This time you're wrong. You just wait an see. An I'm goin to have a patrol too. I'm still constable of this beat, and if them nigger-lovin sons-of-bitches so much as step sideways across any law I'm goin to bust 'em wide open! Now you tell 'em that, 'cause I'm goin to be doin some watchin on my own!"

"Ole pussel-gut's really got on a head of steam, ain't he," Billy said, listening to Ashley stomp across the wooden floor and into the hallway. "Maybe we better lock him up with them Millers again."

"He'll bear close watching," Ike said. He walked over to the window and watched Ashley trot across the courthouse lawn and get into the old car with red flashers mounted on the front bumper. Ashley backed away from the curb, turned and screeched the tires as he raced down Main Street, leaving a trail of blue exhaust smoke.

*   *   *

Ashley drove aimlessly up and down the highway until late afternoon, three miles north, then back, four miles south, then back, north and south again, thinking, agitating, fuming. He drove until he could stand it no longer, then he stopped at the traffic signal, turned across the tracks and sped along Front Street. A cloud of dust followed his car as he raced down the lane to the church. He slammed on the brakes and skidded halfway across the clearing, noticing that the red sports car was not there. He got out anyway and walked into the building.

Miss Landcaster was sitting inside alone, disappointed because no one had come for her first class, and apprehensive because VanDolan had not returned for her. She had waited alone all afternoon in the unfamiliar surroundings. Several times she had thought of walking to Reverend Holbrook's house and waiting there, but decided against it for fear of missing VanDolan completely. When she heard the car come into the clearing she started gathering up her books and crayons and putting them into a box. She was relieved that VanDolan had finally come, but she was angry at him for leaving her alone for so long.

Ashley stood in the doorway, peering into the fading light, his eyes sweeping forward pew by pew, searching but seeing nothing until his gaze struck the flow of blond hair, the white girl in the far corner, her back to him, putting something into a box. He moved swiftly down the aisle.

Miss Landcaster looked up and realized it was not VanDolan approaching her but a huge man, now looming above her, radiating intense waves of anger from his eyes. He examined her visually for a moment, then said, "I'm Con Ashley, the constable. Are you the one?"

"I'm Sylvia Landcaster," she said, startled by his sudden appearance. "I'm very glad to—"

"Are you the one?" he broke in and demanded.

"The one what, Mr. Ashley?"

"The filthy slut who's goin to live with the niggers!"

She flinched, the words striking her like pellets, numbing her senses and making her feel immobile. She stood in the dim light, shocked expressionless, unable to answer or to comprehend, a sickness welling up inside her.

Ashley came a step closer. He pointed a finger into her face and said, "Now you listen to me, you nigger-lovin bitch, an you listen good, 'cause I ain't gone say it but once! You make a false step, just one move outside the law, an it won't do no good for you to yell for ever goddam federal agent in the country! Just one slip an I'll fix that hot little rear of yours so even the niggers won't want it no more! So you better do your whorin out of sight! An I hope that ever one of them black sons-of-bitches you sleep with has got the clap!"

Ashley turned and pounded his way back along the aisle. For a moment she watched him, then she began to sway. She moved backward to steady herself against the pew, but she tripped and fell to the floor.

Ashley went out the door so fast he was not looking, not aware of his path, moving mechanically away from the girl. The peak of his stomach crashed into VanDolan's chest, knocking him flat on his back in the dust. Ashley glared down at the red beard, then stepped over the prostrate body and kicked the front bumper of the sport car with such force he knocked it backward. He grimaced with pain as he put his foot back on the ground and hopped to his car.

VanDolan lay still for a moment, breathing deeply, sucking the air back into his deflated lungs, not knowing exactly what had rammed into him, seeing and remembering only a fleeting glimpse of a prodigious man coming from the church, an imperceptible awareness of being crashed into and knocked to the ground, not purposely but because he happened to be in the line of flight. He heard the dull shriek of tires digging into dirt, then pushed himself upright and sat with his legs outstretched, blinking and grunting. He got up slowly and went into the church.

Miss Landcaster was sitting on the floor, her face white and her eyes expressionless. VanDolan took her hand, pulled her up and helped her move to a pew. "What the hell was that?" he asked, sitting beside her.

"Some big elephant damned near trampled me going out of here. Did he hit you?"

"No, he didn't hit me," she said shakily, her body still trembling. "He said he's the constable. Ashley. He called me a slut and a whore. He warned me."

"You see!" VanDolan shrieked, his face gleaming. "You see! What did I tell you! They're all like that! Savages! All of them! It's like they said it would be! Uncivilized savages! We'll beat them, Sylvia! He hit you, didn't he? We'll defeat them before it's over! Savages! Did he hit you with his fist or with a club?"

She looked at him closely, watching the cataclysmic transformation, knowing that in an instant he had become not a teacher of English but an enraged man spewing venom. Fear gripped her, dominating her impression of the huge red-faced stranger who had shredded her mind with a barrage of hostile words.

She finally said, "Jeffrey! Jeffrey! He didn't hit me! He was so angry when he came in here I don't think he even knew who he was talking to. We'll avoid him and stay out of his way. We didn't come here to defeat anyone, and we won't let one angry man defeat us, either. I'll talk to Sheriff Thornton about this."

"Yes, we won't be defeated," he said absently, his voice calmer.

"Where have you been all afternoon?" she asked. "You should have told me you would be this late coming for me."

He glanced at her, now seeing her again, and said, "I went to forty houses before I could find a place to stay, and then I had to bribe a guy with fifty bucks before he would rent us a room. Ten would have been plenty. These people act like we're some kind of space aliens. They don't realize we're here to help them. One old woman said 'go 'way, white man' and slammed the door in my face. Christ!"

"Is it a decent place?" she asked, still trying to control the trembling.

"Hell, it's a room!" he snapped, annoyed by the question. "I did the best I could. Hasn't got a stick of furniture in it. I went back to town and bought a couple of used mattresses at a surplus store for three bucks apiece, and got some sheets and stuff. I got a piece of rope we can run across the room and then tie up a sheet to give us some privacy."

"Let's go on there now," she said, "and then we'll get supper. I'm not going to hold a class tonight. No one came this afternoon, so we'll have to see Reverend Holbrook again about encouraging the people to come."

They left the church and VanDolan drove through several blocks of the Negro quarters, finally parking in front of a dilapidated shack at the end of a dirt lane. When they were halfway up the steps a giant Negro appeared in the doorway. He squinted his slit eyes at the girl, then said to VanDolan, "You did'n say no white gul comin too."

VanDolan continued up the steps, but Miss Landcaster froze, frightened by the hostile look on the Negro's face. VanDolan said, "Hell, man, I gave you fifty bucks. For that price you ought not care if I bring a baboon in here."

The giant Negro continued to block the doorway and said again, "You did'n say no white gul comin too."

"Listen, fellow," VanDolan said, looking up at the towering black man, "I've paid the rent. Now you either step aside and let us in or give the money back."

The Negro put his hand into the overalls pocket and felt the roll of bills, then he looked at Miss Landcaster and said, "You stay, but don't you scream."

"Jeffrey, let's go!" she said urgently, backing away. "We can find another place. I don't want to stay here."

"Are you nuts?" he said, glaring at her. "This is the only room I could get."

"What does he mean telling me not to scream?" she asked, glancing again at the giant Negro.

"Hell, I don't know!" VanDolan said impatiently. "Maybe he means there are mice in the joint. Now come on before he changes his mind."

Felds disappeared down the hallway when they entered the shack.

VanDolan opened a door on the left and they walked into a bare room with two mattresses on the floor. There was one window with no shades or curtains. A pull string hung down from an uncovered light bulb on the ceiling. The room had a rank smell and was stifling hot. Miss Landcaster stepped back instinctively and said, "Jeffrey, do we have to do this? Is it really necessary?"

"Don't start that again," he said, trying to open the window but finding it stuck. "What's wrong with this place? We'll only use it for sleeping. You must want to go live with that hick mayor."

She shrugged, knowing he would defeat her, then she said, "Does this house have a bath? I really need one."

"No, there's a privy in the back yard, and a water faucet in the kitchen sink."

"Jeffrey," she said, exasperated, "you know I can't bathe in the kitchen with that strange man in the house. What will I do?"

"Damnation, Sylvia!" he said disgustedly. "What'd you expect when you agreed to come here, the Waldorf? Don't you know how to make do? You can bring a dishpan of water to the room when you need to wash. You want one now?"

"Yes, I guess so," she said, frowning. "And where is this privy?"

"Straight out the back," he replied. "You can't miss it. Just go out the kitchen door and follow your nose."

She walked down the dark hall, through the small kitchen and into the bare dirt yard, not seeing the strange giant Negro but sensing his presence. The wooden outhouse was in a far corner of the lot. It was half rotten and leaning to the left. When she stepped inside and closed the creaking door she was in utter darkness. The odor struck her like a physical force, knocking her into a corner filled with spider webs. She stood still for a moment, paralyzed, then something dropped onto her neck and moved. She crashed against the door, fell outside and screamed. When she looked up he was standing over her, staring down with the slit eyes. He said without emotion, "I tole you not to scream, white gul. I don want you scream no mo."

She pushed herself up frantically and ran into the shack, then stumbled along the dark hall and into the bare room. VanDolan was sitting on a mattress, legs crossed, smoking a cigarette.

"Jeffrey, I'm afraid of that man!" she gasped. "He was out there by the privy! I'm afraid!"

"Aw, simmer down, Sylvia," he said, taking another draw on the odd-smelling cigarette. "That big clunk's harmless. You'll feel better soon as you freshen up."

"Jeffrey, I'm afraid!" she said again. "Can't you understand that?"

He got up, walked to the door and said, "I'll wait on the porch. Don't be too long or the Ritz will be closed."

She walked over to the pan of water on the floor.

Upon returning from the cafe, VanDolan parked the car in front of Reverend Holbrook's house and waited while Miss Landcaster got out and walked onto the porch. A ray of light spilled outward as the reverend answered her knock and opened the door.

"Come in, Miss," he said cordially, stepping backward for her to enter.

She came just inside the parlor and said, "Reverend Holbrook, no one came to my class this afternoon. Would you mind passing the word again in the morning?"

"Nome, Miss, I be glad to. I was 'fraid nobody would come at fust. I'll spread de word again."

"I certainly thank you," she said gratefully. "The class starts at ten."

When she turned to leave, he said, "Miss, where you an Mistuh VanDolar stayin?"

"We have a room in a house not too far from here, with a man who lives alone. He's the biggest man I've ever seen, about seven feet tall."

Reverend Holbrook's eyes flashed immediate concern. He said, "Dat be's Hanibel Felds. He's the biggest man in these parts. Nobody else is so tall."

"Yes, he is huge," she said. "We moved in there this afternoon."

Reverend Holbrook stepped closer and said, "Miss, dat's bad. Hanibel, he have spells. It don be safe fo you to be dere when he has a spell. You oughten be dere."

"He does seem strange," she said, watching the expression on the preacher's face, "but that was the only room Jeffrey could find."

He touched her arm and said emphatically, "If Hanibel start ackin lak he havin a spell, you come here right away! Don you stay dere if he don act right."

"I'll come here right away," she agreed. "And thank you, Reverend. I hope we have a class in the morning." She left and went back to the car. Reverend Holbrook stood on the porch and watched them leave, deep concern still creasing his face.

They drove in silence for a block. She turned to VanDolan and said, "Reverend Holbrook says we shouldn't be staying where we are. He says that man's name is Hanibel Felds, and he has some sort of spells. He even intimated we could be in danger."

"Don't let that old geezer scare you," VanDolan replied, unconcerned by the preacher's warning. "We've got a month's rent paid in advance, and I intend to get my money's worth. It might be interesting to see someone have a spell, whatever that is. I thought only dogs have spells."

VanDolan parked in front of the silent shack, now shrouded in darkness. She waited on the porch while he went inside and turned on the light in their room. When he returned she said, "Let's sit out here for a while, Jeffrey. I don't want to go inside yet."

"It is a bit stuffy in there," he said.

They sat on the edge of the porch, listening to the blending sounds of dogs barking, katydids chirping, children shouting, and shrill music coming from the Froggy Bottoms Cafe. The glow from houses and street lights was caught by dust drifting in thin layers, forming a yellow-tinted roof over the Negro quarters.

VanDolan got up and said, "I think I'll go for a walk. You want to come with me?"

"I'm tired, Jeffrey," she said. "Let's stay here."

"I don't want to sit around this damned shack!" he snapped restlessly. "I think I'll go to the Froggy Bottoms and see what's happening there."

"Reverend Holbrook told us not to go there," she said with disapproval. "He said it's a bad place, and it won't help us in our work here if you do things you're asked not to."

"I'll worry about that some other time," he said, not interested in her comment. "Are you coming with me or not?"

"I'm not going to that place," she said, "but please don't leave me here alone."

"Either you come or you stay," he said, going down the steps. Then he turned and said, "See you later."

She stood on the porch and watched him disapper in the direction of the blaring music. She had an eerie feeling that someone was lurking nearby, watching her. For a moment she thought of going to Reverend Holbrook's house and waiting there. She sat on the steps and cupped her face in her hands. She tried to think of how she would conduct her first class the next day.

Hanibel Felds sat at the table in Montique's shack, sharing a meal of canned salmon, onions, dill pickles and crackers. Felds dumped the last bite of salmon on Montique's plate, then turned up the can and drank the juice. He reached in his pocket and said, "I got us Moon Pies too." He handed the small Negro one of the round cakes.

Montique removed the wrapper, took a huge bite and said, "Why you do it, Hanibel?"

"I thought you like Moon Pie."

Montique took another bite and said, "I don mean buy dem Moon Pies. I mean let dem white folk stay at yo place."

Felds squinted across the table. "They give me fifty dollar."

Montique looked at his friend seriously. "Whut good dem fifty dollar gone do if'n it git you killed? You oughten have dem white folk in yo house."

"How they gone hurt me?" Felds asked, more interested in the Moon Pie than the conversation.

"Ain't dem I's worried 'bout," Montique said. "Dey ain't gwine hurt you, but dey sho could git you hurt. You think de white folk gwine lack it, dat white gul livin wid you? Dat fifty dollar won't do you no good is you dead."

Felds squinted again. "Who gone hurt me?"

"Don't know, Hanibel, but dey's folks who could," Montique said, staring directly at Felds. "Dem white men whut put me in dat hawg pen, dey git ahold you, dey dress you out lack a shote. Dem's mean folks, Hanibel."

"I ain't done nothin," Felds said. "I didn know the white gul comin till she showed up. I thought it was jus the man. He give me fifty dollar."

"Whut if'n you has a spell an hurts one of dem white folk in yo house?" Montique asked. "Whut you gwine do den?"

Felds ate the last of the Moon Pie, smacked his lips and said, "I ain't gone hurt nobody. I feel a spell comin, I come to yo place."

Montique said seriously, "You best be mouty kerful, Hanibel. Dem white folk don't mean nothin but trouble. Dey ain't got no business in yo house. Dey sho git somebody hurt bad."

Felds reached into his pocket, took out two more Moon Pies and handed one to Montique. He said, "I ain't done nothin. They give me fifty dollar."

VanDolan walked along the street leading to the Froggy Bottoms Cafe, his sandals kicking up little puffs of dust that spread across his feet. He stopped in the outer rim of light and studied the front of the unpainted building. Three Negro men were sitting on porch benches, watching his silhouetted form as he approached. One of them knocked three times on the wall as the white man came closer. VanDolan ignored their stares as he opened the door and went inside. Only a few people were in the cafe. VanDolan stopped and looked around, noticing that every face was turned to him, all curious, none friendly, some hostile. He took a seat at the nearest table. A young girl came from behind the counter, walked over to him and said, "What you want?"

"What you got?" he asked.

The girl glared. "What you mean what I got? What you want?"

VanDolan pulled on his goatee. "What do you serve? What is your menu?"

She glared again and said, "This a nigger cafe, white man. What you want in here?"

Every eye in the place was fixed on VanDolan, every ear listening. He smiled at the girl and said, "I didn't have anything but a hamburger for dinner, and I want to order something to eat. I'm a civil-rights worker, and I'm living here in the quarters. I came here to help your people."

The girl did not smile. She repeated, "What you want?"

He asked again, "What do you have on your menu? What do you serve?"

"We're out of chicken an fish. All we have left is hamburger, chittlin, sardine, onion, an belly wash. What you want?"

VanDolan fingered his goatee again. "What's a belly wash?"

She intensified her glare. "Belly wash is a belly wash. You want a belly wash? What flavor you want?"

A Negro man got up from a nearby table and came over to VanDolan. He grinned and said, "Come on over an join me, man. Ain't no use sittin here alone. That ain't no fun."

VanDolan followed the Negro to the table and took a seat. The Negro studied him closely, then said, "You want a slug of whuskey 'fore you eat? Makes these Froggy Bottoms vittles go down better."

VanDolan's interest picked up. "You mean bourbon?" he asked.

"Naw, not that crap," the Negro replied. "Swamp juice. Shine. Hundred-sixty proof. Best there is."

"I could sure use one," VanDolan said, taking a closer look at the Negro, noticing that his new companion was no older than himself, husky, kinky-haired and thick-lipped. "I'm Jeffrey VanDolan," he said, extending his hand.

The Negro took the white hand. "Name's Bugger Durr." He turned to the counter and shouted, "Tillie, bring us two big oranges an two glasses." Then he reached under the table, removed a loose plank, stuck his hand beneath it and pulled out a brown quart jar.

The girl came around the counter and set two orange drinks and two tea glasses on the table. She stood there staring at VanDolan.

"Belly wash cost a quarter each," Durr said, holding the brown bottle.

VanDolan put his hand into his jeans pocket, took out some coins and handed the girl a half-dollar. The girl continued to stare.

"Ain't you gone give her a little somethin?" Durr asked.

VanDolan took a quarter from the coins and dropped it into the girl's outstretched palm.

"Tillie, fix us two plates of chittlin," Durr said, now smiling. "An fry 'em some after they boiled." The girl turned and went toward the kitchen. The Negro put the bottle in front of VanDolan and said, "Now fix you a slug."

VanDolan took the bottle, poured an inch of the white liquid into the tea glass, then set the bottle back on the table.

"That ain't no slug," Durr said. He filled VanDolan's glass, picked up the orange soda and poured in a spoonful, then fixed himself a similar mixture. "Halfway in one shot," he said, turning up the glass and draining it halfway in one gulp. VanDolan followed suit but choked on the first swallow. He coughed and hacked, then put the glass back to his lips and drained it halfway. Tears came from his eyes and rolled down his cheeks. Durr smacked his lips, looked across the table and said, "I heard you say you're a civil-rights worker. What you doin here, man? What you got goin in the quarters?"

"Summer project," VanDolan said. The Negro went out of focus for a moment. Then VanDolan squinted and he came back. He said, "I'm gone teach. Got a school in the church."

"Man, that's a gas," Durr said, laughing. "What you gone teach?"

"Readin and rattin." VanDolan shook his head, squinting again.

"All the way," the Negro said, picking up his glass and draining it. VanDolan followed suit again. Durr leaned across the table and whispered, "This project got money behind it?"

"Yeah, we got money," VanDolan said with authority.

"Let me have a twenty an I'll back you up," Durr said quickly.

"Back me up?" VanDolan questioned, his eyeballs vibrating.

"You know, push the project," Durr said, whispering again. "You need help, don't you?"

VanDolan thought vaguely that he was being taken, but he considered the Negro's friendship to be worth the price. He might need him later. He took a twenty-dollar bill from his wallet and handed it to his companion.

Durr took the bottle and filled VanDolan's glass, then filled his own. He said, "Halfway down an we'll go to town!" VanDolan turned up his glass and drained it halfway while Durr took only a sip.

The girl came to the table, put a plate in front of each man, then dumped forks and knives on the table. She said, "That'll be two dollar."

"I'll pay," VanDolan said. "Treats on me." He took out his billfold, handed the girl a five-dollar bill and said, "Keep the shane." Durr glanced at the girl and winked as she turned and went back behind the counter.

VanDolan looked down at the plate, seeing what appeared to be sausage links. He picked one up, put it in his mouth, chewed and swallowed, then took a deep drink from the glass. "What ish that?" he asked, closing one eye and leaning across the table."

"Chittlin," Durr said, not looking up. "Hog guts."

"Hog guts?" VanDolan mumbled. "You mean intestines?"

"Yeah. Hog guts. Good, ain't they?"

VanDolan looked down at the plate again. He crammed another link into his mouth, chewed, and tried to swallow without success. He wheezed when the meat lodged in his throat and started swelling. Durr reached over and pounded him on the back, breaking the obstruction loose. VanDolan felt it slide into his stomach. He drank again and the third link tasted better. "Chittlin," he mumbled, getting the fourth piece down without trouble.

Durr cleaned his plate and looked up at the swaying white man. "You better let me have a ten," he said. "You gone need help on the project."

VanDolan automatically took out his wallet and handed the Negro a ten-dollar bill. He squinted at Durr and said, "You want a smoke?"

"Sure," Durr said.

VanDolan reached into his pocket and pulled out a small tin box. He removed two cigarettes from the box, put one in his mouth and handed the other to Durr.

Durr struck a match and lit both cigarettes. He took a deep draw, blew smoke into the air, then drew again. He looked at VanDolan and said, "Constable Ashley catch you with this pot you'll be in jail 'fore you can blow the smoke out yo mouth. He can smell this stuff a half-mile away." He took three quick draws and said, "Best I throw the butts out the back door. Ole Ashley might come in here an smell it."

VanDolan drained his glass, got up and said, "I got to go now."

"Where you stayin?" Durr asked.

"Big man, tall as a mountain. Name of Hanibel."

"Hanibel Felds!" Durr exclaimed, giving VanDolan a penetrating look. "White man, you got more guts than I thought you had, else you just plain stupid. Hanibel don't like honkies. Let's go on outside an I'll point you in the right direction."

They left the building through a wave of snickering and eye winks. Durr pointed the staggering white man down the lane leading to Felds' shack.

Con Ashley was parked across the street in the shadows, watching. As soon as Durr reentered the cafe, he got out of the car and crossed the street.

Miss Landcaster sat on the porch of the shack, frightened and confused, wondering if her being here alone on the porch of a shack in the Negro section of a small Mississippi town was of value to anyone. VanDolan had insisted it was necessary, but her doubts were increasing. She also attempted to justify the place she was trying to create for herself in such an alien society, among people who were total strangers so unlike anyone she had ever known. What to her in North Dakota and California had been social and racial problems had suddenly become flesh-and-blood people, not philosophies, theories, or abstract humanitarian slogans. She wondered of she were only an uninvited intruder on a stage where she had no part to play, someone who was trying to force herself into these people's lives. Her reception thus far was not what she had expected. In her mind's eye, she would be received with jubilation, the Negroes standing in line to enter her classes. Perhaps she had not been here long enough, had not yet met enough people, and things would eventually change for the better. Whatever her motives had been for coming here, the words of Mayor Grenlee lingered in her mind: *Your project won't be worth two cents to the Negroes, and whatever good it does cannot even begin to balance against the harm it could cause.* The word "balance" made her question her moral right to satisfy a personal desire at the risk of disrupting a possibly solvable problem and leaving behind irreparably damaged relationships, relationships without which the problem could never have a lasting solution. She believed that most of what had been done in the past few years in the name of civil rights was necessary to start a chain reaction of change, but what about now, today? Was her self-imposed presence necessary or foolish, helpful or harmful? She got up and went into the shack, into the dismal room, carrying with her a galaxy of thoughts and questions. She turned out the light and lay on the mattress, vainly hoping for sleep she knew would not come easily, questioning again the wisdom of living in this shack with a Negro man whom even the Negro preacher feared. She hovered for a long period in the narrow avenue between rest and restlessness, sleeping for moments and then awakening in a strange place, startled and confused, then realizing where she was by staring at the bare unpainted walls, then repeating and repeating the same cycle. She sprang to her feet when she heard loud clomping on the porch, uneven footsteps in the hall. She watched wide-eyed as VanDolan weaved into the room and pitched headlong onto the mattress, groaning and snoring simultaneously. She lay back on the lumpy mattress, comforted somewhat by the mere presence of her drunken companion, and sank back into a quagmire of fitful sleep.

Eighteen

Ike drove slowly down the street, looking at the odd patterns formed by new lumber juxtapositioned with old, houses once sagging now made straight by strong beams, new porch supports and replaced planks, each house with an extra room added to the rear, a simple combining of common materials yet a dramatic transformation in a mode of living.

The sewer line was completed on this street, the carpentry work finished, and trucks were dumping gravel for the motor patrol to spread, building a firm base over which the asphalt could be placed. When Ike reached the end of the street he saw painters already at work. One house was a gleaming sea-mist green. Each home owner had been given his choice of color, and the occupants would probably make a rainbow of the lines of houses. On the house next to the green one an initial coat of white had been applied, and a nearby one was pink.

Ike turned and retraced his route, pulling over to let a gravel truck pass. He parked when he saw an aged Negro man sitting on one of the porches. He got out, walked into the yard and said, "Good morning, Uncle Toby. Look's as if they've about got you fixed up already." The man had always been known only as Uncle Toby. He and his wife lived on his government check plus the small amount she earned working mornings as a cook in one of the white homes.

The gray-haired Negro got up and said, "Why, dat be's Mistuh Ike Thonton, sho 'nough it am. Lawd, Mistuh Ike, you looks mighty fine. Come on in an see whut dey done." A broad smile of pleasure dominated his face.

Ike followed the Negro into the house, and they stopped in the front room. Glistening linoleum covered the floor. Uncle Toby continued to smile as he said, "You see dat, Mistuh Ike. Dat's my Chrismus giff way 'fore Chrismus comes. Mistuh Kelley come down here, an he tole dem men to put dis 'noleum in ever room. He tole me I was de best hand he ever had at de mill, an he wanted me to have dis flo as a Chrismus giff. Mistuh Kelley a fine man, Mistuh Ike. Me an him used to hunt deer together 'fo I got too old. He sho know how to shoot a gun."

They walked on through the house and into the new room. Ike looked at the windows still stained with putty, at the white bathtub, the lavatory and commode, things he had always taken for granted because they were there. To this old Negro they were treasures, objects of supreme joy. Ike said, "Looks mighty fine, Uncle Toby."

"Ain't it sumfin," he beamed, lifting the commode seat and then easing it back down. "My wife she gone have a fit don't dey hurry an hook it up. She 'bout nigh bustin a gut to git all dis stuff workin."

They went back through the house and onto the porch. When Ike started down the steps the Negro said, "Mistuh Ike, you ever do much fishin anymore?"

"No, Uncle Toby," Ike said. "I don't have time for it now."

"Dat's too bad. I sho 'member dat time I took you fishin when you were a boy, an we went up Town Creek to Seller's Hole, an you kotched dat fo-pound catfish. You nigh on had a fit. You 'member dat, Mistuh Ike?"

"I sure do," Ike said, remembering fondly. "You had to take the pole and help me get him out. And when we got back to town I showed that catfish to everybody on Main Street."

"Dem wuz good days, Mistuh Ike," Uncle Toby said, a far-off look coming into his eyes. "I sho wish I could hunt an fish some mo, but I's done got too old. But dem wuz good days."

"You're not too old, Uncle Toby," Ike said, smiling. "You still look as spry as a colt. I'll tell you what. First day I can get off we'll go up to Seller's Hole and fish till we get tired of it."

"Sho 'nuff, Mistuh Ike?" he said in anticipation. "You jus let me know when you can go, an I'll dig us some bait."

"That's a promise," Ike said, walking back to the car. He turned and added, "You take care, Uncle Toby. It's been good to see you."

"You come back anytime, Mistuh Ike," the old Negro said, going back to the rocker. "I'll sho dig us some bait."

Ike drove to another street where the ditch digger was still working and found the inevitable audience, among them Reverend Holbrook. He parked the car, walked over to the preacher and said, "Good morning, Reverend. Looks like the project is moving along real good."

"Might go faster if folks like me would stay outen de way," he said, grinning. "But it's goin mighty fine, Mistuh Ike, mighty fine. Don't know what we gwine do when all dis work am finished an we don't have nothin to stand aroun an watch. Guess I'll have to go back to readin de Bible."

Ike said, "Come over by the car a minute, Reverend. I want to ask you something." Reverend Holbrook followed Ike across the street away from the crowd of onlookers. "How's the school doing?" Ike asked.

"I's 'fraid it not gwine do too good, Mistuh Ike. I talked to most ever old pusson in de quarters, an dey jus don't seem instred. Most of dem say dey ruther wait till our own classes start wid de colored teachers from de school. Dey feel more comfortable wid de teachers dey know. I talked to Miss Lancaster last night an promised to help her some mo if I can."

"Maybe if she gets only a few students she'll be satisfied," Ike said. "Did she say anything about dropping the project if enough people don't come?"

"Nawsuh, she didn't. She jus axed me to speak to de folks again." He hesitated, and then he said, "An Mistuh Ike, she told me dey got a room in de house wid Hanibel."

"Hanibel?" Ike said, surprised. "You mean they're staying with Hanibel Felds?"

"Dey sho am," he replied. "I tole her dat were bad, an she oughten be dere, but she say dat de only place Mistuh VanDolar could find. I axed her to come to my house right away if Hanibel seem lack he ackin strange."

"I don't believe this," Ike said, shaking his head. "How do you suppose VanDolan even talked Hanibel into letting them come in the house, much less rent a room? He must have bribed Hanibel real good."

"Don know, Mistuh Ike," Reverend Holbrook said. "It were a big surprise to me too. Hanibel ain't had no spell lately, an he back workin at de mill. It don't seem lack he hates white folks so much when he be's all right, but he could sho change in a hurry. Dem folks ought not be in dat house."

"I'll talk to her about this," Ike said. "I was on my way to the church now to see her about something else. If something does happen that she comes to you for help, you call me."

"I will, Mistuh Ike. I be's 'fraid fo dem folks. I'll call you right away."

Ike drove faster on his way to the church, paying no heed to construction along this street. He was seeing the image of the giant Negro coming at him with a butcher knife, stopping only when Montique hit him with a crutch. He could not imagine what the two young people would do if caught in a similar situation. He parked the patrol car in front of the church and hurried inside.

Miss Landcaster was standing by an easel, marking letters with a piece of crayon. Two women were sitting on the front pew, listening to her explanations. She stopped when she saw Ike enter and come down the aisle. "Good morning, Mr. Thornton," she said cordially. "I'm enjoying my first class, and I have two fine students. Do you know these ladies?"

Ike came around the corner of the pew and recognized Sister Pearley and Sister Dorothy. "I sure do know them," he said, smiling. "I can't say what kind of students they are, but you have two of the best cooks in Stonewall County in your class. You haven't lived until you've tasted some of the dishes these ladies can whip up. If they can learn as good as they can cook they'll soon be teaching you."

The two Negro women exuded pure pleasure, flattered and pleased by Ike's words. Sister Pearley grinned and said, "Lawd, Mistuh Thonton, ain't you a mess! You knows I ought to be at home 'stead of bein here tryin to learn readin an writin, old as I is. It's like tryin to teach a old hound to hunt, an him so wore out an igrunt he can't even find a soup bone right in front of his nose."

Miss Landcaster put down her crayons and said to Ike, "We're pleased you came, and you're welcome to come again whenever you wish. But is this just a social visit, or is there something I can do for you?"

"It's half and half," Ike said. "Half pleasure and half business. I would like to speak to you outside for a moment." He turned to the two women and said, "Would you excuse us, ladies?"

"You go right ahead," Sister Pearley said. "We needs a rest anyway."

Ike followed Miss Landcaster up the aisle and out of the church. They stopped just past the steps, and Ike said immediately, "I talked to Reverend Holbrook a few minutes ago and he said you and VanDolan moved into a house with Hanibel Felds. He is concerned for your safety, and he said he warned you about this."

"Yes, he did," she replied. "He said Felds has some sort of spells. I'm not at all pleased with the arrangement, but Jeffrey says it was the only place he could rent."

"Felds almost attacked me with a butcher knife not long ago," Ike said. "He is potentially violent. I don't believe you realize what a dangerous situation you have placed yourself in."

"I am afraid of that man," she admitted. "He has already scared the wits out of me. I assure you I will be out of that house in a hurry if he does anything that appears to be dangerous." She paused for a moment, then said, "I had another frightening experience yesterday. A man named Ashley came to the church and delivered quite a speech about what he thought of my being here."

"That doesn't surprise me," Ike said. "I knew he would vent his anger some way. Ashley is a problem we haven't yet been able to solve. Did he threaten you?"

"I guess what he said was not a threat but a warning," she replied, remembering vividly. "He intimated dire things if I broke any local law. He was so enraged he could hardly speak."

"I have already told Ashley to leave the two of you alone," Ike said. "If he pays you another visit, please let me know immediately."

"It sounds as if I might spend as much time letting you know about someone starting trouble as I will teaching my classes," she said. "I did not expect this, but perhaps it will prove to be unnecessary."

"I hope so," Ike said, "but just the same, call me if things don't go right. And now for the pleasant part of my visit. Peggy Jo and I would like for you and Mr. VanDolan to attend a cookout at our house tonight and meet a few people. Won't be anything fancy, just hamburgers on the patio."

"I would love that," Miss Landcaster said, surprised and pleased. "I really do want to know the people here. I accept for both of us."

"Fine," Ike said. "Come around six. Go around the courthouse, then three blocks north. Turn left on Pine Lane and we live in the first house on the left. Think you can find it?"

"Yes, I think so," she said, mentally recording the directions. "We'll see you tonight. And thanks so much for the invitation."

As Ike walked back to his car, he wondered where VanDolan was, and why he was not here at the church with Miss Landcaster.

Miss Landcaster left the church at noon and walked back to the shack. When she entered the room VanDolan was still lying on the mattress, snoring. She dropped to her knees beside him and shook his shoulder. He groaned, looked up at her and said, "What you want, Sylvia? Go away! I don't feel good."

She grabbed his shoulder again and shook harder. "Jeffrey, get up! It's noon, and I haven't had anything to eat. You wouldn't wake up this morning and take me to breakfast."

He pushed himself to a sitting position, fumbled in his pocket, took out the car keys and handed them to her. "Go get something by yourself," he said. "I don't want anything. I drank some shine last night with a new friend and my stomach's not in good shape."

"We're supposed to be setting an example," she said, looking at him disgustedly, "and you get stone drunk the first night we're here."

He rubbed his blood-shot eyes. "My new friend, Bugger Durr, says he will help with the project. At least that's worth something."

"Anybody you met in that place and in your condition we don't need," she said emphatically.

"You may not, but I will!" he snapped. "I'm going to start my own class."

She looked at him inquisitively. "Class in what?"

"Civics." He groaned, shook his head and said, "Be a sport and bring me a pan of water from the kitchen."

"Get it yourself," she said briskly.

He got up, staggered backward and leaned against the wall. "How'd your class go this morning?" he asked. "Have any customers?"

"Yes, I had two ladies," she replied. "Very nice people. Sheriff Thornton also came to the church. He invited us to have dinner tonight on his patio and meet some people. I accepted for both of us."

"Crud!" he groaned disgustedly. "What the hell'd you do that for? You ever hear of a hick sheriff inviting civil-rights workers to his house to eat? All he wants to do is get us up there and try to brainwash us with that 'magnolia and moonlight' crap about how good things are here. Jesus, Sylvia, are you crazy? We're here to help the Negroes, not fraternize with the rednecks!"

"We're here to organize and operate a school," she said sharply, "and it certainly won't hurt to make friends with the local people! He asked us to be there at six."

VanDolan walked unsteadily to the door. He turned and said, "When you come back I may not be here. I've got work to do this afternoon."

Ashley turned the key, opened the door and walked into the cell where Bugger Durr was lying on a cot. The Negro came to a sitting position immediately when he looked up and saw the constable. Ashley had a four-foot length of rubber hose in his hand. He sat on one end of the cot, popped the hose against his knee and said, "How you feel, Bugger? You wadden in too good a shape last night."

"I'm O.K., Mistuh Ashley," he replied, watching the hose apprehensively. "All I did was drink a little shine. I need to get out of here and go on to work."

Ashley poppped the hose again and said, "Them other niggers said you was drinkin with that civil-rights bastard. That where you got the money you had in your pocket? Did he give you some money, Bugger?"

"Nawsuh," Durr said. "That's money I made at the mill."

Ashley flicked his arm quickly, slapping the hose against the Negro's face, slashing a red welt across the black skin. Durr placed a hand over the stinging flesh and backed into a corner. Ashley stood up and said, "Bugger, you lie to me, you won't be able to go back to work for a month. Now tell me the truth. Did the white boy give you some money?"

"Nawsuh," Durr said uncertainly. "He didn't give me nothin."

The hose crashed across Durr's head, knocking him sideways. He grabbed his head and tried to move out of the way as the hose lashed his stomach, then caught his face again.

Ashley said calmly, "I'd as soon keep this up all day if you had. Did you earn the money, or did the white boy give it to you?"

The Negro grimaced with pain and said quickly, "He give it to me, Mistuh Ashley."

"What for?" Ashley demanded."

"He were drunk," Durr said, shaking his head. "I sort of talked him out of it."

"Ain't no nigger ever got money outen a smart bastard like that for nothin!" Ashley snapped. "What'd you promise to do, Bugger?"

"Nothin, Mistuh Ashley," he replied, eyeing the hose. "He jus give it to me."

Ashley put all his strength into the swing and the blow knocked the Negro to the floor. He put his foot on the small of Durr's back and lashed him with rapid blows to the shoulders. "You 'bout got enough, Bugger?" he asked calmly.

"Yassuh, Mistuh Ashley," Durr sputtered, "I got enough. Don't hit me no more." He got up and sat on the edge of the cot.

Ashley stood over him. "What'd you promise that bastard, Bugger?" he asked.

"I tole him I'd help with his project," Durr replied.

"What project?" Ashley asked, popping the hose again.

"Some kind of school, to teach readin an writin."

Ashley broke into a spasm of laughter. "You mean you told that white boy you'd teach readin an writin?"

"Nassuh, I din't tell him I'd do nothin," Durr said quickly. "I jus said I'd back the project if he'd give me some money. He were drunk, an he give it to me."

Ashley turned serious again. "Was the white slut there too?"

"What you mean?" Durr asked, perplexed.

"The white girl, goddammit, was she there with you niggers?"

"Nassuh, they weren't no white girl in the cafe," Durr said, startled. "Jus that VanDolan man. He come in by hisself."

Ashley paced back and forth for a few moments, then stopped and said, "You like to drink with a white man, Bugger?"

"Nassuh, I ain't thought much about it," Durr replied cautiously.

"Well, I'll tell you what I'm gonna do afore long," Ashley said, pacing again. "I'm gone arrange a little drinkin party for you an that white bastard, an when I get ready, I want you to do exactly what I say. If you don't, I'll spread your black ass over fifteen acres of ground. You understand me, Bugger?"

"Yassah, Mistuh Ashley," Durr said. "You jus let me know what you wants me to do."

Ashley walked out of the cell and locked the door. He said, "I'll tell old man Clayton to let you out now. I'll just keep this civil-rights money. You git anymore outen the bastard you can keep it yourself." He turned and walked down the corridor.

VanDolan walked down the street, went onto the porch of a house and knocked on the door. When he received no answer he walked to the next house, knocked, and waited impatiently. An old man opened the door halfway, peered out and said, "Yassah?"

"May I have a moment of your time, sir?" VanDolan asked.

"Yassuh, white folk. Whut you sellin?" The old Negro turned his head sideways in order to hear better.

"I'm not selling anything," VanDolan replied reassuringly. "My name is Jeffrey VanDolan. I'm conducting a survey for the National Student Freedom League. Would you mind answering a few questions?"

"Nawsuh, white folk, I don mind," the old man said, blinking at VanDolan. "Whut company you say you wid?"

"The National Student Freedom League." VanDolan repeated. "Are you registered?"

"Nawsuh, I ain't signed up," he replied, grinning. "Whut you given 'way? T'other day Sister Gennie won a 'lectric kivver. Durn things fulla wires. When you plugs it in it hets up lak a bull in a heffer pen. She gwine use it dis winter over her chicken coop."

"No, you don't understand," VanDolan said, shuffling his feet. "I'm not giving away anything. I want to know if you're registered to vote."

"Vote whut?" he asked.

"Vote! Vote!" VanDolan said crisply. "Cast a ballot! Have you gone to the courthouse and registered?"

"Sister Gennie didn't have to go to de cotehouse to sign up. De man brought de card right to de door, an filled it in right dere on de poch."

"VanDolan shufffled again. "What I mean is have you gone to the courthouse and signed the voter registration book so you can cast your ballot in the next election?"

The old Negro cocked his head. "Whut 'lection?"

"Any election!" VanDolan exclaimed. "The next time someone runs for public office are you going to cast a ballot?"

"Don't know nothin 'bout castin no ballot. Couldn throw it fer noways. I's too old. Hit been nigh on fifteen yars since I been able to work."

"Don't be afraid to answer," VanDolan said, hooking his right foot behind his left foot. "I'm a civil-rights worker, here to protect your constitutional rights, your civil rights. Don't be afraid to answer because of the white people. I'm on your side. Now tell me honestly, have they denied you the right to vote?"

"Who?" he asked, blinking again.

"They! The white people! The men in the courthouse!"

"Sister Gennie signed up right dere on de poch. She didn have to go to de cotehouse. Den dey brung de 'lectric kivver to her."

"Goddammit, man, do you know what an election is?" VanDolan boomed.

"Yassuh, white folk, I knows. An speak loud lak dat all de time. I's a lettle deef."

"Are you going to vote in the next election?" VanDolan asked, his face beginning to sag.

"Who's runnin?"

VanDolan danced a jig on the loose plank floor and shouted, "How the hell would I know who's running? I don't live here!"

"Say you don't, white folk. I didn think I'd seed you afore. Whut dat company you say you wid?"

VanDolan put one hand against the wall, leaned forward and

said weakly, "Just one more time, sir. Are you registered to vote?"

"Could you speak louder, white folk? I's a lettle deef."

VanDolan inhaled deeply, then he shouted, "Are you registered to vote?"

"Nawsuh, I ain't never had no regstered shote. De only kind I's ever had is dem swamp rooters."

VanDolan stepped back and mumbled, "You've been threatened. They've warned you. Don't worry. It's your constitutional right. I'm here to help you. You'll be registered before I leave."

When VanDolan started down the steps the old man came onto the porch and said, "White folk, ain't you gwine sign me up? Sister Gennie won a 'lectric kivver. Dey signed her up right on de poch."

"I'll come back tomorrow," VanDolan said. He walked to the next house, climbed the steps and knocked. Three Negro children, ranging in age from three to six, bounded through the door and circled him, eyeing him menacingly. All three, two boys and a girl, were naked. A fat gray-haired woman suddenly appeared and said, "Don't pay no mind to dem younguns. Dey's my granchillum. I keeps 'em durin de day."

"Madam, my name is Jeffrey VanDolan. I'm with the—"

One of the children grabbed him by the leg, almost jerking his feet from under him. He stumbled against the wall. The old woman bounded onto the porch, slapped the boy across the backside and shouted, "Shoo! Git back in de house! You chillen leave dat white man 'lone!" She hit another one across the rear with her open hand and all three rushed back through the door and disappeared. "Scuse me, white folk, whut wuz you sayin?" she asked.

VanDolan straightened himself. "I'm with the National Student Freedom League. May I ask you a few questions?"

"De whut?" she asked, staring at him.

"National Student Freedom League," he repeated.

She looked at him suspiciously. "Whut's dat?"

"It's a civil-rights organization. We're the ones who have started a school in your church."

"Yassah, I knows 'bout dat. I'm gwine go myself dis fall. Whut you want to know?"

"Are you registered to vote?" he asked.

She backed away a step. "Why you want to know dat?"

"I want to know if you've been denied your constitutional rights. We're here to help you. Have you been denied the right to vote?"

"Reveren Holbrook say we all gwine be 'lowed to vote now," she said quickly.

"Have you registered yet?" he asked again.

"Nawsuh. Reveren Holbrook talked to Shuff Thonton, an he say us folks whut can't read an write oughten try to regster 'fore we larn. He say dey ain't gwine 'low no white folks to regster neither, 'lessen dey read an write."

VanDolan's eyes gleamed. He said enthusiastically, "You see! You've been denied! They're lying to you! It's just a trick to keep you from voting!"

The woman became alarmed. She stepped back again and said, "Nawsuh, dat ain't whut Reveren Holbrook say! An Mistuh Hopkins he done made 'rangements for us all to go to school. We gwine start dis fall."

"No, no," VanDolan said, pulling on his goatee, "it's just a trick! They're putting you off, lying to you! They'll never let you vote!"

Shuff Thonton say 'taint no hurry 'cause dey ain't no 'lection fo two mo years. He say dey ain't no hurry."

"We'll demonstrate!" VanDolan said, not hearing the woman. "We'll force the issue and bring national attention! You've been denied, cheated! We'll march for freedom and fill up the streets!"

"Nawsuh, nawsuh, white man!" she said, frightened. "Reveren Holbrook say we do it de Lawd's way. De white folks gwine fix up my house. I's gwine do what Reveren Holbrook say."

"Reverend Holbrook's a fool, a Judas, an Uncle Tom!" he snapped. "He's in with them, trying to trick you! You'll have to march! We're agents of the government! If you refuse to demonstrate we'll have your government check stopped! I'll let you know when we're ready! You've been denied, cheated!"

The old woman was sweating fear, trembling, her eyes bulging. She said, "You go 'way, white man! You go 'way an leave me 'lone! I's gwine do whut Reveren Holbrook say! You come back, I'll tell de shuff." She turned quickly, went inside and slammed the door.

VanDolan stood there for a moment, a triumphant expression on his face. Then he went down the steps and marched to the next house. He raced quickly across the porch and knocked. A young girl clad in yellow panties and a pink bra came to the door. She opened the screen, looked at the white man and said, "Come on in. My name's Clara Mae."

VanDolan stepped inside, pretending not to stare. He said, "Are your parents at home?"

"My pa's in Chicago and my ma works at the Ritz," she replied, visually examining the visitor. "I's fifteen. Nobody stays with me durin the daytime. What you sellin?"

VanDolan shifted his feet as he glanced at the yellow panties. He said, "I'm not a salesman. I'm conducting a survey."

"Salesman who came here the other day gave me these yellow panties," she said, popping the elastic. "Purty, ain't they? It's too hot in here to wear much. You'd be more cool you take off that shirt. You got a extra dollar?"

VanDolan looked at the firm breasts confined by the pink bra. He fumbled in his pocket, took out a bill and handed it to her. "I'm conducting a survey," he mumbled. "I wanted to speak to your parents."

She took the bill, twitched her hips and said, "I'll answer yo survey. You come with me, mister."

VanDolan followed her into an adjoining room.

Nineteen

VanDolan and Miss Landcaster drove up Main Street, around the courthouse and turned north. Miss Landcaster had made herself as presentable as possible under the circumstances. She wore her last clean skirt and blouse, a matching outfit in pale blue. VanDolan's attire consisted of the same jeans and T-shirt he wore when they arrived in Midvale. The shirt bore stains of dust acquired in front of the Froggy Bottoms Cafe. Since VanDolan had fresh things in his suitcase, she had berated him heatedly about his choice of dress for this occasion, but he simply ignored her, stating that his apperance was his own business.

"Turn left at the third block, first house on the left," Miss Landcaster said, excited by the prospect of making social contact with people she would like to know. She had not expected to have this opportunity while in Midvale.

VanDolan remained silent for a moment, then muttered, "Crud!" He turned onto the side street and parked in front of a red-brick house. Several cars were in the driveway. Neither of them realized they were followed. Con Ashley stopped at the corner and watched the couple get out of the red sports car and walk to the door of Thornton's home.

Peggy Jo answered the ring. She extended her hand and said, "You must be Miss Landcaster and Mr. VanDolan. Please come in. We're happy to have you. I'm Peggy Jo."

Miss Landcaster stepped inside first and was immediately envious of the cool sweet feminine smell of clean skin and cologne. She took the hand and said, "Thank you so much for the invitation, and please forgive my appearance. I'm living under unusual circumstances right now."

"You look fine," Peggy Jo said reassuringly. "And please call me Peg."

VanDolan then stepped inside and took the soft hand silently.

Peggy Jo ignored his appearance. "And I'm pleased to meet you, Mr. VanDolan. Just follow me back to the patio. Everyone is outside."

Peggy Jo led them down a hall, through the kitchen and onto the patio. As soon as they came out everyone stood, awkwardly forming a semicircle, looking uncertain and unsure of how they should react to this strange couple. Peggy Jo sensed the strained atmosphere, which was not unexpected. She said, as cheerfully as possible, "Everyone, this is Jeffrey VanDolan and Sylvia Landcaster. I'll make the introductions as we go along. This is Jeff and Sarah Bennett, Ed and Margaret Kelley, Sid and Grace Grenlee, and Major Sylvester Beecham, who is 'batching' this week while his wife Betty is visiting relatives. As you know, the guy at the grill is my husband, Ike."

Miss Landcaster gave each one of them a personal greeting, and VanDolan remained silent. All of them pretended not to notice VanDolan's appearance.

None of Ike's friends had accepted the invitation with enthusiasm, and they all came with a degree of misgivings. None could understand why Ike and Peggy Jo had invited the civil-rights couple into their home, and Grenlee thought it was a foolish thing that could bring unnecessary criticism to Ike. Ike countered with the old saying, 'You can catch more flies with honey than with vinegar,' and he also wanted Miss Landcaster to have more than one impression of Midvale. Despite the misgivings, his guests had accepted the invitation mainly out of curiosity.

Peggy Jo said, "Sylvia and Jeffrey, find a seat and make yourselves at home. We're very informal here." She could think of nothing else to say, so she went to a cooler by the grill and filled a tray with cans of beer. She came back and served Miss Landcaster first, who responded, "Thanks, Peg. This is a treat. I haven't had a beer since we left California."

VanDolan took a can and said, "I thought people in the South drank only mint juleps."

"Not exactly," Kelley said. "I can't stand mint juleps. I'd rather have Scotch or a good sour mash bourbon. If you'd like me to, I can run to the house and get a bottle of Chevis Regal or Jack Daniels."

"There's a bottle of bourbon in the house," Ike said. "Would anyone rather have it than beer?"

"Beer's fine," VanDolan responded. He started to mention the local shine he sampled at the Froggy Bottoms but decided against it.

"Do you have children, Peg," Miss Landcaster asked.

"Lordy yes. We have a boy and a girl who are over at Sid and Grace's house sharing a sitter. They love to turn over the grill and break glass when we have company."

The glacier was showing signs of cracks but was basically intact. The situation reminded Peggy Jo of childhood parties when the boys and the girls lined up on opposite sides of the room, distrustful of each other, coming together only when the ice cream and cake was served.

Sarah Bennett broke a momentary stalemate and said, "Are you a native of California, Sylvia?"

"Oh, no," she replied. "I'm from Trenton, North Dakota. I had never been to California before entering the university there. I'm not well traveled."

"What about you, Jeffrey?" Kelley asked. "Are you a Californian?"

VanDolan took a drink from the can and said, "Right now I'm a Mississippian. I'm from wherever I am at the moment."

Kelley countered, "When you're not in Mississippi, is California your home state?"

"No," VanDolan replied. "My home state is New York. What difference does it make where someone is from? You're here one day, gone the next. It all seems the same to me."

Peggy Joe said, "Why don't you start the hamburgers now, Ike? Does anyone want another beer?"

"I'll take one," Bennett said.

"Count me in too," Kelley echoed.

"What about you, Sylvia, Jeffrey?" Peggy Jo asked.

"No, thank you," Miss Landcaster replied. "One is my limit."

"I'll have another," VanDolan said, feeling a bit better.

After serving the beers Peggy Jo lit tiki torches on opposite ends of the patio.

Kelley said, "Miss Landcaster, I've always wanted to hunt pheasant in your part of the country, but I've never gotten around to it. Are you a sportsman?"

"Oh yes," she replied quickly. "I love the outdoors. I used to hunt pheasant with my brothers. If you ever come to Trenton I can take you to a place where pheasant are as plentiful as field larks."

"I just might take you up on that someday," Kelley said, knowing this would never be.

"I've always wanted to see the Black Hills," Mrs. Kelley said. "Perhaps while you two are shooting birds I could become a tourist. I enjoy eating game, but I'm not a hunter."

"We have fine hunting around Midvale too," Ike said. "Deer, quail, dove, ducks, about everything but pheasant. If you like to shoot pheasants, you would find dove hunting very exciting."

"All of you please excuse me," Peggy Joe said. "I've got a few things to do in the kitchen." She got up and went into the house.

"What about you, Jeffrey?" Major Beecham asked. "Are you a sportsman too?"

"I shoot a fair game of pool," VanDolan replied, "but I've never fired a gun. There's no such thing as hunting in New York City, and I've never had any interest in it."

"You might if you tried," Kelley said.

"I don't think so," VanDolan said, bored by the subject. "I can't see how anyone derives pleasure from shooting animals or birds. I have no desire to try."

"What is your impression of Mississippi, Sylvia?" Grace Grenlee asked, steering the conversation along another course.

"It's very beautiful," she replied warmly. "I haven't seen it all, but I like what I have seen. Perhaps we can take a tour before we leave. I would love to visit Vicksburg and Natchez."

Peggy Jo brought a pot of baked beans from the kitchen and said, "Are the patties ready, Ike?"

"I'm taking them off now."

"Good. I'll bring the potato salad and we're all set. Everyone take a seat now."

Two picnic tables were placed together and covered with red-checkered cloths. Ike lit candles on each end of the tables while Peggy Jo brought out a bowl of potato salad. She said, "This is a serve-yourself meal, so dig in, everybody. There's more beer over there and also tea and ice."

The conversation was temporarily halted as food became the main attraction. Miss Landcaster took some of everything. She was enjoying this bonus experience of sitting on the patio of a Midvale home, eating hamburgers and socializing with the mayor and the sheriff and other local people. It seemed to her a paradox that there could be in one small town such radically different personalities as these people who were trying as hard as possible to make her feel comfortable, and the red-faced constable who had come to the Negro church spewing venom and hate.

All traces of daylight had now disappeared, leaving the patio encased with flickering orange flames from the tiki torches. The meal was finished in a banter of trivial talk, discussions of no importance. Peggy Jo cleared the table, and the group reassembled in chairs scattered around the patio. They remained silent for several minutes, wondering which direction the conversation would take, and who would initiate it. The women especially were now silent, inwardly liking this pleasant young girl but unable to comprehend why she was living by choice in the Midvale Negro quarters, something they would never do under any circumstances. This one fact prevented her from being accepted as merely another female companion and kept her in the class of enigma.

Grenlee finally broke the stalemate and said, "How is your school project coming along, Miss Landcaster?"

"Actually, I'm a bit disappointed," she replied, "but maybe I expected too much. Thus far I have only two students and a promise of a few more next week. I've also been puzzled by my reception."

"How is that?" Grenlee asked curiously.

"I've already told you and Mr. Thornton I didn't come here as a crusader," Miss Landcaster said. "I came because the civil-rights movement is the paramount issue of this decade, and I want to feel that in my own small way I have contributed something to help people who have been denied equal rights. Perhaps I am naive, but my reception has been lukewarm at best. I've received suspicion and indifference along with some appreciation, and this was not expected."

"Maybe I can shed some light on that," Ike said, not wanting to speak but feeling he should. "Many of the people who have come to the South as civil-rights workers came only for publicity and adventure, and they couldn't have cared less about the rights of local Negroes. In many cases local Negro leaders were not allowed to have any voice at all in the projects set up by these people. Their opinions were completely ignored and even ridiculed. Some of the civil-rights workers came only as agitators. They succeeded in smashing all relations between the two races, then they went back to wherever they came from, leaving the locals, both black and white, holding the bag and trying to pick up the pieces. That's why some leaders in the black community take a dim view of civil-rights workers."

"Let me say something," Kelley broke in. "Miss Landcaster, to be extremely frank, you and Mr. VanDolan are as much a curiosity to us as we are to you. This is a rare opportunity for all of us, and I think it would be foolish for us not to exchange honest opinions. Certainly we have diverse points of view, and the worst problem in this country today is a lack of understanding each other, or maybe even a complete lack of attempting to understand different views. We won't start the Civil War again here on Ike's patio, but let's exchange thoughts. If it gets to the stage of throwing bricks we can stop, have another beer, and discuss hunting."

"I couldn't agree with you more," Miss Landcaster said. "I don't have a closed mind, and I wouldn't know how to throw a brick if someone handed one to me with printed instructions. So let's be brutally frank with each other."

"Ike was being kind with what he said about some civil-rights workers," Bennett said. "Many of the civil-rights workers who have come into the state over the past two years have been kooks, misfits, beatniks, and God knows what else. They have swarmed in here like locusts, and once they crossed the Mason-Dixon line they acted as if they had entered a foreign country were everything and anything goes. They made themselves look as repulsive as possible, they made no contact with the white community or tried to make friends in the white community, and they deliberately broke every local law on the books, trying to provoke violence. They did some things here they would never do back in their own hometowns, things that would land them in jail immediately, and they did these things because they knew they had federal protection in whatever they did so long as it was labeled civil rights."

"That's a pretty strong statement, Mr. Bennett," Miss Landcaster said. "What were these despicable acts you speak of? I never saw anything bad on television."

"That's because the cameras were turned off," Bennett said. "You saw only the singing and the marching and the white-black brotherhood. When something bad happened, the cameras were turned the other way. Let me give you an example. Last year one civil-rights group organized a 'freedom march' through the state. They turned off the main highway, went into a town and formed a circle around the town square, where all the businesses are located. There were two hundred of the demonstrators, and the sidewalks were filled with spectators. At a given signal, all of the males unzipped their pants, all the females squatted down, and they urinated in the street. What did that accomplish, and how many friends did it gain? Can you imagine what would happen if two hundred people from anywhere in the South went to New York City, circled Times Square, and urinated in the street? They wouldn't be given the key to the city, that's for sure, or be invited to have tea with the mayor."

Bennett's words were like hot coals in VanDolan's craw, but he decided to remain silent for the moment. Miss Landcaster said, "I have heard that some people who have come here were in fact not here in the interest of the movement. But in a movement as large in scope as this one, don't you agree it would be impossible to weed out the bad? It isn't right to discount the good accomplished by the majority because of irresponsible acts of an uninvited minority?"

"Uninvited, Miss Landcaster?" Major Beecham questioned. "Several of the national civil-rights leaders stated to the entire country that they welcomed anyone who would join the crusade and head south. This was an open invitation to disaster. Any damned rabble-rouser, psychopath or plain damned fool can put a civil-rights pen in his lapel, come south and command a legion of FBI agents as personal bodyguards. I am not a Southerner except by choice, but this makes no sense to me. Does it really make sense to you, Miss Landcaster?"

"Well, Major Beecham," she replied, feeling as if she were being blind-sided from every direction, "this is supposed to be a free country in which any citizen can go anywhere he wishes and campaign for anything he so desires. It would be utterly impossible for the government or anyone else to say who can and who cannot be a civil-rights worker. I agree that the cause has attracted undesirable elements, but to control this would be beyond reason. And thus far no one has mentioned the real tragedy of the civil-rights movement, the murder of civil-rights workers in the South. There are no words you can use to excuse or defend such crimes."

"I agree wholeheartedly," Major Beecham replied. "I would never defend or condone murder. I abhor such actions. But do you know, Miss Landcaster, a household poodle will attack if provoked enough, and there are people in the South and elsewhere who will take the bait. Some of the national civil-rights leaders were probably jubilant when a murder occurred, for without some violence their cause would not have received worldwide attention. They knew this would happen and wanted it to happen, and they were willing to put people on the sacrificial block for the sake of their cause. Just let one isolated murder of a civil-rights worker occur here, and every reporter and photographer in the nation rushes to the scene with cameras and typewriters ready, the story usually written in advance, and then all hell breaks loose in Washington. You would think that violence was invented in the South, when in fact there is more violence in New York or Detroit or Chicago or Los Angeles in one week than there is in Mississippi in a year. Here it gets the spotlight, there it doesn't. In this state, with a population of two and a quarter million, perhaps a dozen people have committed violent acts against civil-rights workers. What sort of a staggering percentage is that? More people than that kill their wives or husbands every day. Yet from what has been written about the state, half the population of the nation believes that all Mississippians are racist murderers. There are people here who have killed civil-rights workers and have killed Negroes, but there are people elsewhere who have killed Jews and Irishmen and Italians and Chinese and Mexicans and Mormons and Native Americans and witches. Violence was not invented in the South alone."

Major Beecham stopped abruptly. He looked around at the silent faces dimly revealed by the flickering light surrounding the now-quiet patio, hearing not even the sound of breathing, seeing that all eyes were turned to him. His face flushed at the realization of his tirade, then he breathed deeply, regaining his composure. He said, "I'm sorry. This was supposed to be a group discussion and I've turned it into a personal harangue. I've had several army friends refuse to visit with us in Midvale because of a sincere fear of being caught in a riot or struck by stray bullets. It's preposterous, ridiculous!"

Miss Landcaster also remained silent, trying to digest the major's unexpected words, then she said, "Admitting that there have been both good and bad elements in the situation, do you really believe that change would have come about in the South without the actions of civil-rights workers?"

"Yes, it would," Marjor Beecham said. "I'll answer this question and then shut up and let someone else talk. The only thing I see that can be attributed to civil-rights workers is that the national leaders used the violence they provoked as a club to get some of the bills through Congress sooner than could have been done otherwise. Other than that I don't believe civil-rights workers have accomplished anything but creating hatred and wrecking communities. The courts and the FBI are responsible for compliance of civil-rights laws in places of resistance. This is not the responsibility of civil-rights workers, although they seem to think it is. No one has attacked an FBI agent or a judge, so it stands to reason that the violence has not been against compliance but against meddling outsiders who have no business taking over the responsibilities of local community officials. There is an abundance of race problems in every state in this country without some people turning their backs on their own junkyards and coming to the South, looking here for problems to solve."

"They came here because your treatment of the Negro is the worst blight on the history of mankind," VanDolan said, getting up and opening another beer. "You Southerners are all alike. You do a lot of yapping about what you would do if people would leave you alone. What you would do is nothing. Without civil-rights workers no changes would ever have been made. All your talk about solving your own problems is just lies and tricks, delaying tactics. You would return the Negro to slavery if you could."

"Mr. VanDolan," Kelley said, reacting to this sudden outburst of accusations, "it may be beyond your ability to comprehend, but we are not responsible for all the Negro's problems. They have brought some of them on themselves, just as white people have. I can hire a Negro and a white man at my mill and pay them the same salary. The white man will have a neat home with flowers in the yard, and the Negro will live in an unpainted shack but will have a case of booze in the closet and the biggest car money can buy parked in his front yard. Not all are this way, but some have not even attempted self-improvement."

"Why should they have been expected to," VanDolan said, "when you have kept them at the level of animals, denying them the right to eat in a restaurant, vote, take part in government, send their children to a school of their choice, or even sit with you in a theater. Do you believe that anyone would want to improve himself under such conditions?"

"Those things you mentioned have happened," Grenlee admitted, "but not in the spirit you intimate, not in hatred of the Negro. They were part of a way of life that evolved generations ago because white people did not want to integrate with Negroes for many reasons. In the beginning it was born of fear. We have never hated the Negro. There has always been a bond of friendship between the white and Negro here that you would never understand, a type of friendship which has never existed between the two races anywhere outside the South, a bond never severed in spite of the bad things we have done and admit we have done. Anytime a Negro here has asked a white friend for money or food or any sort of aid he has received it without question. We have always tried to help the Negro as best we could, and in some cases we could not have done any better. But we're making progress now."

VanDolan took a deep drink from the can and said, "You would have done those same things you speak of for a stray dog. Do you think Negroes are merely cattle, to be kept in barns and fed properly? Your great friendship is a friendship on your terms only, paternalistic terms. And this progress you speak of, is it those toilets you are putting in the Negro shacks? Do you think a few commode bowls will make up for a hundred years of discrimination? You're just trying to trick the Negro into being satisfied for the present, trying to make him lick your hand in gratitude and stay put for a while longer."

"That's not so!" Grenlee snapped. "We're doing that project because we want to, not as a trick. And we're making progress elsewhere, in schools, financing, job opportunities, health care. We're moving as fast as possible."

"You're not moving at all except when forced to," VanDolan countered. "You people are completely out of the mainstream of American life."

"Why are we considered by you to be so different?" Grenlee asked. "What is it that makes us so despised? Is it only the Negro? Are the South's sins the only ones never to be forgotten or forgiven? Are we considered to be out of it because of what has happened in the past to Negroes?"

"You're out of it in every way possible," VanDolan said, his eyes gleaming. "Your sins are not of the past. They're still here. You're a race of savages. You're not a part of the new society."

"Just what do we have to do in order to gain membership in the new society?" Grenlee asked, controlling his anger.

"You can start by ceasing your brutality against Negroes! Put an end to your violence!"

Grenlee stood up and faced VanDolan. "Let me ask you a simple question," he said. "If here in Stonewall County we have a small minority of people whom we believe might be capable of committing violent acts, what would you have us do, round them up, prejudge them on our suppositions, then exterminate them?"

"Yes!" VanDolan replied quickly. "Exterminate them!"

Grenlee looked closely at the bearded youth in soiled clothes and said weakly, "You mean like Hitler did the Jews?"

VanDolan jumped to his feet and shouted, "Yes, goddammit! Like Hitler did the Jews! Exterminate them!"

The two stood there in the dim light, staring at each other, Grenlee experiencing a mixture of revulsion and pity, VanDolan merely staring and shuffling his feet. Grenlee then retreated backward to his chair.

Miss Landcaster got up quickly and said to Peggy Jo, "It's getting late, so I think we better go now. I have some class preparation to do tonight. I really enjoyed the evening, and it was nice of you to ask us."

"We had better go too," Kelley said.

Everyone got up at once, saying abbreviated words of thanks to the hosts. All of them turned their eyes away from VanDolan.

Miss Landcaster said, "It has been a pleasure meeting all of you. And Mr. Thornton, the hamburgers were delicious." She clasped her hands together to stop the trembling.

"We're glad you came," Peggy Jo said. "If you'd like you can go around the side of the house instead of having to go back through the kitchen."

The group moved around the house silently, the atmosphere restrained. They all departed without further words and went to separate cars.

As soon as they were away from the house Miss Landcaster turned to VanDolan and said angrily, "Why did you have to do that? Why must you make everyone your enemy?"

"You fool!" he shot back. "Don't you have any sense? When they were lambasting civil-rights workers they were talking about you, about me! We're civil-rights workers! They were talking about us!"

"We were exchanging opinions and viewpoints!" she said harshly. "They have a right to express an opinion, whether you agree with it or not. Can't you take part in an open discussion with becoming vicious? And how did you become an authority on these people's motives? Do you think you are always right, always the supreme judge? Perhaps Mr. Kelley was correct when he said the worst problem in this country today is a lack of even attempting to understand each other. Exterminate people! My word, Jeffrey! How crude can you be?"

"That's the only way," he replied absently. "That's exactly what must be done. All I said was the truth. They have tried to exterminate the Negro race, and now they must receive a dose of their own medicine. An eye for an eye, a tooth for a tooth."

"My God, Jeffrey," she said, alarmed, "do you really believe that? Are you serious or joking?"

He ignored her question and became silent. They turned down Main Street, crossed the tracks and headed back toward the Negro quarters.

Twenty

Several of the Saturday afternoon sidewalk gawkers watched the bearded boy and blond girl come from the Ritz Cafe, get in the sports car and drive down the street. One said, "That them civil-rights workers who live with the niggers?"

"Yeah. She ain't bad lookin. Too bad she's sleepin with niggers."

"Sheriff Thornton says she ain't that kind of a girl."

"Horse crap! You really believe that?"

"Well, I don't know. Ain't no reason for the sheriff to lie. He ought to know more about it than you."

"How does he know what she does down there at night with them niggers?"

"I don't know, and you don't either."

The crowd of fender-leaners and squatters congregated beside the railroad station observed the small red car as it crossed the tracks and headed toward the Negro quarters.

"That them?" one asked.

"Must be. I heard they got a red sports car."

"Ain't it a shame what a white girl will do nowdays?"

"If she was my daughter I'd lay a strop on her."

"You better not put a strop to that one. Don't you know what them govment fellers 'ud do if you mess with a civil-rights worker?"

"Yeah, I know. It wouldn't be worth it."

"Sheriff Thornton says they ain't doin no harm noways. They just teachin the niggers to read an write. That don't amount to nothin."

"Guess not. They won't be here long noways."

VanDolan turned down the usually half-deserted street which was now crowded with cars and trucks belonging to country Negroes in town for their Saturday visiting. Groups of people sat in chairs jammed together on porches and spilling out into yards. Bands of children raced up and down the street, shouting and kicking up dust. The silent ditch digger looked like a Christmas tree with Negro children as ornaments. Young and old alike watched as the white couple drove by.

VanDolan parked in front of the seemingly deserted shack. As they crossed the yard Miss Landcaster said, "Sister Pearley did my laundry today and I've got to walk over there and pick it up. Would you like to go to the movie when I get back?"

VanDolan twitched his goatee. "What kind of a cruddy show you think they'd have here on Saturday night? An old Roy Rogers flick? You want to go up there and crunch popcorn with the rednecks?"

"Yes," she replied. "I like popcorn. If you don't want to go here we could drive to Jackson. I don't want to sit around this stifling room again tonight."

"I've got a meeting about my class that starts Monday," he said, reflecting no interest in her suggestion. "It has already been arranged so I've got to go. You can have the car and go to the movie by yourself. I'll leave the keys on my mattress."

"Just what is this class you're starting?" she asked curiously. "And why do you have to arrange it on Saturday night?"

VanDolan said with annoyance, "I've already told you. I'm organizing a course in civics and government, and someone is helping me recruit members. I don't want just old women like you've got. You need the car keys, they'll be on my mattress." He hurried up the steps and into the shack as she turned and walked away.

VanDolan went into the kitchen and washed his face and hands in the sink, then went up the musty hall and into the room. He opened his suitcase, took out a clean pair of jeans and a T-shirt and changed clothes. He left the shack and headed toward the Froggy Bottoms Cafe.

The rows of houses were alive with shrill sounds, and the dim street lights competed with the last rays of a rapidly fading sunset. A dog ran out of a yard and barked at the small white man, then circled him, yapping louder. VanDolan walked backward, watching the skinny hound until it turned and ran back into the yard.

VanDolan came around the corner slowly, observing the front

of the cafe, studying the men sitting on the benches. None of them knocked on the wall when they saw him approach. He waded through their indifferent stares and went inside.

All of the tables were occupied by chattering couples. For a moment after VanDolan entered they became silent, some staring at him distrustfully, none friendly. Then they ignored him and the dull roar continued. Bugger Durr was alone at a table in the corner. He stood up and motioned for the white man to join him. VanDolan made his way hurriedly across the room and took a seat opposite Durr.

They looked at each other sheepishly until Durr said, "You want a drink?"

"What kind?" VanDolan asked suspiciously.

"I ain't got nothin but shine."

"They sell bonded whiskey in here?"

"You can get a bottle for a price."

"How much?" VanDolan asked, looking directly into Durr's eyes.

"Five bucks a pint."

VanDolan took a ten-dollar bill from his wallet, handed it to Durr and said, "Get two pints. And you buy the belly wash this time."

The Negro disappeared through the kitchen door and returned shortly with two bottles and a big orange. Each mixed a drink. VanDolan said, "I'm starting a class at the church Monday. I want you to get some people to attend. Young people."

"What kind of class?" Durr asked.

"Doesn't matter," VanDolan replied nonchalantly. "I'll pay you two dollars a head for every person who comes, and pay them a dollar for each class they attend. The classes won't last more than thirty minutes. Tell them to be there at ten sharp Monday morning, at the picnic tables outside the church."

Durr's face beamed. He said, "You want a plate of chittlin?"

"Later," VanDolan replied, knowing he had the Negro hooked. "I've got something to do first. We'll eat later."

They finished the drink and poured another. VanDolan gulped

it down in one swallow and said, "Here's ten bucks for helping me, and I'll pay you Monday night for everybody who shows up. You look out for the whiskey. I'll be back later. I've got something to do now."

"I'll keep it under the floor till you get back," Durr said eagerly. "Then we'll have a plate of chittlin." He smiled as VanDolan got up and crossed the room.

VanDolan left the cafe and walked to a vacant lot at the end of the street. He leaned against an oak tree trunk and waited for his eyes to become adjusted to the darkness. Then he said softly, "You here, Clara Mae?"

The girl stepped from behind a bush and came to him silently. "You got them?" she asked.

"Yes," he replied, handing her a small package.

"What color is they?" she asked excitedly. "I can't tell in the dark."

"Red. You like red?"

"I sho do," she beamed. "I ain't got none on now so I'll slip these on."

"No," he said quickly. "I'll put them in my pocket and you can have them later."

"We can't go to the house tonight," she said. "Mama got off early, an she got company. I knows a place where nobody will see us. It's got lots of pine straw. We can go there now."

VanDolan followed the girl into the thick woods.

Con Ashley parked behind the building and walked to the front entrance. He glanced around impulsively to see if he was being observed, then went inside. Three Negroes stood alongside the counter, waiting as Hankins cut slices of cheese and wrapped them in brown paper. Ashley watched nervously as Hankins put the cheese and several cans into a bag and took money from one of the Negroes. As soon as the men left, Ashley said, "You got everything ready?"

Hankins came from behind the counter and said, "Yeah. It's in the car. You really think we ought to do this?"

Ashley glared at him disgustedly. "You gone back out?"

"Naw," Hankins said quickly. "It ain't that. But what'll we do if he catches us?"

"He ain't gone catch us!" Ashley said harshly. "The bastard's got it comin. You know that."

"He shore has," Hankins agreed. "It needs to be done, so we'll do it. Don't seem like nobody else got the guts."

"You ready?" Ashley asked. "Time we make it out to Jud's an git everthing fixed it'll be about time."

"I better tell my old woman to tend the store," Hankins said. "I don't want to close this early on Saturday night."

Ashley grabbed Hankins by the arm and said menacingly, "You ain't let on nothin about this to her, have you?"

"Naw," he replied quickly. "I put all that stuff in the car while she was uptown this afternoon. She don't know nothin."

"She better not," Ashley threatened. "I'll wait for you out back so she won't see me in here."

Ashley went out the front door as Hankins walked down the hall to their living quarters. In a few minutes Hankins came out the rear door and got into the car. Ashley said, "You sure you didn't for- git nothin?"

"I'm sure," Hankins replied. "I got everthing we'll need."

Hankins drove down the highway and turned onto the gravel road. For a while they said nothing, then Ashley muttered, "Crap!"

Hankins said, "I wouldn't 'a believed it, Con, hadn't you seen it with your own eyes. I just wouldn't 'a believed it. He went too far this time. We got to do somethin afore it's too late."

They drove the rest of the way in sullen meditation, then Hankins turned when he reached the dirt lane. He crossed the clear- ing and parked close by the front steps. Rays of dim light drifted from the window in the front room, and dull thumps could be heard. Coney came to the door, peered out and said, "Hit's Sim an Con, Pa."

The light moved from the room onto the porch, and four

bearded men stood there, watching Ashley and Hanki
steps. Jud said, "We were havin a game of mumbley p
want to play? We got extra knives."

"Naw," Ashley said. "I don't want to play no gam
business to do."

"You want a drink?" Jud asked.

"I could shore use one," Ashley replied. "Then we
penter work to do."

"Fetch a jug, Bester," Jud said, squatting on his h

They all squatted in a circle, waiting for the
Bester came out and handed it to Jud. He turned it
then he passed it to Hankins. When the jug had made
circle, Jud said, "Whut you gone build, Con, a coffin?
somebody?"

"Naw," Ashley replied. "We gone build a cross an
sheriff's house tonight."

"Gawd-a-mighty, Con," Jud exclaimed, "you fell
on thet cross-burnin business again? I ain't never
growed men so tetched in the head 'bout burnin a cr
you want to do it this time?"

"Ain't you heard what's happened in town?" Ashl

"Naw," Jud replied. "I ain't been to town lately.
pened?"

Ashley puffed out his chest and prepared to an
strophic news. He boomed, "Two of them white civil-r
has moved into the nigger quarters!"

Jud looked at Con indifferently and said, "Whut
workers? Thet some kind of govment men, like reven
they better stay way from out here."

Ashley's chest deflated immediately, showing his
ment that his news had not shocked any of the bearded
"Civil-rights workers is them white sons-of-bitches who
town an stirs up the niggers, gits 'em to march in the str
hollerin."

"Whut they want to do thet fer?" Jud asked, s

hy'd anybody want to watch a bunch of niggers sing an holler. I'd
uther go coon huntin."

"Goddammit, Jud!" Ashley roared. Then he suddenly sucked in
 breath, changed his tone to meekness and said, "What I mean to
, Jud, is that civil-rights workers are white people who turn the
 ggers against the white man, git the niggers to run wild, take over
e vote, take over the school, throw rocks an run over the white
an."

"Why don't you jest shoot 'em?" Jud asked calmly. "Ain't no
 se in lettin a bunch of niggers run all over the place."

"One of them is a white girl, Jud," Hankins said, his eyes gleam-
 g, "an she's stayin with that big nigger what got us all in trouble."

"Whut's she doin thet fer?" Jud asked, puzzled again. "Can't she
 d a white man who'd give it to her?"

"She's doin it 'cause she likes niggers better!" Ashley exploded.
 d like to turn a stud hoss loose on that bitch! An there's a white fel-
 w stayin there too." He grabbed the jug, took a long draw and said,
 heriff Thornton had them two sons-of-bitches to his house for
 pper. Had them nigger-lovers right there in his house. I seen it!
 's plottin agin us, Jud."

"Whut you gone do?" Jud asked.

"Burn a cross on his yard," Hankins said.

"Whut fer?" Jud asked. "Why don't you whup them white folks
 shoot a few niggers?"

"You want to go with us?" Ashley asked.

"Naw," Jud said. "I ain't gone burn no cross. Druther sot here
 drink."

"You mind if we build it out here so's nobody will see us?"
 hley asked.

"Don't make me no never-mind," Jud said, drinking again. "Hit
 n't bother me none."

"Get the stuff, Sim, an let's get on with it," Ashley said.

Hankins walked back to the car, opened the back door and
 loaded two-by-four beams, nails, burlap, string, and a saw and
 mmer.

Coney said, "Pa, kin I go into town an see the white girl? I ain't never seen no white girl who is sleepin with a nigger. Kin I, Pa?"

"Maybe later," Jud said. "She ain't gone let you watch it, noways."

"I don't keer, Pa," Coney pleaded. "I jus want to see her."

"I said later!" Jud said firmly. "Now shet up 'bout it!"

"You want me to help?" Bester asked Ashley. "I made a cross once fer a dog whut got killed by a wild hawg. Let me drive the nails."

"That's fine with me," Ashley said.

Bester got up, came down the steps and grabbed the hammer and a sack of nails.

"We'll have to piece a couple of beams together to make it tall enough," Ashley said, "an then base it on an X-stand, 'cause we won't have time to dig a hole an plant it in the ground. Don't put the nail in the cross arm too tight so's we can swing it down flat with the post an get it in the car. We can push the arm back out when we get there."

The other three Millers moved over and squatted on the edge of the porch, watching the construction. Bester pounded away with the hammer, splicing two beams together for the post. Then they made the stand, attached it to the post, put on the cross arm and stood it up. Bester backed off and looked, then he said, "Hit's 'bout the purtiest cross I ever seen. Ain't it nice, Pa?"

"Shore is," Jud said. "Seems a mighty shame to burn it. We could put it out by the hawg pen an look at it."

"You want to finish it while we have a drink," Ashley asked Bester.

"Let me do it," Coney said. "Whut you want me to do?"

"Take these burlap strips an wrap 'em real tight over the cross," Ashley said, "an then tie 'em with string.

"You wrop an I'll tie," Berl said, coming down the steps. "I want to help too."

Ashley and Hankins joined Bester and Jud on the porch while Coney and Berl wrapped the cross. Jud said, "How you gone git that thing in the car, Con?"

Ashley took a drink and said, "When we turn the arm down

straight with the post we can put it through the right front window and push it back as far as it'll go. The rest will stick out the window."

"I don't see why you fellows want to burn that thing anyways," Jud said.

"To let Thornton know we don't like nigger-lovers," Ashley said. "Maybe scare him a little."

"Wouldn't scare me none," Jud said. "Somebody come out here an burn a cross I'd shoot 'em. Whut you gone do if'n he cotches you?"

"He ain't," Ashley said. "We'll light this thing an shuck out like a sow with a hornet on her butt."

"You want somethin to et afore you go?" Jud asked. "We found a shote runnin loose over by the south pasture."

"Not tonight," Ashley said. "We better git on to town with this thing. I could use another drink 'fore we leave."

Ashley and Hankins drank again, then went down the steps, lifted the cross and put it through the window. Ashley said to Jud, "I got a little fun planned for next Saturday night, so you an the boys be shore an stay at home. We'll pick you up here. We'll need a couple of gallons of the strongest corn you can make."

"I'll have it ready," Jud said. "Whut kind of fun are you talkin 'bout?"

"You'll like it," Ashley replied. "We'll see you Saturday."

Ashley climbed across the left side of the front seat. Hankins started the car and drove back toward town.

They drove silently until they reached the highway. Then Ashley said, "If the porch light is on when we get to his house we'll have to wait. If it ain't on, park in that vacant lot down from his house. We'll tote the cross back to his yard, light it an take off. When we get back to the car, drive with the lights off an head for your store. I'll rush on down to Froggy Bottoms an grab me a nigger, an take him to the jail. That way old man Clayton will say I was at the jail if anybody tries to put this thing on us."

Hankins turned off the highway before he reached Main Street. He drove along several side streets until he reached Ike's house. It was silent and dark except for light dimly seen behind drapes. The patrol car and his private car were parked in the driveway. Hankins continued for a half block, then turned into a vacant lot and parked behind a hedgerow. They got out and pulled the cross out through the window.

"Git the kerosene can," Ashley whispered as he turned the cross arm outward. "I'll lean it down by the top an you douse it good."

Hankins soaked the burlap while Ashley held the cross at an angle. Ashley said, "You grab the stand an I'll take the top. When we put it on his yard you come on back to the car an be ready to go. I'll light it an run on back down here."

They moved quickly up the street with their cumbersome burden, glancing about cautiously to detect any sign of life. When they reached Ike's house they set the cross on the yard halfway between the front door and the street. Hankins turned and went back toward the car. Ashley struck a match and held it to the edge of the burlap at the bottom of the post. A small flicker of flame caught in the slow-burning kerosene. When he knew that the fire would stay and work upward, he turned and ran, his huge stomach bouncing up and down like a pumpkin, causing him to grunt with each step. Hankins already had the car in the street, waiting. Ashley jumped in and they drove off into the darkness.

As the flame gradually made a circle around the base of the post, it grew larger and moved upward slowly. It suddenly jumped several feet and sprang to brilliance across the top and arm, lighting up the yard in front of the house.

Ike and Peggy Jo were in the den, watching the late news on television. The children were asleep in the back bedroom. The phone in the kitchen rang and Peggy Jo said with a sigh, "Don't tell me you're going to get called out this late. Let me answer. I'll tell them you're not at home and to call Billy or Sam."

"Better not do that," Ike said, getting up and walking to the kitchen. "I asked for the job, you know."

He picked up the phone and listened. Then he put it down quickly and said, "It was Ron Tullos across the street. He says something is burning on our lawn."

Ike and Peggy Jo hurried through the house and out the front door. They stopped suddenly and stared. Peggy Jo grabbed Ike by the arm and said, "Is that a cross, or am I seeing things?"

"It's a cross," Ike said. He ran to the faucet on one side of the yard, grabbed a garden hose and shot a stream of water into the flames. The cross made a hissing sound as water and fire met. Milk-white smoke poured out and floated upward. Peggy Jo remained in the doorway, unable to remove her gaze from the unfamiliar spectacle. Two neighbors came from their houses and ran across the street, also watching in amazement.

The water quickly gained dominance over the flames, causing more white smoke to boil upward. The neighbor who had called Ike came over to him and said, "What is this, Ike, a prank? It's not Halloween yet."

"Probably just a prank," Ike said, "but I don't think it's funny. They've burned my lawn. Thanks for calling, or it would have been worse."

The man turned and walked back to his house, a puzzled expression still on his face. Ike kept the hose on the cross until it stopped smoking, then asked Peggy Jo to turn off the water while he carried the remains of the cross to the back yard. He came back to the front and they went inside together.

Peggy Jo sat on the couch and said, "What is this, Ike? Is it just a prank? Isn't a burning cross the sign of the Ku Klux Klan?"

"There hasn't been a Klan in Stonewall County for fifty years or more," Ike said. "it's just a prank."

"But why us, Ike? Why?"

Ike knew who had done this, and he knew it was because of Montique and Hanibel Felds and Jeffrey VanDolan and Sylvia Landcaster. He didn't want to frighten Peggy Jo, so he said again, "It was some kids with nothing better to do. It was a one-shot prank, and it won't happen again. I'll find out who it was and talk to their parents. Don't worry about it. I'll take care of it tomorrow."

"I certainly hope it doesn't happen again," Peggy Joe said. "I'm glad the children were asleep. Maybe next time they won't be, if there is a next time."

"Don't worry about it," Ike said again. "I'll take care of it."

Twenty-one

Grenlee and Kelley entered the courthouse soon after Ike came to work that morning. They walked into the private office and closed the door. Ike was behind his desk.

Both men sat in chairs in front of the desk and Grenlee said, "What's it all about, Ike?"

Ike tried to imitate puzzlement. "What's what all about?"

"You know damned well what I mean!" Grenlee snapped. "Who burned a cross on your lawn last night? It's all over town this morning. Most people think it was a prank, but some believe the Klan has come back into the county."

"There is no Klan in Stonewall County," Ike said, leaning back in his chair. "And burning that cross wasn't an innocent prank. I know who did it."

"You do?" Grenlee said, surprised. "Then who was it?"

"Sim Hankins and Con Ashley."

"Hankins and Ashley?" Grenlee questioned. "Why would they do something like that?"

"Several reasons," Ike said. "I threw them both in jail for something they did to Montique. And there's more. My talking to the Negroes about registering to vote, my support of the project in the quarters, and the hamburger cookout at my house for VanDolan and Miss Landcaster could have sparked it. Ashley threatened Miss

Landcaster at the Negro church, and he could have followed them to my house."

"Good God!" Grenlee said. "You mean somebody burned a cross because we had a discussion at your house that almost ended in a brawl? If that's the case, my lawn is next, and then Jeff and Ed and Major Beecham."

"I don't think so," Ike responded. "It was directed only at me. I'm the target."

Kelley said, "Do you have any proof that it was Hankins and Ashley?"

"None at all," Ike replied. "It would be almost impossible to prove. The beams were two by fours and they used burlap wrapping. Those things are as common here as pine cones. But there is one thing. Instead of gasoline, they used kerosene. That thing reeked of kerosene, and it's not so common anymore. But still it would be hard to prove anything. It would be like chasing fog."

"Is there anything we can do?" Grenlee asked.

"Yes there is," Ike said. "Spread the word that this was just a prank. If you have to, lie a little and say the kids were caught and have been punished by their parents. If someone asks for names, just say they were juveniles and the names were not released. The last thing on earth we need here right now is a false belief that the Klan has become active in the county."

"I agree," Grenlee said. "I wish there was some way we could remove Ashley from office before the next election."

"Maybe he will make one mistake too many," Ike said. "He's not through yet. You can count on that."

"Is Peggy Jo all right?" Kelley asked. "How is she taking this?"

"She's fine," Ike replied. "It scared her, but she's fine now."

Grenlee and Kelley got up to leave, and Grenlee said, "If there's anything else we can do, just let us know. We're all in this together."

VanDolan arrived for his class a half-hour early. He sat on one of the picnic tables and waited impatiently, getting up and pacing nervously, then sitting again. He thought of various things he could do to Bugger Durr if no one showed up, especially since Durr had been paid in advance for his services. He took the tin box from his pocket, lit a cigarette and inhaled deeply, then relaxed and regained his composure.

He glanced up the street and saw them all coming at once, a group of twenty teenagers, bounding along happily as they laughed and joshed each other. When they reached the tables, VanDolan said loudly, "Everybody take a seat! My name is Jeffrey VanDolan. What we'll do here is study civics and government."

One boy said, "Bugger Durr told us you'd pay a dollar."

"Everyone will be paid after each class," VanDolan said impatiently. "Take a seat and let's get started."

"We want to be paid before each class," the boy said.

"I said after!" VanDolan snapped, anger in his voice.

The boy blinked his eyes and said, "If you don't pay before each class, you ain't gone have a class."

"Well, all right," VanDolan consented. "I suppose it isn't important." He took a roll of bills from his pocket and handed one to each student, then said, "As you were probably told, I am a civil-rights worker. I have come to Midvale to help your people throw off the shackles of oppression and gain all the rights of citizenship you have been denied for more than a hundred years."

"What's that got to do with civics and government?" a girl asked.

"It has everything to do with it," VanDolan replied tartly, annoyed by the question. "Civics and government is people, and what we're concerned with here is people, your people, the Negro of the South. You have been denied your constitutional rights by the hated white man."

"If you a honkie, how come you hates honkies?" one boy asked.

"Honkie?" VanDolan questioned. "What's a honkie?"

"A white man," the boy answered, causing a wave of snickering.

"Oh. Well, I don't mean all whites," VanDolan said, "just Southern whites. It is only the whites of the South who have denied you your rights. Do you think your life here is anything like the life

Negroes lead anywhere outside the South? Don't be foolish. In California, everyone is equal. Whites and blacks work together and live together, they vote together and go to school together. There is no discrimination, no poverty and no racial tension or racial unrest. Outside the South, everyone is treated equal."

VanDolan stopped and wiped sweat from his brow. He lit another cigarette and continued, "You can have all of these things here, but first we must break the will of the white man. We must force him to give you your constitutional rights. To do this we may have to demonstrate, march in the streets and block the sidewalks."

One boy stood up and said, "My cousin in Greenwood got five dollars ever time he marched in one of them demonstrations last summer. How much you gone pay?"

"What?" VanDolan stammered. "What did you say?"

"How much you gone pay fo marchers?" the boy repeated.

"Pay? We'll talk about that later. I'll make it right with everybody."

One girl stood up and said, "Reveren Holbrook said in church that all folks can vote now, an Mistuh Hopkins said anybody who want to can transfer to the white school this fall. How come you want us to march about that?"

"It's all lies!" VanDolan snapped. "They have been tricked by the white man! He'll lie every time to keep you from demanding your rights. We'll force the issue."

"How much you gone pay, an when we gone march?" the same boy asked again.

"We have to have classes first," VanDolan said, now sweating profusely. "I have to teach you the truth and show you the way. We'll march, but first I must reveal the light."

Another boy stood up and said, "Bugger Durr tole us the class would last a half-hour. We been here that long now. If we stay longer, are you goin to give us another dollar for today?"

"No," VanDolan said. "You have been paid for today, but we must go overtime. There are more things I must explain. You see, the white —"

They all jumped up at once and scampered across the clearing, laughing and shouting and raising a cloud of dust. VanDolan screamed, "Wait! Wait! Wait, dammit. I must explain —"

They were out of sight before he could finish the sentence.

The late afternoon flurry of grocery buying by Negroes on their way home from work at the mill had ended when Ed Kelley entered Hankins' store. Hankins looked up from behind the counter and said, "Well, howdy, Mr. Kelley. Good to see you."

"Got any old-fashioned hoop cheese, Sim?" Kelley asked.

"Yes, sir, I shore have," Hankins said, surprised and pleased that the mill owner had come into his store.

"Give me a slice," Kelley said. "Don't wrap it. I'll eat it here."

Hankins cut the cheese, put it on a paper napkin and handed it to Kelley. He smiled and said, "You don't owe me nothin, Mr. Kelley. It's on me."

"No way, Sim. You can't make a living that way. Man's got to make a living nowdays to support his family." He put a half dollar on the counter, took a bite of cheese and then said, "Ummm. This is good, Sim. Bet you sell a lot of cheese, don't you?"

"Yes, sir, Mr. Kelley, a pretty good bit," Hankins replied proudly. "The niggers like hoop cheese mighty fine."

Kelley took another bite. "How is business anyway? You doing all right these days?"

"Can't complain," Hankins said, leaning against the counter. "I do a right smart of trade at noon and late in the afternoon, an it ain't too bad on Saturdays. We been makin out O.K., thanks to the workers at the mill. I get most of my business from them."

Kelley continued eating for a moment, then said, "How's the kerosene business, Sim? You sell much anymore?"

"Not too much," Hankins replied. "Ain't many folks uses kerosene no more, what with electricity and butane on most of the farms. A few still uses it, but not many."

"Didn't think so." Kelley finished the cheese, leaned against the counter and said, "Just this afternoon I needed some for a camp

215

lantern, and I had to look all over town for it. Only place that even carries it in stock is your place and one of the service stations on the other side of town. Fellow down there said he hadn't sold a drop in about two months. Can't make much money with it at that rate, can you?"

"No sir, you sure can't." Hankins cut himself a piece of cheese and plopped it into his mouth.

Kelley glanced at a shelf of canned goods and said nonchalantly, "Kerosene does mighty fine for burning a cross, doesn't it, Sim?"

The piece of cheese stuck in Hankins' throat. He coughed, then swallowed hard and said, "What you mean, Mr. Kelley?"

"Well, if you used gasoline it would explode immediately into a brilliant flame," Kelley said casually, "and a fellow wouldn't have much time to get away before being seen. But kerosene is a slow burner, and it would give a fellow plenty of time."

Hankins' face paled. He said unevenly, "I don't know 'bout somethin like that, Mr. Kelley. I ain't never had no dealins with burnin a cross."

"I know you haven't, Sim," Kelley said. "A fine citizen like you wouldn't do anything that would harm the town, or especially to hurt your business. If I knew a good man like you would do something like burn a cross, I'd have to ask all the workers at the mill to stop trading here, and that would just about wreck you, Sim. I don't know what a fellow like you would do if, at your age, he lost his business and had to grub wherever he could for a living."

Hankins felt ill. He leaned against the counter to steady himself. "Mr. Kelley, I swear I ain't never burned no cross."

"I didn't say you had," Kelley said, carefully noting the alarm on Hankins' face. "I was just thinking how bad it would be for someone like you to lose everything over something as silly and as useless as burning a cross. I know you wouldn't do a thing like that, Sim. You're a good man. And besides that, you're too smart for such foolishness."

"That's right, Mr. Kelley," Hankins said quickly. "I'm too smart to do somethin foolish."

Kelley walked to the door, then stopped and said, "I want you to do me a favor, Sim."

"Yes, sir, Mr. Kelley," Hankins said eagerly. "I'd be glad to."

"I know you have a lot of influence in the county, Sim, because people respect you for being an honest merchant. I want you to pass the word that burning a cross will not be tolerated in Stonewall County. There will be no more of this foolishness. I'm certain your word will carry a lot of weight. You're my spokesman, and I'm going to count on you to put a stop to this sort of thing once and for all. I'm depending on you, Sim. If anything goes wrong, I'll hold you personally responsible."

"You can count on me, Mr. Kelley," Hankins said. "I won't let you down."

"I know you won't," Kelley said. "I hope all my workers continue trading with you. And that was fine cheese, Sim. I'll see you later."

"Yes, sir, Mr. Kelley," Hankins said, mopping his brow. "You come back anytime."

Kelley started out the door, then turned and said, "Sim, you're like me, getting on up in age, but you have some good years left. Why don't you just forget about the niggers and start enjoying life. Do some fishing, or get an acre somewhere close to town and plant a garden. You always did like to farm. If you need financing, come see me. Start having some fun, Sim. Life's too short now to stay in a stew all the time."

As soon as Kelley was gone, Hankins groped his way around the counter and plopped down in a chair. He tried to think of what he would do if Ashley asked him to help burn another cross. But he was sure there would be no other. Then he thought of Kelley's words, *forget about the niggers and start enjoying life.* He would like to go fishing again, or plant a garden and watch things grow. He decided it would do no harm to look for a suitable acre of land.

Twenty-two

At mid-afternoon Ike left the courthouse and drove down Main Street. His plan to dismiss the cross-burning as a prank had apparently succeeded, and he had heard no more comment on the matter.

Black clouds were forming in the eastern sky, and since there had been no rain in more than a month, the dominant topic of conversation on Main Street was the possibility of a shower. A prolonged summer drought with the resultant crop failure would cause more damage than the burning of a thousand crosses. The success or failure of farmers touched the lives of everyone.

Ike drove for a block along Front Street and then turned left, inspecting the progress on this street. When he saw Frank Parks, Kelley's construction foreman, he parked and walked over to him. "Looks like you're about to finish here," Ike said.

"We'll be done this afternoon, painting and all," Parks said. "If it doesn't rain too much they can shoot the asphalt on this street tomorrow. But I expect it's going to be a few days. Those clouds are boiling up pretty good. For my money, the asphalt can wait a couple of days. We sure need rain."

"A good shower would cool things down and make everyone feel better," Ike said.

Parks lit a cigarette and said, "You know, Ike, I've never worked on a project that gave me as much pleasure as this one. When we finish a house it's like Christmas has come to a bunch of kids. It's a pity we couldn't have done this a long time ago."

"We couldn't have bought this property from Mr. Bingham before now," Ike said.

"I guess so," Parks agreed. "He could have done this himself if he hadn't been such a skinflint. He had me build him a chicken coop a few years ago, and he wouldn't pay me. I stayed after him for about six months, and he finally told me to come and get the coop back. When I picked it up it was full of chicken poop, so I took it straight to the garbage dump. But I got back at him. When nobody was home, I went to his house and boarded up the outside of his kitchen door."

Ike looked up from a spasm of laughter and saw Reverend Holbrook approaching them. The reverend walked up and said, "Sumpin musta got ahold of yo funny box, Mistuh Ike."

"We were talking about Mr. Bingham," Ike said. He shifted the subject. "It's looking good, isn't it, Reverend? Frank says they will finish the houses on this street this afternoon."

"It sho am lookin fine," Reverend Holbrook said. "We had a meetin yesteddy at de church, an when de work is all finished, we gwine have you an Mayor Grenlee and de town boad an all de white folks who's worked down here on de project as guests at a barbeque. We gwine cook some steers de old-fashioned way, dig some big pits, let de coals burn down good, put sweet gum poles cross de pits, split de steers in half an cook 'em slow fo two days. Den we all gwine sot down an et till we can't stand up."

"Man, Reverend, you can start today so far as I'm concerned," Parks said, drooling. "I haven't had barbeque cooked like that since they had those town trade days when I was a kid. Lordy, preacher, I'll have the men goin double time starting tomorrow."

"I'll help too," Ike said, popping the reverend on the back. "I'll be down here in the morning with a saw and a hammer."

"I sho ain't joshin," Reverend Holbrook said. "We gwine have de biggest barbeque since my grandaddy sot fire to a barn an burned up ten cows. We'll et fo three days if it takes it to get all dat meat down."

"I better go now," Ike said, "but I'll see you in the morning. What time do we start work, Frank?"

"Seven sharp. And bring your own bandages."

"Now don't you back down, Reverend," Ike said, starting for his car.

"Ain't gwine to," Reverend Holbrook said, also leaving. "We gwine have us a party."

When Ike reached the tracks he noticed Ashley's car parked beside the station house. He pulled in beside him and said, "Hello, Con. How's business lately?"

Ashley replied indifferently, "Ain't too bad."

"Have a busy night last Saturday?" Ike asked. "Mr. Clayton said you didn't bring in as many drunks as usual but you were at the jail around ten that night."

Ashley looked at Ike suspiciously. "Warn't as many drunks as usual. I do my job. If they get drunk I bring 'em in."

"Yes, I'm sure you do," Ike said, watching Ashley closely. "I guess you heard about those kids burning a cross on my lawn. I caught one of them and he gave me the names of the others. They sure got a lickin from their parents."

"Yeah, I heard," Ashley said gruffly. He had been furious since he heard that everyone had accepted the cross-burning as a harmless prank.

"Well, I better go on now," Ike said calmly, noticing the angry expression on Ashley's face. "Looks like we're going to get rain tonight. You be careful, Con."

Ashley scowled as he watched Ike drive off up Main Street. He pulled away from the station and sped down the highway to Hankins' store. He jumped out of the car and rushed inside.

Hankins was alone, sitting on the counter. Ashley said, "Dammit, Sim, everybody thinks that cross-burnin was just a prank by a bunch of kids! I bet Thornton started that lie hisself. All that trouble we went to was for nothin. A prank!"

"Is that so?" Hankins said, feigning surprise. He was positive Ed Kelley knew who burned the cross.

"You want to burn another one?" Ashley asked. "We burn another one they'll know it ain't no prank."

"Naw, I don't want to do that," Hankins said warily. "We done it once and got by, so they ain't no use to burn another one."

"What the hell you gettin sanctimonious for?" Ashley asked.

"'Taint that," Hankins replied, trying to look unpertubed. "If Thornton knows it warn't no prank, he'd be lookin out for us next time. It ain't worth takin a chance."

"I guess you're right," Ashley said, calming himself. "But you're still goin along Saturday night, ain't you?"

"Yeah, I'll go, but I ain't gone burn no cross."

VanDolan and Miss Landcaster sat on the steps of the shack, watching streaks of lightning slash through swirling black clouds. It was almost dark although there was another half-hour of daylight left.

Miss Landcaster said, "I hope this shack has a good roof. If it doesn't, we'll get the first bath we've had in some time, and this isn't the way I like to take a shower."

"I'll be gone for a while tonight," VanDolan said. "I've got a meeting about my class."

She looked at him curiously. "What are you doing to get all those people? It looked today as if you have around thirty, and I have only four. How are you managing to get so many?"

"I've told you I have someone helping me," he snapped. "How many times do I have to tell you? If you'd get some help, your class would be bigger."

"Reverend Holbrook is helping me."

"Ah, crud," he said sarcastically. "I don't mean that old coot. I better take the car since this storm is coming."

"I don't suppose it would do any good to ask you not to go. This weather looks threatening, and I don't want to be alone."

"I told you I've got a meeting," he replied. "Haven't you ever been in a rainstorm before?" He got up, went out to the car and drove up the street.

She sat on the step a while longer and watched the lightning come closer, creating tremendous booms that shook the loose boards on the porch. A few scattered drops of rain made little volcanic puffs in the yard dust, and then it suddenly came down solidly. She got up and ran into the room. She took a book from her suitcase and sat on the mattress, trying not to look outside at the brilliant flashes.

Felds was sitting at the table in the kitchen, gazing absently out the back door at the rain slashing through the dim light that spilled outside. He put his huge hands on his knees and tapped them up and down, as if keeping time with the beat of the rain. He jumped when a brilliant flash of lightning struck the chinaberry tree at the side of the outhouse, then hunched forward as the shattering thunderclap rocked the shack. For a moment it seemed as if the glass window panes would crash to the floor. Then he heard a scream come from the front room, a piercing scream competing with the receding sound of thunder. He was suddenly thrown backward in time, spun backward through the years, back to the farm in Alabama, back to the creek bank. He grabbed his head in his hands and fell forward on the table.

Felds' huge body shook in agony for a moment. He got up and went to the door. He thought of running down the trail to Montique's shack, but he froze in the doorway, rain pelting against his head and eyes and making splotches on the faded overalls. He stepped back, still looking out into the darkness but not seeing the darkness, not seeing the rain, not seeing the flashes of lightning, seeing instead the creek bank in Alabama, the girl coming on him suddenly, the white girl screaming, and he stood there listening to her scream. Then they came for him in the car with the star on the side because the white girl had screamed. He walked over to the counter and picked up the butcher knife and went silently up the hall to the front room.

She was sitting on the mattress when she looked up and saw him standing in the doorway, the butcher knife in his hand. His eyes were glazed with hatred. She pushed herself backward until she touched the wall, then she looked up at him again. She was too frightened to speak to him and try to convince him to go away and leave her alone.

Felds stepped into the room and said in flat tones, "Don't you scream, white gul."

She could tell by his expression and his voice that he was beyond reasoning, beyond hearing her even if she could speak. He was completely mesmerized, not even of this time and this place. She knew her only chance of survival was to obey his wishes and hope that whatever possessed him would go away.

She closed her eyes in order to escape into a sanctuary of darkness, not wanting to see what was coming. Then she felt the floor shake as he dropped to his knees beside her. She flinched when the knife blade touched her throat.

She pressed her hands over her eyes and started crying, trying to remove herself mentally from this shack and this room and be back at home in North Dakota with her mother and her father and her brothers, walking in fields along streams, hunting pheasants, riding horses on a clear cool autumn morning, dreading at any moment to feel the blade slice into her flesh.

For several minutes she was unaware he had left the room, left her lying there crying. She felt her throat and looked at her hands, and her hands were clean. She sat up quickly, as if awakening from a nightmare. She jumped up and ran from the shack into the blinding rain.

She slipped and fell into mud, then she pushed herself up and ran again, slipping and falling and running and moving by instinct toward the house of the Negro preacher. She was unaware of the darkness or the mud or the blinding rain or the lightning or anything but the necessity to get away from the shack and the giant mesmerized Negro with nonseeing glazed eyes. She finally stumbled onto the porch and pounded frantically with her fists. When the Negro preacher opened the door she tumbled headlong into his arms and cried hysterically.

Reverend Holbrook was instantly paralyzed by fear. He froze in the open doorway with wind shrieking into the parlor, rigidly holding the mud-splattered white girl in his arms. His hand moved instinctively to the back of her head, stroking the wet blond hair. He said softly, "Don cry, chile." He closed the door, led her to the couch and sat beside her, her head on his shoulder, saying again and again, "Don cry, chile."

They sat on the Victorian couch holding each other, experiencing the same unexplainable intrinsic bond that Ike and the Negro preacher had felt when they shook hands for the first time here in this same room. He rocked back and forth, clasping the young white girl as if she were the child he had always longed for but had been denied by either poverty or fate. She was unaware of everything save that someone gentle was holding her, keeping her safe from a horrible nightmare. Reverend Holbrook hesitated to ask what had happened, afraid to know the truth, suspecting that an act had been committed which could rip his community asunder. Visions of holocaust flashed through his mind, the specter of a black-white rape crushing the harmony his people were now enjoying. He summoned his courage and asked, "What did Hanibel do, chile? Did he hurt you?"

She stopped sobbing and said, "No, he didn't hurt me. He frightened me. He had a knife. He didn't know who I was or where he was. He was in some kind of a trance."

Reverend Holbrook shuddered with relief. He said, "You gwine stay here from now on. I'll get Sistuh Lucy to come stay wid us. She live by herself, so she won't mind. You gwine stay here. I'll go get yo things." He got up, went into another room and returned with a raincoat and a robe. "You want me to call Shuf Thonton an tell him 'bout dis?" he asked.

She sat up straight on the couch. "He didn't do anything. He just scared me. Please don't call Mr. Thornton. He just scared me, that's all."

He handed her the robe and said, "You get outen dem wet clothes an put on dis robe. I'll stop on de way an send Sistuh Lucy on up here. Soon as she gets here she'll fix you a hot bath, an you'll feel better. You gwine be all right while I's gone, chile?"

"Yes, I'll be fine," she replied.

He put on the raincoat, took a flashlight from a cabinet drawer and left the house. As he plodded down the muddy street rain beat against him and almost obliterated the narrow beam of light. He stopped at the Negro woman's house and spoke with her briefly, then continued his difficult journey. The shack's front door was still standing open. He climbed the slippery steps, went inside and shouted, "Hanibel! Hanibel! Is you here, Hanibel?" Only the howl of wind-driven rain answered his voice. He went into the room and opened one of the suitcases to be sure he had the right one. He picked it up and started to leave.

VanDolan ran onto the porch and stomped mud from his sandals. He came into the room and stopped short when he saw Reverend Holdbrook standing there, holding the suitcase. He said, "What are you doing here, Preacher? Where's Sylvia?"

"She gone," Reverend Holbrook said, glaring at VanDolan. "She at my house, an she gwine stay dere from now on. Hanibel scared her real bad."

"What'd he do?" VanDolan asked, throwing his wet shirt into a corner. "He say boo to her?"

"I don know what all he did, but he sho scared her," Reverend Holbrook said, still glaring. "An I wants to tell you sumpin, Mistuh VanDolar. You were tole Hanibel could be dangerous, dat he has spells, an you went off an left Miss Lancaster by herself. You oughten to have done that."

"I'm not a nursemaid," VanDolan said, kicking off the sandals. "She's old enough to take care of herself."

"You a evil man, Mistuh VanDolar," Reverend Holbrook said angrily. "I know where you been. I's been told 'bout you bein at de Froggy Bottoms so much, an 'bout you an dat chile, Clara Mae. You a evil man, an someday you gwine face de Lawd!"

VanDolan's face flushed with anger. He walked up to Reverend Holbrook, pointed a finger at his face and said, "Let me tell you something, you Uncle Tom bastard! It's none of your business where I go or what I do! Do you understand? It's none of your damned business!"

Reverend Holbrook walked to the door, looked directly into VanDolan's eyes and said, "You a evil man, Mistuh VanDolar, an someday de Lawd's gwine punish you." Then he turned and disappeared into the darkness.

Twenty-three

It was Friday morning before the ground was dry enough for the paving work to resume. Ike drove into the quarters early to watch the tank truck distribute tar on top of the gravel. Several dump trucks loaded with slag were lined up along Front Street, waiting for the tar application to be finished so they could move in and perform their part of the job. The carpentry work on houses along an adjoining street was completed, and the motor patrol was spreading fresh gravel, building a base for the next paving project.

The tar truck was attracting an audience equal to the ditch digger, and Ike wondered himself if he would ever overcome his boyish delight in watching any sort of construction in progress. Reverend Holbrook joined him, and they were both awed by the bubbling shower of black liquid being shot from pipes on the rear of the truck.

Ike breathed deeply the rank smell of tar. He said to Reverend Holbrook, "Every time a see a house completed or a street paved I think we're one step closer to the barbecue you promised. I have visions of juicy steers simmering on sweet gum poles over beds of hot coals. You haven't backed out, have you?"

"Naw, suh, Mistuh Ike, an we ain't gwine back out. All de ladies done started figurin how dey gwine cook baked beans in wash pots so dey'll be 'nough to feed everbody."

"Much as I'm enjoying this, I have work to do at the office," Ike said, turning and walking toward the patrol car. "You'll have to supervise this by yourself, Reverend."

Reverend Holbrook followed Ike to the car. He said hesitantly, "Mistuh Ike, I needs to talk wid you 'fore you leaves."

"Why sure, Reverend," Ike said. "What is it?"

"Miss Lancaster ain't stayin at Hanibel's house no mo. She stayin wid me. Las Tuesday night, durin dat storm, she come runnin to my house, an she say Hanibel scared her real bad. He almost scared de life outen her, Mistuh Ike, an she axed me not to tell you 'bout it."

"What did he do?" Ike asked curiously.

"She say he didn't do nothin but scare her, that he had a spell. I ain't never seen a pusson so scared. She went to her class de next moanin an she say she fine now."

"I'm sure if he had hurt her she would have told you," Ike said. "At any rate, I'm glad she's out of that shack with Hanibel and living with you."

"I be's glad too," he agreed. "Sistuh Lucy moved into my house an is stayin wid us, an we havin a fine time together." He stopped for a moment and clasped his hands, then said, "Mistuh Ike, dat ain't all I wants to speak wid you about. I's worried 'bout Mistuh VanDolar. He's preachin hate an tryin to pison de young folks' minds. He's payin dem chillun to come to his class ever day, an he tryin to stir up hate. An he's goin 'round pesterin de old folks 'bout votin. Dat man is evil, Mistuh Ike, an I be's afraid of him."

The revelation of what VanDolan was doing came as no surprise to Ike. He said, "What exactly is he saying in that class?"

"He preachin hate 'gainst de white folks, an he talkin 'bout marchin in de streets, puttin on dem protest demonstrations. Dat ain't de Lawd's way, an I be's afraid."

"Maybe the young people won't listen to him," Ike said. "It could be they're just taking his money, and that's all."

"I thought 'bout dat too, an I hope dat's right. But I still be's afraid of what dat man might do."

Ike tried to hide his concern. He said, "You talk to your young people, Reverend, and if anything seems to be developing from this, please let me know right away."

"I will, Mistuh Ike. Lawd knows I will."

Miss Landcaster dismissed her class and started gathering her materials and putting them into a box. All of the women had left the church except Sister Pearly, who continued sitting in the pew. Miss Landcaster turned from the easel and faced the woman unexpectedly. She said, "You startled me, Sister Pearley! I thought everyone had left."

"Nome, Miss Sylvia," she said sheepishly. "I wanted to wait an speak wid you. I done somethin I's worried about."

Miss Landcaster put the box on the edge of the platform and sat beside the women. "Is it something I can help with?" she asked.

"Welsuh, I don know," Sister Pearley said. "I's 'fraid I got Reveren Holbrook in some trouble.

"Reverend Holbrook? How is that, Sister Pearley?"

The old woman clasped her hands in her lap and said slowly, "Miss Sylvia, befo you folks come here de deacons had a meetin wid Shuff Thonton, an den we had a meeting at de church. We all agreed dat de old folks wouldn't try to sign de regstration book to vote befo we larned to read an write. Brother Hopkins, de school man, made 'rangements fo us to start larnin."

"Yes, I know about that," Miss Landcaster said. "But how does that affect Reverend Holbrook now?"

"Reveren Holbrook an de deacons an all us old folks give our word, an now I's done somethin wrong."

Miss Landcaster was even more perplexed. She said anxiously, "What is it you have done, Sister Pearley?"

"Yestiddy afternoon Mistuh VanDolan come to de house an axed me had I regstered to vote an I tole him no. Den he axed me to sign a paper sayin de white folk had kep me from votin. I tole him I hadn even tried to regster yet 'cause we'd agreed not to, but he said if I didn sign he'd have my govment check stopped. I tole him I'd ruther wait an speak wid you 'bout it, but he say I had to sign right den or I would never get another check. I made my mark on dat paper, an he put my name by it. I didn want my govment check stopped, Miss Sylvia. I's too old to go back to work an make a livin now."

Miss Landcaster's face flushed with anger. She said harshly, "He had no right to do that! He can't have your government check stopped. He has no authority to do something like that! I'll speak to him. Don't worry about it any more, Sister Pearley."

The old Negro pushed herself up slowly, relief spreading across her face in the form of a broad smile. She said, "I sho 'preciate it,

Miss Sylvia. We give our word, an if Mistuh Thonton sees dat paper he'll think we lied to him. I don't want Reveren Holbrook an Mistuh Thonton thinkin I done them wrong."

"Just forget all about it," Miss Landcaster said. "I'll take care of it right away."

Miss Landcaster waited until the women left the church, then she walked over to a window and looked toward the picnic tables where VanDolan was holding his class. She watched as he pranced back and forth, waving his arms to emphasize some unknown point he was making to his audience. She wished she could listen to one of his lectures but knew he would not continue if she were present. A frown crossed her face as she thought of the consequences his actions could bring to these people they had come here to help. She continued watching the pantomime performance until the young people got up en masse and scampered away across the clearing. Then she went outside and walked to the tables.

VanDolan was sitting on a bench, disinterested in the fact that she approached and then stood before him. He looked up at her and remained silent.

"Have a good class?" she asked.

"Same as usual."

"What did you teach them, civics and government?" she asked, trying to maintain a calm composure.

"Yeah," he replied, "civics and government."

She said harshly, "What are you doing, Jeffrey? What are you trying to do to these people?"

"I don't know what you're talking about," he replied indifferently.

His attitude irritated her and made her even more angry. "You know damned well what I'm talking about!" she snapped. "Why did you go to Sister Pearley and coerce her into signing a paper saying she had been denied the right to sign the voter registration book?"

He suddenly took an interest in the conversation. "She *has* been denied! All of them have been denied!"

"That's a lie and you know it!" she said furiously. "Sister Pearley hasn't even tried to register. They made an agreement not to. And why did you tell her you can have her government check stopped?"

"They have been denied!" he repeated, rising to his feet. "They have been denied all their lives!"

"What right do you have to interfere with a plan these people have agreed would be best for them?" she demanded. "Who are you, anyway—God? I mean for you to take Sister Pearley's name from that paper, whatever it is!"

"Go to hell!" he stammered. "It's none of your business!"

She stepped forward quickly and slapped his face before she realized what she was doing. The loud clap roared in his ears, temporarily deafening him. He moved back and said fiercely, "You ever do that again you'll wish you had never seen me! Nobody touches me like that! Nobody! Do you understand? Nobody!"

"There's one thing you had better understand yourself," she said, trading him vicious glare for glare. "You're not going to use these people to satisfy a heinous scheme you have embedded in your warped imagination unless you walk over me first! I will stand in your way!"

"You're a traitor!" he said, moving back toward her. "You signed a pledge, just like me, and now you're a traitor! We came here to help these people, and you have been brainwashed! You're no different from that old fool preacher or that hick sheriff! Goddamn traitor!"

"You're right on one thing," she said, overwhelmed with anger. "We came here to help these people. We didn't come to destroy them. You're willing to use them as pawns to justify your own warped ego. You'll have to walk over me first!"

"Bitch!" he shouted, jumping up and down. "Traitorous bitch! I'll report you! I'll have you removed from the project! Traitorous damned bitch!" He was unaware she had run hurriedly across the clearing and left him alone beneath the towering trees, alone to rave hysterically only to himself.

Ike and Peggy Jo were sitting on the patio enjoying after-dinner coffee when the doorbell rang. Peggy Jo went inside and returned with Sidney Grenlee. He relaxed into a chair and accepted coffee, smiled and said, "How goes it, Ike? Has our friend Jeffrey VanDolan exterminated anyone yet?"

"I'm afraid that is exactly what he has in mind," Ike said, not returning Grenlee's humor.

Grenlee had spoken the words in jest and was surprised by Ike's reaction. Peggy Jo also looked at Ike with curiosity. He had not mentioned VanDolan's activities to her.

Grenlee leaned forward and said, "What do you mean by that? If you're pulling my leg, don't. I was only kidding."

"I was in the quarters this morning and talked with Reverend Holbrook," Ike said. "He was extremely upset. He says VanDolan is conducting a hate school and is paying young people to attend. He is also planning a protest demonstration."

"Demonstration about what?" Grenlee asked, the smile now vanished.

"I don't know," Ike said, "but Reverend Holbrook was very concerned. To tell the truth, I am too. I tried to discount the whole thing and suggest it was just a matter of the kids taking VanDolan's money, but that old preacher knows what is going on a lot better than we do. I'm sure he wouldn't push a panic button without reason. I have a strange feeling an ominous cloud is coming our way."

"We can put a stop to that demonstration business," Grenlee said. "Last year we passed a city ordinance making it illegal to hold a parade without a permit. We can refuse to issue them a permit on the basis of public safety."

"I don't think it should be handled that way," Ike said. "Maybe VanDolan hopes you will refuse them a permit, so he can accuse you of denying them the right of free expression. That has happened elsewhere. I believe it would be better to let them march and get it over with."

"You sound as if this thing is already a concrete fact," Grenlee said. "Let's hope it doesn't materialize. If it looks as if it will happen, maybe Reverend Holbrook can talk them out of it."

"Maybe yes, maybe no," Ike said. "I don't want to sound pesimistic, but I believe VanDolan is capable of almost anything."

"What part is Miss Landcaster taking in this?" Peggy Jo asked. "She seemed like the type of person who wouldn't do anything that wasn't in the best interest of everyone concerned."

"I assume she is against it," Ike said, "but I really don't know for sure. She isn't living with VanDolan anymore. Reverend Holbrook said that Hanibel Felds scared her so badly last Tuesday night that she moved out of that shack and is now staying with him and Sister Lucy."

"What did Felds do to her?" Peggy Jo asked."

"I don't know," Ike replied. "She told Reverend Holbrook that Felds didn't hurt her. I know that Felds has some kind of spells and can be very dangerous. I've seen it. I'm glad she is out of there."

Grenlee got up to leave. "Wouldn't it be wonderful if all our race problems could be solved by simply marching up a street," he said.

"If that were so, I would march too," Ike responded. "If only it were that simple."

"Keep me posted," Grenlee said. "I don't have a pipeline to the quarters like you do."

"I will," Ike said. "If something starts happening, you will be the first to know."

Ashley parked his car across the street from the Froggy Bottoms Cafe. He got out and walked toward the building. The bench sitters immediately knocked on the wall. Ashley stepped inside and looked around the room. When he spotted Bugger Durr at a table with two other men he motioned for Durr to follow him outside. They crossed the street and stood on the dark side of the car, away from the lights. The bench-sitters watched them curiously, wondering why the constable did not place Durr in the car and leave immediately. He did not usually have discussions with anyone before beginning the trip north to the pokey house.

Ashley said in hushed tones, "You know where that clearing is on the creek down by the old mill, where you niggers shoot craps?"

"Yassuh, I knows," Durr replied quietly.

"I want you to bring VanDolan down there tomorrow night just after dark."

"What you gone do to him?" Durr asked apprehensively.

"That ain't none of your damned business!" Ashley snapped. "You just bring him down there."

"You gone hurt him, Mistuh Ashley?" Durr asked.

"No, dammit, we ain't gone hurt him!" Ashley roared. He glanced toward the cafe and calmed his voice. "We just gone have a little fun. If you don't show up with him you're the one who'll get hurt! I'll bust your nigger head ever day for the next month!"

"Mistuh Ashley, whut's I'm gone tell that white man to git him to go with me into them woods?" Durr asked.

"Hell, Bugger, that's your business," Ashley replied. "Git another nigger to come too so's it won't be just you an him. They'll be plenty of free drinks an eats, an nobody won't get hurt. We just gone have a little fun."

"I'll try, Mistuh Ashley," Durr said weakly.

"Try hell!" Ashley snapped. "You better be there, 'cause I ain't kiddin! You understand me, Bugger?" "Yassah, Mistuh Ashley, I onderstan," Durr replied, resigned. "We'll be there just after sundown".

Twenty-four

Ashley and Jud rode in the front seat with Hankins, and the three Miller boys in the back seat. When they reached the highway Hankins turned right and headed north.

"Ain't you gone blow the siren, Sim?" Coney asked.

"Shet up, boy," Jud said. "Ain't no siren on Sim's car. Hit's on Con's."

"Ah, shucks, Pa," Coney said, disappointed. "I'll never git to ride in a car with the siren blowin. I thought Sim had one too."

They rode for a moment in silence, and then Jud said, "How come we couldn't a did all this out to the house? I don't like to be gone at night."

"Do you good to get out of them woods for a spell," Ashley said. "You an the boys stay out there too much."

"Is the white girl who's livin with the niggers gone be there too?" Coney asked

"Naw, just the boy," Ashley replied.

"Whut we doin this fer nohow?" Jud asked. "Don't seem like it makes no sense goin to all this trouble. How come you don't just whup the boy?"

"We're not goin to do anything but have some fun," Ashley said. "You an the boys don't have to do nothin but watch. Me an Sim'll do the rest. Do you fellows good to get out of them woods."

Hankins drove slowly when he came into the late afternoon traffic approaching the signals where Main Street met the highway. He caught the light on green and continued north for a mile, then he turned left onto a gravel road that led west and crossed Town Creek at the site of an abandoned gristmill. He pulled off the road and parked behind the dilapidated wooden building, hiding the car from view. They all got out and stretched as Hankins took the key ring from the ignition and opened the trunk.

"You boys tote them boxes an jugs," Jud said, "an I'll bring the shote. You'll have to lead off, Con. I ain't never been in these woods before."

They followed Ashley single file along a trail that ran atop the creek bank for a hundred yards and then cut into a section of thick scrub pine. Low limbs on the trees had almost closed the narrow path, and the springy limbs kept swishing back, slapping each man in the face as the one in front moved forward. Jud stopped for a moment and said, "Dammit, Con, these limbs is about to knock my brains out. How fer we have to go?"

"Just a short piece, Jud," Ashley replied. "We'll go slower an it won't be so bad. I ain't been here for a spell myself an didn't know the trail is closed up like this."

They continued for a short distance along the nearly non-existent path before coming into a small circular clearing surrounded by tall longleaf pines. The ground was bare except for a thin layer of pine needles. They had now come back close enough to the Negro quarters so that music from the Froggy Bottoms Cafe jukebox could be heard in the distance.

Jud put the pig carcass on the ground and said, "You boys git some wood an start a fire afore hit's too dark to see. An we gone need forked branches to make a spit fer roastin the shote."

The three Millers disappeared into the woods as Hankins spread newspapers on the ground and started emptying the contents of two of the boxes. He took out a full hoop of cheese, six loaves of bread, a gallon jar of dill pickles, and three dozen Moon Pies. They also had four jugs of corn whiskey.

"Gone be a fine party," Ashley said, picking up a jug and drinking deeply, "a mighty fine party. You'll be glad you come, Jud."

Bugger Durr sat alone at a table in the cafe, nervously picking his fingernails with a penknife. He glanced anxiously toward the door each time someone entered, hoping it would be VanDolan. He knew if he did not locate the white man soon he would be in trouble, for VanDolan would meet Clara Mae somewhere in the darkness and disappear into the woods. He finally got up and walked to the door, signaling for another Negro to go with him outside.

They walked a short distance from the building, out of hearing range of the men on the benches, then stopped. "We better find him quick," Durr said, glancing up and down the rapidly darkening street.

"Where we gone look? I don't know nothin 'bout where that white man goes."

"Maybe he ain't left the house yet," Durr said. "Let's walk over there an see. He should of been at the Froggy Bottoms a half hour ago."

The Negro man with Durr was forty years old, six-feet-six tall, and thin as a fence post. He walked with long uneven strides and looked like a black mixture of Don Quixote and Ichabod Crane. His first and only name was Dragline, and when an occasion arose for him to affix his signature to an account ledger, Dragline was the only name he used. He earned a precarious living by driving a daily route through the Negro section of Dry Ridge, peddling grocery items and sundries off the back of a Model-A Ford pickup truck. He was known in both the white and Negro communities as a carefree man who would never refuse a free drink or turn down the chance to participate in a prank. Durr selected him as his partner in this venture because he knew that for the price of free food and drink and a five-dollar bill the tall man's mouth would be closed forever, no matter what occurred.

The two men walked along the street leading to Felds' shack, Dragline thinking of the food and whiskey he had been promised, and Durr contemplating what would happen to him if he failed to deliver the human package. Just as they reached the gate, VanDolan came from the shack and across the yard.

"We been lookin for you, Mistuh Jeffrey," Durr said, stepping in front of VanDolan to block his route. "We want you to go with us sommers."

"Haven't got time," VanDolan said, trying to move around Durr. "I've got to meet someone."

"Won't take long," Durr said, stepping sideways, blocking VanDolan again. "You'll be back in plenty of time for yo meetin."

"What is it you want, Bugger?" VanDolan asked impatiently.

"We wants you to go with us to a gatherin," Durr replied.

"What kind of a gathering?" VanDolan asked suspiciously. "Sort of a clan gatherin."

"You mean the Ku Klux Klan?" VanDolan exploded.

"Oh nawsuh, nawsuh!" Durr said quickly, afraid he had blown

the whole thing with his poor choice of a word. "It's a eatin an drinkin group, both white men an colored men, what gets together ever now an then to have a little fun. Ain't far from here, just down the crick a ways. Take us 'bout ten minutes to make it there."

"Sounds stupid," VanDolan said, trying again to move around Durr. "I've got to go now. Will you please get out of the way?"

Durr was frightened, desperatedly trying to think of something that would persuade VanDolan to go with them. He said, "Constable Ashley gone be there, Mistuh Jeffrey. You drink some with the constable he might come in handy with yo project. Man around here becomes a friend if'n you drinks with him."

VanDolan suddenly stopped trying to escape. He calculated the value of this new information, weighing possibilities, wondering if he could somehow use the dumb redneck constable to remove Sylvia Landcaster as an obstacle in his course of action. He said, "I guess I can go, but I can't stay long. I've got to meet somebody a little later."

Durr wiped sweat from his forehead. He grabbed VanDolan by the arm and led him briskly down the street, saying in rapid sentences, "You gone have fun. Ain't far from here. 'Bout ten minutes. This here is Dragline. I got a flashlight. Ain't far. We'll be back afore long. Eats an drinks. Kind of a gatherin. You gone have fun."

Bester sat on the ground beside the fire, slowly turning the improvised spit that held the roasting pig over glowing coals. The meat popped and bubbled, sending a spray of juice downward into the flickering flames, causing puffs of brilliant orange to explode on the coals. The small clearing with its wall of thick pines and roof of interlaced limbs resembled a giant tepee built by nature. The thin green pine needles turned a yellowish hazel in the gentle glow of the campfire.

The other men were squatting in a circle, drinking from a jug and eating dill pickles. Hankins cut a wedge of cheese, took a large bite and said, "Don't believe that nigger's gone bring him, Con."

"He'll be here," Ashley said, sucking the briny juice from a pickle. "He's just runnin a little late. He knows to be here."

"I don't keer if they never git here," Jud said. "Can't see no sense in askin niggers to et with us. I ain't never took no meal with a nigger."

"How come the white girl ain't comin?" Coney asked. "I'd druther they bring her than that man you been talkin 'bout. I ain't never seen a white girl whut's livin with niggers."

"You kin see her some other time," Jud said. "Don't want no woman 'round when I'm cookin a hawg. Ain't nothin but men spose to et a whole hog together."

"Listen!" Ashley said sharply, becoming alert. They all became silent and could hear a thrashing in the woods. A small beam of light cut through the outer rim of the thicket. "That's them," Ashley whispered. "They're comin now."

The tramping sound became louder, then Durr suddenly broke through the wall of the clearing and released a limb he had pushed forward when entering. The pine limb swished backward and caught VanDolan in the face, knocking him to his knees. He shook his head and shouted, "Goddammitt! Damm you, Bugger!" Then he crawled into the clearing and looked up at the circle of men.

Jud took a drink from the jug and said, "At least he knows how to cuss."

Dragline broke through the wall and stepped on top of VanDolan, causing himself to trip and crash to the ground. Ashley looked at the long prostrate body and said to Durr, "Hell fire, Bugger, what'd you bring that freeloadin bastard for? He'll eat up everthing we got."

VanDolan pushed himself to his feet and looked around at the strange assembly, then decided it was already time to depart. He was moving back toward the woods when his eyes caught on the roasting pig, the whole carcass rotating over coals and sending out the hypnotic aroma of meat cooking over open flames, a scene straight out of Sherwood Forest. He took a second and more penetrating look at his hosts, seeing them now as quaint characters he could endure for a short time for the sake of both absorbing local color and satisfying the yearnings of his stomach.

Ashley said, "This here is Mr. VanDolan. These folks is Jud Miller, Coney Miller, Berl Miller, an Sim Hankins. That's Bester Miller over by the fire. You come in here an git a drink, Mr. VanDolan."

VanDolan surmised that none of them intended to do any handshaking. He stepped into the circle beside Coney and squatted awkwardly. Berl ran his finger through the small jug handle, flipped the jug to the back of his wrist, turned it up and gurgled, then he passed it to VanDolan, who had carefully watched the technique. He crooked his finger through the handle, turned the jug up and poured whiskey over his chin and chest. The strong fumes caused his nostrils to vibrate rapidly. He set the jug back on the ground, then picked it up with both hands, put it to his lips and drank. A crestwave of molten lava ran down his throat and splashed into the pit of his stomach. He bounced up and down on his haunches, clutching his throat and croaking, "Water! Water!"

"Git Mr. VanDolan some water, Sim," Ashley said. "He seems to be havin a problem."

Hankins took a tin cup from one of the boxes and filled it with clear corn whiskey from another jug and handed it to VanDolan. He grabbed it eagerly and drained it before he jumped up and started coughing, hacking and wheezing. He jogged around swiftly in a circle, holding his throat and muttering inaudible words.

"He do a pretty good turkey trot, don't he," Jud said, amused by the antics of the strange boy.

Almost immediately VanDolan felt a warm benevolent glow pulse through his veins, a floating sensation that eased the pain in his throat and stomach. He stopped his motion, turned to the circle of men, blinked his eyes and said sheepishly, "Got something caught in my throat." Then he returned to the circle and squatted.

While VanDolan held everyone's attention, Dragline picked up a jug and proceeded to help himself. When Ashley noticed what the Negro was doing, he jumped to his feet and shouted, "Git yore goddam nigger lips offen there, Dragline! I ought to stomp hell outen you! I ain't drinkin from a jug with no nigger! You want some whiskey, git a cup!"

Dragline reached into a box, grabbed a tin cup and filled it to the brim, then drained it in one gulp. He smacked his thin lips and filled the cup again. "That's good whuskey, Mistuh Ashley," he said. "Kin I have some cheese an pickle?"

"Yeah, git some," Ashley said without enthusiasm, "but don't eat the whole hoop. I don't see how you put so much in that belly of yourn an still look like a chicken snake." Durr came around the circle and joined Dragline with the whiskey and cheese.

VanDolan picked up a jug and took a generous drink, and this time he escaped with only a mild spell of hacking. He was feeling more and more neighborly. Jud gave him a piercing look and said, "You a coon hunter, boy?"

VanDolan looked up at the wide-brimmed black felt hat and the bushy beard. "No, sir, Mr. Miller. I don't do any hunting."

"How come?" Jud asked.

"Well, you see, I —"

Bester broke in and said, "Pa, this shote's done. Somebody give me a hand an we'll bring it over there."

Berl got up and took one end of the spit. They brought the smoking carcass over and put it on the newspapers. Jud cut one side of the pig into small chunks. "Better wait a few minutes afore eatin," he said, sucking the juice from his fingers. "Hit's powerful hot."

"Let's make a round," Ashley said, picking up a jug. When it came VanDolan's turn he downed the same amount as the others. He was swaying slightly.

"You still raisin them white rabbits, Dragline?" Hankins asked, watching the Negro drool at the sight of the meat.

"Yassuh, I sho is," he replied, smacking his lips. "Ain't nothin I enjoys more than watchin rabbits hunch."

"God-a-mighty, nigger," Jud said, glaring at Dragline, "you mean you raises rabbits jest to watch 'em hang up?"

"I sho do," Dragline said as he filled the cup again. "I kin sot three-fo hours on end an watch them rabbits go at it. Hit's a pure pleasure to watch."

"They done brought a loco nigger in here," Jud muttered. He picked up a chunk of meat and put it into his mouth. "Ain't too hot now," he said. "Let's et."

VanDolan put a piece of roast pig in his mouth. He chewed for a moment and then stopped, not wanting to swallow so he could savor the taste longer. In all his experience he had never eaten meat that was so good. He finished the small piece, took a drink from the jug, then picked up a large chunk.

All conversation ended as the men concentrated on devouring the roasted pig. Jud cut the other side into chunks. Soon nothing remained but a skeleton and they gnawed the bones. A chorus of burps resounded across the clearing as the jug was passed again.

VanDolan pushed himself up unsteadily. He staggered backward and said, "Is been a pleasure. Got to go now. Late for a meetin."

"Have one more drink with us afore you go," Ashley said. "Sort of a farewell salute." He filled a tin cup and handed it to VanDolan. "All the way in one shot."

"Thank you, sir," VanDolan said, putting the cup to his lips. He held his breath and downed the entire contents, then belched violently. For a moment he thought everything he had eaten was coming up. He clutched his throat and staggered around the clearing, muttering to himself. The pine trees were spinning madly, the ground rotating, making everything blend into a vague blur. He stopped and fell backward, then lay still.

"He's gone," Ashley said. "Git the stuff, Sim."

"Whut you gone do?" Durr asked anxiously.

"Give him a haircut," Ashley said.

Bester and Berl held VanDolan in a sitting position while Ashley took a soup bowl from a box and placed it on top of VanDolan's head. Then he took a pair of scissors and started clipping the hair. Dragline came around in front of them. He squatted and watched. He clapped his hands together and shouted, "Yeeeeehaw! Do it, white folk, do it!"

"Shut yore goddam mouth!" Ashley snapped. "You want ever nigger in the quarters to hear you?"

Dragline bounced up and down on his haunches, his eyes gleaming. He said in quieter tones, "Lay it on, Mistuh Ashley, lay it on!"

When Ashley finished cutting the hair he took a shaving mug, brush and straight razor from the box. He lathered the soap and shaved the part of VanDolan's head beneath the soup bowl. "Better take off them whiskers too," he muttered as he lathered VanDolan's 'cheeks. "Anybody who'd wear a beard is a son-of-a-bitch nohow."

"Whud'd you say?" Jud asked, starting to get up.

"Didn't say nothin," Ashley replied quickly. "I'm gone shave his cheeks an leave a tuff of that red hair on the point of his chin." He scraped the hair from VanDolan's cheeks and upper chin, then put the tools back into the box. "Git him on out of here now, Bugger," he said.

"We make it to the woods we can tote him all right," Durr said, "but how'll we get him through that thicket?"

"Drag him by the feet," Ashley said. "It won't hurt him."

"Whut's I'm gone say to him 'bout his head when he wakes up?" Durr asked, frowning.

"Tell him he got drunk an done it himself," Ashley replied indifferently.

"Let me have one mo drink an a piece of cheese 'fo we go," Dragline said.

"Damn, Dragline," Ashley said, "you must have a belly like a stove pipe. I ain't never seen a nigger who could hold so much."

Durr walked over to VanDolan, ran his hand into the jeans pocket and withdrew a tin box. "You folks want some good smokes?" he asked. "He gits these cigarettes in some feren country. I'll leave them for you." Durr dumped the cigarettes on the ground and put the box back into the jeans pocket. Then he took a packet of white powder from the other pocket. "This here is white snuff," he said. "You don't dip it and put it in your mouth. You sniff it up your nose. I seen Mistuh Jeffrey do it in the cafe. You puts some in the palm of your left hand and puts it to the nose. Then you takes a finger on your right hand and closes the right side of the nose. Then you sucks hard and sniffs it up the left side of the nose. Like this." Durr went through the procedure without using the powder. He threw the packet on the ground.

Dragline finished the drink and slipped a chunk of cheese into his pocket. He came over and grabbed one of VanDolan's feet. They pulled the limp form through the wall of the clearing and disappeared into the darkness.

Jud picked up one of the cigarettes, lit it and inhaled deeply. Then he sniffed some powder up his nose and passed both of them. He said, "This snuff is different. What'd he say it is?"

"Feren, I think," Sim said. "Or maybe the cigarettes is feren. I don't remember."

They all squatted again in a circle, puffing and sniffing until the white powder and the cigarettes were gone. Jud suddenly jerked his left leg, looked at Bester and said, "Dammit, boy, quit kickin me!"

"I ain't teched you, Pa," Bester said."

"You callin me a liar, son?" Jud asked.

"What you need is a drink, Jud," Ashley said. "But first I'll have a snort myself." He turned up the jug, missed his mouth and saturated his shirt with whiskey. "Goddammit, Sim," he said, "what'd you hit my arm for?"

"You must be crazy," Hankins said. "I ain't touched you."

"You sunda bitch, you callin me a liar?" Ashley asked, glaring at Hankins.

"You call me that again I'll ram my fist in yore fat gut," Hankins snorted.

"I seen him!" Jud said. "I seen him hit yore arm, Con."

"Sunda bith sunda bitch sunda bitch!" Ashley said.

Hankins drew back his fist, swung at Ashley and missed. He fell forward and rammed his head into the ground. He looked up and said, "Whut'd you hit me for, Con? I didn't do nothin."

"I ain't touched you," Ashley said.

"You callin me a liar?" Hankins asked.

"I seen him, Sim!" Jud said. "He poked you right in the mouth."

"You're a goddam liar," Ashley said.

Jud swung at Ashley and caught Berl on the side of the head, knocking him into Bester, who immediately kicked him in the stomach. The circle was suddenly transformed into a mass of flailing arms and legs. Coney crawled out of the wild melee, stood up and shouted, "Pa! Pa! I don't feel so good! Let's go home!"

They stopped as suddenly as they had started. Ashley looked around with a blank expression and said, "What's all the commotion about?"

"Whut conunotion?" Jud asked.

"Let's go home, Pa," Coney repeated.

"Suits me fine," Jud said. "Git them jugs an thet box. You lead, Con. You the only one whut knows the way out."

"Follow me, men," Ashley said, walking as if he were stepping over a fence. "Stay in close. Don't nobody get lost."

The weaving line of men crashed into trees and fell over bushes, following the staggering leader through pitch-black darkness. Ashley did not know where he was but would not admit it. They continued walking, certain they would eventually reach the road.

Coney broke the silence and said, "Pa, my feet feels funny. They's cold slam up to the knees."

"Mine too," Jud said. He reached down and felt around him, then he shouted at Ashley, "Dammit, Con, we's walkin right down the middle of the crick! Whut the hell you tryin to do?"

Ashley mumbled absently as he turned right and led them up the bank. He continued following the creek and finally reached the mill. They got into the car without further comment. Hankins put the car into reverse, backed up rapidly and rammed into the rear of the building, scattering boards over the top of the car. He grunted and shifted gears, then pulled onto the gravel road and drove slowly toward the main highway.

"Wash a fine party," Ashley said, leaning out the window and letting the wind strike his face.

"Git yore hands off my hat," Jud said.

"I ain't touchin you," Ashley replied.

Jud mumbled again, then leaned back and started snoring.

Ashley repeated to himself, "Wash a fine party."

Twenty-five

Miss Landcaster walked down the street and stopped at the edge of the clearing, listening to the blending of Negro voices coming from the church. On an impulse she decided to attend the morning services, and Reverend Holbrook did not know she would be present. She stayed outside until the hymn was finished, then she went into the building and took a seat in the back pew. Only those in the two back pews noticed she was there.

The church seemed different from when she used it each day as a schoolroom. Then it was an almost-empty box void of personality. Now it pulsated with life, reflecting the vibrancy of the congregation. She watched the choir leader stand and raise his arms for the beginning of another hymn. There were young and old people present, black in varying degrees, all classified as Negroes but some evidently of mixed blood. Most wore their "Sunday clothes," prized garments donned only for church services, funerals and weddings, suits and dresses always buried with the owners. The worshippers seemed to fit this stark building, to belong and to share with it some secret unknown to her, to possess an understanding one to the other which was far beyond her ability even to vaguely comprehend.

She sat spellbound, listening to a hymn explode with life as she had never before heard, music coming not from the lungs but from the heart, spiritual offerings far greater than anything dropped into a collection plate in a magnificent cathedral. She was saddened when the song ended, for she wished it to continue endlessly.

Reverend Holbrook walked to the edge of the platform and looked directly at his congregation. Then he said in subdued tones, "Brothers an sisters, does you believe in God an de Bible?

"Yes," echoed the listeners.

"Does you want to be saved?"

"Yes."

"Does yo *really* want to be saved?"

"Yes."

"Does you want to go to heaven?"

"Yes."

"Does you believe you can go to heaven if'n you don't believe in God an God's word, de Bible?"

"No."

"Can you go 'gainst God an be saved?"

"No."

"Can you sin 'gainst de Lawd an be saved?"

"No."

"Ain't no way to get to heaven, is dey, 'cept by de will of God?"

"No.

"Brothers an sisters, don tell me no lie here in de Lawd's House. Does you *really* believe in God and de Bible?"

"Yes."

He turned and walked behind the pulpit, looking again at his congregation as he said in stronger tones, "Brothers an sisters, dey is evil turned loose in dis community, evil dat comes from de debil, not de Lawd. Someone is preachin de gospel of de debil, not de Lawd, an who-some-ever amongst you listens to dem words of hate is doin de work of de debil, not de Lawd."

He picked up a Bible, held it over his head and said louder, "You sees dis, brothers an sisters, dis is de word of de Lawd, God's word, de word of Jesus. Let's see what dey say."

For a moment he held the Bible in outstretched hands, then he opened it and placed it on the pulpit. He spoke slowly, "You has heard dat it been said, an eye fo an eye, a toof fo a toof. But I say unto you, dat you resist not evil, but who-some-ever shall smite you on yo right cheek, turn to him de other also. An who-some-ever makes you go a mile, go wid him twain. You has heard dat it been said, love yo neighbor an hate yo enemy. But I say unto you, bless dem dat cuss you, do good to dem dat hate you, an pray fo dem dat despitefully use you an persecute you, dat you may be children of yo Father what am in heaven, fo He makes de sun rise on de evil an de good, an sends rain on de just an de unjust. Be ye perfeck, brothers an sisters, even as yo Father which am in heaven is perfeck. Do it de Lawd's way, brothers an sisters, do it de Lawd's way an you gwine be saved!"

He took a handkerchief from his pocket and mopped his brow, then continued, "Blessed be de poor, fo dey's is de kingdom of God. Blessed be dem dat hunger now, fo dey shall be filled. Blessed am dem dat weep now, fo dey shall laugh. Blessed is you when men shall hate you, an when dey shall separate you from dey company, an shall reproach you, an cast out yo name as evil, fo de Son of man's sake. Rejoice in dat day, an leap fo joy, fo behold, yo reward is great in heaven, fo in lak manner did dey fathers unto de prophets. Love yo enemies, do good to dem dat hate you. Love yo enemies, an do good, hopin fo nothin again, an yo reward shall be great, an you shall be de chillun of de Lawd. Be merciful, as yo Father is merciful. Wid de same measure you mete it shall be measured to you again. A good tree don bring foth corrupt fruit, an a corrup tree don bring foth good fruit, an ever tree is known by its own fruit, fo of thorns dey don gather figs, and dey don get grapes from a bramble bush. Brothers an sisters, de Lawd say, 'Why call me Lawd, Lawd, an do not de things which I say?'"

He stopped again and turned his head down, pressing his hands over his eyes as if praying; then he looked out over his people as if seeing someone not present, speaking as if speaking to someone not in the room, "De Lawd say who-some-ever comes to Him, an hears His sayins, an does dem, he is like a man who built a house, an digged deep, an laid de foundation on a rock, an when de flood arose, de stream beat meanly on dat house, an couldn't shake it, fo it was founded on a rock. But he dat heard an didn do, he am like a man dat widout no foundation built a house on de ground, again which de stream beat meanly, an right away it fell, an de ruin of dat house was great."

He left the pulpit and came to the edge of the platform, now seeing his congregation again, speaking to them individually, "Brothers an sisters, love is a rock, an hate am like sand. We's jus startin to build a new house now, us colored folk, we's jus startin, an if we build dat house on love it gwine stand like de house on a rock, an if we build dat house on hate it gwine wash away like a bed of sand. It may take a little while longer, jus a little while longer, to build a house wid a foundation den it do to build one widout a foundation, but it gwine last a heap longer, an we gwine be on dis earth a powerful long time. I's not preachin fo de colored folks to be lak sheep, but I says ack like de Lawd say fo you to ack, love yo enemies an you gwine be rewarded someday. If you does everthing in hate an vengeance, you gwine win somethin like de thorn tree what gives bitter fruit. You might get de tree, but you ain't never gwine enjoy de fruit. An what is anythin wurth if'n you can't enjoy it? We got to do it de Lawd's way, den it will last. Don listen to prophets of de debil. Don listen. You listen, you gwine be sorry. Don get you a mark of Cain. Jus cause some of yo white brothers got de mark, don you get one yoself. Jesus an His deciples were persecuted turrible, but dey didn preach no hate, throw no stones an bottles. Dey built a house on a rock, a house dat's still standin, an de house of dem Romans washed away. Moses he didn listen to de Lawd, an when dey reached de promised land, de Lawd wouldn let Moses enter. Dat's de way it gwine be wid us, brothers an sisters. We go 'gainst de Lawd, we gwine see de promised land, but we ain't gwine never enter."

He stepped down from the platform to the main floor and said, "Brothers an sisters, de Lawd's way might take longer, but it be's a house built on a rock. Dem dat cries today gwine laugh tomorrow, dem dat's hongry today gwine be full tomorrow, if dey do it like God say. Love yo enemies, do what you do in de name of de Lawd an you gwine be a chile of God foever an foever. Let us now sing hymn number forty-six."

When the song began Miss Landcaster got up and walked out of the church and across the clearing. She stopped in the shade of a tree and listened to the music, spellbound again, feeling as if she had somehow been suddenly reborn into a world previously known to her only as words in a newspaper or scenes on a television screen. She felt as if she now had the ability to at least try to comprehend and to understand.

VanDolan awoke shortly before noon. He lay still for several minutes, trying to remember, seeing the campfire and the men and the roasting pig, then a blank. He pushed himself to a sitting position and was immediately overwhelmed with nausea. He lay back down immediately, waiting for the room to stop spinning, feeling sweat run from his pores. His head throbbed, causing a pounding sound of drums in his ears. He sat up again, this time knowing the nausea would not recede. He put his hand over his mouth and stood shakily, then staggered down the hall and reached the back steps just as he retched violently into the yard.

He leaned against the back of the shack, cursing himself for having drunk the corn whiskey, wondering where he had been and what he had done after leaving the men. The hot sun drew the nausea up again, like water from a swamp, so he climbed the steps and went back inside.

For several minutes he sat at the kitchen table, trying to regain some semblance of normalcy. A gnawing thirst crept through his body. He got up, went to the sink and turned on the tap. He put his mouth beneath the stream of water and drank deeply. As soon as the water reached his stomach he became sick and vomited into the sink. He cupped his hands and splashed water on his face and head, letting the cool dampness remove some of the feverish burning. He was not immediately aware of the smoothness of his cheeks, but the second time he rubbed water onto his face his hands froze.

He stood there bent over the sink, feeling again, this time knowing. He grabbed a small mirror off the wall and looked, seeing the small tuft of hair perched on top of his head like an inverted bird's nest, the red muff on the point of his chin. He threw the mirror to the floor, shattering it. He jumped up and down, screaming, "Murder! Murder! Bastards! Murder!" He turned quickly and ran down the hall, bursting through the front door and running blindly down the street toward the shack of Bugger Durr, infuriated, half insane, violated, robbed of his badge of identity.

The sudden violent motion brought back the sickness, and he stopped long enough to vomit. He did not notice the people staring at him and snickering, snickering turning into laughter, curious people coming from their houses and looking. He ran again, and when he reached the shack he dashed onto the porch and pounded the door with both fists. Durr came outside reluctantly. He had been waiting all morning, dreading this visit.

VanDolan's face was white and his eyes glazed. He stammered, "Traitor! Bastard! You'll pay! I ought to kill you! White nigger!"

Durr stood there silently, knowing VanDolan would not listen if he spoke, waiting for him to calm, looking for any sign of sanity. They faced each other, VanDolan's eyes transmitting venom, Durr's reflecting fear and anguish. Durr finally said, "Mistuh Jeffrey, what you talkin about?"

"My head! My head! Goddammit, my head! You know!"

"Mistuh Jeffrey, you done that yoself. You got dronk, powerful dronk, an put on a show. You done that yoself."

VanDolan breathed deeply. His nostrils quivered as the foul breath swooshed back out. For a split-second he had doubts, wondering if he could have violated himself in a drunken stupor, then assured himself it was impossible. He said, "Liar! Goddam liar! You'll Pay! All of you will pay!"

The flesh on Durr's face drooped like warm candle wax. He said as convincingly as possible, "Mistuh Jeffrey, I swear 'fo God I ain't touched you."

VanDolan pondered the various complexities of his situation, realizing that revenge is one thing and stupidity another. He knew they would all lie and he could prove nothing. He had become rational enough to know he had further use for Durr, and perhaps the constable too, and if he alienated them now it would seriously hamper the success of his plans. He made a quick decision to seemingly accept this outrage as an act he committed himself. There would be time later for revenge. He said to Durr, "Loan me a cap until I can buy one. I must have a cap."

Durr was relieved by VanDolan's changed tone. He said quickly, "I got one! I got a huntin cap you can have! I'll get it now! I swear 'fo God, Mistuh Jeffrey, I ain't touched you.

VanDolan covered his head with his hands as Durr rushed into the shack.

Reverend Holbrook sat in a rocker on the front porch, enjoying the late afternoon calm. Miss Landcaster came out and took a chair beside him, and they rocked in unison. She had been thinking all afternoon about the sermon, the pleading urge for peace and brotherhood and love and patience. It did not fit the philosophy she assumed all Negroes have. She had heard in California that such words come only from an "Uncle Tom," a white man's Negro who has deserted his own race in favor of the white community. She knew this was impossible with Reverend Holbrook. In the short time she had been in Midvale she had become convinced that the only lasting solution to problems faced by both races would come from mutual respect, understanding and cooperation as friends, not by violence. It would come from the heart, not the fists, and it would have to be agreeable to both races living as friends, not adversaries. Yet she could not comprehend why all Negroes, including Reverend Holbrook, could help but have bitterness toward the white race as a whole, how Reverend Holbrook could express himself free of hatred as he had done.

She continued rocking and said, "I heard your sermon this morning."

"I knows. I saw you when you came and when you left."

251

"I hope you didn't mind."

"Everbody be's welcome in God's House, Miss Sylvia," he said. "I hope you come ever Sunday."

She stopped rocking and said, "I want to ask you something that might sound like a personal probe, but it isn't. You can tell me it's none of my business and I will understand."

He stopped rocking too. "You go right ahead an ax anything you wants to."

"Those things you said in church today, do you really mean them?"

"Yessam, I do."

"Why?" she asked falteringly, not wanting to press.

"'Cause I believes in God an God's word, Miss Sylvia," he said simply.

"That I understand," she said, "but it seems unlikely that you wouldn't have bitterness in your heart."

"Miss Sylvia," he said, looking deep into her eyes, "I knows what you thinkin, dat I ought to hate de white folks 'cause of what some of dem has done to my people. If I hates de white folks, I'd have to hate some colored folks too. Dey's mean colored folks de same as white folks, an de Lawd will judge us all. Ain't no man born wid hate in his heart, he puts it dere. I knows some white men who pure hates a colored man, an dey kill a colored man quick as dey would a snake, but not all white folks dat way, so why go on hatin everbody. An I knows some colored folks who got nothin but hate an vengance in de heart. Some folks can't foget de past. If I hates all de white folks fo what some did, den where do it go from here? If we don't all stop right now an fogit de past, an fogive each other, an start livin in peace as brothers an sisters under de Lawd, den whut we gwine do? Where we gwine go? We gwine go on hatin till we all kills each other, an dey ain't nobody left? Whut's de purpose? We all got to live together, we can't jus up an leave de earth, so why let hate ruin our lives? Dey ain't no room in my old heart fo hate. I wants to be de white man's fired, not his enemy, an I ain't ashamed to say it. I wants us all to live in peace an friendship, an dey ain't no way we can do it wid hate in our hearts. To fogive is de work of de Lawd, an to hate is de work of de debil, an we all gwine stand befo judgment someday."

"You make me feel ashamed of my shallow reasoning," Miss Landcaster said. "There are so many things I don't know."

"Nobody knows all de answers but God, Miss Sylvia" he said, "an nobody never will. I wants to say one more thing to you, Miss Sylvia, an I don't want you to take it pussonal, 'cause you a fine lady, an I's glad you's here. I knows most everbody in de county, an us colored folks can talk wid most of dem 'bout votin an schools an such an dey won't be no trouble, long as we can talk as friends. We already has talked widout no fear or hate. What stirs up trouble is when strange folks comes in an tries to foce things. Somethin I'd ask de white folks do widout no trouble makes dem stubborn as mules if strangers tries to foce it on dem. Dat's jus de way dey is. In de long run us folks here in Stonewall County gwine have to settle our problems amongst ourselves."

Miss Landcaster knew that this old Negro preacher had tried to explain in his simple language a problem so far-reaching in all its complexities that no one could completely comprehend except those who had lived it. She touched his wrinkled hand and said, "I'm glad I got to know you, Reverend Holbrook. It was worth my visit here. I'll never forget you, not for the rest of my life."

Twenty-six

Coney stayed behind at the house when the others went into the woods just after daybreak on a hunting trip. Soon after they were gone he started the long trek into town. He left the gravel road and cut through the woods, walking briskly up and down sharp ravines, raw cuts in the clay earth, beneath tall lackadaisical pines, feeling carefree and exhilarated at the prospect of seeing the white girl Ashley said was living with niggers. He laughed to himself when he thought of their Saturday night escapade, wondering what reaction the white boy had the next morning when he discovered Ashley's prank. A mother fox squirrel momentarily attracted his attention by barking at her young, chasing them in leaping acrobatics from one high limb to another. Then he lost interest and continued.

He left the woods and crossed the baseball field behind the high school, then walked through a residential section, around the courthouse and down Main Street. He attracted the occasional glances the Millers always drew when they made one of their rare appearances in town, tall bearded men with wide-brimmed black helt hats, faded blue overalls and brogan shoes, a curiosity. He did not notice the stares as he passed along the last block before reaching the highway. He waited for the traffic signal to turn green, then moved across the tracks and kept a steady pace toward the Negro quarters.

Coney reached Front Street and stopped when he heard the roar of a truck spreading tar on a side street. For a few minutes he joined the crowd of onlookers, grinning with pleasure at seeing something he had never before witnessed. He drew the attention of several Negroes who wondered who this lanky white man was and why he was here. One who noticed him with more than idle curiosity was Lon Marcey.

When he remembered the more promising spectacle awaiting him at the Negro church, Coney lost interest in the paving project and left the crowd, walking transfixed again, past the house of Reverend Holbrook and down the street leading to his final destination. Lon followed slowly in the patrol car, staying two blocks behind, watching and wondering why one of the Millers was heading toward the church, speculating the reason this white man who had never been known to spend even one day away from his father and brothers was now alone in the Midvale Negro quarters.

Coney stopped when he reached the clearing in front of the church. He looked toward the picnic tables, seeing the funny white man now wearing a blue cap, standing before a group of young Negroes, talking and waving his arms. He moved to the left and skirted the edge of the clearing, then squatted behind a bush and watched the door of the church, looking and waiting for the white girl to appear.

Lon parked the patrol car a block back from the church and walked to the edge of the clearing. He stepped behind a tree and watched the white man squatting behind the bush. He did not have even a vague idea why this unexpected incident was taking place, what purpose the man had in being here, but he suspected that no good could come of it. He stepped from behind the tree and walked quietly along the edge of the clearing toward the bush.

Coney glanced up at Lon when he heard footsteps approaching, but he did not move. He looked back at the church and continued squatting. Lon stopped beside Coney and said, "What you doin here, Mistuh Miller?" He was not sure which of the Miller brothers he was confronting.

Coney replied without looking up, "Nothin."

Lon moved a step closer and said, "What you want, Mistuh Miller? What business you got here?"

Coney continued staring at the church. "I want to see the white girl."

Lon stepped in front of Coney and said, "You better move on out of here, Mistuh Miller. You ain't got no business here at all."

This time Coney looked. He arose and said, "You the nigger what come out to the house an drawed down on us, ain't you?"

"I'm Deputy Lon Marcey. I'm not lookin for trouble, so why don't you just move on out of here nice an quiet-like. You got no business bein here."

Coney reached into his pocket, took out a knife and flicked open the long blade. He said without emotion, "Ain't never been drawed down on before by a nigger."

Lon backed up a step. "Mistuh Miller, I don't want trouble. You put that knife away an just walk on out of here."

Coney advanced slowly and didn't answer, the knife gripped in his right hand.

Lon backed up again. "I'm tellin you for the last time to put up that knife. I'm not goin to back up any more. You better stop now before somebody gets hurt."

Coney moved forward steadily, every muscle in his body tense, ready to spring. He made a sudden quick move and Lon felt the blade slash into the flesh of his upper left arm and rip downward. He jumped backward as blood dripped from his fingers and splashed into the dirt at his feet. He pulled the pistol from its holster and fired.

Coney dropped to his knees and looked up at Lon still without emotion. A trickle of blood ran from his mouth and caught in the black beard. He rose to his feet, stepped forward and said, "You oughten to have done that. I was just goin to cut you up some. Now I'm gone kill you."

Lon fired again as Coney made a sudden rush toward him.

Coney stopped and stared at Lon, then toppled backward and lay motionless, the wide-brimmed hat still on his head.

Lon was momentarily unaware of people rushing from the picnic tables and the church, forming a circle around him and the lifeless body. He stood there with the gun in his hand, dazed, staring into nothingness, searching for an answer he could not find. He returned to reality when Miss Landcaster stepped in front of him and said, "What is this? What has happened here?"

"Send someone to a telephone quick!" Lon said, turning to her. "Get Sheriff Thornton down here, and an ambulnce too. Hurry!"

"You go!" Miss Landcaster said, pointing to a young boy. He

turned and ran across the clearing. She took the belt from her dress and put it around Lon's arm, twisting it tight, then she looked at Coney and said, "Who is this man, and why was he here?"

VanDolan was standing at the edge of the circle, staring at the body. He said shrilly, "It's one of them!"

"What do you mean, one of them?" Lon asked.

VanDolan immediately realized he was getting himself involved in something that would be of no benefit to him and possibly a hindrance. He said, "I thought I recognized him, but I was mistaken. I've never seen him before."

"Do you know who he is?" Miss Landcaster asked Lon again.

"He's one of the Millers," Lon replied. "They live out in the north part of the county."

"What did he want? Why was he here?" Her eyes reflected both curiosity and fear.

"I don't really know," Lon replied. "He said he wanted to see you."

"Wanted to see me?" she questioned, even more perplexed. "Why?"

"I don't know," Lon repeated. He swayed and dropped to his knees. He said, "I didn't want to shoot him."

Miss Landcaster knelt beside Lon and twisted the belt tighter, slowing the stream of blood to a trickle. She said, "I don't understand why he would want to see me. If that is what he wanted, why didn't he just come into the church? I would have been glad to speak with him. I don't understand any of this."

The crowd of Negroes moved back when they heard the screech of automobile tires coming into the clearing. Ike, Sam and Billy jumped from the car and ran to Lon. Ike glanced at Coney, then he knelt beside Lon and Miss Landcaster. "What happened?" he asked, completely baffled, unable to comprehend the presence of Coney Miller alone in the Midvale Negro quarters.

"I followed him here from up on Front Street," Lon said, his eyes beginning to wander. "He went to that bush over there an squatted. I came up an asked him why he was here, an he said he came to see the white girl. I told him to leave, that he had no business here. Then he came at me with a knife. I didn't shoot him till he cut me. Then he came at me the second time an I shot again. I begged him to put up the knife an go away. I didn't want to shoot him, Mistuh Ike."

Ike got up and walked over to Coney. He felt his wrist and dropped the arm back to the ground. He said, "Billy, you and Sam take Lon to the hospital. I'll wait here for the ambulance, only now it's a hearse. I'll bring Lon's car to the courthouse." He turned to the crowd of onlookers. "All of you people clear out of here. There's no point in your being here."

The crowd began to drift away as Billy and Sam helped Lon to the patrol car. Lon looked back and said, "I didn't want to do it, Mistuh Ike. I didn't want to shoot him."

"I know, Lon," Ike said. "We'll talk about it later."

The ambulance came into the clearing as the patrol car left. Two men with a stretcher cart rushed to the body. One of them said, "Is he alive?"

"No," Ike replied. "Take him to the funeral home and call the coroner. I'll come by there later."

They lifted the body onto the stretcher, put it into the ambulance and sped away.

Miss Landcaster looked at Ike, anguish in her eyes. "Am I the cause of this?" she asked. "He said he came here to see me. Am I somehow responsible? Please tell me the truth. I want the truth."

"I don't know why he was here," Ike said, wondering why Coney thought it so important to see her. "It would be hard to say who is responsible, but don't blame yourself for this. It's not your fault."

"Can I ride with you to Reverend Holbrook's house?" she asked.

"Yes. Let's go now."

They walked up the street to the patrol car and made the short drive in silence. Ike was thinking, knowing within himself that Coney Miller was a tragedy not of his own making, that Coney was dead because his father happened to stop in Stonewall County in 1935. He could as well have been in Texas or California or Montana. The answer to what Coney Miller could have been, or might have been, was lost forever in a pool of blood in front of the Midvale Negro church.

Ike sat in his office, trying to find a reasonable explanation for what happened. He wondered if Coney had gone to the church to harm Miss Landcaster, what he would have done if she had come outside. Any conclusion he reached he knew would be sheer speculation. There would never be an answer, for the only one who could supply a true answer was now in the funeral home, awaiting the trip back to the woods.

Billy and Sam came in with Lon following. Lon's arm was heavily bandaged and in a sling. Ike was surprised. "What the devil are you doing here?" he said to Lon. "Why aren't you in the hospital?"

"I'm not hurt bad, Mistuh Ike," Lon said. "I didn't want to stay out there. I'll be fine here."

"You ought to be in bed!" Ike said harshly. He changed his tone and said, "Do you want to stay out at your father's farm until this thing blows over?"

"No, sir, Mistuh Ike!" Lon replied emphatically. "I'm not goin to run. I'll be here when they come. That boy forced me to shoot him, an I'm not goin to run from it."

"We'll all be here," Ike said. "All of you stay here in the office while I go to the Miller place with the hearse."

"Don't you want us to go with you?" Billy asked, concerned. "You shouldn't go out there by yourself."

"I think it will be better this way," Ike said. "Wait here at the office until I return."

Ike sat on the front seat with the driver and his assistant, giving directions to the Miller shack. They rode silently along the gravel road until Ike said, "Turn at the next right and pull up to the house."

The driver turned up the narrow lane and drove across the bare dirt clearing. When he parked in front of the shack Ike got out and knocked on the porch floor. The two funeral home men stood beside the hearse, nervously wishing for this mission to end. Jud and the two brothers came around the side of the shack. They stared at the black hearse without speaking.

"It's Coney," Ike said, brushing his arm against the pistol strapped to his side, being sure it was there. "He's been killed."

"Who done it?" Jud asked without emotion.

"One of my deputies," Ike replied, watching Jud closely. "Coney attacked him with a knife. He had to shoot him."

"Which one?" Jud asked.

"It was one of my deputies," Ike said nervously.

"Which one?" Jud demanded.

"Lon Marcey," Ike replied, knowing he had to tell them.

"The nigger?" Jud asked.

"Yes."

One of the funeral home men said, "You want us to handle the funeral, Mr. Miller?"

Jud stared at him. "We bury our own."

"You want to purchase a casket?" he asked uncertainly.

"We make our own," Jud said. "Put him on the porch."

The two men took the stretcher from the hearse and placed the body on the sagging planks. One of them said, "I hate to mention it in your time of sorrow, Mr. Miller, but you owe us twenty dollars for ambulance service. You want to pay now, or had you rather we send you a bill?"

Jud ignored the question. He said to Ike, "What'd he shoot him fer?"

"I told you," Ike said. "Coney came at him with a knife and cut him pretty bad. He had to shoot. What was Coney doing at the Negro church?"

"He wanted to see the white girl."

"Why? What for?"

"He wanted to," Jud said. "Ain't you ever wanted to do somethin?"

Ike walked back to the hearse. He turned and said to Jud, "Is there anything we can do for you?"

He received no answer. Jud stood silently between Bester and Berl, all of them staring with hostile eyes. Ike said, "Let this be the end of it, Jud. Let it go. I'm sorry Coney is dead, but he forced my deputy to shoot. Don't start trouble over this or somebody will get hurt."

Jud still didn't speak. He watched Ike get into the hearse, watched the long black vehicle pull away and disappear around the bend in the lane. He turned to Bester and said, "You an Berl git some boards. I'll fetch the hammer an nails."

"We gone kill the nigger deputy, Pa?" Bester asked.

"Yes."

"We gone do it today?"

"No. Hit'll be time enough fer thet later, after we bury Coney."

Ashley was waiting at the courthouse when Ike returned. He met Ike in the hall and followed him into the outer office. He said anxiously, "What you gone do, Thornton? You got a murder on your hands. Is the nigger deputy in jail yet?"

Ike turned and faced Ashley. He leaned against the counter and said, "No, he's not in jail, he's in my office. And he's not going to jail."

"How come?" Ashley asked, feigning surprise. "He killed Coney Miller, didn't he?"

"He shot in self defense," Ike said, annoyed by being questioned by Ashley. "Coney came at him with a knife."

"You gone arrest the white girl?" Ashley asked.

"Arrest the white girl," Ike repeated incredulously. "Arrest her for what?"

"Goddammit, I don't know for what!" Ashley exploded. "Hell fire, Thornton, think up somethin! It's her fault! You can't let that slut git a white man killed an do nothin! Arrest her for whorin with the niggers!"

"Get out of here!" Ike snapped, not wanting to even look at Ashley. "You sound like an idiot! I'm busy! Just go away!"

"I'll fix her!" Ashley said, his stomach heaving with excitement. "She'll foul up sooner or later, an I'll fix her! She ain't gone git Coney killed for nothin!" He turned and left as Ike walked into his private office.

News of the perplexing death of Coney Miller spread over Midvale and furnished the grist for conversation mills. Interest in the incident did not involve sympathy for such an unknown person as one of the Miller brothers. It was puzzlement over why Coney Miller was in the Negro quarters in the first place, and why he placed himself in a position to be killed by a deputy sheriff. It was the general consensus that his presence at the Negro church had something to do with the civil-rights workers, but the connection between a member of the Miller clan and the two white people living with the Negroes was impossible to establish. It was unbelievable that any Miller could have the vaguest interest in the civil-rights movement or any movement.

These hermitlike men had never been known to concern themselves with anything or anybody, and the idea that one of them had suddenly thrown himself into the forefront of a cause bordered on the realm of fantasy. Most people attributed the shooting to the simple fact that Coney Miller had been in the wrong place at the wrong time and had refused to leave peacefully. He brought it on himself. All were in agreement, however, that they would not like to be in the shoes of Sheriff Thornton or the Negro deputy, for it was a foregone conclusion that the bearded men of the pine hills would not let the matter drop easily.

Ike was also of the opinion that the incident was not ended. The emotionless reception the Millers gave him when he delivered Coney's body had not lulled him into complacency; instead, it had given him even more cause for concern. All of his deputies were instructed to maintain extreme caution for the next several days. He also suspected that Con Ashley had played a major role in whatever it was that lured Coney Miller to the Negro quarters. That Ashley would blame it all on Miss Landcaster was to be expected.

Ike sat at his desk, agitated because of involvement with the Miller clan at a time when he wished his hands free of everything except VanDolan's threatened demonstration. He was in deep thought when Billy rushed into the office and said, "Those damned Delong brothers are in town! They've already cut up one man, an they're holed up in the Froggy Bottoms Cafe."

Ike got up quickly and strapped on his pistol. "Is Sam here?" he asked.

"He's out at the car now," Billy replied.

Ike went to the gun rack and handed Billy two shotguns. "We'd better take these too. What about the man who got cut?"

"He's already at the hospital," Billy said. "They laid his stomach open. The whole bunch is drunker than hell."

"Damn!" Ike said, wishing this had not happened at this time. "Get some cuffs and leg irons."

When Ike started for the door Lon stepped in front of him and said, "Let me go too, Mistuh Ike. I can still handle a gun."

"You better stay here," Ike said. "You're in no shape to get mixed up in something like this."

"Let me go, Mistuh Ike," Lon pleaded. "I'm all right. You'll need all the help you can get with that bunch."

"Well, all right," Ike agreed reluctantly. "You go with me. Billy, you and Sam go on ahead now. Don't try to do anything until we get there. We'll be right behind you."

The Delong brothers were three Negro men in their middle forties who lived in the south end of the county, somewhere inside the dense Pearl River swamp. They had created for themselves an even more isolated life than the Millers. Any fact about them, where they had originally come from or how long they had lived in the swamp, was unknown. Sometimes they peddled catfish door to door in the lower end of the county, and during winter months they sold firewood to farm families. They had never been friendly with anyone, black or white. They came into Midvale twice a year for staple supplies, bringing along several jugs of homemade swamp juice whiskey. Almost each visit ended in the Stonewall County jail on charges ranging from public intoxication to disturbing the peace to resisting arrest. They were harmless until they became drunk, then they changed drastically. They were usually given a wide birth during their infrequent rampages in the Midvale Negro quarters, and local Negroes refused to file charges against them out of fear.

Ike had forgotten about the Millers as he raced through the Negro quarters to the Froggy Bottoms Cafe. Only twice before had he encountered the Delong brothers, and each time he and his deputies found it necessary to physically overwhelm them in order to jail them. Both previous clashes had almost ended in gunfire. The two patrol cars skidded to a halt in front of the cafe. Ashley was across the street, leaning against his car, a rifle in his hands. He didn't move as Ike got out and came to him. Negroes were huddled in small groups around the building, watching.

"Are they inside?" Ike asked, looking from Ashley to the cafe.

"Yeah," Ashley replied. "They got that big-titted gal who works in there cornered. Them sonsabitches will come out after a while, an when they do I'll put some hot lead in their asses."

"While you're standing out here waiting, what's going to happen to the girl?" Ike asked.

"Who gives a damn?" Ashley said. "It'll be one nigger rippin up another. I shore as hell ain't goin in there an get carved up 'cause of some nigger bitch."

Ike turned and walked back to the patrol cars. He said, "Sam, you and Billy come in the back door. I'll go in the front. Lon, you come in after me. Be careful, and don't do anything foolish. All we want to do is get them out of there and to the jail. Don't take unnecessary chances."

Ike waited until Billy and Sam disappeared around the side of the building. Then he moved to the door, opened the screen and stepped inside. His shotgun clattered to the floor as he was grabbed from both sides and flung violently against the wall. He did not have time to think before the knife blade was pressed against his throat.

When Billy and Sam came from the kitchen they froze when they saw the two men holding Ike against the wall, the long blade of a butcher knife at his throat. The girl was lying on the floor, and one of the men sat beside her, popping her face with a knife blade. The two deputies knew not to make a sudden move and excite the Delongs. Lon stepped through the door, a pistol in his hand. The two men holding Ike glanced at Lon for a moment, then they slammed Ike to the floor and pressed the knife back to his throat.

"What we gone do, fellows?" Lon asked, looking at Billy and Sam.

"I don't know," Billy said. "We wouldn't get halfway across the room before they'd slice Ike ear to ear. You think they'd listen to reason?"

"Naw," Lon said. "They don't want to reason with nobody. Maybe if I shoot one of them through the head the other two will listen." Lon cocked the hammer on the pistol and took a step forward.

"Watch out, Lon!" Sam said excitedly. "You're gonna get Ike killed an yourself too. Don't move in on them!"

"They're goin to kill him anyway," Lon said, moving closer. "They're real mean, these fellows, real mean. They'd just as soon die right here an now, they're so tough. These bullets probably won't do nothin but bounce off their heads."

"Watch it now, Lon!" Sam said again. "What you tryin to do?"

"I'm gone let 'em kill me an Mistuh Ike, an soon as we's dead, both of you can load 'em up with buckshot." Lon stopped when the two men looked up at him. He stared straight into their eyes and said, "You fellows might think that 'cause I'm black too I won't shoot you, but I will. I had to kill a white man this mornin 'cause he came at me with a knife. If you're not up off that floor by the time I count to five you'll never know what hit you."

The two Negroes looked at each other, then at their brother sitting by the girl, then back to Lon. He said slowly, "One, two, three, four, five." They did not move. The explosion rattled the windows as the gun went off, splintering a hole in the floor two inches from one of the Negro's knees. They both jumped up and backed into a corner. Ike rolled sideways quickly, then scrambled to his feet and grabbed the shotgun.

Billy and Sam rushed forward with shotguns leveled. The man sitting by the girl dropped the knife and got up slowly. Ike said, "All of you lean against the wall with your backs to us! Do it quickly! Sam, you and Billy cuff their hands behind them." Ike sank into a chair as Billy and Sam handcuffed the brothers. Ike sighed and then said, "God-a-mighty, Lon, remind me to give you a raise soon as we get back to the courthouse! I thought I was a goner that time."

"What I need instead of a raise is a nerve tonic," Lon said, dropping into a chair beside Ike. "I don't think I could cut another day like this."

The Negro girl was still sitting on the floor, dazed. She suddenly jumped up and ran out the front door. Ike watched her disappear. He said to Sam and Billy, "Get these three on up to the jail. We'll be along as soon as I get the strength."

"Will do, boss," Billy said poking a shotgun barrel into one Negro's back. "But don't stay down here too long in case them Millers show up at the courthouse."

Ike had forgotten about the Millers. He frowned at the thought of them and got up and walked out of the cafe.

Ashley came up to Ike and said, "You let me have them niggers for a while you won't have to worry 'bout them comin into town again anytime soon."

"Why didn't you go in and get them yourself?" Ike asked. "Seems you're a little late now."

"I still wouldn't risk my hide for a nigger whore," Ashley said. "If you want to do it that's fine with me." He turned and walked back to his car.

Ike waited until the brothers were loaded into the back of Billy's car, then followed them back toward the jail. Lon remained silent until they reached the tracks. Then he turned to Ike and said, "You think them Millers are really comin in after me, Mistuh Ike?"

"Not today," Ike replied. "They'll come, but not today."

"I hope they don't come at all," Lon said, staring out the window. "I didn't mean to shoot that boy. I swear I didn't. He made me do it."

*   *   *

VanDolan entered the cafe just after sundown. He went straight to a table and joined Bugger Durr without greeting him. He said immediately, "I have a few things for you to do."

"You want a drink or somethin to eat?" Durr asked.

"Haven't got time," VanDolan replied tartly. "I have a round to make." He leaned across the table and said softly, "I want you to have that constable here tomorrow night about eight. Tell him if he will wait around outside he can catch Miss Landcaster drunk. Do it any way you can, but do it. Have him here about eight."

"What for, Mistuh Jeffrey?" Durr asked, surprised. "How come you want me to do that?"

"She's got to be out of the way for a couple of days," VanDolan said, still whispering. "I'll give you twenty dollars."

"I'll try," Durr said without enthusiasm, "but is you sure you know what you're doin? That man is mean, Mistuh Jeffrey, real mean."

VanDolan ignored the comment. "We'll march Thursday morning," he said. "Everyone can assemble at the church by ten. I'll pay ten dollars to each marcher you bring."

"How much for me?" Durr asked.

"Two dollars per head."

Durr said hesitantly, "Mistuh Jeffrey, what is this march gone be? Is they likely to be trouble?"

"There will be no trouble," VanDolan replied. "All we will do is walk to the courthouse and back. It won't take long."

"If that's all there is to it, how come you're willing to pay so much money?" Durr asked suspiciously."

"It's none of your business," VanDolan said, getting up from the table. "I have to go now. Have Ashley here tomorrow night."

VanDolan left the cafe and walked along the street leading to the shack. When he reached the gate Felds was sitting on the front steps. He had not seen the giant Negro since the night Miss Landcaster left the shack, and he assumed the incident had caused Felds to temporarily move out and stay elsewhere. He crossed the yard, stood in front of Felds and said, "Where have you been lately, Mr. Felds? I haven't seen you around." Felds squinted at VanDolan and remained silent." You know, Mr. Felds," VanDolan said, stepping closer, "I think you can help me. How would you like to be sheriff of this county?"

Felds blinked and said, "Whut?"

"How would you like to be sheriff of this county?" VanDolan repeated.

"Whut you mean?"

"You help me and I will help you," VanDolan said, watching Felds closely. "If all the Negroes register to vote you can elect a Negro sheriff. You would fit the job fine. You could drive a patrol car and carry a pistol. If you will march with me Thursday I will see to it that you are elected sheriff."

For a moment Felds had wild visions flash through his mind, things he had never before even imagined; then he got up, stared at VanDolan and said, "You must be tetched, white man."

"We'll talk about it again," VanDolan said as Felds walked into the shack. "You think about it." VanDolan then left the yard and disappeared beyond the streetlight.

Hankins and Ashley made the trip from town to the Miller place without speaking. They parked in the darkness, crossed the porch of the shack and silently entered the front room. The crude pine casket sat on the floor, and light from a kerosene lamp cast shadows along the walls. The Millers were squatting in a circle in the middle of the room, drinking from a jug. Coney's wide-brimmed black felt hat was a part of the circle. Hankins and Ashley took their places automatically, seemingly unnoticed by the bearded men. The jug was passed to them without any sign of recognition. They continued squatting for an hour in the dimly lit room, drinking in silence, not offering condolences, not asking what anyone would do. Hankins and Ashley got up and looked into the casket, and then they left as silently as they arrived, still seemingly unnoticed. The car headlights flashed across the clearing and disappeared down the lane, allowing darkness to again engulf the shack set in the edge of the pine woods.

Twenty-seven

Montique finished shining the shoes and accepted the coins with a broad smile. No one else was waiting, so he said to the shop owner, "Mistuh Bradley, I's goin to de cotehouse. I be back in a minute."

"Are you going up there to get a marriage license?" Bradley asked, laughing.

"Naw, suh," Montique replied, hobbling out the door. "I ain't got no such foolishness as dat on my mind." He moved slowly up the street and across the courthouse lawn and into the courthouse. He went down the hall and into the sheriff's office. He peered over the counter and said to Mrs. Fleming, "Is Mistuh Thonton in?"

She looked at the small gray head barely visible over the counter top. "Yes, Montique. He's in his office. Just go on in."

Montique hobbled into the office. "Moanin, Mistuh Ike. Can you see me fo a minute?"

"Sure," Ike replied, pushing away a sheaf of papers. "Have a seat. What brings you away from the shop this time of morning?"

Montique propped his crutch against the wall and slid into a chair. He said seriously, "Dey's somethin I ought to tell you 'bout, Mistuh Ike. I fears trouble comin."

Ike leaned forward and asked curiously, "What is it, Montique? Is Ashley bothering you again?"

"Nawsuh, ain't dat. It's 'bout dat VanDolan man. Las night he come to my shack an said he'd pay me fifteen dollars to march wid him Thursday, said it would look good fo de demonstration to have a colored man marchin wid a crutch. He say dey gwine march Thursday moanin."

"He told you this last night?" Ike asked, his suspicions now confirmed.

"Yassuh, he sho did. He come to my shack. I tole him I wadn't innerusted in no marchin, an he say think it over an be at de church by ten Thursday moanin."

"Did he give you any additional details?" Ike asked.

"Nawsuh, dat's all he say. I thought you'd want to know 'bout dis, Mistuh Ike. I ain't messin wid dat man."

"I appreciate the information," Ike said gratefully.

"You be's mos welcome," Montique said, pushing himself up and retrieving his crutch. "A heap of folks is takin dat man's money, but I don't want no part of it. I be's scared of dat man."

"Thanks again," Ike said as Montique started out the door. "You come back anytime."

Ike got up and walked to a window overlooking Main Street. He watched the small Negro hobble down the sidewalk and disappear into Bradley's Barber Shop. He continued staring out the window, trying to visualize a mass of people marching up Main Street, led by a high-stepping VanDolan holding a drum major's baton. He turned to the counter and told Mrs. Fleming he would be gone for a short time, then went out to his patrol car and drove toward the Negro quarters.

VanDolan stopped speaking when he saw Ike park at the edge of the clearing and come toward him. He left the picnic tables and walked hurriedly toward the sheriff, not wanting his students to hear whatever it was that Thornton had come to say.

They met halfway across the clearing. For a moment they stared at each other silently. Then Ike said, "May I have a moment of your time, Mr. VanDolan?"

"Yes, but let's go over by your car," VanDolan replied, glancing back at the picnic tables.

They walked to a tree at the edge of the clearing and became silent again. Ike spoke first, "I heard what you have planned for Thursday morning."

"So?"

"It would have been nice of you to come and tell me."

"I knew you'd find out anyway," VanDolan said indifferently.

After another period of silence, Ike said, "Just what is it you plan to do?"

"Conduct a protest demonstration."

"Exactly what is that?"

"We will march up Main Street to the courthouse and protest."

"Protest what?" Ike asked.

"Your inhuman treatment of Negroes, the injustice of your way of life."

The last of the sequences of silence ended with Ike's question, "Do you realize you will be breaking the law if you don't get a parade permit?"

"We don't need a damned parade permit!" VanDolan exploded. "It's every citizen's constitutional right to protest! You can take your parade permit and cram it! Do you expect to arrest everyone who marches? Will you turn dogs loose on us?"

"I don't recall saying anything about dogs or arresting people," Ike said, warming up to VanDolan's temperament. "I only asked if you know it's illegal to hold a parade without a permit. Did you apply for a permit? If you didn't, you will be breaking the law."

"You break the law every time you discriminate against these people and deny them their constitutional rights. Yet you have the gall to speak to me of law-breaking."

Ike forced himself to remain calm. He said, "If someone has something they wish to discuss or protest, why don't we do it here in the church, or in the school auditorium? Why in the streets? Why do you feel you must march up Main Street?"

"Because it draws attention to the problems."

"What do you want, attention or solution?"

"They go hand in hand. One breeds the other."

Ike leaned back against the tree trunk and said, "Do you mean to tell me that marching up Main Street will breed solutions to all our racial problems?"

"Yes," VanDolan said emphatically. "We draw attention to your racial injustice and this gains national sympathy. Then you are forced to stop your discrimination and treat Negroes equally with whites. The end result is the ultimate objective, and everyone strives for the end result."

"If this is true, why are you paying these people to march?"

VanDolan's face flushed. He said angrily, "Why are you so concerned over a simple protest march?"

"I'll tell you why," Ike said, stepping closer. "These are people's lives you are playing with, not toys you can break and throw in a corner when you are finished with them! Do you even realize what the results could be of this game you are playing just to amuse yourself? I see you as a magnet, drawing every undesirable hothead we have right out of the woodwork."

VanDolan's body went rigid. His lips trembled as he said, "I know about your hotheads! They have already come out of the woodwork!" He jerked the cap from his head and shouted, "You see! They did this to me! I know! I know!"

Ike looked at the thatch of hair on top of VanDolan's head. "Someone here did that to you?"

"Yes, goddammit!" VanDolan shouted, slamming the cap back on his head.

"Who?" Ike asked, puzzled.

"Some of your redneck hotheads!" VanDolan said furiously.

"Why didn't you come tell me when it happened?" Ike asked.

"Come and tell you?" VanDolan stammered. "Why? You would have done nothing."

"Are you so sure?" Ike asked. "You did not even give me a chance to investigate this."

"You have already been given a chance!" VanDolan boomed. "Many chances! I know about your Southern justice! Beat us with clubs! Spill our blood in the streets! Kill us, goddammit, kill us! We'll destroy you in the end! Savage bastards!"

Ike backed away and watched in awe as the enraged VanDolan jumped up and down, stomping the ground with his sandals. All the young people at the picnic tables stared in puzzlement as he retreated quickly to the patrol car and drove away.

Ike went straight to Grenlee's insurance office. He walked briskly past the secretary and into the private office without knocking. Grenlee said humorously, "Barge right on in, Ike. That 'private' sign doesn't mean anything."

"Can you call a town board meeting for tomorrow morning?" Ike asked without smiling.

"Yes," Grenlee said, becoming serious. "What's it about?"

"The protest march will be held Thursday morning. We have to decide what to do."

"Thursday morning," Grenlee repeated. "Are you sure?"

"Yes. I'm positive."

"Is there anything we can do to prevent it?"

"Absolutely nothing."

"Can you meet at nine in the City Hall?"

"I'll be there."

Bugger Durr left the mill early and walked along the tracks toward the station house, hoping that Ashley would be parked there as usual in midafternoon. He moved slowly and counted each crosstie, picking up pieces of slag and throwing them into a ditch beside the embankment, balancing himself on the rail for a distance, arms outstreached, then counting crossties again, walking with reluctance, frightened by the role he had been assigned in VanDolan's plot involving the white girl and Ashley. To lure VanDolan into a harmless rendezvous with a bunch of pranksters was one thing, but to become entangled in a scheme involving a white girl was another. He knew Ashley would not play jokes with her. Speculating about what Ashley might do or could do to her almost made him refuse VanDolan's money and have no part in this. But with a few more dollars from VanDolan he could purchase a washing machine for his mother and a new television set for himself.

He tried to convince himself that the worst Ashley would do to the girl was to lock her in jail for a couple of days. He salved his conscience somewhat by telling himself he was merely passing information that would lure Ashley to the cafe at a precise time. Whatever happened afterwards would be none of his affair. Yet with all his self-administered ointment the dread was still there.

When he reached the station house, Ashley's car was there. He walked to the driver's side and said, "Howdy, Mistuh Ashley."

Ashley looked around to see who had greeted him. He grunted and returned his gaze to the highway.

Durr kicked a rock beneath the car, then twisted his body and said, "Mistuh Ashley, I knows somethin you might want to know."

Ashley turned to him again and said gruffly, "What you want, Bugger?"

"I can tell you somethin 'bout the white girl."

Ashley's eyes glinted. He leaned out the window and said cautiously, "What is it, Bugger? Don't you fool with me."

Durr spoke slowly, forming his tale carefully. "I ain't foolin, Mistuh Ashley. That white girl been drinkin some lately down at the Froggy Bottoms."

"You lie!" Ashley snapped. "If she'd been there I'd a seen her. What you tryin to do, Bugger? I ought to get out of here and stomp you in the ground!"

Durr jumped back mentally, momentarily stunned by Ashley not believing him. He regrouped and said, "She been comin an goin by the back door so's you can't see her. That white girl can drink shine with the best of 'em.

Ashley jumped out of the car and said, "Bugger, you lie to me I'll bust you wide open! How come you tellin me this?"

"I ain't lyin," Durr said, his voice trembling. "I just thought you might want to know. You park outside the cafe 'bout eight tonight, you'll see."

"If you're lyin to me," Ashley said, "you better stay out of sight for the next month!"

"I ain't lyin, Mistuh Ashley," Durr said again, stepping backward. "I got to go now." He turned and trotted hurriedly down the railroad tracks toward the quarters.

Ashley got back into the car and stared at the highway, seeing the white girl drinking with the Negroes, drinking and giggling. He slammed the car into gear and shot across the highway, racing up Main Street and around the courthouse. When he reached the jail he took a gallon jug of corn whiskey from the truck of the car and went inside, hiding the jug behind the door. He knocked on the living quarters door and said loudly, "You in there, Ance?"

The old man came to the door and said, "Yeah, I'm here, Con. What you want?"

"I need one of them master keys," Ashley said restlessly. "I got to go upstairs now an come back in a little while. If I have a master key I won't have to bother you again. I know you like to watch television."

"Well, O.K.," Clayton said, "but bring it back to me soon as you're done with it." He took a key from a huge ring and handed it to Ashley. "Anything special happening?" he asked.

"Naw, just drunks." He waited until Clayton was back in the living quarters, then he unlocked the bottom door, retrieved the jug of whiskey, took it upstairs and hid it in a broom closet. He came back down the circular stairs, locked the door and left hurriedly.

Main Street was almost deserted when VanDolan came from the Ritz Cafe and got into the red sports car. He drove to the quarters and parked in front of Reverend Holbrook's house, then went onto the porch and knocked.

Reverend Holbrook came to the door and was surprised to find VanDolan there. He said distastefully, "What is it you want here, Mistuh VanDolar?"

"I need to see Sylvia," he said, disappointed that she had not answered the knock herself. He did not want to have verbal or physical contact with the preacher.

"She in her room," Reverend Holbrook said. "I'll tell her you's here."

VanDolan walked to the edge of the porch and stared aimlessly across the yard while he waited. He turned quickly when he heard her footsteps in the parlor. She opened the door and said coolly, "Yes, Jeffrey? What is it?"

He forced his most innocent look. "I thought you might like to go to the movie. I'm tired of sitting around that shack by myself."

Her inclination was to respond negatively to anything he suggested, and his friendly gesture caught her by surprise. She still did not trust him, but she weighed possibilities. Perhaps if she went with him they might talk and try to dissolve their differences, work together again rather than oppose each other. She said reluctantly, "Is going to a movie all you want to do?"

"That's all," he replied. "I thought you would enjoy it."

"I'll get my purse."

When she returned they walked across the yard and got into the car. He looked at her innocently again and said, "I have to stop by the Froggy Bottoms Cafe. One of my students sent word he has see me. It won't take but a minute. Then we'll go uptown."

"Why do you always have to meet someone in that place?" she asked, seeds of doubt germinating in her mind.

"It's where he said he would be," he replied cagily. "And besides, why do you call it 'that place'? The Froggy Bottoms is not as bad as you have been led to believe. It's just a cafe."

"According to Reverend Holbrook, it's more than 'just a cafe.'"

"Christ, Sylvia," he snapped, his voice harder, "have you ever heard of a preacher saying something good about any place but his church? He would probably think the movie theater is bad. We won't be there but a few minutes." He started the car and drove toward the cafe. She decided to humor him and not spoil their possible reconciliation so quickly.

VanDolan parked beside the building. He got out and opened her door. She looked up at him and said, "I'll wait here."

"It's no wonder you don't have more people in your class," he said, staring at her. "You come here to help the Negroes and gain their trust, yet you hold yourself aloof from them. You act as if you're too good to be seen in their only restaurant. And besides that, I don't want you sitting out here alone." He grabbed her hand and pulled her from the car. "It won't hurt you to go with me for just a few minutes."

She walked hesitantly past the benches where the Negro men watched her silently, glancing in surprise at each other. VanDolan opened the door and she stepped inside. Every eye in the room turned to her, piercing her already thin composure. VanDolan stepped beside her and said, "He's not here yet. Let's take a table and wait. He won't be long."

She forced herself to sit but did not look right or left. She stared straight ahead, unable to glance about and see the people who were visually dissecting her.

VanDolan said, "I'll get something to drink while we wait, and stop looking so frightened. There's nothing here but people. They're not cannibals."

For a moment her fear made her feel foolish. She realized she was among people who would not be seen in Reverend Holbrook's church, but this was not necessarily a reason for dread. She tried to relax and dispel her apprehensions. VanDolan went to the counter and ordered two drinks. He winked at the girl as she reached beneath a shelf and poured an inch of moonshine into the glasses. Then she filled both glasses with ice and soda. He put a five-dollar bill on the counter and returned to the table. He gave Miss Landcaster the glass with the whiskey and said "Cheers," watching as she sipped the orange-colored liquid.

"What is this?" she asked, frowning. "It tastes odd."

"Negroes call it belly wash," he said, smiling. "It's a Big Orange. I have it in here all the time. It grows on you."

She suddenly stared at him curiously and said, "Something is different about you. What happened to your beard, and why are you wearing that cap?"

"I shaved, and one of my students gave me the cap," he said indifferently, brushing aside her question.

She took another sip of her drink and said, "How long are we going to wait? We'll miss the movie."

"I guess he's not coming," VanDolan said, glancing at his watch. "Go on out to the car. I need to stop in the john out back. I'll come around the side of the building." He watched as she went out the front door. Then he disappeared through the kitchen.

Ashley got out of the car immediately when she came from the cafe. He blocked her path and said roughly, "You been drinkin?"

The shock of his presence rendered her speechless for a moment. She looked into his hostile eyes and said nervously, "No. I was with Jeffrey, waiting for one of his students. We are going to the movie."

He moved closer. "Don't lie to me! Let me smell your breath." She jumped backward when his nose touched her mouth. "Stand still, goddammit!" he boomed. The men on the benches watched with interest as he put his nose back to her mouth and sniffed. He grabbed her by the arm and said, "I can smell it! Let's go!"

She resisted, pulling against him and struggling to break free, shouting, "Jeffrey! Jeffrey! Come out here, Jeffrey!"

"I'm gone give you a choice," he said, gripping her arm. "You can come with me peaceably, or I'll carry you. Which will it be?"

She stopped struggling and examined the situation, deciding it would be best to go with him and try calling Sheriff Thornton from the jail. She grimaced, "You're hurting my arm! I'll go with you! Please let go!"

He loosened his grip and pulled her to the car, then pushed her onto the back seat and drove away. VanDolan stood in the shadow of a tree and watched until they disappeared before he went back into the cafe.

Ashley did not speak during the trip to the jail. When they arrived, he pulled her across the yard and into the bottom level. The loud sound of television drifted from the living quarters and into the somber hall. He unlocked the massive steel door and pushed her up the winding, circular stone stairs, stopping on the top landing to retrieve the jug of whiskey from the broom closet; then he unlocked the upper door and pushed her into the corridor separating the two rows of cells.

Ashley shoved her along the corridor and stopped when they reached the cell occupied by the Delong brothers. The three men watched curiously as Ashley set the jug on the concrete floor and said to her, "You want to see some real niggers? Take a look in there. Them's real niggers. Cut up another nigger yesterday just for the hell of it."

She looked into the shadowy cell at the three men who were staring at her and the constable, men with black beards and wild kinky hair. Ashley unlocked the door and set the jug inside the cell. "You fellows have a drink on me," he said. "Go ahead! It's good corn whiskey."

The brothers looked at him suspiciously, not understanding why he would bring whiskey to their cell. One of them picked up the jug, removed the cap and sniffed, and then sipped cautiously. He gurgled deeply, then passed the jug to the others. Ashley said, "Just look at them niggers go. They like that corn. Makes 'em crazy as loons. What you think about it, nigger-lover?"

Miss Landcaster turned her face away from the cell. He grabbed her and shoved her against the bars. "I said look, goddammit!"

She watched the Negroes pass the jug back and forth, drinking deeply. She tried to turn her head but couldn't. She said through clenched teeth, "I want to call Sheriff Thornton! I have a right to make a call!"

"You got a right to watch them niggers!" he said, holding her face against the bars. "You want to innergrate, I'm gone let you!" He shoved her inside the cell and locked the door. "Now go ahead an innergrate! Them's real niggers, not them powderpuff kind you're teachin to read an write."

She watched the men take the jug and retreat into a corner. She grabbed the bars and screamed, "Let me out of here! I want to call Sheriff Thornton!"

"You ought not carry on like that," Ashley said, laughing. "You love niggers. Them's your friends in there with you. I'm gone leave you now."

A man in a cell across the corridor watched silently as Ashley played out his drama. He then shouted, "Hey, fellow, you can't leave that girl in there!"

Ashley turned and said, "What you in for, mister?"

"Robbery."

"Robbery," Ashley repeated. "I thought you might be waitin transfer to the looney hatch. You want in that cell too? She look pretty good to you? You're the wrong color. She don't like nothin but niggers. You're out of luck."

The man repeated, "You can't leave her in there!"

"Watch," Ashley said, turning to leave. "You folks have a good night." He walked back down the corridor and slammed the steel door shut.

Miss Landcaster pressed her back against the cell bars, watching the men continue drinking, noticing the changes in their expressions, seeing the tempo of their breathing increase. She moved sideways into a corner as they put the jug on the floor and walked toward her, fanning out as if trapping an animal. She screamed as the first blow knocked her senseless. Then a fist into her stomach spun her halfway across the cell. She fought back automatically until another until blow to her face caused her to crumple and lie still on the floor.

The man in the opposite cell shouted out the window, screaming for help, trying vainly to attract attention. He picked up a chair and pounded the floor frantically. The desperate racket ricocheted through the tomblike chamber, bouncing away from the steel door and echoing back through the cells.

Ike was sitting in the den watching television when the phone rang. He went into the kitchen and picked up the receiver. When he returned to the den he said to Peggy Jo, "I've got to go to the jail. Mr. Clayton is all excited about something. I won't be gone long."

"Did he say what it is?" she asked.

"He was jabbering so fast I couldn't understand anything he said," Ike replied.

Ike drove to the jail and became alarmed when he saw Clayton standing on the steps, motioning desperatedly for him to hurry. He rushed across the yard and said sharply, "What is it? What has happened?"

"Upstairs!" the old man gasped. "In the cell! Hurry!"

Ike raced up the stairs and down the corridor, first noticing the man alone in a cell, mesmerically pounding the floor with a chair. He looked into the opposite cell and saw a woman's body lying face-down on the floor, blood staining the concrete beside her. The Delong brothers were passed out in a corner, one of them holding an almost-empty jug.

"What is this?" Ike asked. "What has happened here?"

"I don't know," Clayton puffed. "I was watchin television an heard a poundin noise. When I come up here this is what I found. I don't know how the woman or the jug of whiskey got into that cell."

"You don't know who she is or how she got here?" Ike asked, finding Clayton's statement unbelievable.

"I sure don't, Mister Ike. I don't know anything."

"Go downstairs and call an ambulance," Ike said harshly, "and call Billy and Sam to come here. Give me the key and I'll get her out of there. Hurry!"

Ike went into an empty cell, removed a blanket from a cot and spread it in the corridor. Then he unlocked the cell and stepped inside. He rolled the woman onto her back and stared for a moment, then said in surprise and anguish, "Sylvia Landcaster! My God!"

The man in the opposite cell stopped pounding and said, "I seen it all, Sheriff! That constable did it. He fed them niggers whiskey, and then he put her in the cell with them. I begged him not to, but he wouldn't listen. I tried to get help but it took awhile before anyone heard me. Them men would 'a killed that girl if they hadn't passed out when they did. They gave a terrible whuppin."

"Ashley!" Ike muttered. Anger surged through him as he picked up the girl's limp body and placed her on the blanket.

Clayton ran down the corridor and said, "The ambulance is on its way. Is she all right?"

"I don't know," Ike replied. "Did you let Con Ashley up here tonight?"

"No, I didn't, Mistuh Ike," Clayton said fearfully. "I gave him a master key this afternoon. He said he had some drunks to bring up later. He never brought the key back."

Ike heard the scream of an ambulance siren a couple of blocks away. Billy and Sam both ran down the corridor and looked at the girl. "What happened, Ike?" Billy asked.

"It's Sylvia Landcaster," Ike said. "She's been beaten to a pulp. You and Sam find Con Ashley and bring him to the office. I don't care what time of night it is, just find him. I'll stay here until the ambulance leaves, then I'll go to the courthouse and wait for you there."

"Did Ashley have something to do with this?" Sam asked.

"Go now!" Ike said urgently, not answering. "Bring Ashley to the courthouse!"

Ike paced back and forth, waiting impatiently for Billy and Sam to return. The picture of Sylvia Landcaster lying in a pool of blood fanned his smoldering anger. He walked into his office and out again, moving constantly until he heard the sound of footsteps coming down the dark hall.

Ashley came in ahead of Billy and Sam. He said nonchanlantly, "What you want, Thornton? I'm gettin tired of your deputies shovin me around."

Ike stared at the puffed red face. "Why'd you do it, Ashley?"

"Do what?" Ashley replied indifferently.

"What did she ever do to you?"

"I don't know what you're talkin about," Ashley said, pretending annoyance.

Ike grabbed Ashley and shoved him against the counter. "Answer me!" he demanded. "What did she ever do to you?"

Ashley moved sideways out of Ike's grasp and said nervously, "If you're talkin about that bitch I put in jail, she was drinkin, an I got witnesses."

"Why did you put her in the cell with those Delong brothers after you fed them whiskey?" Ike asked, his eyes blazing with fury.

"You know how mean they are when they get drunk. Why?"

"She wants to innergrate, so I let her," Ashley said.

"You sadistic bastard!" Ike shouted, his hands trembling. "Those men almost killed her!"

"I don't see how come you're so upset," Ashley said, backing up again. "She ain't nothin to you."

"Nothing to me," Ike repeated, stepping close again. "She's a human being, or do you even know what that is? Do you realize what you've done to her? Do you even care?"

"I ain't done nothin to her," Ashley said, becoming alarmed. "Them niggers might have, but I ain't."

"You've served your last day as a constable," Ike said. "You're finished, through. You'll sit in jail until we decide what charges to file against you."

"You kiss my ass!" Ashley snapped, alarm changing to anger. "Who the hell you think you are?"

Ike's fist caught Ashley in the stomach, spinning him along the counter. Ashley bent double for a moment. Then he straightened up and said, "You ought not to have done that! I done took enough from you! I'm gone stomp the livin hell outen you!"

Ike moved quickly, smashing his fist into Ashley's face with a blow far beyond his normal strength. The huge man staggered for a moment with surprise in his eyes, then toppled backward to the floor. Ike stood over him and said in gasps, "Get him out of here! Get him out of my sight! Take him to the jail!"

Sam and Billy helped Ashley to his feet. He swayed and shook his head. "I'll git you for this, Thornton! We ain't done yet!"

"Get him out of here before I do something I'll regret!" Ike screamed. Sam and Billy led Ashley out of the office and down the hall.

Ike leaned against the counter and let his anger cool, then turned off the lights and went outside. He drove down the deserted Main Street, past the silent stores and the darkened Ritz Cafe. Then he turned north to the county hospital. He went into the building and to the reception desk. The nurse on duty was Betty Brown, a high school classmate. He said to her, "Hello, Betty. I'm looking for the room of Sylvia Landcaster."

She's in one-oh-one, Ike. The doctor just left. I'll walk down there with you."

They walked down the quiet hall and into the dimly lit room. Miss Landcaster's face was battered, and she had a strap around her chest. Ike stared at her for several moments, then said, "Will she be all right?"

"She has bruised ribs and contusions all over her face and chest," the nurse said. "Dr. Lowry doesn't think she has internal injuries. She should be fine but it will take time for her to recover." The nurse hesitated, then said, "Ike, isn't this the civil-rights worker who is living in the Negro quarters?"

"Yes, it is."

"Who did this to her? It's horrible."

"Con Ashley is responsible," Ike said wearily. "He didn't do the actual beating, but he arranged it."

"My God, Ike, why?" she asked. "Why would he do such a terrible thing?"

"Who knows, besides Ashley and God," Ike said. "Maybe some of us haven't come as far from the jungle as we think we have."

They walked back up the hall to the reception area. Ike said, "Take care of her, Betty. Do the best you can." He turned and left the building.

Twenty-eight

Ike came from his private office and said to Lon, "Go down to the quarters and tell Reverend Holbrook what has happened, if he hasn't heard already. Ask him to go to the church and tell Miss Landcaster's class she won't be there. I have a meeting now at the City Hall or I would go myself."

"Yessir, Mistuh Ike," Lon said. "You want me to stay down there or come back to the office?"

"All of you should stay here in case I need you," Ike replied. "Billy, call the hospital and tell Peggy Jo I will come by there as soon as I can. She went there early this morning."

"Ashley is kicking up a ruckus at the jail this morning," Billy said. "He's bellowing like a bull in a slaughter pen."

"Let him bellow," Ike said, turning to leave. "He may have a long time to sit and think about what he did."

Ike left the courthouse and walked to the City Hall. Only Ed Kelley had arrived early for the meeting. When Ike entered Grenlee said, "That was a terrible thing that happened at the jail last night. Con Ashley ought to be shot."

"He's finished as a constable," Ike said. "The district attorney is already looking at charges that can be brought against him. I don't think he will be out of jail anytime soon."

"What is all this leading to?" Grenlee asked. "That Miller boy gets himself killed down in the quarters, and now this girl gets beaten up in the jail. What's happening here?"

"I don't know," Ike replied. "I feel like I'm caught in a suction pump and can't get out."

"I've got more news," Kelley said. "Frank Parks told me this morning that the workers in the quarters won't go back to the project until this demonstration business is over. I suppose they're afraid to get caught in the middle of it."

"When will they go back?" Grenlee asked apprehensively.

"As soon as they are sure there will be no trouble. You can't really blame them."

The other board members all came in together and took seats at the conference table. Grenlee said, "I suppose you know why we are here. There will be a protest march in the morning, and we need to decide how to handle it. Whatever we decide will be carried out by

Ike and his deputies."

"Have they applied for a parade permit?" Kelso asked.

"No," Grenlee replied. "Ike informed the organizer, Jeffrey VanDolan, about the law, and he hasn't applied for a permit. I am sure he won't."

"I say arrest the whole bunch the second they step across the railroad tracks," Branch said.

"That is exactly what VanDolan would like for us to do," Ike said. "His purpose is not to protest but to attract attention."

"Just what is it they intend to do?" Bennett asked.

"March to the courthouse and make a protest, then return to the quarters," Ike said. "So far as I know, that's all."

"What do you suggest we do, Ike?" Kelso asked.

"Let them have their march and hope that is the end of it."

"Do you believe the march will end it?" Bennett asked.

"As I said, I hope so," Ike said, "but no one knows for sure. Sometimes people like VanDolan are used as bait to provoke violence and draw attention to the cause. If no one here takes the bait, it ends."

"What if someone does throw a brick or a bottle?" Bennett asked. "What then?"

"We will protect the demonstrators as best we can," Ike said. "But who in Midvale will throw a brick at a local Negro teenager just because he or she is marching up Main Street?"

"I don't know anyone personally who would throw a brick," Bennett said, "but the streets and sidewalks are public property. Who can say how many people will be here, and where they come from?"

"Good point," Ike said. "We'll just have to cross that bridge when we come to it."

"I still don't see the purpose in fillin up the streets with niggers," Branch said. "I told you when we had the meetin about those houses that you can't do anything for a nigger an expect him to appreciate it. You help a nigger an he'll stab you in the back every time."

"Which ones have stabbed you?" Grenlee asked.

"You come look at my account books an you'll see!" Branch snapped. "A nigger ain't got no responsibility. They're liable to sit down right in the middle of the street an start eatin Moon Pies, like a bunch of friggin monkeys. You just wait! You'll see!"

"Now that you have established yourself as an anthropologist we can proceed with our business," Major Beecham said to Branch sarcastically.

"Do you think Roy should run an editorial in the paper asking for calm during the demonstration?" Grenlee asked.

"It would just draw attention to the demonstration," Kelley said. "An editorial in the paper would be an invitation for everybody in the county to show up out of curiousity."

"I guess you're right," Grenlee agreed. "No editorial. We've covered all that we can, so hope for the best. The meeting is adjourned."

Everyone left immediately, not lingering over coffee as usual. Ike said to Grenlee, "Can you be at the courthouse a half-hour early in the morning? I suppose you and I will meet this delegation."

"I'll be there," Grenlee responded.

Kelley was waiting outside when Ike came from the building. He stopped Ike and said, "Will you see Miss Landcaster this morning?"

"I'm going to the hospital as soon as I get back to the office."

"Tell her I have arranged to pay the hospital bill," Kelley said. "I called Doc Lowry this morning and told him to take good care of her."

"I'll tell her," Ike said, surprised and pleased. "I'm sure she'll be glad to know she has friends here."

When Ike reached the office Claire Landrum, owner of the Ritz Cafe, was waiting for him. He said, "Hello, Claire, what brings you to the courthouse this time of day?"

"I want you to deliver something," she said, handing him a package. "It's not much, just a nice robe. Give it to Miss Landcaster and tell her I'm sorry about what happened. I liked that girl, and I don't think she meant harm to anyone."

"I'm going to the hospital now," Ike said, again surprised. "I'll be glad to deliver it."

"Tell her if she doesn't like that hospital food let me know. I'll bring her a country-fried steak, blackeyed peas and cornbread, and a peach cobbler."

"I could use that myself," Ike grinned.

As the woman turned to leave, she said, "She's a nice girl, Ike. She didn't deserve what she got. Somebody ought to shoot Con Ashley."

Ike went out to the patrol car and drove to the hospital. He walked down the hall, opened the door to room 101 and peeked inside. Miss Landcaster seemed to be asleep. Her face was covered with purple bruises, and her left eye was badly swollen.

When he entered the room she turned to him and tried to smile.

"Good morning," Ike said, unsure of what he should or could say to her. He noticed flowers on a stand next to her bed. "Where did you get the roses?" he asked awkwardly.

"Peggy Jo brought them," she said. "She left just a few minutes ago. They're beautiful, aren't they?"

"Yes, they are." Ike put the package on the bed. "Claire Landrum at the Ritz Cafe sent this to you, and Ed Kelley asked me to tell you that your medical bills are paid in advance. You don't have to worry about that."

She opened the package and ran her fingers across the soft robe. She started crying. Ike touched her hand and said, "I'm sorry. I'm so sorry. We're not all bad. Don't judge us all by this."

"I don't judge anyone," she said, wiping tears from her cheeks. "That will be done by an authority higher than me." She stopped sobbing and said, "I want to go home just as soon as possible. I can't stay here now."

"You can think about that later," Ike said. "Right now you need rest."

She touched the robe again and said, "Tell Mrs. Landrum thank you for me, and also Mr. Kelley. I appreciate everything. Has anyone told my class I won't be there?"

"Reverend Holbrook has taken care of it. I am sure he will

come by here today." Ike walked to the door and said, "Please get some rest. I'll see you later."

As soon as he closed the door she cried again. The words rang in her mind, *Don you ever hate nobody fo any reason, Miss Sylvia. To fogive is de work of de Lawd, an to hate is de work of de debil, an we all gwine stand befo judgment someday.*

Ike sat behind his desk, waiting for Lon to come in. Billy and Sam were seated before him. Lon entered and took a chair beside them. Ike said to Lon, "What did Reverend Holbrook say when you told him about Miss Landcaster?"

"He cried like a baby," Lon said. "I pure hate to see a grown man cry. He said to tell you if there's anything he can do just let him know. He went right on out to the hospital."

"Did you find VanDolan and tell him?" Ike asked, curious about VanDolan's reaction.

"Yassuh, I did," Lon replied. "He turned white as a bucket of lard, but he didn't say anything. He just muttered and walked off."

"I've called this meeting to make plans for the demonstration tomorrow," Ike said. "It starts at ten. I want you to be honest with me, Lon. Had you rather have no part in this?"

"No, sir, Mistuh Ike," Lon said emphatically. "This is my town too. If anything bad happens it will hurt my people more than anyone. I'll do anything you say for me to do."

"Good," Ike said. "We need all the help we can muster. The city police will direct traffic at the highway, and the rest is up to *us*."

"How many people are marching?" Sam asked.

"I don't have any idea," Ike replied. "VanDolan is paying young people to participate, but I don't know how many. Lon, you stay down at the station. Bill and Sam will meet the marchers at the tracks and walk with them to the courthouse and back."

"What are we supposed to do if someone does start trouble?" Billy asked.

"Ask them to move on, and if they don't, arrest them," Ike replied. "Don't arrest anyone unless you have to, but do it if it's necessary. One of you take the person to the jail and the other remain with the marchers."

Mrs. Fleming opened the door and said, "I hate to bother you, Ike, but someone is here to see you."

"Thanks," Ike said, getting up and coming around the desk. "If there is anything the three of you need to discuss, go ahead and do so."

Ike stepped into the main room and froze when he saw Bester Miller standing beside the counter, a rifle in his hand. The bearded man said to Ike, "Pa wants you outside." Then he turned and left.

Ike went back into his office and said calmly, trying to hide the anxiety, "The Millers are here. Billy, you and Sam get shotguns and come out behind me. Lon, you stay in here."

Ike took a shotgun from the rack and walked slowly down the hall, trying not to attract the attention of anyone in the other offices. He opened the side door and stepped outside. The three Millers, all with rifles, were standing on the sidewalk. Billy and Sam came out and took positions on each side of Ike.

"We come fer the nigger who killed Coney," Jud said without emotion.

"What did you say?" Ike asked with disbelief.

"We come fer the nigger," Jud repeated.

Ike took a step forward and said, "Jud, this in 1965, not 1895. You better bring yourself forward a few years. If you're trying to make a point, you've made it, so just go away peacefully. If you don't, somebody will get hurt."

Jud said again, "We come fer the nigger."

Ike shook his head in frustration and tightened his grip on the shotgun. He said, "I'm not going to tell you again, Jud. Let it go. If you don't move on, all of you are going to jail. Coney was killed because he attacked a law enforcement office with a knife. Let it go now before it's too late."

Ike watched the rifle barrels come up, and then he heard the click of hammers. He glanced behind him as Lon came out, a shotgun in his hands. Ike said harshly, "I told you to stay inside! Get back in there and let us handle this!"

"No, sir, Mistuh Ike," Lon said, "I'm not gone do that! If I hide now I'll be hidin the rest of my life. You Millers want me, here I am!" He stepped between Ike and Sam.

Jud raised the rifle and pointed it at Lon. Ike cocked the hammers on the double-barrel shotgun and said, "Billy, Sam, the first one moves a muscle, blast him full of buckshot!" Ike pointed the shotgun at Jud. "You might get that bullet in Lon, Jud, but you and your boys will die for it. Is it worth it? If you want to kill your boys, go ahead and pull the trigger."

Jud continued aiming the rifle at Lon. He glanced right to left, seeing four double-barreled shotguns pointed at him and his sons. He calculated that eight loads of buckshot would come their way instantly, cutting them in half. He would never know if his bullet killed the Negro or not. He decided the odds were against them. The rifle barrels came down. He said to Ike, still without emotion, "We ain't done yet. Come on, boys. Hit's a long trek back to the house."

Ike's hands trembled as he watched the bearded men saunter slowly up the street. A rush of air came from his chest, sounding like a wheeze. They all looked at each other and uncocked the shotguns. Lon said to Ike, "You think they'll come back?"

"I doubt it," Ike replied. "Jud was as relieved as we were to see those gun barrels come down. He just had to give it a try."

"I think I need to go an change my britches," Billy said. "Ole Jud'll never know how close I came to blowin his head off."

"It was close," Ike said, "and Jud knows it. I don't believe he'll repeat this performance."

VanDolan entered the Froggy Bottoms and looked around. He joined Bugger Durr at a table. "Is everything fixed for tomorrow morning?" he asked."

"They'll all be there before ten," he replied. "You want a drink?"

"Yes."

Durr got up, went to the counter and returned with a Big Orange and two glasses. He raised a plank beneath the table, took out a bottle and poured clear liquid into the glasses.

"Put some more in mine," VanDolan said.

Durr handed him the bottle. "Sheriff Thonton finds out what we did to that white girl, he'll kill us," he said.

"He'll never know unless you blab it out!" VanDolan said harshly. He turned up the glass and drained it. "How did we know that idiot constable would get her beaten to a pulp? Forget it and keep your mouth shut. Are you going to march at the head of the line with me?"

"I'm not gone be there," Durr said.

"What do you mean you're not going to be there?" VanDolan asked, drinking again.

"I'm not gone march," Durr replied, looking directly at VanDolan. "I'm through, Mistuh Jeffrey. They's been a man kilt down at the church, an now that white girl all messed up. I been doin everthing you asked, but I'm done now. I ain't gone do no more."

"You don't have a choice!" VanDolan snapped. "You're in this as much as I am!"

Durr leaned across the table and said, "You 'member the first night you come in here? Ever man in here was ready to dump yo guts on the floor. I'm the one who stopped them. You never knowed it, but if it warn't for me, you'd be dead or in a hospital right now. If you want to, we can start again right at the beginning. I got a switch blade in my pocket, an if you want me to, I'll take it out an empty yo guts right on this table."

VanDolan looked at Durr with fright. He said quickly, "There's no need to get mad. You don't have to march. We can still be friends."

"I ain't mad," Durr said, glaring at VanDolan, "I'm just tellin you. I ain't gone do no more. An after that march I wants the rest of my money."

"You'll get it," VanDolan said nervously. "I've got to go now. I have an appointment. Here's five dollars. I want the rest of the bottle."

"You can have it for nothin," Durr said, refusing the money and handing VanDolan the bottle.

VanDolan put the bottle under his shirt and left hurriedly. He trotted down the street, still dismayed by the sudden change in

Durr's attitude. When he reached the shack, Felds was sitting on the front steps. He sat beside him, took out the bottle and said, "You want a shot?"

Felds looked at him but didn't answer. He got up to leave but stopped when VanDolan said, "Are you going to march tomorrow? You would look good in a sheriff's uniform."

Felds still didn't speak. VanDolan took a bill from his wallet, handed it to Felds and said, "Just to show you I have faith in you, here's a twenty-dollar advance on your first month's salary as sheriff. Be at the church before ten in the morning." Felds took the bill and put it into his pocket.

VanDolan got up and left the shack. He walked to a small clearing at the end of the street. He stood still for a moment, drinking from the bottle. Then he whispered, "You here, Clara Mae? It's me."

She came from behind a bush, giggling. "You bring me somethin?" she asked.

He took a dime-store bracelet from his pocket and handed it to her. "It's from a store in New York called Saks. It will look real good on you." She giggled again as she put the bracelet on her arm, then she took him by the hand and led him into the woods.

Twenty-nine

The morning was dry and hot, no different from any other July day in Midvale except for an imperceptible tension blanketing Main Street like fog. Merchants glanced out their store fronts, looking toward the railroad tracks. Shoppers made decisions about purchases more quickly than usual. Even lumbering dogs seemed to be trotting faster. Cars and trucks ordinarily seen in town only on Saturday were parked by the station house. The Ritz Cafe was doing a brisk business in coffee.

Reverend Holbrook walked down the street to the church, walking slowly like an old man pulling a full cotton sack. His face was twisted with anxiety. He stopped at the edge of the clearing and watched VanDolan flail his arms wildly as he gave instructions. He crossed the open space, came up to VanDolan unnoticed and said loudly, "May I have a word wid everbody?"

VanDolan looked at the preacher with annoyance. He shrugged and said, "Go ahead, but make it fast."

The crowd became quiet as Reverend Holbrook faced them and said, "Our Father which am in heavin . . . Hallowed be yo name . . .lead us not into temptation, but deliber us from evil . . . fo yo's is de kingdom, an de power, an de glory . . . fo if you fogives men dey trespasses, yo heavenly Father will also fogive you . . . but if you fogive not men dey trespasses, neither will yo Father forgive yo trespasses." He stopped momentarily, looking at each face in the crowd, then continued slowly. "De Lawd is my shepherd. Ever one of you best 'member dat de lawd is watchin. When you walk up dat street, de Lawd gwine be wid you. He gwine see. Do what you do de Lawd's way. You can't hide from de Lawd. He gwine be watchin." Then he turned and left.

VanDolan turned back to his audience and said, "Fall in in rows of three. Hanibel Felds and Dragline will be in the front row with me. You know what to do, so form up."

Fifty Negroes, mostly teenagers, moved into rows as they laughed and shouted at each other. The few old people looked afraid.

Montique hobbled into the clearing. He had left his job at the barber shop in order to see the formation of the parade. Groups of curious Negroes formed a spectators' gallery at the edge of the clearing. Montique's eyes bulged with fright when he spotted Hanibel Felds at the head of the line. He hopped as fast as he could to Felds and said excitedly, "Whut you doin, Hanibel? Whut you doin in dat line?"

The giant Negro looked down at the small crippled man and said, "I'm gone be shuff."

"Is you havin a spell, Hanibel?" Montique asked, not believing the words.

"I'm gone be shuff," Felds repeated.

"You git out of dere an go wid me!" Montique said, taking Felds by the arm. "You ain't got no business on de street! You gwine git yoself in trouble!"

Felds shoved him aside and said harshly, "I'm gone march!"

"I'll buy us some salmon," Montique said desperately, "an some cheese, an some Moon Pies an belly wash. You go wid me, Hanibel! We'll go to my place!"

VanDolan came to Montique and said, "Get out of the way! You had your chance to march and turned it down, so get out of the way!" As soon as Montique hobbled off, VanDolan raised his arm and shouted, "Let's go!"

Dragline took a bottle from his pocket and drank from it. Then he clapped his hands and shouted, "Yeeeeeehaw! Do it, white man, do it!"

Montique stood at the edge of the clearing and watched as the rows of marching people passed by him and moved up the street toward the railroad tracks.

The three deputies were standing beside the station house when they saw the marchers approach. Billy said, "Here they come. Sam, you march on the left side of the column, and I'll take the right."

Several farmers were sitting on truck fenders, watching silently. One of the spectators at the station house was Sim Hankins. His hands trembled when he spotted Hanibel Felds at the head of the marchers.

The city policeman stopped traffic on the highway as the line crossed the railroad tracks. Strangers who were travelling the highway north and south blinked with curiosity at the line of marchers led by a giant Negro in overalls three sizes too small, another Negro almost as tall as the giant but two hundred pounds thinner, and a small white man with a blue cap on his head. Spectators on the sidewalks, both white and black, watched silently as the procession moved up Main Street to the courthouse lawn.

Ike and Grenlee stood on the front steps of the building, both of them feeling uncomfortable with the situation, wondering what would be said to them and what they could say in return. Grenlee popped his knuckles nervously.

VanDolan halted the marchers ten feet from the steps. The ones in the rear came forward, forming a semicircle around the leaders. For several moments the marchers stared silently, blinking their eyes. Then a young girl stepped forward and said, "I wants to protest."

"Protest what?" Grenlee asked.

"Votin," she said hesitantly.

"Are you old enough to register?"

"Nawsuh."

"Then why are you protesting?"

"My mamma is old enough."

"Has she tried to register and been denied?" Grenlee asked.

"Nawsuh," the girl answered, squirming nervously.

"Then why are you protesting?"

"Because."

"Because what?" Grenlee demanded.

The girl became totally confused. She said hesitantly, "Just because."

"What she means," VanDolan broke in quickly, "is that she's protesting your refusal to let everyone register."

"No one has been refused," Grenlee said. "The old people agreed to wait until they learn to read and write."

"We intend to change that!" VanDolan snapped.

A young boy then stepped forward and said, "I want to protest."

"What is it you wish to protest?" Grenlee asked.

"I want to go to the white school."

"Have you applied for a transfer?" Grenlee asked.

"Nawsuh."

"You have to make a transfer application. Talk to Mr. Hopkins and he will tell you what to do."

The boy stepped back and smiled, seemingly relieved that his part was ended.

Ike looked over the crowd. He came down the steps and said, "Why are you here, Uncle Toby? What is it you wish to protest?"

The old man cast his eyes downward. "Mistuh Ike, dat white man tole me if I didn march he'd have my govment check stopped. I can't git along widout my check. I's too old to work anymore."

"He lied to you, Uncle Toby!" Ike said furiously. "No one can have your check stopped! If that's your only reason for being here, you can leave now if you wish."

"I think I will, Mistuh Ike," he said. "I didn know." The old man turned and walked back across the courthouse lawn. VanDolan's face flushed as he hooked his right foot behind his left foot.

Ike turned to Dragline. "Why are you here?"

"Lawdy me, Mistuh Thonton," Dragline said, grinning, "I's done walked up that street a thousand times an I ain't never befo been paid to do it. I's havin fun."

Ike then turned to Hanibel Felds. "Why are you here?"

Felds said, "I'm gone be shuff."

"What?" Ike asked incredulously.

"I'm gone be shuff," Felds repeated.

Ike turned to VanDolan and said, "Did you tell him that?"

"It's true," VanDolan replied, shuffling his feet. "He can be sheriff. If enough Negroes vote they can elect a black sheriff."

"Do you realize what you have done to him?" Ike asked angrily. "He's mentally unstable, and you have filled his mind with a fantasy."

"I haven't done anything," VanDolan said. "He can be sheriff."

Ike turned back to the crowd and said, "Has anyone else got a protest?"

"What about police brutality?" VanDolan quipped.

"None of my deputies have ever been brutal to anyone," Ike said. "As for what Constable Ashley has done, his days in law enforcement are ended."

VanDolan said nothing. He didn't want to pursue this matter further for fear his role in Sylvia Landcaster's beating would be revealed.

Ike walked back onto the steps and said, "If any of you have a protest, you can come into my office now. Mayor Grenlee and I will discuss any problem you have. If you have no protest, I suggest you leave now and return to your homes."

"Mistuh Thonton," Dragline said, "if you don't mind, I's gone march back down the street an give this man his money's wuth. I purely enjoys it."

"Any of you who wish to march back are free to do so," Ike said. "It's your choice. If you don't want to march, leave now."

VanDolan looked around frantically as the crowd drifted away. He shouted, "Wait! Wait! We have to march! Stop!" His army dwindled down to himself, Dragline, Hanibel Felds, and ten teenagers. "Fall in!" he cried. "We march now! Fall in and follow!"

Dragline clapped his hands and shouted, "Do it, white man! Do it!" The procession moved back across the courthouse lawn and down the middle of Main Street.

Hankins leaned against the station house wall, watching them come closer and reach the tracks, seeing the giant Negro in the lead. He suddenly darted into the open and rushed headlong into Felds, knocking him to the ground. VanDolan and Dragline jumped back as Hankins kicked the downed Negro in the stomach. Felds jumped to his feet quickly and grabbed Hankins, lifting him from the ground and smashing him into the side of a truck, momentarily stunning him. Hankins shook his head and flew back into Felds, his arms swinging wildly. Felds picked him up again and threw him back into the truck door.

The unexpected commotion caught Sam and Billy by surprise. As soon as they realized what was happening, they joined the fray, stepping between the two men. Hankins charged again, and Billy and

Sam dragged him to the station house, pinning him against the wall. Lon pushed Felds away with his one good arm.

VanDolan jumped up and down, shouting, "You see! You see! Savages! We can't protest! We'll march again! I'll get help! You see! You see!"

Dragline watched the fanatical outburst and decided he had discharged his debt to VanDolan. He slipped away silently and walked down the railroad tracks. Five of the other marchers ran when the fight started. What was left of the procession moved forward again toward Front Street. VanDolan continued jumping up and down, shaking his fist and shouting. Several spectators who witnessed the encounter between Hankins and Felds shook their heads in dismay and walked away.

After lunch, Ike drove out to the hospital. He was in an almost jubilant mood, grateful that the protest march was peaceful except for the clash between Sim Hankins and Hanibel Felds. His light-hearted feeling was dimmed when he entered the building and was reminded of his reason for being here.

Miss Landcaster was in better spirits. She smiled when Ike came into the room. "I talked to Dr. Lowry this morning," she said, "and he said that if I insist, I can leave tomorrow, and I did insist. I'm going home."

"I'm glad it makes you so happy," Ike said.

"I'll fly out of Jackson tomorrow afternoon and be home tomorrow night," she said, her eyes reflecting anticipation.

"Peggy Jo and I will take you to the airport," Ike said.

The smile faded as she said, "No, you can't do that. I talked to my father, and he will meet me in Jackson and fly back with me. He wanted to come here, but I told him no. He is very angry about what happened and he blames everyone here for it, and I don't want him to come to Midvale in the mood he's in. It would be very unpleasant for everyone, including me. A bus leaves for Jackson at nine in the morning and I'll meet him at the bus station there. It will be better this way."

"We'll pick you up here and take you to the bus station," Ike said.

"I want you to know something," she said seriously. "I wouldn't have made it through this without you and Peggy Jo and my other friends here. I'll never forget what you have done for me at a time when I really needed friends."

"We hope you leave here with some memories of Midvale besides bad ones," Ike said, getting up to leave. "I have to go back to the office now. I'll see you in the morning."He left without telling her about the protest demonstration, thinking it would serve no purpose for her to know of VanDolan's activities.

Hankins left his store just before dark and drove to the Miller shack. He had been brooding all afternoon, consumed with a burning anger, humiliated that the giant Negro had struck him in public for everyone to see. He was thoroughly shamed and confused, knowing he must do something but unable to decide what it should be.

He pulled into the clearing as the last rays of daylight caught the tips of pine limbs. Jud and the two brothers were sitting on the porch, staring blankly at nothing. Hankins got out of the car and said, "Howdy, Jud."

"Howdy," Jud said in return. "Where's Con?"

Hankins sat on the steps. "They got him locked up in jail. That white girl got beaten up by a bunch of niggers an they're blamin it on Con."

"How come?" Jud asked.

"Well," Hankins said, scratching his head, "them niggers was in jail. Con took some whiskey up there an got 'em drunk an put the girl in the cell with 'em. They beat the stew out of her."

Jud grunted and said, "You want a drink?"

"Don't mind if I do," Hankins replied.

"Fetch a jug, Bester," Jud said.

Hankins waited to say more until Bester returned with the whiskey. He turned up the jug and drank. Then he said, "The niggers had a march this mornin in town. They walked to the courthouse an did some talkin an then marched back. That big nigger what got us all throwed in jail was at the front of the line with the white boy. Me an the nigger set to it down at the tracks, an he hit me right there on the street."

"You kill him?" Jud asked."

"Naw, I couldn't," Hankins replied dejectedly. "Them deputies grabbed me an drug me off 'fore I could get back at him. Them niggers keep on, they gone take over the whole county."

"Whut you gone do?" Jud asked.

"I dunno," Hankins said, scratching again. "I dunno, but somethin's got to be did. That white boy keeps stirrin 'em up, they gone be like a swarm of hornets."

"Don't you know how to git rid of hornets?" Jud asked.

"How's that?" Hankins asked curiously.

"Burn the nest."

Hankins took a deep drink from the jug and thought silently for a moment. Then he handed the jug to Bester and said, "Warn't for the nigger church they wouldn't have no place to meet, would they?"

"Warn't for the nigger church Coney wouldn't be dead," Berl said.

They all remained silent for a few moment. Then Hankins said, "When we gone burn it?"

"Tonight'd suit me," Jud said.

"Can't do that," Hankins said. "We ain't got the stuff."

"All it'd take is some coal oil," Bester said.

"We can't use kerosene," Hankins said quickly. "We'll have to use gasoline."

"How come?" Jud asked. "Ain't you got kerosene at your store?"

"We can't use kerosene," Hankins replied firmly. "It ain't no good for burnin a church. It don't burn fast enough."

"When you want to do it?" Jud asked.

"Tomorrow night," Hankins replied. "I'll git the gasoline an pick you up here just after dark. We'll have to park up by the bridge an walk through the woods along the crick. We don't want nobody to see us."

"Won't take long," Jud said.

"I wish I could git that big nigger in the church an burn him too," Hankins said.

"Me an Berl'll hawgtie him an bring him along," Bester said.

"Naw, it'd be too risky," Hankins said. "We'd just end up in jail with Con."

"You want some deer meat?" Jud asked. "We got some in the house."

"I guess," Hankins said.

"Fetch a chunk, Berl," Jud said.

Hankins took another drink and said absently, "They ought to be some way I can git that big nigger."

Thirty

Ike opened the front door and picked up *The Daily Record*, a statewide newspaper, then went into the kitchen and poured a cup of coffee. He sat at the table and glanced at the front page. His eyes caught one headline, and his face paled as he read the article. He slammed the newspaper down and said loudly, "Dammit to hell!"

"What's the matter with you?" Peggy Jo asked, coming into the room. "You'll wake the children."

"Listen to this," he said, picking up the newspaper. "'Violence hits Midvale demonstration.' That's the headline. Here's some of the article. 'A peaceful demonstration in Midvale turned violent Thursday when a local white man attacked one of the black civil-rights workers. He was subdued by police officers before a serious riot could develop. No arrests were made. The demonstrators had marched to the courthouse in a protest demonstration led by white civil-rights leader Jeffrey VanDolan of California, who is head of the Midvale project. Prior to the incident Thursday, a white female civil-rights worker was severely beaten inside the Stonewall County jail. VanDolan said there would be a demonstration in Midvale Saturday to protest violence against civil-rights workers, and he called on volunteers to join with local civil-rights workers in the protest rally.'"

Ike dropped the newspaper and said, "This is an open invitation to mayhem."

Peggy Jo put her hand on his shoulder and said, "Don't be so upset. There wasn't trouble yesterday except for the incident at the end of the march."

"Those were local people," Ike said. "God knows who will be here tomorrow.'"

"What will you do?" Peggy Jo asked, becoming concerned too.

"I don't know," Ike replied. "Sometimes I wonder why I got myself into this mess. I could have a nice quiet job at the high school. I need to call Sid Grenlee and talk to him about this, and then it will be time to pick up Miss Landcaster."

"Will you tell her about this?"

"There's no need for her to know," Ike said. "It would only upset her. Let her at least leave here in peace."

Reverend Holbrook, Sisters Pearley, Dorothy and Lucy were standing outside when Ike parked beside the Midvale bus depot. Peggy Jo and Miss Landcaster walked over to them as Ike went inside to get the ticket.

Sister Lucy grinned as she handed Miss Landcaster a small box and said, "I brung you some fried chicken an biscuits. You can't get no good vittles on dem airplanes, an you needs yo strength. You et ever bite of dis."

"I will, Sister Lucy," she said, taking the box, "but I'll share it with my father. He's never eaten Southern-fried chicken. I know he'll enjoy it, and I thank you so much."

Sister Pearley smiled, "Dis ain't much, Miss Sylvia. Me an Sister Dothy made 'em together. You gwine need 'em someday." She took two aprons with lace borders from the bag and held them up for Miss Landcaster to see. The intricate needlework was perfect, and Miss Landcaster knew it took the two women hours of work to create them.

Miss Landcaster accepted the aprons gratefully and said, "You shouldn't have gone to so much trouble for me, but I do appreciate it."

Reverend Holbrook had been holding his hand in his right coat pocket, grinning like a fox who has outsmarted the dogs. "I brung you somethin too," he said. He removed a small yellow box from the pocket and placed it in her hand. "A white lady gave dis to my granmammy durin de Civil War when she was a house servant on a plantation in Georgia. When de Fedral troops was comin de white lady didn want dem to have de box, so she gave it to Granmammy."

Miss Landcaster looked at the solid gold jewelry box set with red and blue stones and small diamonds. She said immediately, "I can't accept this. It must be one of your most cherished possessions. I thank you so much, but I cannot accept it."

She tried to give it back, but he wouldn't take it. He said, "I want you to have it, Miss Sylvia. It's yours now. What's a old man like me goin to do wid a box like dis?"

She knew he would be hurt if she refused his gift, so she put the box into her purse. "Thank you," she said. "I'll take care of it, and I'll treasure it always."

Ike came from the building, handed Miss Landcaster her ticket and said, "I've checked your suitcase to Jackson. You're all set."

They looked down the highway when they heard two loud blasts from the bus horn. They moved back out of the way as the bus pulled in. The three women stepped forward and kissed Miss Landcaster on the cheek. Sister Lucy said, "You take care of yoself, chile. You hear?"

"I will," she said. "And all three of you remember that you don't spell *cat* with a *k*."

Reverend Holbrook took her hand and said softly, "God bless you, Miss Sylvia. God bless you. We'll miss you, chile."

Peggy Jo looked into Miss Landcaster's eyes as one woman who knows another's pain. She said, "Good luck, Sylvia. Let us hear from you."

Ike took her hand and they exchanged penetrating glances in silence. She reached up impulsively and kissed him on the cheek. Then she turned and said, "Good-bye, all of you." She boarded the bus quickly.

The odd group stood on the concrete apron and watched the bus pull away and gain speed. They could see the outline of a young face pressing against the window glass, looking backward.

Reverend Holbrook cleared his throat, took a handkerchief from his pocket and wiped his eyes. He said falteringly, "Got some trash in my eyes. Wind must of blown it."

"The same wind hit all of us," Ike said.

They walked away in silence.

After taking Peggy Jo home, Ike drove to Grenlee's insurance office. The secretary was not present so he went into the private office. Grenlee looked up from his desk and said, "Good morning, Ike. Have a seat."

Ike took a chair. "I tried to call you earlier but nobody answered."

"I was a bit late getting to the office," Grenlee said. "I tried to hang myself on a garage rafter."

"If you did that, I presume you've seen the morning paper."

"That I have."

"Well?"

Grenlee leaned back and said, "Is there any way this thing can be nipped in the bud?"

"I don't think so," Ike responded

"Are you going to talk to VanDolan?"

"Yes, but I don't expect results. Even if he did back down, it's too late now. The call has been sounded."

"What should we do?" Grenlee asked.

"I'll call the governor and request state troopers be sent here.

We don't want to alarm people but it would be foolish to take chances. If we do have trouble, my small force can't handle it alone. I'm not willing to run the risk."

"Are we supposed to meet the protesters again at the courthouse?" Grenlee asked.

"I assume so," Ike replied, "but you will have to be there alone at first. I need to be on the street with my deputies. If nothing happens, I'll join you."

"Good enough," Grenlee agreed. "I still hope you have success with VanDolan and stop this thing before it starts."

VanDolan was sitting on the steps of the shack when Clara Mae entered the yard. For a moment he pretended not to see her. She stood directly in front of him, scraping her foot in the dust. He finally looked at her and said, "What are you doing here? I told you to never come here."

She cast her eyes downward. "You tole me you'd come to my house an you didn't."

"I'm busy," he said, "and I'll be busy the rest of the day. Just go back home and I'll see you later."

She put her hands behind her back and said, "We got to talk some, Mistuh Jeffrey."

"Dammit, Clara Mae," he snapped, "I'm trying to think! What do you want?"

She looked directly at him and said, "I's missed my period. I think I's fixed."

"What do you mean?" he asked angrily.

"I think I's fixed," she repeated.

"Dammit, Clara Mae, I'm going to fix you all right if you don't say what you mean!"

"You already has fixed me. I's missed my period. Mamma gone whup me good when she find out."

VanDolan got up and came down the steps. He said harshly, "I've got to go. We can talk whenever you decide to make sense."

She stepped in front of him and said loudly, "I think I's pregnant, Mistuh Jeffrey! Fixed! Mamma gone whup me good!"

He stopped suddenly and glanced around to see if anyone was nearby. "Keep your voice down, dammit!" he said. "Why don't you get on top of the house and bellow!" Then he looked at her kindly and said softly, "It couldn't be me, Clara Mae. I've taken precautions."

"You the only one I been with since you came."

"Then you were fixed to begin with!" he roared. He put his hand over his mouth, surprised by his own booming voice. He glanced around again and noticed the patrol car coming down the street. "Take this ten dollars and go buy yourself something," he said urgently. "Go on, now. We'll talk later. I promise."

She accepted the bill and walked from the yard as Ike drove up and parked.

VanDolan tried to regain his composure as Ike got out of the car. He said with simulated pleasantry, "Hello, Sheriff Thornton. What brings you here?"

Ike leaned against the gatepost. "It's good to see you in such a jolly mood. What was the matter with your girlfriend? She looked upset."

"She's not my girlfriend," VanDolan responded. "She's just one of the workers."

"Is she going to march tomorrow?"

"I don't know. We didn't discuss it."

"Let's you and I discuss it," Ike said. "Who is going to march?"

"All those who are opposed to injustice," VanDolan replied.

"Why are you doing this to us?" Ike asked.

"You have done it to yourself," VanDolan said. "You will get exactly what you deserve."

Ike knew it was useless to try to reason with VanDolan. He started to leave, then turned back and said, "Miss Landcaster left for home this morning."

"It's fine with me if she wanted to leave," VanDolan said. "That's her business."

Ike stepped closer to VanDolan and said, "My deputy Lon

Marcey did some investigating, and we know you set Miss Landcaster up for that trip to the jail. You brought her to the Froggy Bottoms that night and went in with her. You paid a girl to put moonshine in her drink so she would have whiskey on her breath. When she went out the front door you didn't go with her. You went out the back door and disappeared. Con Ashley knew exactly when she would come out that door. You paid Bugger Durr to lure him there. You set her up, and you almost got her killed."

VanDolan paled. He said uncertainly, "I don't know what you're talking about. You can't prove any of that. It would be my word against a Negro."

"I'll tell you what I should do," Ike said. "I should go to the jail and tell Con Ashley you said he planned the whole thing by himself. Then I should take you up there and put you in the cell with Ashley. If I do that, you will know firsthand what it feels like to beaten senseless."

VanDolan backed away and said, "I'm a civil-rights worker. If you so much as touch me I'll call in the FBI."

"I wish you would," Ike said. "I'll request them to investigate your role in Miss Landcaster's beating. That would make an interesting newspaper story."

"You're crazy," VanDolan said. "You're just trying to threaten me. It won't work. I've got things to do, so I've got to go now."

He walked away rapidly as Ike went back to the patrol car.

When he reached the railroad tracks, Ike turned on a sudden impulse and drove in the opposite direction, south across Town Creek, along a gravel road and then down the dirt lane leading to the Negro cemetery. He parked at the edge of the plot of lonely earth bounded by woods and cotton fields and tall growths of sagebrush. He walked through the sea of graves covered with pots and pans and glass bottles. He stopped at the grave and read the inscription, *Doshie, loved by all, missed forever and forever, God grant her peace. Mother, companion, member of a generation, a way of life.*

He imagined he could see her standing there, short fat body, red-checkered apron, head tied in a cloth, fat hands, twinkling eyes, shoes slit down the sides to relieve the pressure on her corns, round black face. He thought back to the carefree days of his youth when he had no conception of what was to come.

Ike suddenly realized there would never again be a Doshie, never again be a relationship with a Doshie such as the one he experienced and enjoyed. It was gone now, gone forever, never to return. It saddened him. He looked at the grave marker again and said, "I'm sorry it had to end this way, Doshie. I'm sorry."

As he walked back to the patrol car the sunlight seemed to bathe the hodgepodge of grave markers with a golden glow. He looked back once, then got into the car and drove down the dusty lane.

Hankins turned off the street at the Town Creek bridge and parked alongside a narrow lane leading down to the water. He said to Jud, "We'll walk from here. It's less than a half-mile down the crick bank."

"How many cans you got?" Jud asked.

"Three. That ought to be aplenty."

"We could burn the whole dern cotehouse with that much," Jud said. "Me an the boys will spread the gas an sot the fire. You kin stand watch an let us know if someone is comin."

They took the cans from the car trunk and moved into the woods. Hankins said, "I been here before, so I'll lead. If we run into anybody we can hide in the bushes an wait. Ain't likely to meet nobody in here at night, though."

"Shet up an go," Jud said. "Let's git this done with an go back to the house. I ain't et, an I'm hungry."

Hankins led them through silent woods disturbed only by an occasional cracking of dry limbs and bubbling water. They stayed close by the creek bank, passing behind Montique's shack and stopping at the edge of the clearing on the south side of the church. Noises drifted through the stillness from the nearby Negroes' houses and the Froggy Bottoms Cafe. The dark church was too far away to be touched by the dim glow of street lights.

Jud said, "Ain't gone be nothin to this. We ought to be gone from here in 'bout ten minutes. You stay here, Sim, an let us know if anybody comes down this way."

Hankins remained at the edge of the clearing and watched the three forms disappear in the direction of the church. Jud entered first and said, "I'll start down at the other end an work back. Bester, you start here an work that way. Berl, you take the middle. Slosh it on good, boys, an she'll go up like a tinder box."

Jud's footsteps made dull thuds as he walked to the far end of the building. He tripped on the platform, then got up and threw gasoline right and left, working his way back to the center of the church. He felt cold liquid splash over him and said harshly, "Watch out, Berl! You throwin thet dern stuff on me!"

"I couldn't see you, Pa," Berl said sheepishly. "Let's hurry an git out of here. This place scares me."

"Ain't nothin in a nigger church to scare nobody," Jud said. "You done?"

"Yessir, I'm finished."

"You done, Bester?"

"Ain't got a drap left."

They moved back to the door. Jud said, "You boys git on out there with Sim. I'll blast her off an come a'runnin."

Jud waited until Bester and Berl had crossed the clearing, then he struck a match on the sole of his shoe and threw it into a puddle of gasoline on the worn floor. The entire building exploded at once. Fire sprang in all directions. A streak of flame shot across the floor and leaped onto Jud's gasoline-soaked overalls, instantly turning him into a glowing orange ball. He screamed and rushed outside, running wildly in a circle. Then he fell to the ground and rolled over and over.

Bester watched the ball of fire shoot from the church. He stared in horrified disbelief as it circled and fell. He shouted frantically, "Hit's Pa! He's afire! He's burnin up!"

They rushed into the clearing and stopped short when the intense heat drove them back. Bester shouted, "Run fer the crick, Pa! Run fer the crick!" The ball of fire continued rolling back and forth, over and over. Bester and Berl took off their hats and tried to beat out the flames but only burned their hands.

The entire clearing glowed orange-yellow. The old building popped and roared as flames leaped high above the pine trees. Leaves rustled across the ground as they were sucked toward the raging inferno.

When Hankins heard shouting and the sound of footsteps running down the street toward them he said, "We got to go, boys! We got to go! They ain't nothin we can do for Jud now!"

Bester and Berl took one last look at the twisting form of withering flames, then turned and ran into the woods. Hankins' eyes caught on the silhouetted outline of the giant Negro, standing at the far end of the clearing, watching like an all-seeing gargoyle, springing up at him from the darkness. He cursed, then ran into the woods and disappeared.

Ike jumped instinctively when the phone rang. He listened for a moment, then shouted to Peggy Jo, "Somebody has set fire to the Negro church!" He rushed out the front door without hearing her reply.

The volunteer fire department siren on top of City Hall shrieked and wailed as he rushed toward the Negro quarters. He could see a glowing dome in the distant night sky.

When he reached Front Street, people were running ahead of him in the direction of the fire. He turned on the siren and sped down the street, skidding to a halt at the edge of the clearing. The church had collapsed into a huge bed of glowing embers. Firemen shot water across the ground, preventing the fire from spreading into the woods.

Lon ran to the car and shouted, "Over here, Mistuh Ike! Over here!"

Ike followed Lon to a spot on the south side of the church. Billy and Sam were kneeling beside a charred body. Several Negroes stood close by, staring wild-eyed. "Can you tell who it is?" Ike asked.

"Not from this chunk of charcoal," Billy replied. He handed Ike a wide-brimmed black felt hat and said, "This was lying on the ground just over yonder."

"Millers," Ike muttered.

"It's got the initials J.M. scratched on the inside band," Billy said.

Ike turned the singed hat over in his hands and examined it. He said, "It's probably Jud, but we'll never know for sure unless we find the other Millers."

"You want us to start looking for them?" Billy asked.

"No, you won't find them," Ike replied. "We may never find them. They're probably long gone from here. We can look later. Has anyone called the funeral home?"

"Yes," Lon said. "I called them when I called you."

"We'll probably end up burying this body ourselves," Ike said.

"Mistuh Ike," Lon said, "they's a lot of strange people in the quarters. They been comin in since dark."

"All of you patrol down here until midnight," Ike said, "and be back by daybreak. If anything looks wrong, call me at once."

As Ike walked back through the crowd he came upon Reverend Holbrook kneeling in the dust at the edge of the clearing, swaying back and forth, chanting, "Dey's burnt my church, dey's burnt my church."

Ike knelt beside him and said, "Don't worry, Reverend Holbrook. We'll build another one right here in the clearing."

"It won't be de same as de old one, Mistuh Ike," he said, looking up through tired eyes. "Dey's destroyed de House of de Lawd, and it won't be de same ever again."

"We'll build a church you'll be proud of," Ike said, helping the old man to his feet. He walked with his arm around him to steady his trembling body. Then he helped him into the patrol car and drove away from the glowing mound of coals.

Thirty-one

Hankins was restless all night, seeing images of Jud Miller encased in flames, Coney Miller dead and Con Ashley in jail, the giant Negro coming into his store and pointing an accusing finger, the giant Negro marching in the street and then throwing him into the side of a truck, the all-seeing giant Negro watching as Jud miller went up in flames. In his mind all of these events were linked, parts of a chain leading back to the giant Negro.

He arose at daybreak and paced back and forth in the kitchen, constantly building an anger that overwhelmed him. He was unaware when his wife came into the kitchen and made breakfast, unaware of her concerned glances and the frightened expression on her face. He ate the sausages and eggs automatically and drank the steaming coffee without relish. Then he went into the bedroom.

Her eyes flashed horror when he returned with the shotgun. She pleaded, "Leave it be, Sim! It ain't worth it! You know what Mr. Kelley told you! Let it go!"

He paid her no heed as he walked by her without recognition, getting into his car and driving away. She ran to the front of the store and watched as he disappeared in the direction of the Negro quarters.

He looked neither right nor left as he turned down the lane leading to the shack, seemingly unaware of anything but his destination. He parked the car, then walked into the yard and shouted, "You! Hanibel Felds! Come out here, nigger!"

Felds came out of the shack with a shotgun in his hands, taking a position ten feet in front of Hankins. Both men glared at each other, eyes transfixed, Hankins seeing legions of niggers sucking oranges and spitting the seed through their teeth, Hanibel Felds seeing the white men with the pincers. Both guns fired simultaneously, both loads of buckshot making thuds as they tore into flesh. For an

313

instant both men continued staring. Then they toppled backward into the dust.

VanDolan slipped out the back door when he heard the shouting. He peeped around the corner of the shack just as the two guns fired. He ran down the street, screaming, "Murder! Murder!"

Patrol cars converged on the shack instantly. VanDolan ran back and stood by the bodies, panting, "I saw it all! I saw it all!"

Lon ran into the yard and was joined by Billy and Sam.

Billy stared at the bodies and said, "What in hell happened here?"

"I don't know," Lon said, "but it's sure bloody. They're both dead. One of you call Mistuh Ike and an ambulance. It's best I stay here." Billy turned and ran from the yard.

A crowd gathered rapidly, some of them leaning against the fence. Lon said to them, "You folks move on back! There's nothing to see." They dispersed momentarily and returned.

When Billy returned, they stood around uncertainly until Ike arrived. He came into the yard and looked at the bodies. He winced and said to Lon, "How did this happen?"

"I saw it all!" VanDolan said before Lon could answer. "Hankins did it! He called Hanibel out of the shack! Called him a nigger! Hankins started it!"

"You don't know who started it," Ike said, not really speaking to VanDolan. "Nobody knows."

"I know!" VanDolan repeated. "I saw it all!"

"Nobody saw it all but them," Ike said absently.

The ambulance turned off Front Street and screamed down the lane to the shack. Two men got out and brought a stretcher cart into the yard.

"Can you carry both bodies?" Ike asked.

"Are they both dead?" the driver asked.

"Yes."

Ike turned quickly when a rock crashed through the rear window of his car. Another bounced off the top of the ambulance, and another fell into the yard. The crowd at the fence scampered out of the way. Ike shouted to the ambulance drive, "Get those bodies out of here! Hurry!" He saw more rocks coming from a small group assembled across the street. He said to Lon, "Do you know those people?"

"I've never seen them before," Lon replied.

Montique hobbled around the corner of the shack just as Felds' body was put into the ambulance. He looked at Ike in fear and said, "Is it Hanibel, Mistuh Ike?"

"Yes," Ike replied. "He and Sim Hankins killed each other."

"I tole him!" Montique said in anguish. "I tried to make him go wid me! I tole him!" He turned his gaze to Ike. "Can I ride wid him?" he asked.

"Yes, but hurry. They're ready to leave."

Montique climbed into the ambulance. The driver turned on the siren and sped up the street.

Another rock crashed through a side window of Billy's car. Ike said, "Billy, you and Sam get out of here. Go to the station house and stay there. Lon, stay down here as long as you can. I'll be at the courthouse for a while and join all of you later."

A Negro of about twenty-five was standing across the street, watching. He wore a white T-shirt, jeans, and white jogging shoes. As soon as the patrol cars left he came up to VanDolan and said, "Are you Jeffrey VanDolan?"

"Yes," VanDolan replied, curious about the stranger.

"I'm Greg Martin of the League's state headquarters in Jackson," he said, not offering a handshake. "I've come to take over. Where is your meeting place?"

"What do you mean by 'take over'?" VanDolan asked suspiciously.

"You're not being pushed out," the man said quickly, detecting resentment in VanDolan's attitude. "You've done okay in setting this up, but from here on out it's not a job for an amateur. You'll still march at the head of the line and be the project leader, but I'll whip this thing into final shape."

"We meet at the picnic tables by the burned church," VanDolan said without enthusiasm.

"Have your people there before noon," Martin said. "My group will be here by then. I'm going to look around some now and I'll see you later."

Ike was in his private office with the door closed, thinking of all the things that had happened in Midvale during the past few weeks. They all seemed to be parts of a tragic play drawing rapidly to a climax. He was startled when Mrs. Fleming opened the door and said, "There's someone here to see you."

A man in the uniform of a state trooper came in. "I'm Captain Bill Waller," he said, extending his hand.

Ike shook hands and said, "Ike Thornton. I'm glad to see you here. Things look a shade rough. How many men did you bring?"

"Fifteen. I brought extra tear gas guns and masks for your men."

"We wouldn't know what to do with tear gas guns unless you furnish printed instructions," Ike said. "If it comes to that, your men will have to handle it."

"We won't use tear gas unless we have to," the captain said, "and we won't fire it except under your orders or in self-defense. If a riot does break out, my men know what to do."

"The best thing for you to do is deploy your men around the railroad station house and at the foot of Main Street," Ike said. "I have only three deputies, and we'll be down there with you."

"How bad does the situation look?" Waller asked.

"Not good," Ike replied. "There are people in the quarters I've never seen. We had a double murder down there this morning, but it was caused by a lot of things that have happened here lately and not just this protest march. They have also picked the worst day possible to stage this march. Everybody in Stonewall County comes into town on Saturdays. Anything can happen."

The captain said, "I'll go on now and deploy my men. We'll see you later."

Greg Martin stood on a picnic table and surveyed the crowd assembled around the ashes of the burned church. In his audience were local Negroes, strange Negroes, young white girls and boys dressed in T-shirts and jeans, and several clergymen. Martin studied the faces, then said, "There's been a local leader murdered here this morning, shot down at his own home. Are we going to let this man die for nothing?"

"No!" responded the crowd.

"The church was burned last night," he continued. "That's how much respect they have for the Negro community. Burned the house of God. Are we going to let this go for nothing?"

"No!" came the echo.

"We're tired of the white man's injustice!" Martin shouted. "We're tired of waiting and listening to lies! What is it we want?"

"Freeeeeedom!"

"When?"

"Now! Freeeeeedom now!"

"All right, then!" Martin shouted. "Let's march for freedom now!"

VanDolan watched as Martin jumped from the table and raised his arms as a signal for everyone to form behind him. Then he hurried over and took his place beside Martin in the front row. The procession moved up the street, clapping and chanting, "Freeeeeedom, freeeeeedom." Several local Negro spectators became mesmerized by the chant and joined the marchers.

Clara Mae ran to the head of the line and walked backward in front of VanDolan. She said loudly, "Mistuh Jeffrey, when we gone talk?"

"Dammit, Clara Mae," he said harshly, "can't you see what's happening? Get out of the way!"

"You said you'd see me today," she said persistently, backing up continuously.

"We'll talk tomorrow," he said, glancing sideways at Martin. "I'll meet you tomorrow afternoon at two at the big tree. That's a promise. Now get out of the way!"

"Can I march?" she asked.

"Yes, dammit!" he shouted. "You can march!" She dropped back and joined the rear of the column.

Reverend Holbrook and Lon were standing in the middle of the street, blocking the marchers just before they reached Front Street. Martin signalled for the column to stop. Reverend Holbrook said loudly, "You can't do dis! It's not right wid de Lawd! Go back to yo homes!"

"I don't know who you are, old man," Martin said, "but you've got thirty seconds to get out of the street."

"You can't do dis!" Reverend Holbrook repeated.

"Are you deaf?" Martin shouted. "I said move it!"

A rock sailed from the crowd and hit Reverend Holbrook on the side of his face, knocking him to his knees. Lon helped him to his feet and out of the street. Blood trickled down his cheek and onto the frayed white collar.

Martin raised his arm and the chanting started again. The procession moved onto Front Street and headed toward the railroad station. The marchers now numbered over two hundred.

Ike stood in the middle of the street just past the tracks, with Billy and Sam on each side of him. He raised his arms when the column reached him. When they stopped, Martin stepped forward and said, "What is it you want?"

"What is it *you* want?" Ike replied.

"Freedom," Martin said.

"Tell me what it is you want and we'll talk," Ike said. "There's no need for this."

"You're a little late," Martin said. He raised his arms and the procession moved forward again, clapping and chanting.

Crowds of people stood by the station house and on the Main Street sidewalks, watching the sheriff and his deputies back up as the marchers moved forward.

Ike looked at the faces in the procession, mostly strangers but also familiar Negro faces he thought would not be present, teenagers who only two days before had required pay to do what they were now doing of their own volition, adults whom he believed did not really know why they were on the street or realize the possible consequences, all of them led by a chanting young Negro and a young white man wearing a blue cap.

A pickup truck stopped on Main Street ahead of the marchers, blocking the way. Other cars and trucks came down the street and stopped, forming a wall. Horns blared. Someone shouted, "Get them niggers out of the street!" Two men in the back of a truck threw eggs, splattering the demonstrators. Someone else shouted, "What the hell you think you're doin?" Then, "Git them sonsuvbitches off the street!"

A rock flew out of nowhere, striking a demonstrator on the shoulder. Then suddenly a barrage or rocks came at the demonstrators and from the demonstrators, smashing store windows and car windshields and bouncing along the sidewalks. Ike looked at the corner and saw the trooper captain watching him, waiting. He hesitated for a moment, then shouted, "Fire them!"

He looked up as canisters sailed above the crowds. Muffled explosions sent tear gas swooshing downward into the screaming people. Other canisters bounced along the street and exploded. Ike saw a trooper fall to the asphalt when a rock smashed into his head. He ran to the captain and said, "What can we do?"

"We'll drive them back into the quarters and seal it off!" he shouted. "Come with me and I'll get masks for you and your men!"

Ike rubbed his stinging eyes and followed the captain to a patrol car.

The battle followed the same pattern back to the Negro quarters, troopers moving in and firing gas, demonstrators pulling back, screaming and cursing and hurling bottles and rocks, then troopers moving again, firing more gas. The troopers finally pushed the demonstrators back into the quarters and formed a ring along Front Street, firing at people as they darted out and hurled missiles, then scurried down side streets and rushed out again. Ashley stood by the cell window, listening to the boom of tear gas guns. He shouted for Clayton, then banged a chair on the cell floor and bellowed. The old man rushed down the corridor and said, "What's wrong with you, Con? You lost yore mind?"

"What's goin on down there?" he asked excitedly.

"The niggers is havin a riot," Clayton replied. "That's state troopers doin the shootin. They got tear gas."

"I knowed it!" Ashley shouted. "I knowed they would do it! Let me out of here, Clayton! Let me out!"

"I can't do that, Con, an you know it."

Ashley leaned against the bars and said, "You ever seen a white man after a nigger gets done with him with a knife? Belly laid open an guts hangin out? Them niggers is liable to be up here to the jail any time now. They come up here, they'll slit your throat an dress you out like a shote. Them troopers need all the help they can git, so you better let me out of here."

Deep fear came into Clayton's eyes. He asked with anxiety, "You really think the niggers will come here?"

"Hell yes, they will!" Ashley snapped.

"Will you come back soon as the fightin's done?"

"Yes, goddammit! Let me out 'fore it's too late."

When Clayton opened the cell door Ashley rushed out and said, "Loan me a pistol and your car keys! Hurry up!"

They went downstairs and Ashley waited in the hall while Clayton went into the living quarters. The old man returned quickly and handed Ashley a pistol and the car keys. Ashley said, "I'll be back soon. Watch out for the niggers!" Then he ran out to the car and drove away.

Ashley followed the route they used the night they met VanDolan in the woods. He would come in the back way to the quarters and avoid being seen. He parked by the abandoned mill and followed the path to the small clearing, then plunged into the pine thicket. Tear gas guns could be heard in the distance. He was startled when a voice said, "Hold up!" Bester and Berl stepped into the path.

"God-a-mighty, you boys give me a fright!" Ashley said. "Where's Jud?"

"He's dead," Bester said. "Burned to a crisp last night at the nigger church."

"Damn them sons-a-bitchin niggers!" Ashley snapped. "We'll git 'em! They'll pay for this!"

"Taint the niggers," Bester said calmly.

"What you mean?" Ashley asked. "The niggers is the cause of Jud bein dead."

"'Taint the niggers," Bester repeated. "We ain't never had no business with niggers before 'cepin when one stole a hawg. Hit's you, Con. Allus comin out to the house an talkin 'bout nothin but niggers. Warn't fer you an Sim, Coney or Pa wouldn't 'a been at thet nigger church." Bester suddenly snatched the pistol from Ashley's hand. He and Berl whipped out switch blades and flicked them open.

"You fellows got it all wrong," Ashley said, eyeing the knives. "I always been your friend. Ain't I drunk with you an eaten meat?"

"Yeah," Bester said, moving forward, "an allus talked 'bout nothin but niggers."

Ashley backed up and said desperately, "You fellows mess with me, the law'll git you for sure."

"Naw they won't," Bester said. "Not 'less they look all over Texas. Soon's this ruckus is over, we're leavin. We wouldn't 'a stayed here all this time 'cept for Pa wantin to live out there in them woods."

"You're makin a mistake!" Ashley said, backing against a tree, his eyes filled with terror. "I'm your friend! It's the niggers who're against you!"

"You know how to hide a body to keep it from being found?" Bester said. "You split it open an fill it with sand, then you sink it in the crick. Sometimes it never comes up, an sometimes hit's months 'fore what's left of it floats out. I calculate hit's goin to take a full bushel of sand to fill up thet big gut of yourn."

"You're crazy"! Ashley said, wild-eyed. "You've both gone crazy!" He suddenly rushed forward. Bester's hand caught him in the chest, ramming the knife in to the hilt. Berl's blade slashed into his neck. Ashley stopped and looked at them in horror, feeling the blood flow, feeling the two knives embedded in his body. He staggered and swayed, then he stumbled backward and fell. Bester and Berl dragged him toward the creek.

Nightfall came and the battle still raged in the Negro quarters. An hour after dark two fires cast an orange glow into the night sky. When the fire truck arrived it was met by a crushing onslaught of rocks and bottles, smashing windows and making dull thuds as they bounced off metal. The truck backed up quickly, and the men watched the flames helplessly.

Ike walked up and down Front Street, listening to the screams and the pop of tear gas canisters, sounds he never dreamed of hearing in Midvale. He wondered how many people were hiding under beds, how many were peeping out darkened windows, how many had run to the woods, how many had their hearts in what they were doing, how many would forget and how many would never forget.

Shortly before midnight the last tear gas canister was fired and the last rock hurled. The fires burned down to a dull glow. The troopers pulled back to the station house and watched a steady flow of cars come from the quarters and turn north on the highway to Jackson. All but one patrol car of troopers left. Ike told his deputies to leave too. Then he drove home and parked in the driveway.

Peggy Jo rushed into his arms when he came into the living room. She cried, "I've been out of my mind with fear! Is it over?"

"This part of it is," he said. He held her close for a moment, then closed all the windows, trying to block the smell of drifting tear gas from entering the house.

Thirty-two

Ike arose early and left quietly, not disturbing Peggy Jo. He drove around the courthouse and gazed down Main Street, then crossed the tracks and stopped at the beginning of Front Street.

He got out of the car and looked at the flowing stream of broken glass, rocks and empty tear gas canister. Then he began walking, trudging down one street and up another, looking, seeing the burned-out shell of the motor patrol, the charred skeleton of the ditch digger. He could feel eyes following him, peering out windows, faces hesitant about coming out and greeting him, sharing with him the hurt and the pain. The half-painted houses on one street looked grotesquely ridiculous, like partly-finished stage sets.

When he came to the shack of Hanibel Felds, VanDolan was standing beside the red sports car, tying a suitcase onto the luggage rack. Ike stopped and watched him silently. VanDolan turned and saw him. "I'm leaving now. We won after all."

"Won?" Ike said blankly.

"Yes, we won," VanDolan repeated.

Ike looked at him quizzically. "What is it you've won?" he asked.

"We brought attention to the situation," VanDolan replied. "You're in the spotlight now. If you continue your discrimination federal agents will come here. We won."

"No," Ike said, shaking his head, "you've won nothing. When people turn against each other in hatred and violence, nobody wins. The aftermath of this will be with us for another generation, maybe longer. It may never end. We've all lost."

"That's your opinion," VanDolan said, getting into the car. "I say we won." He revved the motor, then turned and said, "So long, sport. You have a nice day."

Ike stood in front of the empty shack and watched the car move up the street and disappear. He walked again, feeling the eyes, some pained, some regretful, some hopeful, but many of them hostile. He came to the clearing and saw Reverend Holbrook standing alone, looking silently at the giant pile of ashes, the remains of his church. Reverend Holbrook turned and saw him, then came to him. Ike said, "Is it all gone?"

"I don know, Mistuh Ike, I jus don know. Jesus never quit, an Moses never gave up."

"Maybe we can pick up the pieces and start over," Ike said, "and have a new beginning."

"I'll pray fo it, Mistuh Ike. I'm gwine hold services dis moanin under de trees. I'll ask my people to foget an fogive an live in peace as brothers an sisters under de Lawd. I'll try, Mistuh Ike. I knows it's de will of de Lawd."

"We'll all try," Ike said. "It will take longer now, but maybe we'll get there someday."

They looked back at the empty clearing, at the scorched earth. Then they turned and walked up the street, walked side by side, together.

If you enjoyed reading this book, here are some other books from Pineapple Press on related topics. To request a catalog or to place an order, visit our website at www.pineapplepress.com. Or write to Pineapple Press, P.O. Box 3889, Sarasota, Florida 34230, or call 1-800-PINEAPL (746-3275).

BY PATRICK SMITH:

A Land Remembered. This well-loved, best-selling novel tells the story of three generations of MacIveys, a Florida family battling the hardships of the frontier, and how they rise from a dirt-poor Cracker life to the wealth and standing of real estate tycoons. (hb, pb)

The River Is Home and *Angel City*. Smith's first novel, *The River Is Home*, revolves around a Mississippi family's struggle to cope with changes in their rural environment. Poor in material possessions, Skeeter's family is rich in their appreciation of their beautiful natural surroundings. *Angel City* is the powerful and moving exposé of migrant workers in Florida in the 1970s. (hb)

Forever Island and *Allapattah*. Widely recognized as the classic novel of the Everglades, *Forever Island* tells the story of Charlie Jumper, a Seminole who clings to the ancient ways and teaches them to his grandson. When their simple existence is threatened by developers, Charlie fights back. *Allapattah* is the story of a young Seminole in despair in the white man's world. "Allapattah" means crocodile, a creature that becomes Toby Tiger's obsession and that he must wrestle to set himself free. (hb)

A Land Remembered Student Edition. This best-selling novel is now available to young readers. In this edition the first chapter becomes the last so that the rest of the book is not a flashback, and also the language and situations are altered slightly for younger readers. **Volume 1** (hb & pb) **Volume 2** (hb & pb)

OTHER FICTION:

For God, Gold and Glory by E. H. Haines. The riveting account of the invasion of the American Southeast 1539–1543 by Hernando de Soto, as told by his private secretary, Rodrigo Ranjel. A meticulously researched tale of adventure and survival and the dark aspects of greed and power. (hb)

Nobody's Hero by Frank Laumer. Based on a true adventure of an American soldier who refused to die in spite of terrible wounds sustained during the battle often known as "Dade's Massacre" that started the Second Seminole War in Florida. (hb)

Black Creek by Paul Varnes. Through the story of one family, we learn how white settlers moved into the Florida territory, taking it from the natives—who had only been there a few generations—with false treaties and finally all-out war. Thus, both sides were newcomers anxious to "take Florida." (hb)

Confederate Money by Paul Varnes. In 1861, as this novel opens, a Confederate dollar is worth 90 cents. We follow Henry Fern as he fights on both sides of the war. Through shrewd dealings he manages to amass $40,000 in Confederate paper money, and finally changes his paper fortune into silver and gold. (hb)

The Bucket Flower by Donald Robert Wilson. In 1893, 23-year-old Elizabeth Sprague goes into the Everglades to study the unique plant life even though warned that a pampered "bucket flower" like her cannot endure the rigors of the swamp. She encounters wild animals and even wilder men, but finds her own strength and a new future. (hb)

My Brother Michael by Janis Owens. Out of the shotgun houses and deep, shaded porches of a West Florida mill town comes this extraordinary novel of love and redemption. Gabriel Catts recounts his lifelong love for his brother's wife, Myra—whose own demons threaten to overwhelm all three of them. (pb)

CPSIA information can be obtained at www.ICGtesting.com
Printed in the USA
BVOW02s1821031013

332567BV00001B/4/P